I0737699

When I See You

A Novel by

C.L. Haynes

Copyright © 2023 by C.L. Haynes
All rights reserved.
Printed and Bound in the United States of America

ISBN: 978-0-578-37851-0

Jessica Tilles, Editor
TWA Solutions, Cover and Interior Design

Library of Congress Control Number: 2023934531

First printing April 2023

This is a work of fiction. Names, characters, businesses, places, events, and incidents are either the products of the author's imagination or used in a fictitious manner. Any resemblance to actual persons, living or dead, or actual events is purely coincidental.

No part of this book may be reproduced, stored in a retrieval system or transmitted in any form or by any means without the the prior written permission of the publisher—except by a reviewer who may quote brief passages in a review to be printed in a newspaper, magazine, or journal.

For inquiries, contact the publisher.

Dedication

For my wonderful husband, who told me that writing this book wasn't a silly idea. That if I enjoyed doing it, then I should keep doing it. Thank you for always supporting me in my choices and for being the love of my life. I'm forever yours.

And to my dad. He was easygoing and happy. Hardly ever angry, kind, well liked, and always did the right thing, and the best Papa to my kids. I see a lot of him in myself, and that's what has helped mold me into the person I am today. I love you, Dad, until we meet again…

Acknowledgments

This book is a journey of creation and imagination. I would like to thank one of my best friends in work and life for traveling on this journey with me. I have known L.T. for over ten years and she has been there for me both professionally and personally. She always had my back and was a source of objectivity and support when I needed it. Thank you for listening to me as I read you every word of this book nightly over the phone. It was often the highlight of my busy days. Thank you for your support and for being one of my biggest fans. I love you, sister.

I would also like to thank Jessica Tilles of TWA Solutions. Her professionalism and assistance in editing were priceless. Her expertise, guidance, and patience were invaluable. I never could have done this without her. Thank you so very much. I'm forever grateful.

And to my favorite author, TL Swan. Your excitement and willingness to give back to others is inspiring. Thank you so much for encouraging others, and me, to get the story out of my head and just start writing. Your excitement about writing is contagious. Look at what I did! I never would have done this if it weren't for your inspiring words of wisdom.

Chapter 1

Seriously? Another trauma patient?

I'm exhausted. This is my fourth, twelve-hour shift in a row, and now, in my eleventh hour, here it comes. A hot holy hell mess of a trauma admission. Stretching my neck from side to side and taking a deep breath, I eye the vacant seat at the nurse's station. A thirty-second sit-down would be nice, but I can't help but think of all the things I have yet to do to complete my day and get ready for this trauma admission. Leaning against the wall, and looking around, this unit has seen its share of trauma, death, and sickness. It's a highway for doctors and nurses, rushing to tend to their patients. The cold tile floors blend into even colder glass doorways framed in gray metal that separate patients from loved ones. Cold, sterile, and clean—nothing attractive to write home about. This is where I work. This is where I spend my life, saving people.

Taking another deep breath, my mind shifts into overdrive. My adrenaline kicks in and I'm focused. No more whining about how tired I am, or how I could be on the beach with my friends. It's time for my "let's do this" attitude.

I often wonder why people don't know how to go on vacation and play nice and not hurt themselves. What is wrong with people? They come to the beach, drink too much, lay in the sun, fry themselves under the Southern sky, and do stupid stuff while saying to their gang of drunken friends, "Here, hold my beer while I try this."

Hearing the sirens in the distance quickly approaching, I run down the routine in my head. First, admit the trauma patient, assess, and reassess. Make sure I see and examine the whole body from head to toe. Second, do whatever it takes to stabilize him. Third, which is always the hardest, is dealing with the awaiting family.

Accidents are called accidents because no one is ever ready, let alone prepared, for one. No one has time to accept their fate. It happens super quickly and is usually devastating. It catches families off guard, and parents and spouses ache for their loved ones. That's why it's called a trauma. Not only is it physical trauma, but it's also highly emotional trauma. Empathy, understanding, support, and education. That's how nurses deal with the families of the injured. You take care of the patient first and make sure you do a damn good job doing it because families will watch your every move. Then, you take care of the families. If there is any time left over, you take care of yourself, but that's a big *if.*

So, I became a trauma nurse. The rush of fixing an emergent situation and the expertise of great teamwork—I love it. It all unfolds like a well-oiled machine. Each patient is someone's loved one. This is a mom or dad, sister or brother, son or daughter, a coworker or friend. It's always someone who is devastatingly important to someone else.

The trauma patient arrives to the ICU and so it begins. A rush of adrenaline pumps through my veins as two nurses, a patient care tech, and two trauma doctors descend upon the patient. We hook the patient up to the monitor and begin our assessments. Doctors sound off orders left and right, as staff bring in needed supplies to stabilize the patient.

This patient has a GSW to the chest. A gunshot wound, to the left chest, which went clean through, missing the heart. Now, that's what I call a miracle. The patient is on a ventilator to protect his airway and is under sedation, for now. The word on the street is that this is a gang shooting and the TICU, Trauma Intensive Care Unit, will now be on lockdown. The hospital stays on lockdown until police can ensure there will not be any gang-related retaliation. Ensuring the safety of hospital staff and patients is top priority. The police don't want a confrontation to occur in the hospital, and frankly, neither do I. But there are those days when I ask myself, "Please remind me again why I became a trauma nurse?" The stress of these situations can be overwhelming sometimes.

Liz, my good friend and coworker, looks up at me and frankly states, "We do this for the greater good." I roll my eyes and shake my head.

"How did you know what I was thinking? It's as if you were reading my mind."

"Because we think alike. That's why we work so well together." We smile and get to business.

Thankfully, this patient is stable. His vital signs are rock solid and his oxygenation is great for someone with a gunshot wound in the chest.

The plan is to let him rest overnight and wean him off the ventilator in the morning. After an hour of fast-paced assessing and medical care, we silently declare another stable victory. It's understood that critical care nurses measure success by "another patient who is stable and alive at the end of a shift." No one died on my time. My patients are all accounted for and have pulses when I punch out. That, my friend, is what we, in the medical profession, call a "good day in the TICU!"

"Hey, Mindy?" Liz calls out to me with music in her voice.

Oh shit. Here it comes. The question of the day. I know that tone, and she wants a favor, and I'm not going to like it.

She stares at me with a huge smile. "So, let's talk about tomorrow, shall we?"

Instead of answering her, I give her that you've-gotta-be-kidding-me look. After a long pause, I shake my head. "No, let's not talk about tomorrow. The answer is no! Whatever the question, just assume the answer is no!"

She stares at me like she's waiting for me to change my mind.

"What, Liz? Don't look at me like that. Don't even ask. The answer is no! No, no, no. Don't even think about it." Turning to walk away, I hear Liz's pleading.

"Oh, come on, Mindy? *Please?* We are so short-staffed tomorrow and we really could use another nurse. I'll give you your patients back, including this new admission you just worked so hard to stabilize. And, by the way, administration is offering incentive pay. I know you said you wanted some extra cash. Here's your extra cash. Ask and you shall receive." She glares at me with a devious grin smeared all over her face. If she wasn't such a good friend, I swear I'd tell her to suck it, but I'm a pushover for a friend in need.

"Really, Liz? You know this is a bribe, right? How much extra money are we talking about here?" Although I'm selling myself to the devil, money talks. What else have I got to do tomorrow? My life sucks lately, so why not make some extra cash? That's my thinking, right? So what if I'm exhausted, my feet hurt, and I haven't even eaten or peed all day. So, this is me, talking myself into, yet again, another overtime shift, and justifying it.

Liz smiles at me, for she knows me too well. Just by asking how much extra money I can make, she's got me. I'm on the hook. All she needs to do now is reel me in! Damn it! I'm so easy to read, it's pathetic. Being my friend and coworker gives her an advantage, and she just cashed in on it. No good nurse wants to see their coworkers suffer and "circle the drain" on a bad day. Caving in, I agree to work. In a moment of weakness, she took full advantage of the situation and trapped me with cash! Why did I agree to this? Instantly, I regret it and wonder, *What have I done?*

The next morning, Mr. Turner, the patient with the gunshot wound to the chest, is my patient. His name is Todd Turner. Hmm, kind of catchy. Makes me think of Tina Turner as I hum a Tina hit.

Mr. Turner is an average-looking, well-built male with a few tattoos, but nothing stereotypical of a gang member. We easily wean him off of the ventilator and he awakens with no problems. Relief passes over me, as I no longer anticipate a physical struggle with a large man who probably doesn't want to be in the hospital. I certainly don't want to piss off a "gang" member.

"Hello, Mr. Turner. I'm Mindy and I'll be your nurse today. You're in the hospital and you're doing well and you're safe. You're in Memorial Hospital. How do you feel?"

"Pissed off."

"Well, I can understand that. It's not every day you recover from being shot. Are you in pain?"

"Actually, I'm doing okay. My pain is minimal, and your soothing voice has helped me. Thank you for that and for actually caring."

"You're welcome, Mr. Turner. I just want you to get better so you can get out of this ICU. Let's work on some breathing exercises, and later this morning, we'll be getting you out of bed and walking. The sooner you ambulate, the sooner you can get out of the hospital."

"Sounds like a good plan to me. I'm ready to get out of here. I've got a lot of business to deal with."

"I'm glad you're enthusiastic. I'll be back in a bit to get things rolling." I reach for his call bell, which is out of his reach, and place it in his lap.

"Here is your call bell. If you need me before I make my next rounds, just push this red button and I'll answer."

The morning routine is always fast and wicked. We have patients coming and going, patients getting up and out of bed, and multiple doctors requiring my attention. There is always a lot of commotion in the mornings. To add to the controlled chaos today, the police are on hand, and they are visiting Mr. Turner. Apparently, he is the law-abiding victim that witnesses say he is. He was in the wrong place at the wrong time.

Sergeant Houser told me there was a drive-by shooting near The Catch, a well-known bar and hangout for the local biker clubs, The Creeks and The Vipers. The two clubs have been getting into it lately, and that drive-by is just another example of that violence. Since the police have cleared Mr. Todd, the hospital has lifted the lockdown on our unit, and business, as usual, can resume.

From a distance, Doctor Dan Cooper, a first-year surgical resident, is talking smack about Mr. Turner. Immediately, I stop what I'm doing and listen from around the corner of the nurse's station.

"Yeah, a gang member, probably doing drugs or stealing. You know they are all involved in bad shit. It's always something with them. They think they are above the law and always taking the law into their own hands. He probably deserved it and got what was coming to him."

His mouthing off instantly pisses me off and I fly into defense mode. I don't like confrontation, but making an assumption about a situation he knows nothing about, and something that is my business, I'm going to get in his face about it. I'm known as the nurse who is always in a good mood and hardly ever gets pissed off or cranky. But trust me, when I go over the edge, all bets are off. There is a running joke between me and Liz. If I say to her, "I'm going over the edge" or "I'm gonna lose my shit," she goes on red alert and is immediately on standby for the show. Folks better watch out!

"Excuse me, Doctor Cooper. Did I just hear you right? Did you just say that my patient probably deserved this? Did you just make a generalization about gang members, of which you know nothing about?"

Doctor Cooper opens his mouth to reply, and I put up my index finger to halt his effort. "Wait a minute, Doctor Cooper. We are here to care for and take care of all patients, regardless of their background, nationality, or the cause of injury. Everyone deserves the same care, regardless of the situation. I take great offense to your comment that someone deserved this. *You*, my dear, sir, are *just* a first-year resident. *You* have a lot to learn. *Stay* out of my way and out of my patient's room. Keep your opinions to yourself. It's inappropriate to gossip about a patient's medical information. Didn't your momma ever tell you that if you don't have anything nice to say, then don't say anything at all? Now, Doctor Cooper, close your mouth and walk away. Go ahead, turn around, and walk away. Don't speak and don't make excuses. We're done here."

Doctor Cooper is speechless and hangs his head in embarrassment as I strut down the hallway, pissed off. That situation is now under control, but I'm still simmering. I get so upset with these young, inexperienced residents. They think they know the answer to everything. Yesterday, they were just medical students. Today, they are doctors with no bedside experience and think they know all the answers. *Jeez, get a clue, buddy.*

Walking into the break room, my heart is pounding out of my chest. My heart rate must be at least 150. Shit, I hate confrontation, but he deserved it. He's been getting on everyone's nerves for weeks and I couldn't stand it anymore. A headache is coming on now, too. That damn adrenaline rush gets me every time. Time for a quick bathroom break, a deep breath, and a moment to chill out before I go see Mr. Turner.

Liz walks into the break room, smiling from ear to ear. "Way to shine 'em up, sister. I knew you had balls, but now I know for sure. I'm proud of you. He deserved that and needed to hear it. I saw you getting ready to go over the edge, and I knew it was coming. That was awesome!"

Looking up at Liz, I laugh. Being assertive is not my thing. It's not that I can't do it, I just don't like to do it. Getting along with everyone and not making waves is more of my cup of tea. A people pleaser is who I am. But I also know my shit, so don't mess with my patients!

As I walk out of the break room, I take a deep breath and smile. Nurse Mindy is calm, cool and collected and back on duty.

Walking into Mr. Turner's room to assess his pain control and get him out of bed, I notice he has a huge grin on his face. "What's up with you, Mr. Turner? You look like the cat that ate the canary?"

"Well, I just witnessed my nurse handing a new doctor his ass on a silver platter. It was the best thing I've seen in a long time. He deserved it, I have to say, and it made me feel all warm and fuzzy."

The corners of my mouth form into a small grin, and my cheeks redden. "Did you now? I'm sorry you had to hear that. It was unprofessional of me to say those things in an area where you could hear them."

"Oh no, Mindy, that was the best show I've seen in a while. I think he had it coming to him and his condescending attitude needed adjusting. Let's hope he listens to your advice and adds this to his list of life's lessons."

"I hope so. Now, Mr. Turner, let's get back to you and get you walking in the hallway."

"Please, call me T. All the people that are special to me, that I care about, call me T."

"Mr. Turner, I don't think I would be comfortable calling you that. I'd like to call you Mr. Turner and keep it professional, if you don't mind."

"No, not at all, Mindy. Whatever you want. You're the boss. Please lead the way."

We slowly walk into the hallway for his first ambulation attempt. He holds my arm around the biceps, for support as I escort him out of his room. He grips the handrail with his other hand. As we proceed down the hallway, I get an uneasy feeling in my stomach. The hairs on the back of my neck rise. He's holding my arm, but his fingers are rubbing the inside of my arm as we walk. You know, kind of like the caring, caressing motion your loved one might do if they were holding your hand. It makes me feel uneasy. My inner voice tells me to just keep walking. Just as I settle my thoughts…

"Gee, you really do smell good."

"Excuse me?"

"Well, I smelled your fresh scent when you walked in this morning. I like it."

"Thank you, Mr. Turner, but it's called soap. Now, let's stay focused and just keep walking. Let's see how far you can go, but remember, you need to save energy for the trip back to your room."

Nope, it is not my imagination. He is feeling up my arm. How gross. Now I have Goosebumps, and my conscience is telling me, *Get this man back to his room and off your arm as fast as you can.*

Once Mr. Turner settles back in his room, Doctor Benjamin, the head trauma surgeon, arrives to see him.

"Mr. Turner…Todd, you are doing remarkably well. You will be able to get out of the TICU this afternoon. You will be transferred to the step-down unit."

"Thanks, Doc. I wouldn't be doing this good if it weren't for the great Mindy here. She is one fine nurse and a firecracker, you know. I like that in my women." He looks at me and winks. "Can I take her to the stepdown unit with me?"

Nausea and uneasiness fill my stomach. My gut is *never* wrong, and I don't like this. Something is off, but I can't put my finger on it. My wheels are turning and I decide to file that thought into the imaginary file cabinet in my brain. You know, that place where you keep important things stored that you want to recall later? I'll put this one in the top drawer, the most important drawer. Trivial stuff falls into the bottom drawer.

Smiling, Doctor Benjamin shakes his head. "I'm afraid not. She's one of our best nurses. We need her here in the ICU, but you will be just fine where you are going. Those nurses on the step-down unit are extremely capable of managing a patient with your condition."

Mr. Turner accepts his fate and doesn't harass Doctor Benjamin any further as I start the transfer process.

Later that day, as Mr. Turner is leaving the ICU, he calls me into his room. "Mindy, you have been a great help to me and I thank you. I've enjoyed watching you all day. I saw you speaking with that annoying visitor earlier. You know the one with the red baseball cap? It looked like he was giving you a hard time. Do you need my help with that situation or anything at all?"

What? He's been watching me? There's that uneasy feeling again.

"No, Mr. Turner. Thank you for the concern, but I can handle it. I took care of the situation and it was resolved. No problem."

"You truly are a caring and sweet person. Can I please give you a big hug before I leave?"

Instantly, I think, *Oh, hell no!* Some patients you don't mind hugging—believe me, I'm a hugger—but I don't want to hug this man. That uneasy feeling is a true sign. Go with your gut, *always*, I say. He's giving me a big smile and the creeps all at once. Seriously, he's been watching me? He's weirding me out.

"Mr. Turner, it has been my pleasure taking care of you. I wish you all the best in your recovery and thank you for the kind words. They mean a lot." I extend my hand for a formal handshake instead of a hug.

He takes my hand and shakes it, encircling my hand with both of his. My neck hairs stand at attention again. He shakes my hand and lightly squeezes.

"Really, Mindy, if you ever need anything, please don't hesitate to ask. I'm forever grateful to you for my care." He reaches into his wallet and hands me his card. "Here, take this. You never know when you may need it, or me." He smiles.

"Thanks, Mr. Turner, I'll remember that. Have a good day and good luck." I glance down at the card as the orderly wheels him out of TICU. The card reads:

Todd "T." Turner
The Creeks MC
President

Watching as he heads for his new room, I glance down at the business card again. Did I take care of a biker? I had no idea. Maybe that's why I always felt on guard around him. I'll file this in my brain's top drawer, too. Placing the card in my scrub pants pocket, relief consumes me as Mr. Turner exits the unit. The tension in my shoulders dissipates as I return to the rest of my responsibilities of the day.

Chapter 2

It's finally my day off. Good, can I sleep in? Nope. I get up so early for work that I can't even sleep past seven in the morning on my day off. Crap. Getting up, I head to the kitchen to make myself some coffee. What will I do today? I sit and evaluate my life. Right now, I'm trying so hard not to feel sorry for myself. Pulling the cup down from the cupboard, I pour a cup of coffee that automatically brewed from my setting it last night. Sitting at the table, I hold the cup of steaming goodness to my lips. I'm healthy, have a good job, a roof over my head, a few good friends, and a great family support system. Then why do I have the blues? Nodding with a smirk, I realize why. It's because of him. It's always been because of him. Brad was a jerk, and we broke up. It's been three months now, but I'm still angry and hurt. Should have seen it coming, I guess.

A hopeless romantic, it's only natural that I live at the beach, which is my dream place. I see in-shape humans every day, running on the beach—tanned, toned, and muscular. Gorgeous. Women and men alike. Bikinis everywhere. Then there is me. My stomach has not seen sunlight since I was a chubby kid at three years old when it was cute to see a fat kid in a bikini. Now, I'm a few pounds heavier than I should be, but nothing some discipline, exercise, and healthy eating can't fix.

So, with that thought, it's time. Time for me, finally. I'm a caregiver. Every day, for days on end, I take care of people. Holidays, nighttime, daytime, weekends, you name it, and I'm there. I'm a fixer. I'm a surgical nurse who fixes people. Do you think I can fix myself? Nope, but I'm sure going to try. So, here goes.

After putting on bike shorts and an oversized T-shirt, I stretch and jump on my bicycle. It's time for Mindy. Let's go for a bike ride.

Making my way down the path, I see the sights. There sure are a lot of people out early in the morning, getting all healthy and shit. I laugh to myself as I watch beach yoga in progress. Lined up in a perfect row parallel to the ocean surf are ten-toned and skinny women. All of them look like clones with their perfect-fitting yoga pants and sports bras, doing downward dog on their straw mats. Asses in the air and heads down. Good luck, girls. If I could bend like them; just think of the sex positions I could do! I giggle and keep pedaling.

I'm meeting Liz for an early dinner at the beach. Calypso Bar and Grill is one of my favorite places. It sits exactly on the beach. While the beach is pristine with its white soft sand, the view from the restaurant is exquisite. Palm trees line the walkways from the restaurant doors down to the outdoor sitting area, a popular spot for those wanting a quiet place to enjoy a good meal. Tables covered with white linens sway in the breeze from the surf as the table candles flicker. Seagulls sometimes badger sunbathers as they wait for them to leave a few morsels in the sand for consumption. The real treat is watching the occasional pelican dive for its meal or the rare dolphin break the surface as it swims by. It's an art mastered to perfection.

Painted white with an ocean blue ceiling to represent the sky, Calypso's elevated balcony is beautiful and provides the perfect backdrop. The stunning sun setting on the beautiful blue-hued ocean makes it a popular place to dine. It boasts a large covered area for outside dining and listening to the surf while enjoying the smell of the sea. Ceiling fans circulate air during the excessively hot summer months. It's a perfect setting for a dinner scene in a movie. Just adorable.

This evening, I'm wearing a cute summer dress to hide the thighs I'm so desperately trying to bike away. Do you know how much fire I could start by my thighs rubbing together? Beach bonfire, here we come. All things considered, there is a casual and relaxed feeling about me. This is going to be a great outing with my friend.

Liz enters the restaurant. Who can miss her? She is stunning. Taller than me, about five feet nine, and well built. That cleavage is to die for, if you know what I mean. She looks great in her summer dress, with her summer tan and summer hair. She's wearing it down, flowing and lightly curled. She's beautiful and confident. She used to be a model in her teen years, and had a great future ahead of her, but went to college and became a nurse instead. Stupid girl. She's a great friend and an even better nurse, but I often wonder what her modeling career would have been like if she continued it past high school? She sees me across the room and waves.

Waving back, I catch a glimpse of a Greek god out of the corner of my eye. Trying not to look without being too obvious, I notice two men at the bar. Both are tall, dark, and handsome. They are sporting casual shorts and collared polo shirts, but their matching black leather-strapped watches promote a businessman persona. Their hair is wavy and dark, and they have the perfect tan. Their chiseled features add to their hotness. Holy hell, where did they come from and how long are they staying? They are beautiful.

The taller of the two is intently watching Liz's every move. He hasn't taken his eyes off of her, and she's clueless as always. I don't even think she notices him. The shorter man, and more attractive of the two Greek gods, has his nose in his phone and is oblivious. Either he is deep in a conversation or just a workaholic who can't even put his phone down. *Geez, buddy, enjoy life, and shut the phone down. You're at the beach, for God's sake.*

Liz and I are enjoying a great, relaxing dinner. I casually sneak a peek over to the bar area. Yup, the gods are still there, hanging out. We talk nonstop, sharing plans for better living, future vacation plans, and, of course, do a little bitching about work. Because, let's face it, sometimes you just need to vent to someone who gets it and won't be all "judgy."

After an early dinner and two frozen margaritas later, we call it an evening. We both have work in the morning and at 5:00 a.m. Wake-up is mighty early. It sucks to be an adult sometimes.

As we stand to leave, I catch a glimpse of the Greek god duo. The taller man stands as we do. Shorty is still on his phone and is still oblivious. The taller man approaches Liz as we head toward the door.

"Excuse me, miss. May I have a word, please?"

Looking at Liz, she is just as clueless.

She looks at me and then looks at this tall drink of water and then back at me. "Yes? May I help you?"

"I hope so. I don't mean to be rude, and I'm not a stalker, but I couldn't help noticing your beauty from across the restaurant. I would love to buy you a drink."

I glance at him and then back at Liz as I sense my pulse quicken.

"Why thank you, sir, but I'm just about to leave. You should have approached me earlier. I have a super early morning and I really must be going. But thank you so much for the offer." Liz looks at me. "Okay, let's go. I'm ready."

Standing there, I look from the Greek god to Liz and back at him as we walk away. Damn, such confidence in this girl. It's impressive and my mouth is on the floor.

"And why aren't you staying for a drink?"

"Girl, I don't have time for that. He should have come over and asked earlier. He is awfully handsome, though, isn't he?"

"Ya think? Damn, girl, they make statues out of men like that. I can't believe you blew him off. He's putting a little tingle in my jingle, if you know what I mean. And his buddy, who is always on the phone, is even hotter, Liz. It's a shame he is so preoccupied with technology. He missed the whole show, but I certainly didn't miss him."

"Mindy, you're a trip." She giggles. "I didn't even see them the whole time we were there. You really checked them out, didn't you?"

"Hell yes! How did you miss that? Really, Liz, sometimes you are so clueless. How you missed those gorgeous men I will never know. Just like you don't realize how beautiful you really are. Men are always checking you out. It's amazing to watch, actually. I caught a glimpse of them the minute you walked in, and he never stopped eyeballing you the whole time.

"See, Liz, I'll prove my point. Did you even notice those two bikers over there watching us? They are both sitting on their bikes just watching the sights, so to speak."

"I can't say that I did. I guess I'm focused on myself. I didn't even see the men. Is that bad?"

"Well, one is rather handsome, with large arms and a clean-shaven face. You know, a clean-shaven face is my favorite. The other one has a beard and a weird tattoo on his face. I can't tell from here what it is, but he is definitely checking you out."

"Well, bikers aren't my type, so I guess I just never really check them out. Maybe he was checking you out, Mindy? Did you ever think of that?"

"Yeah right. Like that would ever happen. You're so oblivious it cracks me up. Oh well, as they say, another one bites the dust."

We laugh and exchange hugs as we leave to get into our cars. Back to the old grind, bright and early in the morning.

∾

Restless, I'm tossing and turning and can't get to sleep. Thoughts of the Greek gods enter my mind. Damn, how does God make such a perfectly physically attractive individual? And how did Liz say no to that?

I can only imagine being with someone that beautiful—to be the envy of every woman. To have a man like that on my arm. Damn, the thought makes me tingle. *Stop it*, I tell myself. Romance of that nature doesn't happen to me. Someday someone will love me for me. For who I am and for my personality. I mean, people tell me I'm cute and all, and too nice to date, too. So, should I become a bitch? Would that make me look more attractive? I don't want to be cute. I want someone to call me fucking sexy as hell, and say that I'm his everything.

Maybe I shouldn't be so nice, easygoing, and easy to please. Why is it that all the bitchy hot women get all the hunks? But for us nice girls, and the 'goody-goodies,' the kind of girl you bring home to Mom, always ends up taking a back seat? "Good things come to those who wait," my mom always said. Well, shit. I'm thirty-ish years old and prime for the picking. I want a man ready to bring it home already!

Chapter 3

There is a lull in the day's activities at work. Most of the patients are napping and appear stable, while others are quietly visiting with loved ones. No call bells are beeping and the nurse's station is void of conversation. There is an uneasy quietness in the unit. Everyone knows you never say the Q (quiet) word at work. For if they do, it usually isn't long before all hell breaks loose. I take advantage of this rare moment and sneak away for lunch.

Liz is busy dealing with a committee report and won't be back on the unit for two more hours, so I'm in charge until she returns. Just as I swallow my first bite of food, the trauma pager I'm carrying for Liz goes off. The alert on the screen states: Thirty-five-year-old male. Near drowning, facial injury, intubated, helicopter arrival five minutes. Here we go again.

Leaving my lunch, I set up the only open room available—the one directly across from the nurse's station. It's my room, my admission. I prepare the room and alert my staff as to the admission that will most likely be a hot mess.

Five minutes later, my phone rings with a report. "Hey, Mindy, this is Kris from the trauma room. I've got that level-one trauma headed your way. I'll give you a report when I get there, but he's intubated and sedated. Multiple facial injuries, but the rest of the CT is negative."

"Okay, Kris, I'm on it. Thanks."

The patient arrives, and boy, is he a mess. The team attaches him to the monitors straight away. His pulse is racing but steady. His blood pressure is stable. Unfortunately, his face is badly broken, his eyes are swollen shut, and there is blood everywhere. He has two black eyes, a broken nose, and facial swelling. I have never seen such severe swelling before. I can't even open his eyes to check his pupils.

There is a large hematoma above his left eye and a deep laceration above his right eyebrow, which will need stitching for sure, but that can wait. He is on a ventilator to protect his airway. Can you imagine the swelling in his throat if his face is this bad? Thank God, they intubated him in the ambulance because all that swelling in his face and neck has caused pressure on his airway.

We finish our assessments and cover him with warm blankets to protect his internal body temperature. Pain control and neurological assessments begin every hour to monitor his brain function.

Apparently, this man was on a Jet Ski and hit a wave, at an unknown high speed, just right. He lost control and flew off the Jet Ski. He, unfortunately, was heading right for the jetty and hit his face on the rocks. His face took most of the impact. Thankfully, bones will heal, although it's going to be painful for a while. This poor guy is going to be sore. His head CAT scan was negative for a brain injury. That is the most miraculous thing I've ever seen with this type of injury. I can't believe it.

The IV sedation for him continues and I start a continuous pain medication infusion, too. We need both medications to keep him safe and comfortable as I don't want to lose his airway. Jesus, what a mess that would be.

He has other minor injuries, such as scrapes and bruises, and a broken right femur. A few other lacerations that will need stitches, but overall, he's damn lucky. I find out from the Emergency Department nurse that his name is Kyle Masterson, and he was hanging out with friends, just enjoying a day on the ocean, when this happened.

Kyle is now resting and sedated, so I step out of his room to call and see if there are visitors for him. A man answers the waiting room phone.

"Is there a visitor for Kyle Masterson?"

"Yes, this is he."

"You may come in, please. If you walk to the end of the hall, I will buzz you in."

"Thank you. I'll be right there."

Buzzing in the visitor, I quickly return to the storage room to get some needed supplies and IV fluid. I want to make it back to Kyle's room before the visitor, so I can greet him. I don't make it in time. He's already in the room. Damn, I hate not being in the room when a visitor comes in for the first time. It's always a shock for visitors to see their loved ones in a state of a medical emergency, especially when there are a lot of machines and tubes in the room.

The visitor is already at the foot of the bed, staring at the body in the bed. His back is to me, with his head hung low. He's sniffing as I enter the room. Oh man, he's crying. I don't want to invade his privacy, but I'm holding an armful of heavy supplies that I'm barely balancing.

"Hello, I'm Mindy, and I'm Kyle's nurse for the rest of the day."

The man turns around. "Hello, I'm David, Kyle's brother."

As I look up to meet this man, eye to eye, I lose control of my balancing act. All my supplies tumble to the floor and my heart stops in my chest as I gasp at the sight of those blue eyes looking back at me. I recognize him instantly—the Greek god from last night. Holy shit, he's here in front of me. I would know that silhouette anywhere. It's burned into my memory because those two men from last night were picture-perfect, both too good to be true.

"Here, let me help you with that." He bends over to help pick up the mess I've made.

"It's okay. I probably shouldn't have been carrying so much, anyway. I was trying to get it all in one trip. That's what I get for being in a hurry."

Taking a longer look at my patient in the bed—holy hell! I'm convinced, one hundred percent. This is the Greek god from last night! No way! Can't be. Can it? I'm trying not to stare, but how can I not? *Oh, my God.* I look back at David. His hair color is the same dark brown, almost black. They have the same physique—broad shoulders, muscular arms, a toned stomach, and long legs. My senses heighten as I reassess this situation. This man is here with his brother, who is now my trauma patient. *The man in the bed is his brother*, I repeat to myself. *His brother!* They look alike from what I can see of his physique. I can't tell facially since my patient is so busted up, but the hair color matches. The puzzle pieces fit together. *Holy shit, this is my shorter Greek god. The phone man!* His face is still so swollen and distorted, but that body, it's a winner. They match…oh no; he was so pretty, but now, not so much. The once perfect profile of Mr. Hotness is now the face of someone even his brother barely recognizes.

A cold sweat breaks out under my scrubs. I don't say one word about last night's encounter, because David is too preoccupied and he never really noticed me last night, anyway. He wanted Liz, not me. He never even saw me. Suddenly, I'm internally fretting and feeling nauseated.

"Will you excuse me for just one moment, please? I'll be right back." I walk around the corner and frantically text Liz.

How much longer before you are back on the unit?

My phone beeps her reply. *30 minutes, why? Are you ok?*

Yup! But come see me ASAP when you are done with your meeting. Do not pass go! Do not collect $200! Do not stop! Focus and find me FIRST!

OK, see you soon. You are freaking me out!

Returning to Kyle's room, I attempt to look professional, calm, and cool. David looks up at me. He's clueless. He has no idea who I am. He was so busy gawking at Liz all night; he didn't even notice me. That's the story of my life, always the friend in the shadows, watching the fun from the sidelines. Never front and center in all the attention.

Moving on, it's time to play ICU nurse. The role I have perfected and truly love. When Liz arrives on the floor, I'm going to corner her. She needs to know that the man that asked her to stay for a drink, which she blew off, is now standing in my patient's room. I can't believe it. She is not going to believe me.

I spend some time with David in silence as he assesses the situation.

"Sit down in this chair before you fall down, David. You're not looking so good yourself. I don't need two patients in one room. Please sit before you fall down."

He grabs the chair and plops down, exhausted and spent. I have seen that look many times before. David hangs his head and props his elbows on his knees while holding his head.

"What am I going to tell my parents? Do I say, 'So, Mom, your sons were idiots by being wild and reckless and now Kyle is half dead'?"

Pulling up the other chair and positioning it next to David, I am on the same level as him. I place my hand on his shoulder to offer comfort. This is something I do all the time. It is so natural to me that it takes me a moment to realize David's arm is rock solid under that T-shirt sleeve. I can feel the strength under that T-shirt as Superman comes to mind. I reel my mind back to the present and decide against taking my hand away. It would look awkward to pull my arm away when consoling a family member is so perfectly normal.

"David, your brother is not half dead. Yes, he is very badly busted up, especially facially. The swelling definitely makes it look ten times worse. His facial injuries will require the attention of an ENT surgeon, I'm sure. Doctor Benjamin, who is the trauma surgeon, has already contacted the facial surgery team for a new consult. They will be up here later today to examine Kyle. Until then, he will remain sedated."

It appears David intently hangs on to my every word, as he doesn't seem to take his eyes off my lips. Like most loved ones, I'm sure his thoughts are chaotic and he wants to ask a hundred different questions but not knowing where to begin.

"David, your brother will need to stay sedated for a while. He needs to rest as his body starts the healing process. There is a lot of facial swelling and one can only assume the swelling has extended into his throat. Kyle has to stay on the ventilator until his swelling decreases. If we remove it too soon, his trachea may be too swollen to allow airflow, depriving his lungs and body of needed oxygen. This is why we say we are protecting his airway for him until he is able to do it himself."

After I explain all the equipment in the room and answer his many questions, I can't help but stare at him and think of all the X-rated thoughts I had about him and his brother last night. The shorter phone guy was yummy. My stomach clenches as I watch David watching Kyle's every breath as he sleeps.

"So, we don't know how long that could take, do we?"

Shaking my head, I sigh. "No, I'm afraid not. Every person is different. The doctors will make sure Kyle's lungs are strong enough to handle the extra work of breathing. Once he is strong enough, we can remove the tube. It's a process, David. One day at a time. To Kyle's benefit, he's young, healthy, and appears in good shape. This will help him out tremendously."

"Thank you so much for explaining all this to me. I'm sorry, I forgot your name again?"

"It's Mindy."

"Thank you again, Mindy."

"You're very welcome. You can ask me anything, and if I don't know the answer, I will find you someone who does."

"When can he have visitors?"

"David, the Trauma ICU is a very busy place. We allow one visitor at a time, and immediate family only. That would include parents, spouses, siblings, and adult children only. Who else should be on Kyle's visitation list?"

"Just my mom and dad. I'm his only sibling, and there is no spouse."

"Okay, do I need to add a girlfriend or something like that?"

"No, it's just us for now. It's been like that for a while. We both were taking a break from women for a while. That's what this trip was all about. Just hanging out with each other and enjoying a vacation. We both needed a break. You know? Time to decompress, enjoy life, and time with each other. We both have stressful jobs and, ironically, estranged women we needed to get away from. The bullshit needed to end, so we decided on a whim to getaway. We both had available unused vacation time, so we just packed up and left on one day's notice. We didn't even tell our parents we were out of town. We wanted to just unplug and sow some wild oats for a week. Look where that got us." His eyes tear up. "My brother, who doesn't look like anything I've ever seen before, is on a breathing machine. I know what you said, Mindy, and I understand, but you have to admit, he looks pretty bad."

"David, the swelling is so distorted that yes, it looks bad. But I promise you, the swelling will eventually go down. Your brother is still in there. He's just sedated."

"Thank you, Mindy, for taking the time to explain all that to me. Now I can call my parents and explain the situation a little bit better. Hopefully, they won't freak out too badly. If you will excuse me, Mindy, I'm going to take a break for a while; go grab a bite to eat and call my parents."

"Please, take all the time you need. I need to do a few things to care for him now, anyway. This is a great time for you to leave for a little bit. Go take a break and breathe. I've got him, and I'll be right here with him for a while."

"Okay, thanks. I'll be back later."

Hearing David's pain hidden in his deep exhale as he exits the room toward the elevator, I stare at Kyle. This once beautiful face, now swollen and misshapen in my care. I never expected this today. The Greek god in a bed before me, at work no less.

Chapter 4

Vhile taking the patient's vitals, I spot Liz walking by. "Liz, hey! Come here quick."

"What's up? What's with the anxious text earlier? You're being weird." She says as she enters my patient's room and stands at the foot of the bed.

"Liz. Seriously. Look at this patient. I mean, really look at him." I squeal. "What do you see?"

"Okay. I see an intubated patient who looks like he just got into the worst fistfight of his life and lost. His face is a mess."

"Okay, is that it?"

"Well, I see a right leg that looks broken without looking at his x-rays. I'm not sure about a head injury, though. Oh, and, he's got great hair and a beautiful smooth rippled chest."

"Exactly!" I screech. "Look at his body, Liz."

"How can I miss it, Mindy? It's amazing. So trim and fit."

"Exactly, like a Greek god?"

"You think all rippled men look like Roman gods, Mindy?"

"I didn't say anything about Roman gods, Liz. I said Greek gods! I don't usually say Greek very often, do I?"

From the look in her eyes, the light bulb comes on. Her eyebrows shoot up and her hands wave wildly.

"Oh, my God! Is this the guy from last night at the restaurant?"

"This, my dear friend, is my cell phone man with the black leather watch!"

"What? You mean the guy at the bar? The shorter one, the one who never looked up from the phone, but you spotted him anyway?"

"The exact one, Liz. Can you believe it? His name is Kyle Masterson and the tall guy is his brother, David."

"Come on! Are you serious? Are you sure? How do you know? What happened? Tell me, Mindy."

"Geez, Liz, slow down. You're firing questions at me one after the other, and I need time to answer."

She smiles at me because she knows I'm right.

"So apparently the guys were down here on a weekend getaway, kind of living it up, I guess. David said they both have stressful jobs and were trying to escape from work and unforgiving, estranged old girlfriends. I guess today they were out on the jet skis and Kyle hit a wave and it threw him off. He went flying into the rocks at the jetty. He was nearly drowning and has all of these facial fractures and a broken right femur. So far, it doesn't look like he has a brain injury. Luckily, the CT scan so far is negative. Can you believe it? Liz, I can't believe these are the same guys we saw last night. What are the chances?"

"So, what is Doctor Benjamin saying about the prognosis?"

"I guess if his CT scan stays negative and doesn't show any head bleed, and he can wean off the ventilator in a timely fashion, then hopefully he can make a full recovery. Although he'll need some facial surgery, too, I bet. He has a broken eye socket on the right and bad swelling. The ENT surgery team is seeing him later this afternoon, and ortho will be fixing his leg tomorrow."

Liz looks around and whispers to me, "So where is his hot bother?"

"He stepped away for a break and a bite to eat. I think he was getting up the nerve to call his parents. They don't even know he is here yet. They just took off and never told anyone where they were going." I look at her inquisitively. "OMG, Liz, for someone who blew him off the other night, you seem so eager to see him now. At a time like this, no less."

"Oh, come on, Mindy. You have to admit his name fits him."

Looking at Liz, my forehead wrinkles with confusion. "I don't get it. What does that mean? I think I'm missing the point."

"Duh, the perfect man? The famous Michelangelo statue of David? Don't you think he looks like that?"

I roll my eyes. "Now I get it, Liz! Geez, I think I'd have to see him naked, to be sure. You know, for comparison." We both giggle. "But seriously, Liz. I've got to get him cleaned up before David comes back. Do you have a few minutes to help me?"

"Sure, let's get to it before we have a room full of visitors." Liz closes the heavy sliding glass doors and pulls the curtain together for privacy.

In the ICU, all rooms are private and all doors are glass for easy viewing of patients.

We start at the head and work our way down, just like our mommas taught us. His hair is in disarray. I comb it back and see it naturally part. It's beautiful, and jet back. The waves in his hair are apparent, now that I have properly combed it.

His face is a mess and needs tender loving care. I gently wash his forehead and cheeks and slowly remove the dried blood from his eyebrows. The sutured laceration above his right eye now becomes evident.

"Oh man, Liz, this is going to hurt when he wakes up. It is so swollen. Maybe a small ice pack will help. I'll check with Doctor Benjamin about that when we're done."

Liz is cleaning his arm and chest.

"Hey, Liz. I think I found dimples. I'm cleaning his cheek and I can see a dimple. Well, well, well, that makes him even cuter now, doesn't it?"

"Sure does, in my opinion, you know that. Gosh, Mindy, take a look at this chest, would you?"

"Why? What's wrong with it?"

"Girl, absolutely nothing! It's perfect. It's smooth, firm, warm, and ripped. He's got a fine six-pack for sure. No love handles here. Just solid muscle. And look at that?"

Looking in the direction where she's pointing, the perfect completion of the abdominal cavity, the famous V that leads to the lower pelvis—the fun zone. It's amazing. Defined and muscular. There is a small trail of black hair that travels from his navel to the top of his pubic hair. Then there is the "forbidden fruit" area. His hair is well-groomed, just as I imagined it would be. A man who looks this good takes care of himself everywhere. Manscaping is a beautiful thing.

Looking up to see Liz watching me with that I-know-what-you're-thinking grin, I tilt my head. "What?"

Saying nothing, she just smiles at me. She catches me gawking, and there is no way out of it. She knows me too well. I'm busted!

"Well, would you just look at that? Isn't that impressive?"

"Liz, you're horrible. How can you say that about a patient?"

"Oh, come on, Mindy. It's human woman nature. Check it out, it's huge, and it's not even hard. Can you imagine what it would be like at its full potential?"

"Jesus, Liz, focus."

She smirks and we move on. It's a good thing we are the only two in the room and behind closed doors, because the words "horribly unprofessional" come to mind. Seriously, she is right. That is a divine piece of art, and I can only imagine its beauty at full length. I'm feeling that tingle as my cheeks flush and my womanhood feels a slow burn. Man, I need to stop it. *Pull yourself together, Mindy, this is work.* This is a patient…although a seriously delightful distraction for a few minutes, I must admit.

Kyle's bed bath is complete, and he looks so much better. The swelling has not improved, and won't for a few days, but at least all the old dried blood from his face is gone. At least part of him is visible, and, yes, definitely dimples. Score!

An hour later, it's time to do another neuro assessment and check Kyle's brain function. I decrease his sedation and wait for signs he may wake up a little bit to participate. In the meantime, I check his pupil function.

I gently open his swollen eyes and see the most beautiful shade of ice-blue eyes looking back at me. If only they were really looking at me. They have that sedation look, that nobody's-home look. His pupils are equal and reactive. Thank goodness. So far, so good.

Kyle's heart rate increases. A sudden cough and an alarm from the ventilator alerts me. He's awakening. Going to his side, I take his hand in mine. He slightly, but weakly, grips my hand. Did I imagine that? I don't think so.

I lean in close to him. "Kyle, squeeze my hand if you can hear me." He squeezes my hand. Kyle squeezes my other hand on command, too. His grip is strong, and he's holding tight as if he doesn't want to let go. I explain to him that he is in the hospital and safe. He squeezes my hand again. He is following commands; this lets me know his cognitive brain function is intact. This is a huge relief. An assessment of his lower extremities shows the strength in his legs is weaker, as expected, considering his leg injury. But he can wiggle his toes.

"Kyle, you have a breathing tube in place to help you breathe. Try and remain calm. You are safe and your brother knows that you are here."

He squeezes my hand several times when I mention David. His heart rate increases.

"Don't worry about David, Kyle. He is safe and here in the hospital waiting room."

He relaxes the grip on my hand as I talk more about David. This leads me to believe that he is worried about his brother at a time like this when he is the one on a ventilator.

After my assessment is complete, and not wanting him to be awake too long, I re-sedate Kyle. It would be too uncomfortable for him to be wide awake on a ventilator with that type of injury. Once the swelling has gone down, then it will be better.

Standing in the doorway, watching the monitors, I also watch him breathe. He looks better for when his parents come to visit but is still shocking nonetheless. Just as I turn to leave to check on another patient, I run headfirst into a solid brick wall of muscle. I bounce off so quickly that two strong arms catch me and steady me.

"Ooh. I am so sorry. I should really watch where I'm going."

"No worries. I just kind of snuck up on you there. I was just watching you as I walked up the hallway. You are very focused and observant." He smiles.

"Thank you. I try to pay attention to the little subtle details a patient is sending. Sometimes, it makes all the difference. And now your brother looks so much better. I don't want your parents to freak out too much, you know? Anything I can do to help Kyle look better is my goal."

"Well, Mindy, he looks one hundred times better than before. You did a great job on his face. He is starting to look more like himself. Swollen as hell, but better."

"Yeah, those cheeks are to die for," I say as my cheeks blush. Shit, why did I say that? My mouth filter didn't kick in as usual and my brain engages before I have time to shut it! God, I'm so embarrassed. I quickly try to recover from a situation in which there is no way out.

"What I mean is, I'm sure that face and those cheeks have made many a woman swoon over him. I'm sure women must get in line to get a chance to talk to him and make a lasting impression." With my back to David, I try to hide my embarrassment and put myself in check. *Calm down, Mindy, and get rid of the blushing cheeks. You are giving yourself away already.*

"Actually, Mindy, Kyle is kind of a shy guy. He doesn't go out much, and it takes him a long time to approach women. Although he is definitely a good-looking guy. How can he not be? He's related to me. We share the same gene pool. You know, that tall, dark, and handsome type?"

"Yeah, I know. I can definitely see it." What the hell did I just say? My conscience and mind are screaming at me. *Oh, shit, Mindy! Shut the hell up. You are digging yourself into a big hole and never coming out.*

Shaking my head, I hang it low. My mouth engages before my brain. Strike two! God, I think I'm hopeless.

David looks at Kyle in the bed and then at me. I understand his question without him saying a word. "Yes, David, you can touch him. Hold his hand and talk to him. He is lightly sedated enough to be comfortable, but not so deep that he can't hear you. He probably won't remember any of this, but for now, he should be able to hear you."

"How did you know what I was going to ask?"

"I've been an ICU nurse for a long time, David. I know the look. Please, feel comfortable and touch him, it's okay. It actually helps and proves to be soothing to patients. Don't be afraid. Pull up a chair and sit with him. I promise it's okay."

David pulls the chair next to the bed, sits down, and reaches for his brother's hand. "You're going to be all right, bro. You've got this great nurse taking care of you. I'm here and I'm not going anywhere, I promise. Just rest and do as she says. She's pretty smart, you know, and she's got your back. She's cute, too, so that's helpful." He smiles as he looks up at me.

Ugh, my conscience says, *There is that word again. Cute.* Well, I guess if I look on the bright side, at least he didn't call me a bitchy old nurse. It could always be worse.

David inhales sharply, which alerts me something is going on. I whip my head around and look at the heart monitor. Kyle's pulse slightly elevates. "What just happened?"

"I felt him squeeze my hand, Mindy. He actually did it." David is grinning from ear to ear as he looks at me.

"He does follow commands, David, and he can hear you. See? He is responding and his heart rate is showing you that he is a little bit awake. That is such a good sign, but I don't want Kyle agitated, okay? He seems okay, but in a few minutes, I'm going to give him more sedation so he can rest."

"Okay, I'll make it quick." He turns those amazing crystal blue eyes back on Kyle and I see him tear up. "Kyle, man, you got this. Just rest. Mom and Dad are on their way and I'm here. You are going to be fine. I love you, man."

With that, Kyle squeezes David's hand again. I shake my head to David in acknowledgment that it's time for him to rest as I increase his pain medication and sedation medication.

David looks at me. "What can I do for you? How will I ever thank you for taking such good care of him?"

"David, there is nothing you need to do for me. Just be with him and be safe. You don't need to thank me. I do this because I love it. It is my pleasure, and my reward is to see Kyle get out of the ICU."

"Well, thanks anyway. I can tell you love your job; it shows. We are so lucky to have a nurse like you."

<h1 style="text-align:center">Chapter 5</h1>

It's an hour before the end of my shift, and I look into Kyle's room through the closed glass doors. He looks peaceful. His vital signs are stable and his breathing is slow and steady on the ventilator. David is there, never leaving for a moment, just like he promised. I watch David as he stares at his brother. Continually looking between the monitor and Kyle, watching for any signs of change in his condition. His eyebrows furrow as worry is constantly visible on his face. The love of a brother, his best friend, is evident as I watch through the cold glass door.

As I think for a moment, maybe there is something David can do for me. Is this the appropriate time to ask? I look around and assess the situation first. Kyle is under sedation and resting on the ventilator. My other patient is sleeping and stable. I have a few extra minutes on my hands.

Sliding the glass door open, I quietly sneak in and take a seat next to Kyle. "Hey, David, you look like you could use a break."

"No, I'm good. I'm just keeping him company. What's going on with you these days?"

"Actually, David, there is something I've been meaning to discuss with you."

He turns to face me. "Oh boy, this sounds serious. What's up?"

"Well, it has nothing to do with Kyle's medical condition, so you can relax."

"Okay, what else is the matter then, Mindy? You're making me nervous?"

"Nothing is the matter, you can relax. I just have a question. I know this may not be the appropriate time, but I was wondering if you would meet one of my friends?"

"You mean like on a date?"

"No, like soon. You sort of actually met once, but I'm not sure you would remember."

"How could we have met already? I've only been in town a few days. I haven't really met or been with anyone?"

"You'll see."

"Is she hot?" He grins.

Smirking, I roll my eyes. "God, David, you men are all alike. So typical, but will you do it?"

"Sure, for you I will. I have a deep respect for you, Mindy. I'll do it for you."

"Thanks, I appreciate it, and I think you will be pleased."

"So, when do I meet her?"

"Who said it was a she?"

He sees right through me. "Um, Mindy, I'm sorry if I gave you that impression, but umm…" He can't find the correct word to say to be polite and politically correct, so I help him out.

As I snicker, he sees right through me.

 "Ha, you think you're funny, don't you?"

"Yup, I had you going there for a minute, didn't I? Actually, she is my best friend and a faithful coworker. I just thought you may be interested in a sensible, smart, and drama-free kind of woman. She is kind of hot, too, so that's always helpful."

"Well, that sounds like a winner to me, Mindy. When can I meet her?"

"How about now?"

"Um, I'm not shined up appropriately to meet anyone, you know? I like to look less worn out. You know, more hot and handsome."

"Oh, I know, but you've already met her. You'll see. I'm sure it will be okay."

"Okay, Mindy, my fate is in your hands. Bring it on!"

"Trust me, David, this is going to be so good. It's going to blow your mind."

I, and my devious alter ego, excuse ourselves from Kyle's room. I immediately scour the unit for any sign of Liz and find her walking up the hall. "Hey, what are you up to?"

"Getting ready to give shift report in a few minutes. Why? What's up?"

"I need you for a few minutes. Can you spare five minutes?"

"Sure, where are we going?"

"To the Greek god's room. I need a favor."

"What kind of favor?"

She knows I'm up to something. You don't work with someone for ten years and not know their moods, their looks, and their tone of voice. I try to play it off. "Oh. You'll see."

We walk up the hallway, and David has his back to the doorway. Gosh, even his back looks good. All toned, muscular, and firm. Those big broad shoulders are amazing. Liz inhales sharply and I smile.

"Mindy, what are you up to?"

"Just follow me for a minute. Come here and trust me, would you?"

She exhales heavily, but does it. I know she will be happy about it when he turns around.

We walk in the door. "Excuse me, David, there is someone I would like you to meet."

He turns around and those piercing blue eyes light up and lock on Liz. He smiles with those perfect white teeth shining brightly. I see a dimple, too. Right there on his right cheek. Consider Liz hooked. She is a sucker for dimples. "You? I would know that face anywhere. So, now can I buy you that drink?"

"David, this is my good friend Liz, Liz Bennett. Liz, this is David Masterson."

David extends his hand to shake hers. Their eyes meet, and I can see the smoldering fire begin from here. Score! Mindy's love connection service strikes again.

"Hi, David, it's nice to meet you."

Taking a step back from their personal space, I look at my friend. By the look on her face, she is awe-struck. Those amazing crystal blue eyes and that holy hell hot body have got her hooked. She is speechless, and she is never speechless. Her cheeks are flushing.

"Well, David, now you know why she couldn't stay and have a drink with you last night. We weren't blowing you off. We really did have an early wake-up this morning. Nurse life starts at the crack of dawn."

"Now I understand. So, you really weren't blowing me off. Duty calls, as they say."

"That's right. I'm sorry I couldn't stay but you know, I can't come to work exhausted from staying out too late. I need to be on my toes at work. It's crucial."

"I'm so thankful. Now, in hindsight, I'm glad you did go home. I would much rather you be here taking care of patients and my brother than out late with me."

"Actually, Mindy is the one who convinced me it was time to go home early."

"You were there, too, Mindy?"

"See, Liz, I told you. He didn't even see me last night. Yes, David, I was there. I was standing right next to Liz when you approached her to ask her to stay and have a drink."

"Get out! I would have noticed you."

"Nope. You didn't." I laugh. "But I saw you, and Kyle, too. You were watching Liz all night, and Kyle was at the bar with his nose in his cell phone. He hardly ever looked up once. Believe me, I was watching." Oh, God, the mouth engaged again before the brain could shut it down. Strike three! My conscious mind tells me to walk away before I keep letting out more embarrassing secrets. My blushing cheeks fire up again.

Walking out of the room, I go to my computer and do nursing things, leaving David and Liz alone for a minute. I look up over my computer and into the room to see Liz smiling and blushing. This is a good thing.

A few minutes later, Liz approaches with a shit-eating grin on her face. "He's nice, isn't he?"

"Mind, he asked me out. He said all the right things. How could I say no? But a part of me is cautious. He's too smooth, you know?"

"Maybe you're just worried because he's so damn hot."

"Well, there's that, of course. But I can tell he's done this before, many times. Not this exact situation, but you know what I mean. He's been popular with the ladies. It's obvious."

"So, play hard to get, and take it easy. He's a little preoccupied right now, anyway. Just go for coffee in the cafeteria for now. Keep it on your terms and make him work for it."

"Not a bad idea Mindy, he does have a lot on his plate right now, and his brother is the priority most definitely. But he is the one who did the asking."

"So, do something to distract him and calm him at a time like this. You know how stressed families are when they feel helpless."

"Oh, I could give him something to distract him!" she says in that devilish seductive voice of hers.

"Liz! Down, girl! You know what I mean."

"I'm just kidding, but it would be a fun distraction for sure. Just the thought warms my lady parts!"

"Oh, my God, Liz, you're too much."

Returning to Kyle's room, I complete my final shift assessment and say goodnight to David.

David looks up and grins from ear to ear. "So, you're the matchmaker now, are you?"

"Yup, I'm a woman of many talents: nurse extraordinaire, friend, and matchmaker. Now if I could only find myself a match, that would be something." I sigh and look at Kyle, then back at David. "David, it's been a long day for you. You need some rest, too, you know."

"I will. I just want to stay a little bit longer into the night, then I'll go back to the hotel. Will I see you tomorrow?"

"I'm off tomorrow, but I will be back on Thursday. I'll see you then, and if Kyle isn't my patient, I will come by and check on him and say hello. Okay?"

"That would be nice," he says, with a defeated look on his face.

Placing my hand on his shoulder, this time it doesn't feel weird at all. He covers my hand with his. "Stay strong and take care of you. You need to rest, too. We've got him, so rest while you can. He will need you strong for when he wakes up."

"Thanks a million, Mindy. Have a good night."

Walking to the car with Liz, she looks like the cat that ate the canary. "So, spill it, Liz. I want the details."

"There isn't a whole lot to tell. He said he noticed me last night and couldn't keep his eyes off me. He said he thought I was a mirage. Just a vision of a hot, sexy beach babe. Not real, just his mind playing tricks on him and wishful thinking."

"And you fell for that line of shit?" I laugh because I know she did. Hell, I would have, too.

"How could I not, Mindy? Look at him. I need to at least give it a try. I may never get a chance with a Greek god again. How many people can say they went out with a real Greek God before? If he's willing to buy me a drink, I'm going!"

"Good Lord, Liz! You're killing me. You know I'm living vicariously through you, right? Well, at least let me know when you're going out so I can spy on you guys."

"You got it, Mind."

"I just had a crazy thought, Liz. Do you even think he is Greek?" Laughter ensues and I shake my head as we both get in our cars and head for home.

Chapter 6

My cell phone is ringing. Another unknown caller. I don't answer it. They call back. I ignore it again. The third time, I answer the damn phone because now I'm pissed.

"Hello?" I yell into the phone, short-tempered and bitchy. Silence. What the fuck? I'm so sick of this. I need to block this number. I hang up and immediately block the number. That will teach you to mess with me, shithead!

Ten minutes later, my cell phone rings again. Now I'm more pissed because I think it's another bogus phone call. The caller I.D. reads: *Mom*. I clear my throat to make sure I don't sound so pissed off because she will sense it and know something's up. That mother's intuition gets me every time.

I answer the phone, with all my stomach jitters safely tucked away for now. "Hey, Mom."

"Hello, honey. I was wondering if you want to come for dinner? It's your favorite."

"Oh, is that a passive-aggressive way to bribe me, Mom?"

"You know it!" She boils over with laughter. "Honey, we miss you and want to hang out for a while. Do you have plans?"

"Nope, you caught me on a good night. I'll be over later. How's five-ish?"

"Sounds great. See you then, honey."

∾

"Hey, Mom, I'm here," I yell as I roam through the house. I find my parents chilling on the back patio with cocktails in hand.

"Hey, guys, what's up?" I walk outside. "Mom, the house smells so good." There is nothing as good as going home to Mom's cooking when she is making my favorite meal. "The kitchen smells like Grandma's kitchen. It's amazing. Brings back such great memories."

"It sure does, honey, and thanks for the compliment. If I could be half the cook that woman was, then I'll be excited."

"Well, I'll let you know when I taste it. Gram always made a wicked good chicken cacciatore. We'll see if you live up to her reputation." I laugh as my mom throws the dishtowel at me.

"Smart ass. I've got to go check dinner. I'll be right back."

"I'll help. What can I do?"

"Well, grab the lettuce and tomatoes and help me with this salad. You know how I hate to cut up all this stuff."

"No worries, I'll do it. You just concentrate on the chicken so you don't fuck up my favorite dish of all time."

"Ooh, girl, I'll get you for that." She smiles. We laugh and catch up as we prepare dinner for the three of us. "So," she pauses, "have you heard from Brad lately?"

"Why would you ask me that, Mom? You know we don't talk."

"Well, I bumped into Mrs. Tyler at the store the other day and your name came up in conversation."

"Did it now? How so? I'm dying to hear this one!"

"Well, I probably shouldn't tell you this, but she said Brad was depressed and so sad since you left him. That he regretted not fighting for you harder and making you see how good you were for him."

"Well, Mom, I haven't told you the story as to why and how we broke up in the first place."

"No, you haven't, honey, and I didn't want to ask too many questions. I figured you would tell me when you were ready."

"Well, that's a first. You always have a hundred questions for me. Okay, Mom, here are the cold hard facts."

I take a deep breath. This will shock my mom, I'm sure, but she needs to hear it so she will get off my back about Brad. She thinks he was Mr. Wonderful because that's the only side of him he revealed to her and my dad. Well, shocker, he was a slime ball, a cheater, and emotionally abusive. But she doesn't know a thing, yet. Here goes nothing.

"So, Mom, I don't feel sorry for Brad being depressed at all. Actually, I'm sure that's just a line of crap he's feeding his mom, so she will feel sorry for him. He certainly didn't look all that depressed when I caught him balls deep inside another woman in our bed!"

Mom whipped her head around so fast, she made herself dizzy. "*What?* Are you fucking kidding me?"

"Mom, your language!" I'm laughing; all smiles because I know I can tell my mom anything, and she will be cool with it. She is a great mom and is my best friend. But she is a mom, so I don't tell her everything.

"Nope, Mom, I'm not. He really is a bastard. Some of the things he used to say to me were so demeaning and hurtful; it was ridiculous. He used to say things like, 'Just be happy you have a boyfriend. I could always go find someone better, you know?' Or he would say, 'You always look so plain-Jane. Can't you be a little sexier and sluttier, you know, like that thin hot girl over there?'

"He was always eyeing for something better and demeaning me. He even threatened me once. He said if I didn't start putting out more, he would go find it somewhere else. Well, he was true to his word on that one. I'll give him credit for that. He went and found someone else. Actually, he found several others to help him keep his word and to sleep with. I just happened to catch him in the act."

"Shit, Mindy, how did it happen? Inquiring minds want to know?"

"He forgot that he had given me a key to his place last spring. Remember when he went away for 'business' and he needed me to watch Pedro, his dog? Well, he never asked for the key back, so I kept it, thinking I would surprise him one day. Well, the joke was on me.

"Well, I never mess up my schedule, but this particular week, I switched shifts with Liz, so she could go to an appointment. But I never took myself off work in my datebook. So, I showed up to work on my day off, by mistake. They actually were well-staffed that day, believe it or not, and didn't need me. I thought since I had a bonus day off, I would go to Brad's and make him breakfast before work. That's easy to do when my day starts at 6:30 a.m., right? Well, I thought it was a good idea. That is, until I walked into his apartment and found him in bed, having sex with another woman! He didn't even see me at first, and he was doing things to that woman that were so out of character for him. It was a side of Brad I didn't know.

"That chick was handcuffed to the bed and blindfolded. Brad was like a madman. He was all rough and caveman-like with her, Mom. Using foul language and slapping the shit out of her ass. I don't know how they didn't put the bed through the wall, with all that ferocious banging. I thought the headboard was going to break. And all that yelling and moaning. Jesus, it was like watching a rough porno flick. He was an animal.

"So, I watched for a few minutes, and when they were done, and her blindfold was removed, I stood tall in the doorway and cleared my throat. Loudly. His head snapped around and the woman was in shock. She couldn't move, since she was shackled to the bed. All she could do was look at me. And I wanted to look at her! I wanted a good look at the slut who was fucking my boyfriend."

"Mindy! T.M.I.! I don't need all those types of details, Jesus. Just saying he slept with someone else would have been enough."

"Well, Mom, you wanted to know, now you know. He never made me feel like I was enough. He always made me feel like I was the one who always had to improve, measure up, and be grateful. That I should be thankful that I had a man on my arm such as him. He even told me once how hot he thought he was, and that I should be tending to his every need because there were plenty of other women who would jump at the chance to have him. Do you know what that was like for me, Mom? To think that you're never enough for your man? It fucks with your head, Mom, that's what it does. So, I told him I was tired of all the threats and since he was enjoying himself with his 'plenty other women in the world,' he could have them because I was done. He didn't deserve me!"

"Oh, Mindy, I'm so sorry. I had no idea. Is there anything I can do now to help you?"

"No, Mom, just listen and be supportive, and please, get off the Brad train, okay? No more talking about him and wondering if I'm over him. It's done and long over. I've worked really hard to move on. Feeling good about myself helps and my confidence is returning. I'm getting there. Now, can we eat already? I'm starved. Let's see if you're cooking really measures up to Grams."

"Sure, honey, let's get your dad."

Dinner and dessert were phenomenal, as expected. It really is nice to come home once in a while for family dinners. It warms my soul and keeps me grounded. I'm forever thankful.

Chapter 7

My work cell phone beeps with a new text. "Mindy, please come to the front desk when available."

Oh shit, am I in trouble? Now what? God only knows what kind of mess I'm in. I approach the nurse's station desk and see a delivery man holding one dozen long stem yellow roses.

"Excuse me, Miss. Are you Mindy Harper?"

"Yes, may I help you?"

"Um, um Miss, these are for…for you," he stutters. "I was given explicit instructions to…to deliver these…these to you, and only…only you."

"Well, thank you, they are super gorgeous. And they smell amazing. These are the biggest roses I have ever seen. Who are they from?"

"Um, I can't…can't tell you. You need to sign…sign for them and then I can give…give you the card." He stares at me, then looks me up and down. Ooh, there is that awkward, uneasy feeling in my gut again. What the hell, he's just the delivery guy. My conscience brings me to reality. *Relax, girlfriend. Reign in your inner detective-ness. He's just a shy guy with a speech impediment. Cool your jets.*

After signing the receipt, I thank the delivery man, and he walks away, stopping halfway down the hall toward the elevator. He looks over his shoulder, straight at me. He waves, and it makes me feel uncomfortable, but I'm friendly and don't want to be rude, so I wave back.

"Holy shit, Mind. This is the hugest bunch of roses I have ever seen," Liz says, with excitement.

"Right? I have no clue who they could be from."

"Well, you're never going to know if you don't open the card, shithead."

"All right already. Hold your horses, lady." I open the card with shaking fingers.

For an Exceptional Nurse
With Gratitude and Love,
T.

"Oh my God, Liz! Do you know who this is from?"

"Nope, haven't a clue."

"Yes, you do. Think. Remember the patient I had last week that was sort of giving me the creeps? You know, the guy who wanted a hug when he left the ICU and then gave me his business card?"

"You mean the guy that was shot in the chest?"

"Yup, that's the one. He is the president of The Creeks Motorcycle Club, according to his business card. But I didn't know that until after he had left the ICU. That's when I looked at his card."

"Well, that's just great, Mind. Just what you need. Quiet, little ol' Mindy with a biker hot after her ass!"

"Hey, nobody said he was after my ass. He's just sending me a thank you, that's all. You know, out of respect."

"Okay, girlie, you keep thinking that. And when the biker gang shows up to kidnap you for a gangbang, I'll be the one to call the police for you."

"Jesus, Liz. Stop it. I happen to know The Creeks Motorcycle Club is a non-profit motorcycle club that does a lot of good for people in our area. They even do Toys for Tots and stuff like that."

"How do you even know that, Mindy?"

"My mom has a friend whose brother is a Creek, if I remember correctly. I never really heard my mom talking about them as being bad boys."

"Well, just remember, Mind, I warned you and I've got your back."

"Got it, Liz, and thanks. And hey, you never know when I might need a bad boy biker at my side to make a 'statement.' You know, to ward off evil spirits?" I laugh as I walk away.

"Yeah, Mindy the Biker Bitch. In black leather and shit. Now that would be a sight."

Cracking up with laughter as I walk into Kyle's room, I stop in my tracks. There is an older woman at the bedside, holding his hand and weeping. She looks up at me. "Hi, I'm Samantha, Sam, Kyle's mom."

"Oh, hello. I'm Mindy. I'm his nurse today. It's a pleasure to meet you." I shake her hand. "Mrs. Masterson, may I get you something? You're trembling."

"No, dear. Just take good care of my baby, okay?"

"I'll do my best, Mrs. Masterson."

"Please call me Sam. Samantha sounds so formal and snooty, and I am anything but formal."

"Okay, Sam. Do you have any questions for me? I know David has been updated, but you probably have a million worries."

"David actually did a good job filling me and Bob, Kyle's father, in on all the details. We just finally got into town last night and this is the second time we have gotten to see him. He actually looks a little better, I think."

"Sam, I haven't seen him in two days, and I can tell you he looks a hundred times better. The swelling on his eyes and cheeks has improved so much, I'm shocked at how good he looks, actually."

"So, what do you think the plan will be for today?"

"Doctor Benjamin and the trauma team will be around soon to evaluate him. Feel free to stay in the room so you can have a chance to talk to the team and discuss the plan of care. Okay?"

"I would love that, thank you."

Looking at Kyle from his mother's angle—holy hell, he's beautiful. His facial features are returning to normal and man, he's something. He takes my breath away. Good Lord. When all this is over and he is awake, I don't know how I will ever look him straight in the eyes without blushing. I have a bad habit of not being able to hide my facial expressions and wearing my feelings on my face. That's why I never lie. You can always tell. Better to tell the truth and live with it, then lie and be fake, a lesson learned the hard way.

Doctor Benjamin walks into the room just as I finish my assessment. "Hello, I'm Doctor Benjamin from the trauma team. And you are?"

"I'm Samantha Masterson, Kyle's mom." Her voice is shaky. I can hear the stress in every word she says. I can't imagine how helpless she must feel. To see her baby laying in a bed, tubes, and wires everywhere, and knowing she is not the one to fix him. That she has to leave all her trust in medicine, and God, to heal him. That it's all resting on the shoulders of doctors and nurses she doesn't even know, to keep her child alive. It's a complete and utter surrender of control. It's a parent's nightmare.

She takes a deep breath. "So, what's the prognosis, Doctor?"

"Kyle is doing exceptionally well, and the swelling has gone down significantly in his face and eyes. I believe the ENT surgeon, Doctor Max, is planning on taking him to surgery this evening to fix all the broken bones in his face."

"Do you know when that will be? I need to let my husband know of the plan?"

"I'm not sure. Doctor Max just texted me and said sometime this evening. I think he needs to finish office hours first and then he is heading this way. As soon I find out the exact time, I'll have Mindy let you know."

"Thank you, I really appreciate it."

"Mrs. Masterson, there is one more thing I want to discuss with you."

Sam looks up at Doctor Benjamin with that impending doom of fear in her eyes.

"Although Kyle was removed from the water rather quickly, all things considered, there is a chance he may not wean off the ventilator as quickly as I would like. You see, salt water is not a good thing for the lungs. Now, he is young and obviously in shape."

Now that's an understatement, if I do say so myself.

"So hopefully he will be able to overcome that issue. The plan is, once his facial surgery is completed, we hope to wake him up and wean him off the ventilator. He may or may not do well. We have to take it one step at a time and see how it goes.

"If the surgery is completed tonight, then we will let him rest overnight and try to wean him off the ventilator tomorrow. That is, providing he has a good stable night."

"I understand, Doctor Benjamin. Thank you for taking the time to explain all that to me. Let's hope it all goes smoothly."

I watch as Sam exhales and cries. I approach, and she looks up at me with eyes reflecting a sad mother.

"Sam, you have the best ENT surgeon working on him tonight. Hang in there. Okay?"

"I will, thanks. I think I'm going to go call my husband and give him the update."

"Okay. I'll be here when you get back. Take your time." My heart feels a pang of empathy as I watch Sam slowly walk to the elevator, crying.

Chapter 8

Doctor Max took Kyle to surgery two hours ago. He told Mrs. Masterson that it would be at least a three-to-four-hour surgery. She is patiently waiting in his room for any news from the surgery team.

Mindy and I head out for the day. On our way past the cafeteria, we see David sitting alone at a table in the cafeteria. "Hey, Mindy, I see David sitting over there looking all lonely. I think I'm going to go over to say hi."

"I think you should, Liz. I'll see you this weekend, okay?"

"You got it. Have a good night and stay out of trouble, okay?"

"I make no promises." Mindy laughs.

I approach David, who is deep in thought and scrolling through his phone.

"May I sit down?"

"Why, of course. I would love that."

"How would you like to buy me that drink now?" I raise an eyebrow.

"What will it be, madam? Bad hospital coffee, tea, soda, or a bottle of water?"

"Hmm, such decisions. I guess I'll have Diet Coke, please."

"My pleasure, but keep in mind, this wasn't exactly the type of drink I had initially offered. I had more of a cocktail in mind."

"Well, my dear David, so did I, but this will do for now. When Kyle is better, then we can grab that cocktail. How does that sound?"

"Sounds like a date and a promise to me," he says with a huge grin on his face.

I strike up a light and easy conversation and the talk is casual. You know, the typical "What brought you to the beach? What do you do for a living?" type of conversation.

"So, David, what made you decide to be a police officer?" Now I know why he is so physically fit. Police officer. Isn't it ironic? Nurses are frequently hooking up with police officers and firefighters. I wonder why?

Maybe the mutual need to serve the public? Or is it just the attraction of a man in a uniform?

"When I was a kid, I saw a man push an elderly woman out of the way as he was running down the street. He had stolen something from a store, and the police were chasing him. The cop jumped a fence and tackled the robber, handcuffed him, and arrested him. The cop also pulled the man up to his feet and dragged him over to the woman he almost knocked over. He made him apologize to her in front of everyone. It was awesome. From that moment on, I knew I wanted to help people and keep the bad guys away. Now, as an adult, I realize how much more complicated reality is, but the premise is the same."

"That's the sweetest story, David. See, you never know how childhood events can shape and mold someone's future."

I watch David's every move, burning his features into my memory as we sip our sodas.

"I just want you to know, the minute I saw you walk into that restaurant, I was stuck on you."

"Stuck on me? What does that mean? Like gum on the bottom of your shoe?"

He chuckles. "Oh, come on, Liz, you know. Like I couldn't get you out of my mind. You drove away and my heart skipped a beat and I felt so deflated."

"Come on, David, that is such a line of shit if I've ever heard one." My inner voice yells at me. *Seriously, Liz, He's just a player, looking for a good time while on vacation.* I think about that for a moment. His boys' week away on vacation ended with his brother being admitted to the ICU. Maybe he is a good guy and telling the truth? Time will tell.

"Your heart skipped a beat? Seriously? Is that the best line you've got? David, I'm not buying it." I beam as I take another sip of soda.

"Listen, Liz, I'm a man of my word. I speak the truth. I'm a police officer and proud to admit a detective, too. I believe in the truth. I need the truth and I expect the truth. I will not lie to you, especially when I'm trying to make a good impression."

"I'm sorry, David. I didn't mean to offend you. I'm just saying that line sounded a little corny and rehearsed."

"Okay, Liz, how about this for the honest truth? I was having a drink, minding my own business, when I glanced up to look around and watch the sunset over the ocean. I saw you walk in, and I actually felt my heart skip a beat. I inhaled sharply and felt a warm rush all the way to my crotch. Your beautiful face caught my every cell on fire. Liz, you're absolutely beautiful. You have that girl-next-door look. You know, the girl everyone wants to date? Subtle makeup, yet stunning, with no crazy wardrobe. You have that classy, sassy look. I was drawn to you instantly. I needed to talk to you. I wanted desperately to talk to you."

My brain is in overdrive. Okay, this guy's good. Now that he is telling me the truth, or so he says, he's slowly working his way into my system. The wall of protection I have built around me is crumbling brick by brick. Oh, he's good, so very good.

"I saw you walk in with such poise and grace, yet tall and confident. I knew I needed to meet you. I had to hear your voice, smell your perfume, and touch you. So, I walked over to you. You know the rest of the story. You turned me down flat, without a second look. I was deflated. The ache in my body, I felt to my core."

He looks at me with those bright blue eyes. Good Lord! I don't think I can resist this man even if I want to.

"So, Liz, how's that for honesty?"

"Impressive."

I raise my Diet Coke in a toasting fashion. He smiles and those beautiful white teeth shine, and I melt. I mean, I melt everywhere. I can feel the warmth, the burning, and the yearning all the way down to my neglected vagina. I'm actually dripping wet. It's official, I'm on fire, and wanting him to touch me. I'm a mess with desire. How do I hide this from a man who wants honesty? Maybe I shouldn't hide it. Maybe if he wants honesty, then brutal honesty he shall have.

"Okay, if we are being honest, David, answer me one question."

"Sure. Ask away. I'm an open book."

"So, that night after Mindy and I left the restaurant, how come I saw you leave with that redhead? You know the one. She was wearing a black sundress with a gold belt and gold strappy sandals. The one with tits bigger than Dolly Parton's."

David's complexion immediately pales to ghost white.

"Busted. So how into me are you actually, if you left with another woman?"

David holds my glare as he swallows hard and I can see his Adam's apple bob up and down with his swallow. His jaw clenches and those little muscles in his cheeks tighten. I can tell he's trying to find the right words without blowing his chances with me.

"I'm waiting," I say, all sassy and bitchy.

"Well, Liz, first of all, I'm not a sleaze bag, if that's what you're thinking. I don't get in the habit of taking women home with me. What you witnessed was my attempt to have a walk on the beach with a pretty woman, and then see what happened. I know it sounds so cliché, but it's the truth. I have a strict rule: no sex on the first date. And most of the time, no sex on the second date either.

"And for full disclosure here, Liz, I didn't ever think I would see you again, so when she came up to me and asked if she could buy me a drink, I accepted. Nothing happened on our walk, just conversation. I escorted her to her car afterward and gentlemanly shook her hand goodbye. It was a very uneventful evening, except for the moment I saw you, of course."

"Thank you for your honesty, David. You have no idea how much I respect that value in a person."

"Hey, wait a minute here."

The look of confusion is on his face, loud and clear. My inner voice is yelling, *Liz, you've just been had, and in a big way!*

"If you left with Mindy, how did you see me leave with the redhead? That was like an hour later?"

I freakin' knew it! He figured it out. Now, who's the one who has to fess up? Smooth move, Liz, way to get caught red-handed in espionage. I'm a little panicked as I realize now I'm the one who has to give full disclosure. Damn!

I look at those piercing crystal blue eyes and can't lie. "Stop hypnotizing me with those beautiful eyes of yours." I blurt out, my mouth engaging before my brain. He says nothing and just keeps smiling and waiting, forever patiently waiting. He is like the cat that ate the canary, looking all proud of himself.

"Full disclosure it is. I guess I will uphold the standard of truth time you have set. David, I did notice you at the bar. Who didn't notice you? You and Kyle are like two perfectly sculpted men out of a fitness mail-order catalog. Mindy calls you both the Greek gods. That's the nickname Mindy gave you both the night she saw you at the bar. You know, the tall, dark, and handsome type? The make-me-lose-my-breath-and-get-weak-in-the-knees kind of man."

"Yes, Liz, I know what Greek god means. Go on, please. I'm listening."

"After I left the restaurant, I started to drive home and regret my answer and how I spoke to you. The vision of you standing at the bar, watching me, while you were chewing on your swizzle stick, drove me insane. To be honest, it brought heat to my womanhood that I haven't felt in a long time."

"Is that so?" He raises an eyebrow as he looks at me and listens, actually blushing.

"Stop looking at me like that. Just shut up and listen." I blush. "I turned around and headed back to the restaurant. My intention was to approach you at the bar and tell you I had second thoughts, and that you deserved a chance. But when I got there, I chickened out. So, I sat there in my car for a few minutes to gather my thoughts and get up my nerve to go back in the bar and look for you. That's when I saw you walking out with that redhead in tow. She looked oh so comfy on your arm."

"Exactly. That was the problem! She was a clingy bitch who wouldn't let go of me the whole time. She didn't understand personal space and was all up in mine every minute. It was like she couldn't even walk. She was literally trying to climb up my body the whole time. So, after a short walk, I graciously escorted her to her car. I was polite, but my thoughts were like, *Bye, Felicia.* There was no hookup for me. I went home with Kyle, thinking of you!

"You actually came back for me? I can't believe that. I'm so intrigued by you and very happy to hear you say that I was driving you insane. I think that's how you put it."

"I believe everyone deserves a second chance, David. This is yours, right here and right now. Don't fuck it up."

"Oh, I don't plan to, Lizzy. A toast to second chances."

We raised our cans of Diet Coke and clinked them together.

"Lizzy? You're calling me Lizzy?"

"Yup. I kind of like it. It's endearing."

"I don't know. It makes me sound like a kid."

"Well, to me, it's more personal and intimate."

"Well, I don't dislike it, but don't call me that at work, okay? It's too cutesy."

"Deal." He smiles.

"It's getting late, David, and I really need to get going. I've got a full schedule tomorrow. Thanks for the soda. I'll see you in the morning, okay?"

"I look forward to it, Lizzy," he yells as I walk away.

Chapter 9

Doctor Benjamin has been in to assess Kyle this morning, so we will wean his sedation and wake him up. He will be foggy and disoriented and will need coaching through this process. I'm excited for his family to speak with him and have their Kyle back. It's heartwarming and soothing to my soul to watch that first interaction after extubation. He will look more like himself without that tube in his mouth, and he can finally speak. It's so rewarding.

I inform David and his parents of today's plan. Everyone anticipates the moment they can hear Kyle's voice, and secretly, I am, too.

As the sedation wears off, Kyle begins to stir. Slowly, he is becoming more restless and tense. His pulse and blood pressure are rising. The ventilator alarms as he realizes there is something in his throat. He bites on the breathing tube, which totally occludes all the airflow to his lungs. The loud ventilator emergency alarm screams out and flashes red. I look up and see the panic on everyone's faces.

"Mr. and Mrs. Masterson, this is a normal process for someone who is weaning off the ventilator. Lots of things happen at once, and sometimes it is difficult to watch. Trust me when I say this is expected and I'm prepared to handle it. Why don't you all take a break and let me work with Kyle for a little while? He needs my encouragement and guidance if we are going to get that tube out today."

David takes my cue and looks over at his parents. "Mom, Dad, let's leave Mindy to her expertise and let's go get one of those horrible hospital coffees. Mindy needs some time with Kyle to work her magic."

David glances to me as I mouth the words 'thank you.' He nods and winks.

I reach over and hold Kyle's hand. He immediately squeezes my hand. "Hey, Kyle. It's Mindy, your nurse. You're doing just fine. We need to get this breathing tube out of your mouth, so listen to me. Okay? I'm going to help you through this." He holds my hand even tighter and my stomach clenches. My inner voice kicks in and has to add her two cents. *Such a strong hand grip, he has Mindy. And look at those long fingers. You know what they say about long fingers. Just imagine!*

I can't take the noise in my head anymore. I cough and clear my throat. *Focus Nancy Nurse,* I tell myself. I look at the man before me in this industrial hospital bed. He's a helpless work of art, so handsome and broken. I focus and say out loud, "Time to get this masterpiece to come back to life."

"Kyle, in order to do this, I need you to try to remain calm. I will coach you through the whole process. I need you to try to relax as best you can, and listen to my voice. I'll be here with you. I'm not going anywhere." There is a small nod of his head in understanding. It's subtle, but I saw it. He starts to open his eyes, but they are still a little swollen, but with some effort, he should be able to open them.

I reassure Kyle this is going to be a process and I will help him. "Listen to me, Kyle. Take slow, easy breaths and think of calming your nerves." I can feel his tense muscles relax under my fingers. That's it, Kyle, easy in and easy out. You've got this. I'm right here with you, and I'm not going to let anything happen to you. You're doing great. Keep up with this great breathing and we should have this tube out in no time."

Doctor Benjamin arrives and we discuss Kyle's progress.

"He is doing great and following my lead. He is listening to my instructions and remaining calm." Doctor Benjamin decides, based on my assessments and his lab work, that Kyle is strong enough and ready to extubate. We remove the breathing tube and take the ventilator away, and then ask Kyle to say hello. It's important for us to hear his voice, to make sure there is no damage to his vocal cords.

"Hello," he says in a froggy voice. "Where am I and what the hell happened?"

"You are in Memorial Hospital. You had a jet-ski accident. Don't you remember anything?"

"I remember I was out in the deep reef area and the waves were awesome. It was a lot of fun, and then nothing but blackness. I don't remember anything else."

"Well, your brother David can tell you the rest, but I believe he said you hit a large wave and went flying off the jet-ski. You hit the rocks on the jetty just right and landed in the hospital here with me."

"And who are you?"

"I'm Mindy, your nurse. I've been taking care of you a lot since you came in last week. It's so nice to finally hear your voice."

"Can you come here, so I can see you and thank you properly?"

I look up at Doctor Benjamin with concern. He shares my concern as his facial expression drops, showing worry. I can always tell because his forehead starts to wrinkle, and he becomes very pensive. Doctor Benjamin nods and I understand. I move directly in front of Kyle, standing at the foot of the bed.

"Okay, Kyle, look at me for a minute. Kyle, open your eyes and look at me, please." He opens his eyes and those beautiful ice-blue eyes are visible but unfocused. He stares into space, motionless. I glance at Doctor Benjamin and proceed. "Kyle, do you see me?"

Kyle attempts to speak. His voice is hoarse at first. He coughs and clears his throat, then slowly says, "What the hell is going on? I don't see anything. My eyes are still closed. Why won't they open? What's happening?" he yells.

I rush quickly to the side of the bed and hold Kyle's hand. I sit down in the chair and calmly talk to him.

"Kyle, turn your head to the right and open your eyes. What do you see?" I watch him intently and scrutinize his every move. His eyes are now open a little more and I can see the beautiful blue before me.

"I see blackness. I see nothing. But my eyes feel like they are open, Mindy. Why can't I see you? What the hell is going on?"

Doctor Benjamin stoops down to Kyle's level to examine his pupils. Both pupils are reacting normally to light, thankfully. So, what the hell is going on? Doctor Benjamin flicks his fingers in front of Kyle's eyes. Nothing happens. No blink reflex. No tracking of his eyes with movement. I'm shocked and stunned. My heart is beginning to break for this man who is in the prime of his life, now with a vision problem.

Doctor Benjamin meets my eyes and gives me that silent, sad look. That look that needs no words, but says *this is bad.* He explains to Kyle that he thinks Kyle may have some eye injury from his trauma we didn't anticipate. An ENT physician will need to do further evaluation.

"Kyle, I need you to try to remain calm and let's try to keep the eye pressure to a low normal level, if possible. Getting upset and raising your blood pressure could be dangerous to your eyes, so try to rest until the eye specialist can evaluate you. Okay?"

"Sure, Doc, it's easy for you to say. You can see!"

"I will explain these new findings to your parents, and I will call the eye doctor right away. I'll keep you posted. I promise."

I'm standing against the wall, not saying a word. Just observing and processing the situation. What will Kyle do? His life, as he knew it, is potentially over. He will need to adjust his entire lifestyle. No driving, no views of the ocean, no looking at women? How's a man of his beauty going to survive that?

"Hello? Are you there? Mindy?"

"Yes, Kyle, I'm here. I didn't go anywhere. How are you doing? Are you in pain?"

"My leg aches a little, but I'm fine. I feel like my cheeks are so fat, and that I'm talking with a lisp. What happened to me?"

I tell the story to Kyle of his accident again. From experience, I can tell he is shocked and amazed that he even survived. "I'm so lucky considering I hit the jetty. I can't believe I didn't smash my head to pieces. That's so crazy. I must have had a guardian angel looking out for me. I'm so grateful to be alive, you know?"

"Yes, Kyle, I know, and I'm grateful you're alive, too. Now, this is a lot for you today, so do me a favor. I want you to rest and try to take a nap while you don't have any visitors. You have been through a lot. Your body needs to catch up and rejuvenate. Okay?"

I'm watching Kyle's every move closely as I rest my hand on his arm for support. He's trying to be calm and put together, but I can tell he's struggling. He just discovered he can't see. I'm sure he wants to lash out in anger, but he's being extremely stoic at the moment. Suddenly, his muscles tremble. Is it from fear or anger? I'm sure a little of both. I can't even imagine how he must be feeling.

"Mindy?" he softly whispers.

"Yes, I'm here."

"What are you doing right now?

"I'm just sitting here with you for a few minutes in case you need anything. What can I do for you?"

"Um, I don't mean to be rude, but I could use a few minutes to myself to process all this if you don't mind?"

"No, not at all, Kyle, but please remember I'm right outside if you need me." I give him the call bell and place his finger on the button for the nurse so he can feel it. "All you need to do is push down on this button if you need me. I'll be there, I promise. I'll be back soon to check on you."

As I quietly slide open the door to leave, he is sobbing. There it is. The crack in his reality. The realization of his diagnosis and his now "dark" life.

My heart breaks for him. I quietly close the sliding door and see his family walking up the hallway. David looks at me, as tears well in my eyes. I quickly pull it together. I don't want to make the family more upset by them seeing me upset, too. I'm supposed to be the strong one, the one to keep it all together for the patients and family.

"Hi," I say to David and his parents. "Um, before you go in there to see Kyle, can I speak with you all for a minute, please?"

"Sure," says Mr. Masterson, "Is everything okay?"

"Well, I just wanted to get an update from you about your knowledge of Kyle's plan of care and what went on so far."

David tells me about the conversation they had with Doctor Benjamin. They know Kyle's current condition and they are anxiously awaiting the eye doctor's evaluation.

"Just so you all know, I was just politely asked to leave David's room. He wanted some time to be by himself and process his diagnosis. He is angry and concerned, understandably so. I also think he is afraid. He hasn't said those exact words to me, but I can tell. No one knows if this is permanent or not and I'm sure this is scary. When I left, I could hear him quietly sobbing. Please give him some time to process all this. Okay? I will be by to check on him shortly, but he has his call bell button if he needs me sooner."

"Mindy." I look at the tear-filled eyes of Sam, Kyle's mom. "Thank you for all you've done. I rest a little easier knowing you are here taking care of him."

"Thank you, Sam. I just want what's best for my patients. Whatever I can do to help, please don't hesitate to ask me."

Sam leans over and gives me a big hug. I glance at David and see his teary eyes and my heart breaks.

Chapter 10

Doctor Keller has been in to see Kyle and examine him. Hopefully, he can determine why he can't see.

All of Kyle's family is in the room as Doctor Keller is giving his update. He begins with the obvious announcement. "Kyle, your blindness is most likely a result of the blunt force trauma you suffered when your face hit the rocks at the jetty. I believe that the force of the impact caused such swelling in your face that it put pressure on your optic nerve. This high pressure is not good for the nerves. It causes decreased blood flow to the eyes and, in your case, blindness. What we don't know is if this blindness is permanent. It can be reversed in some cases, if treated quickly."

"So, what do we need to do, and what's the plan?" asks Mr. Masterson.

"Well, quickness is the key. So, I will continue with the steroids he has already been on, just increase the dose. I'm also ordering an MRI to make sure there is no visible damage we need to surgically fix. Then, unfortunately, we wait. Time will tell if his vision returns. It could go either way."

There is silence in the room as everyone processes the news when a soft voice comes from the bed. "Well, let's get to it. Let's get this MRI done. Seconds could mean everything for me. Let's get the show on the road." Kyle says with affirmation.

Doctor Keller makes his way into Kyle's room later that afternoon. His parents are anxiously awaiting the news. I'm anxious, too, and swiftly follow him into the room so I can hear the prognosis as well.

"Well, Kyle, the MRI was very diagnostic and helpful. It looks as though you have a partially severed optic nerve. The small break in the nerve is enough to be contributing to your blindness. The good news is that I can repair it. The bad news is that I don't know if it will change your outcome. We could take you to surgery and fix it and it may never make a difference. The facial swelling you suffered definitely played a role in your injury. But fixing it definitely gives you a chance at future sight, versus doing nothing, and staying permanently blind."

Kyle takes in a huge, deep breath and blows it out. I'm sure he's processing the decision, but in my mind, it's a no-brainer. I patiently wait for his decision. There is silence in the room, and then that beautiful voice.

"Hey, Mindy, can you come over here for a minute, please?"

"What's up, Kyle?"

"I want your opinion on what Doctor Keller just told me."

"Kyle, it's not up to me. It's up to you and your family. This is your life. You all have to decide what to do. All I can ask you is, what is your gut telling you?"

"It's telling me that you have seen me from the very beginning and my progress. You have seen how I have improved, and although I can't see you, I can tell you are sweet and care about your patients. Break it down for me in simple terms, please?"

I look up at Mr. and Mrs. Masterson and then at David. They all give me the nod to go ahead. I take a deep breath as my inner voice is yelling, *Oh shit!*

"Kyle, I can't tell you what to do, but I can tell you what I would do if it were me. I would feel like some chance at seeing is better than no chance of seeing, so I would have the surgery as soon as possible if it were me."

"My thoughts exactly! So, Doc, how soon before I can have the surgery?"

"As a matter of fact, Kyle, I've already booked the O.R. for this afternoon, so we can get this done ASAP. Time is vital, so I'll see you in the pre-op area. Don't be late."

"Oh, I'll be there. No worries about that." As he flashes that killer smile and dimple.

Hours later, I send Kyle off to the operating room, wishing him good luck and "I'll be here when you get back" support.

Suddenly, he raises his hand in the middle of the hallway, stopping the orderlies from wheeling him away. "Waite, hey Mindy!"

I walk back over to Kyle and reach for his hand. "What's the matter, Kyle?"

"Nothing. I just wanted to say you're the best, and selfishly, I wanted to get one last big relaxing breath of you."

"Excuse me, what do you mean?"

"Mindy, when I wake up after surgery and can finally see you, I might not have the courage to tell you this face to face, so I thought I better tell you now. Every minute you were in my room, I knew it. I could sense you and your light perfume of amber sent my mind reeling. You could never sneak into my room. I know you tried several times not to bother me. I could always sense your presence, and I'm grateful for it. And you always smell amazing. That was always a bonus, so thank you. I will think of you and that amazing perfume scent as I drift off to sleep for surgery."

My insides clench and I blush. "Thank you, Kyle. That's very sweet. Now just don't worry and I'll see you soon. Everyone will be here when you get back." I pat his hand and squeeze his shoulder as I nod to the transport orderly to continue wheeling Kyle to the O.R.

With Kyle safely tucked away in the operating room, I see David wandering the halls. What the heck? He's acting like a lost puppy. I approach him and before I can say one word, he blurts out, "Do you know where I can find Liz? I need to see her for a minute." He looks haggard and worn out.

"David, are you okay? You look so distracted and confused."

"Yes, I'm fine. I just really need to see her for a minute."

"Okay, let me page her hospital phone for you."

I get a text back and inform David. "Hey, Liz said she is sitting outside in the courtyard having lunch."

"Thanks a million, Mindy." He takes off at a fast pace for the elevator. What the hell? He's being so strange.

I text Liz and give her the heads up. *Hey, lady, the Greek god is headed your way. Hope you're not eating tuna, lol.*

She texts back the middle finger emoji as I crack up laughing.

Chapter 11

Itry to relax for a few minutes while eating lunch outside in the courtyard. Thanks to Mindy for giving me the heads up, I try not to look so obvious watching out for him.

As I raise my cup of iced tea to take a sip, I see him approaching. I fumble with the drink and almost spill the whole damn thing in my lap, but my quick reflexes catch the cup and avoid disaster.

"Hi, Liz. Can I join you?"

"Sure, please sit. I'm sure you are having a long day and can use the fresh air. How are you and your family doing?"

He gazes at me and straddles the picnic table bench, facing me.

I notice his masculine form and how he is sitting. His muscular thighs are apparent as his pants cling to his thighs and highlight his toned body. All this muscle and now it's positioned up close and personal. My womanhood clenches as I'm burning with desire and trying to hide it. I quickly adjust my position and face him so I don't appear distracted by his bulges—all of them, not just his thighs.

"Liz, I need to tell you something."

"I knew it. You're married with kids, aren't you?"

"Liz, close your eyes and be quiet and listen to me."

With a tilted head, I give him the side-eye and he definitely gets the message.

"Please, Liz, trust me. Close your eyes, please, and listen. And no, I'm not married with kids." He snickers.

I do as he asks with bated breath. My insides melt from the fire burning within. *Lord, help me.*

What was that? What's he doing? With eyes tightly closed I wait. David scoots up, causing the bench to move. He's sitting close to me; his body heat warms me. His cologne is making me dizzy with desire and I might self-combust any minute, or better yet, fall off the bench!

David slowly cradles my face, pulling my face in closer to him. His moist, warm lips touch mine. He subtly moans, which creates a need in me so deep, I want to jump him right there on the picnic bench. I respond willingly, deepening the kiss. David's tongue roams my lips, causing my lips to part. He conquers my mouth and savors the warmth within as I weave my fingers deep within his wavy hair.

So captured by David's passion, I don't realize how lost I am in the moment until someone yells from across the courtyard, "Get a room already! You're making the rest of us jealous!"

Now embarrassed, I pull away, breathless and blushing. I look into his perfect blue eyes. "What was that for?"

"Liz, let me explain. This whole time Kyle has been sick, I have been worried to death about him. He is my best friend and I'm freaking out here. I know I need to be strong for my family and for him. Thinking of you and the anticipation of our upcoming date, whenever that may be, has been the one bright spot in all of this. I can't wait for some alone time with you, and considering who knows when that will be, I decided to break the ice now."

"Oh, I'd say the ice is broken, David. It's like broken and melted everywhere." I smile. "That was an incredible kiss. I'm a little embarrassed, but I would like for you to try to break the ice again, but I'm at work, you know?"

"I know, and I'm sorry. I just couldn't wait. All I've done for a week is think of you, and wonder how good you would taste. It's been keeping me up late at night, tossing and turning in restless fits. It's a little selfish of me, but I couldn't help it. I kind of go after what I want. I've just never done it in a hospital courtyard before." He smiles.

"Well, that makes two of us. I'm thinking it was pretty effective, though. In my opinion, it made a statement. It made a statement in front of a lot of people, actually. And I like that. Thank you for making me the topic of conversation. You know how the hospital gossip hotline works." I sinisterly laugh. I look at David's moping face. "Just so you know, David, that comment was not meant to hurt your feelings. Just the opposite, actually. I'm proud to now be the topic of conversation in rumor city today. I can't wait to be the envy of every woman. It's not every day a tall, dark and mysterious man hunts me down to make out with me at lunch. This is the best lunch I've had in a very long time. Thank you so much, Mr. Masterson."

"Well then, my dear Liz, you are very welcome. How about a drink after work tonight? I can meet you wherever you want?"

"I would love that. I'll buzz by Kyle's room on my way out. This way I can say hello to everyone, and then we can head out. Sound like a plan?"

"Works for me."

"Well, I've got to get back to work. Catch you later." I lean over and plant a tender kiss on David's lips. I smile as I get up from the bench, and notice the pup tent in his pants. I guess I know where the warmth of my kiss went.

David smiles as he watches Liz walk away and has a serious conversation with his manhood. *Down, boy! This is one fine woman. Have patience and class. Easy does it.*

Chapter 12

I hear that soft soothing voice even in my sleep. I remember her saying, "Kyle, it's me, Mindy, your nurse." Hmm, my nurse. I like the sound of that. My nurse, just for me, no one else. Well, in another life, maybe. Now I can't even see her to talk to her. I might as well say it's all imaginary. Because now, it's all professional business. So much for my fantasy coming to fruition. Over the years, I have had many fantasies about nurses. Their pure white uniforms, those long legs in white stockings wearing red, come-fuck-me pumps. Now I have a chance for my fantasy to come true. I've finally met a real ICU nurse, and I can't even see her. What the fuck is that all about?

"Kyle, open your eyes for me. It's Mindy. You are all done with surgery and you're back in your room in the ICU."

She has this calming way about her. It's soothing and understanding. She amazes me, and she doesn't even know it.

I've heard her talking with other families and coworkers. She can be firm when she needs to be, especially when it's for the benefit of her patients. Although I don't think she has a mean bone in her body, at least I haven't heard any Mindy attitude yet. She's so damn sweet.

I'm sure she doesn't even realize that I could hear her and another nurse, Liz, I think it was, talking about me and David. I was still pretty sick, but I can remember something about "Greek gods" and how anatomically perfect we are. Now that's a compliment. I also remember them talking about my chest and how smooth it is. I wanted to jump up and interject in their conversation and say, "Girls, it takes a lot of work at the gym to look this good," but somehow, I never had the strength to do it. Someday, I'm going to tell her. I'm sure she will be so shocked and I can't wait to see her blush. When I finally come clean, I bet the look on her face will be priceless. I can't wait to see her, to meet her face to face.

"Kyle, open your eyes, honey, it's me, Mom. Please, take your time and try to open your eyes."

Trying to find the strength to speak, my throat is sore and my mouth is so dry that it tastes like second base. Although weak and worn out, I find the strength and squeak out, "Mom, where's Mindy?"

"I'm right here, Kyle. Your whole family is here with you. Can you open your eyes yet? It may be difficult. They are still a little swollen."

"I'm trying, Mindy, but everything is dark, still so dark."

"It's going to take time, Kyle. Let me see those beautiful blue eyes of yours."

I struggle and finally get my eyes open to mere slits, but enough that my parents can see my eyes. They seem so happy, but I'm still concerned and worried.

"Hey, Bro! Nice to see you in there. I haven't seen those baby blues in a while."

"Yeah, well, maybe if I could see your baby blues, then I would be just as happy!"

"Well, Kyle, the surgery went well," Doctor Keller says. I didn't hear him come in, but I'm happy to hear his voice. "There were no complications, and I repaired the break in your optic nerve. Now we just have to wait. There is no time limit here, Kyle. It will be one day at a time, so don't get discouraged."

Doctor Keller continues and outlines the treatment plan for me. "You will continue on steroids and eye drops to help decrease the swelling within your eyes, and a low dose blood pressure pill for now. The blood pressure pill is not permanent, but right now, you need to remain calm and try not to get too excited. We don't want to raise your blood pressure, especially your internal eye pressure. That could cause permanent damage. Calm is key, so try to relax and be patient. All right? Any questions for me?"

"No, I guess not. I'm sure I'll have a few by tomorrow."

"You rest up, Kyle. You did good, and I'll check in on you tomorrow morning on rounds. Try to sleep and rest. Goodnight."

"Kyle, are you in pain? Do you need any pain medication? Do you want a warm blanket?" Mindy asks her typical nurse questions.

I don't answer her. I just shake my head.

"Kyle, give yourself some time. Things will be better tomorrow. But for now, all we can do is wait and pray."

"Mindy, can you leave me alone for a while, please? I need some time to think. I would like everyone to just go and leave me alone." The anger in my voice is clear.

"Okay, honey. You get some rest and we will see you tomorrow," Mom says.

I nodded, as I'm sure Mom and Dad are upset that I asked everyone to leave, but I need time to digest all of this.

"David? Can you hang back, please?"

David sits in the chair next to me, and we both are silent.

"Damn it!" I slam my hand down on my thigh, remembering my newly repaired femur. "Fuck that hurt!" I shake my head in disgust. It's as if I can see David. "I know you're smiling at me, big brother. I can feel it from here."

David lets out a small laugh but says nothing. He sits there and waits. He knows me and knows I will talk when I'm ready.

"You know, D., I really thought I would wake up and this nightmare would be over. I would see again like before. I'd be normal again. What am I going to do if this is permanent, bro? How will I work? Shit, I'll never see any hot woman and I'll never have sex again! This has to get better; it just has to." My fears finally revealed, I try hard not to cry.

"Kyle, buddy, stay positive. It's only been a few hours since the surgery. I'm sure there is some swelling just from the surgery. Give your body time to heal. And when you're ready, I'll tell you all about the hot nurses around here. Okay?"

"Sure, maybe I'll take you up on that later. I'm feeling angry and let down right now. I just needed to vent and let it out for a minute, you know? If you don't mind, I think I want a nap right now."

"You got it, man. It's getting late, anyway. It's almost the end of the day shift, so just chill and remember what the doc said, low excitement and rest."

"Easier said than done, D., but I'll try. Night, bro, and thanks for hanging with me all day."

"I wouldn't have it any other way. Sleep well, brother."

Chapter 13

Looking at my watch, I realize it is the end of our shift, so I'm sure Liz will be heading this way very soon to see David. Right about now, she should be giving her shift report and walking our way. Since Kyle is sleeping, David and I exit his room as we run into Liz.

"Hey, what's up, Liz? I've been so busy; I've barely had a chance to talk to you since you left for lunch."

Liz starts to blush and I immediately look over at David. He has a huge grin on his face and I put two and two together. I knew it, the rumor mill is correct. These two were making a scene in the courtyard!

"Oh, my God, the rumors are true! What happened? Tell me now!"

"Just a little ice melting." Liz smiles. "David, would you excuse me for a minute?" Liz takes my hand and leads us away from Kyle's room for a quick hallway girl chat.

I look at my friend, who right now looks like a kid with her hand caught in the cookie jar. "Uh-huh. You mean the gossip is true? Five more minutes in the courtyard and lunch would have been X-rated for everyone to witness? So, what now?"

"Well, I wouldn't go that far, Mindy. But it was awfully heated. This guy's good. I mean, really good. I'm in so much trouble here Mindy. We made plans for tonight. David is taking me out for that drink he promised me. It's going to be a good night. I have a good feeling about this. I'll see you tomorrow and fill you in on all the details." She says as she gives me a quick hug goodbye.

"Don't even think about calling out tomorrow just because you were out too late tonight, Liz! I know where you live, and I will come get you and drag your ass to work in the morning if I have to!"

Liz waves me off and walks away. It's nice to see Liz smile over a man. It's been a long time, and she deserves someone special.

❧

I punch out and head to my car. With one leg in the car, I see more advertisements decorating my windshield. *Can't hospital security keep solicitors off the property? I'm tired of always getting crap on my windshield.* I grab the piece of paper from under the wiper blade, ball it up, and throw it into my bag. *I'll throw it away when I get home.*

I grab my mail from the mailbox and head for my apartment door. The usual routine I always follow. Get the mail, shower, eat, watch TV and fall asleep with the remote in my hand. Tonight feels different, though. I can't figure out why, but something is off.

Sorting through the mail, I remember the paper from the windshield I balled up and threw in my purse. I grab the wadded-up paper and something catches my eye, so I look more closely at the wrinkled paper. What the hell? My name is on the paper. Opening the crumpled mess, I lay it flat on the kitchen counter and flatten out the wrinkles with my hands.

Staring at the paper, I'm speechless and confused. This is not paper at all. It's a photo of me and Liz, sitting at a dinner table laughing. I turn the picture over. There is writing on the back, with a black Sharpie marker that reads:

Mindy, you're so beautiful in this dress.
I want you so badly.
When can I have a date?

I start to shake and feel nauseous. Who took this picture and where did it come from? This picture…is from last week, when Liz and I went out to dinner. This was the night we saw the Greek god brothers! Oh. My. God. Is someone watching and following me? What creepy person has my personal information? My mind is reeling in three different directions and I'm starting to freak out.

I immediately call Liz. She doesn't answer. Of course not! She's having a great time with Mr. Wonderful and I'm having a nervous breakdown. What am I going to do? *Think, Mindy. Think!*

Okay, I look around my apartment because now I'm freaking myself out. Everything looks the same, no forced entry, nothing disturbed. I grab a kitchen knife and quietly walk around my apartment.

What am I doing? What if someone is here? Do I really think I have a chance to win in a fight or confrontation? Fuck no! So, I do the only sensible thing I know to do. I leave my apartment, get in my car, and lock myself inside. At least I can make a fast getaway if I have to.

After I call Liz again and get no answer, I leave her a 911 text, our emergency code to each other. It means we have to stop whatever we're doing, no matter what, and call the other one back. I have never used it before today. I sit in my car, anxiously waiting for my phone to ring. Nothing. Five more minutes, nothing.

What am I going to do? She's probably having a great time locking lips with Mr. Greek god. She'll be so distracted that she'll never hear the phone. *Think, think, think, Mindy!*

I've got it. It's a little like breaking the ethical rules, but plausible. I immediately call my work and get the charge nurse on the phone.

"Hey, Sara, it's Mindy. I need a huge favor."

"What's up, girlfriend?"

"I need you to go to Kyle Masterson's chart and give me the number of his brother, David. It's listed as his emergency contact."

"Mindy, are you all right? You sound winded and upset."

"Yeah, I'm good. I just realized I forgot to give him some important information he asked for when he was at the hospital. I need to call him now, before I forget again, and give it to him. It's time-sensitive, otherwise, I would wait until tomorrow."

"Okay, Mindy, here it is. Good luck and be careful."

"Thanks, Sara, and I'll see you in the morning. Night."

I frantically dial David's number. No answer! Are you fucking kidding me? I scream at my phone as I look at the screen. I try again. This time I text and say, "Have Liz call Mindy 911." And now I wait. I have no idea what they are doing. They could be in the middle of hot oily sex for all I know, but I don't care. I need her, and I need her now!

My phone rings one-minute later. "Mindy, what the hell is going on? You never 911 me? Are you ok?" she asks in a panic.

"No, I'm not Liz. I'm freaking out here. I just got a note left on my car, Liz. Which wouldn't be a big deal, except it's a picture of you and me. It was taken when we were out to dinner the other night. The person wrote on the back and didn't sign it. I didn't even see the note until I got home and was going through the mail. Now, I'm scared shitless. I even checked my house for intruders."

"What? That's crazy, Mindy. Where are you?"

"I'm locked up tight, sitting in my car outside my complex. I was too afraid to stay inside. I figured if I saw anything weird, I could hit the gas and make a run for it."

David's talking in the background. "Tell her to stay put. We'll be right there."

"I heard him. Thanks, Liz."

"Be careful, Mindy. Eyes open and doors locked. We're on our way."

I'm panicking and trying to look calm in my car on the phone. I'm looking around for anything out of the ordinary and I see nothing. My mind is reeling, of course. Who sent this? What do they want? Why did they follow me and Liz? What if they know where I live? What if they are watching me now? The list of questions goes on and on. It's endless. I start feeling like I might have a panic attack when I see Liz's car pull up next to me. I'm so relieved, I almost want to cry. I jump out and hug her tight, trembling under my scrubs.

"God, Mindy, you're shaking to death. Take a deep breath and calm down."

David pipes up. "Tell me from the beginning what happened?"

I give him the story and he wants to go inside and check the place out before we go back in there. And that's just fine with me!

"Mindy, what apartment is yours?"

"It's number 3B."

He starts walking toward my door when I realize I still have the keys. "Here, David, you'll need these." I toss him my keys.

He takes off for my door and doesn't look back.

I look at Liz. "Honey, I'm so sorry I ruined your night. All you wanted to do all day was go out with him, and I ruined it. I'm so sorry."

"Mindy, you didn't ruin anything. You're like a sister to me. If you need me, I'm here. And David was amazing about it. I think he's a little protective of you, too, you know?"

"Me? Why would he be protective of me? He really doesn't even know me outside of being Nancy Nurse."

"I think that's why he is protective of you. He watches you take care of his family in every way. Not only do you do an amazing job with Kyle, but you are always checking on the needs of his family. That is super important to him. You have won him over and you don't even know it. He has such respect for you."

"And you know this how, Liz?"

"Well, I can tell, for one thing, and he told me. We were just talking about his family and how everyone is coping with Kyle's diagnosis when you called. His parents love you, too, you know."

"I'm just happy they feel like their son is getting quality care, Liz. Although, having two perfectly stunning men to look at all day helps." A small laugh escapes me.

David returns and gives us the all-clear. We head back to my apartment and I immediately open a bottle of wine. It's just what I need to calm down a bit.

"Anybody want a glass?"

"No thanks, Mindy, we're good. You have some and come sit down and relax."

David starts firing questions at me so fast that I can't handle it, and I start crying.

"Mindy, I'm sorry. I didn't mean to upset you. I'm just trying to put some pieces together."

"I know. I told you everything. Actually, there isn't much to tell. I just feel like something is off and I can't put my finger on it, you know? I'm just a boring nurse with a boring life. Who would want to bother me? I don't get it."

"Mindy, you are a very attractive young woman. People envy that and want to be a part of that. People are crazy. You don't even know if this was sent by a man or woman. It could be anybody, friend or foe, coworker, acquaintance, etc. Are you sure there haven't been any other strange signs or happenings that you're aware of?"

"No, David. The only thing recently was a large bouquet of flowers that was sent to me at work the other day, but that was legit. They were sent by a former patient I had taken care of the week before, who was just sending a thank you. I really can't think of anything else."

"All right, at least we covered everything, for now at least. Do you feel okay to be alone, or do you want Liz to stay with you tonight?"

I look at Liz and don't even need to speak a word.

"I'm staying. You don't even have to ask. You can drive us both to work in the morning, no worries."

"Thanks, Liz, you're the best. I'm sorry, David, for messing up your date night. I really am."

"Mindy, don't even worry about it. I think we'll just reschedule this hot date for tomorrow. What do you say, Lizzy?"

"I'm in. I'll go wherever you want, but I'm getting that cocktail come hell or high water tomorrow night." We all laugh and Liz looks at David. "Come on, I'll walk you out and you can drive my car back if that's okay?"

"Sure, that works, and tomorrow night I'll drive you back after the end of your shift."

"Perfect, Mr. Masterson. It's a date for sure. Mindy, I'll be right back. I'm just going to walk him out."

Chapter 14

As David and I approach his car, he grabs me by the arm and spins me full circle into his chest.

Laughing like a teenager, I look up at him. "Thank you for being so understanding—"

Before I could finish my sentence, his lips connect with mine. His warm body molds perfectly with mine as he holds me around the waist, deepening the kiss.

I moan, and David responds with a soft cry of his own. The kissing becomes electric, our tongues touching and roaming. As I buckle at the knees, David has a good grip on me. His strength is amazing. Rock-solid arms hold me up as I lose self-control and grab his head. With fistfuls of hair, I intensify our kiss. It's the most heated kiss I have ever experienced. I want more, but right now, I, regrettably, know being a best friend to Mindy must take priority.

Out of breath, I slowly pull back from the kiss and look up at David as he holds his gaze.

"Jesus, Liz, you're killing me here. Why did you stop? That was so perfectly hot." David flashes a devilish smile.

"David, you made my knees buckle, for God's sake. That never happens. It's a good thing I did stop or you would have had to pick me up off the ground." I glance up at his electric blue eyes and share an equally devilish grin. "I have to be a good friend and go back inside to Mindy. My desires need to take a back seat, just for tonight."

"Oh, so you desire me, huh?"

"What I meant was, my friend needs me. That should be the priority."

"I think I just heard you say that your desires need to take a back seat, Liz. What do you really mean and want, Lizzy?"

I stare at David because I don't know what to say. He just put me on the spot. I wonder if this is one of those times when he wants honesty.

Should I tell him my innermost wants or save something for later? It may be too soon to be completely honest with him. Before I can reason out my thoughts, David makes the decision for me.

"It's truth time, Lizzy. Always the truth, remember? You tell me your truths, and I'll share mine."

"Okay, if you promise to really be honest, David. I mean it."

"Always, Liz. Haven't I proven I'm already honest? You go first."

"My wants, if I could really have it my way tonight, which we already established we can't, will have to wait for another night. But, for the sake of honesty, I would want you, naked, covered in baby oil, underneath me! I would be in the position of power and I would fucking take you and rock your world!"

"Christ, Liz! You say something like that to me and then send me home? How unfair is that? You're sending me home with a boner a mile long! How the hell am I going to sleep tonight? You will be on my mind every minute. Because my truth is, I've wanted to have you since the first minute I saw you. I want you on a beach blanket under the stars. There, I would find and taste your amazing lips, whisper in your ear, nibble on your earlobe, kiss your neck, and work my way down to your beautiful breasts. From there, we would see how far I could go and what would happen."

"Gosh, David, you must think I'm a slut. Here you are talking all romance on the beach and taking your time, and I just jump into a scenario with you naked underneath me. I didn't play the romance card at all. I went straight to the let's-fuck-and-be-nasty card. I feel horrible, what you must think of me. I'm so embarrassed. I think I really have to go now before I ruin any chance of another date."

I turn away quickly to leave, and David steps in front of me, blocking the way. I look down in complete embarrassment.

"Liz, stop. Look at me. Please." He raises my chin with his finger and stares into my eyes.

"Listen to me. Your desire was the raw truth and I'm so thankful for that. Never has anyone been so completely honest with me like that on a first date. I admire you and I'm proud of you. It makes me want you even more. You have no idea how bad I want you. Since the first moment I saw you, Liz. You're amazing and you just proved it. Now, go inside and support Mindy, and realize that I desire you, too. Every inch of you."

"Good things come to those who wait, I have been told."

"Damn straight, Lizzy. I'll be waiting, and I'll see you at the hospital tomorrow. Sleep tight and dream of me. Good night."

"Night."

I head for Mindy's door as David waits to make sure I get inside safely. I wave goodbye and close and lock the door. I lean my back against the door and sigh, as Mindy looks up and watches my every move.

"Oh my, I know that look, Liz. You're whipped. The magic of the Greek god has struck the 'I'm hooked on you' cord, hasn't it? I can tell, and all he has to do is reel you in, right?"

"Most definitely, Mindy. He's too perfect so far. I'm waiting to see something negative about him, but I haven't yet. I hope I don't mess this up."

"One day at a time, Liz, and thanks for staying tonight. I really appreciate this, you know."

"Anything for you, sister! Now, I need a shower and some jammies. Can I borrow a sweatshirt and leggings? And then let's watch a chick flick. We might as well take advantage of this free time together and enjoy the night in, right?"

"Most definitely. I'm on it! I'll have a chick flick ready in ten minutes, so get a move on," Mindy yells as she heads down the hall to her room in search of clothes for me.

Chapter 15

Kyle's family has been at his bedside most of the day today. He is struggling with his emotions. One minute he is calm and sweet, talking to me as if we are old friends, and the next minute he is barking orders, being rude and ordering me around all morning.

"Please and thank you would be nice to hear, Kyle. I'm your nurse, not a servant, you know."

Of course, I feel horrible after saying it, but he needs to hear it. I mean, he's got a huge lifestyle change now. I should cut him some slack, but shit, he just pissed me off, and it popped out of my mouth. When no one else is in the room, I will have to apologize. I don't want his family to know that I let a cranky patient get the better of me. It's unprofessional, but I felt better for a few minutes after I said it, in all honesty.

I've made peace with Kyle after my outburst and I'm on my way to check in on him. I gave him some space, as he wanted to rest awhile and listen to the sports news channel on television.

As I approach his room, there is an unknown woman at Kyle's bedside. Her back is to the glass door, and she is facing Mr. and Mrs. Masterson. She is blonde and well-dressed in a beautiful summer dress. Her hair is perfect and the diamonds gracing her neck and ears speak volumes, as well as her perfectly red-manicured fingers and toes. She silently makes me aware of her vanity and is probably a woman of high maintenance, I presume. Her total look exudes money and pampering. *Who the hell is this chick? She's not on the visitation list. Should I go in there?* I wait as I have another patient to attend to right now. But rest assured, I've got my eyes on her.

As I get ready to make my rounds, an alarm chimes at the nurse's station on the cardiac monitor. It's Kyle's room. I walk over and study the screen. There is a spike in Kyle's heart rate and blood pressure that sets off the alarm. I check the alarms and all look well, so I assume he probably is in pain but doesn't want to interrupt his visit to ask for his medication. I take the initiative to go get his medication for him, but something stops me. As I pass his room, very loud voices are coming from within. I stop dead in my tracks and back my ass up to peer into his room. There, at the bedside, is the blonde bombshell, looking directly at Mrs. Masterson. She's pointing her index finger directly at her face. What the hell? I wait and listen, as I try to make it not obvious that I'm eavesdropping.

She says, "You know I only want what's best for Kyle. I want him home now, where he can get the best possible care. This is ridiculous, Samantha. I want to talk to someone in charge, and I want it now!"

Oh, hell no! Who does she think she is? This is not happening. I look up at Liz, who is walking down the hall toward me. She knows my look and nods in approval. "Go ahead, Mindy. Shine 'em up, sister," she says with that sinister grin.

I slide open the glass doors and enter Kyle's room. "Good morning," I say in a warm, nonconfrontational way. "How are you, Mr. and Mrs. Masterson?"

The bombshell opens her mouth and answers for them. "We are not good, not good at all. We need to see someone in charge, and it needs to be now."

"Excuse me, and you are?"

"I'm Patricia Marks, Kyle's fiancée," she proclaims, with her shoulders held high and her fake boobs pointing at me like two headlights in a winter storm.

"Well, Patricia, I'm Mindy and I'm the nurse in charge of Kyle's care. I have been his nurse pretty much since the beginning of his hospitalization."

"Well then, Mandy. You must be well-versed in the inadequacies of his current care. I demand to speak with this so-called eye doctor of his. His loss of vision is thoroughly unacceptable."

Is this chick for real? Who the hell does she think she is? She is pissing me off and I can feel my blood simmer. I'll be professional, but it's time to bring it! Bring out the assertive Nurse Mindy, the don't-fuck-with-my-patients bad-ass nurse attitude.

"Patricia, first of all, my name is Mindy, not Mandy. I'd appreciate it if you address me properly. Secondly, I don't believe you have the proper clearance to ask for Kyle's medical information. As a matter of fact, you don't have the proper clearance to even be in this room today. Visitation is immediate family only," I retort with assertiveness, pride, and authority. I hold my head high and straighten my shoulders. I've grown two inches taller by just standing up straight.

"I am family. I'm his fiancée."

As I watch Samantha Masterson turn five shades of red, I catch a glimpse of David leaning against the back wall. He is leisurely leaning on the doorjamb with his arms crossed in front of him. He is looking straight at me and shaking his head in a "no" fashion.

I give David a wink of acknowledgment and proceed.

"Ms. Marks, like I have said before, you are not approved to be on the visitation list. Kyle has approved all visitors and you're not one of them. Please gather up your belongings and leave."

"Oh, dearie, I think you are mistaken. My fiancée would want me here, wouldn't you, Kyle? We have a long history together and don't leave each other's side for more than a few days. When I got the call he was here, I knew I needed to be right by his side, where I belong. Now get me that doctor. And I need to speak with the charge nurse now."

"Actually, Patty, you see this room here? This space and everything in it is mine, all mine. And I'll have you know I am the charge nurse! I am in charge of this patient and the people in this room. It is my responsibility to be the patient's advocate when they are unable. I have the authority to protect my patient, and I will, always. So, Patty, gather up your shit and leave. And if you don't, I'll be more than happy to get you a security escort!" I say with complete convincible authority.

My peripheral vision gets a glimpse of Kyle and his parents. They all have smiles on their faces, and appear to approve of my assertive behavior.

And…she continues to have her temper tantrum. "Tell me why I'm not included on this list. Doesn't the fiancée top the list?" She is huffy and pissed off.

"Actually, I was told there was no wife, no fiancée, or no girlfriend to put on the list. So that must mean you are the estranged old girlfriend who wouldn't give up the hope of marriage I was warned about." My inner voice hums, *Touché,* for me. Maybe now she'll get the message.

I reach for my work phone to call security when the deep voice of

Mr. Masterson booms.

"Patricia, that's quite enough. You have been here long enough. Leave now or I will drag you out myself. Kyle has been done with you for months, and you won't accept it. Kyle has been through enough already. He doesn't need your immature, spoiled brat breakdowns. Get over it already and do us all a favor and leave."

Patricia looks at Kyle and reaches out to hold his hand. He feels the familiar contact and immediately pulls away. "Patricia, leave. Mindy is right. You don't belong here, and I certainly don't want you here."

Patricia looks around the room at all the blank faces. They are all without emotion as they wait for her to make her move.

"Is this how you really want it, Kyle? For me to leave and be escorted out?"

"Yes, Patricia, I have wanted you gone for months now. Maybe now you will finally get the picture. Leave and don't come back. I've been done with you, done with the drama, and just done for a long time. I'm over it!"

With more drama than an award-winning actor, she grabs her designer purse and leaves with a loud huff. Though not before the slamming of the glass doors, just to make a scene and add attention to herself, I'm sure. As she is leaving, the clicking of her high heels fades as she heads down the hallway to the elevator. I internally sigh in relief and look up at Mr. and Mrs. Masterson.

"I'm so sorry I was rude to her, and a little unprofessional. It takes a lot to make me that mad, but she managed to do it in about thirty seconds."

Kyle pipes up. "Mindy, please don't worry. She had it coming to her, and she's a spoiled rotten bitch. I'm so proud of you for finally showing a tough side. You're always so nice. It's nice to know you got some spunk in you. I was beginning to wonder if you were human, or just an angel. I've never heard a bad thing come out of your mouth. It's always positive and compassionate. Finally, I heard the confidence David told me you had. You're a little firecracker. Nice job, lady, and I'm proud of you."

"Why thank you, Kyle. I appreciate that. I was worried you would be pissed at me."

"No way. How could I be mad at someone who has helped me and my family in such a crazy time? I feel so lucky to have you on my side. Please relax, and no worries, I promise."

I smile and blush, and Kyle's family catches a glimpse of my emotions. I turn my back to them and ask Kyle, "So, are you ready to work some of that anger out?"

"Well, Mindy," he says in a flirty voice, "what did you have in mind?"

'Kyle!" his mom yells from across the room. "I'm sure Mindy didn't mean it that way. Do you always have to act like such a flirty teenager?"

"Well, Mom, I can't see, so I might as well have some fun. Sorry, Mindy, I didn't mean to embarrass you."

"Actually, I'm good with it, Kyle. Just remember, two can play that game," I say with sarcasm. "But seriously, I mean, are you ready for physical therapy to come and work with you? You need to learn to maneuver with that healing femur and weight bear on that foot. You've got to learn how to distribute your weight properly and start to walk."

"I'm ready, Mindy. I need something physical right now, and it sounds great to me."

Kyle's family decides it's time to grab a bite to eat and leaves Kyle to his "time of working out his frustrations class" as his mom calls it.

David follows me out the door and gently grabs my elbow. "Hey, Mindy, can I have a word?"

"Sure, what's up?"

"I just wanted to apologize for that scene you walked into back there. Patricia is *not* his fiancée, nor does Kyle even have one. She's delusional and can't get over the fact that Kyle broke up with her long ago."

"David, you don't need to apologize. It's none of my business. I just didn't want her to upset Kyle any more than he already is. He has a lot to deal with, and his life may drastically change permanently."

David just stands there and listens to me as I'm on a roll.

"She didn't need to bust in here, all high and mighty like she owns the place, and start barking orders. That's what pissed me off. I'm in charge here, and while Kyle is my patient, I'm in charge of him. She can go pound sand for all I care. I was just too happy to make her leave. I guess I'm a little territorial and protective of my patients, you could say."

"You think?"

"I'm just passionate about nursing and my patients, David. I'm proud of that."

"And we are all proud of you, Mindy. The looks on my parents' faces were priceless. I wish I could have taken a picture for you. It was awesome. They have wanted her and her drama gone for a long while, and I think you just achieved the impossible. Congrats."

"Well, thanks, I guess. Listen, David, I really need to go check on my other patient. Tell Kyle physical therapy will be with him in about fifteen minutes, okay?"

"Will do, thanks again, and bravo, Mindy." He's clapping as he walks back to Kyle's room.

Chapter 16

Kyle is sitting up in bed, rubbing his head, which immediately concerns me.

"What's wrong, bro? You don't rub your head unless you have a huge decision to make. What's going on?"

"Can you tell me more about Mindy, David?"

"Like, what do you mean? Her nursing job and stuff? You already know that. You've been talking to her every day she's been working. She's an exceptional nurse and a good friend to Liz."

"Who the hell is, Liz?"

"Oh, she's the hottie I saw that night at the restaurant. The night we went out before your accident, remember?"

"You mean the girl you asked out? The tall beauty who blew you off because she had an early morning the next day?"

"Yep, one and the same. Bro, she is so sweet and fine. That ass of hers is to die for. And those long luxurious legs, topped by the breasts that won't quit. I'm so hooked already."

"Jesus, David, stop it. I'll get a boner just listening to you, and then what will I do? You can tell me how you got back together with her later. Right now, I want to hear about my nurse."

"Oh, it's *your* nurse now, is it?"

"Damn straight. I feel very protective of her, too. Please tell me all about her. I want to know everything."

"Well, bro, she is really cute. She is probably five feet five, or so, with blue eyes and light brown hair that has been highlighted with these pretty auburn streaks. Her hair is shoulder length, and it looks all soft and flowy. She wears it up in a ponytail often, especially while she's at work."

"Wait just a minute, David. You've seen her outside of work? What were you doing? Where did you go? Why are you alone with her?"

"Calm down, Kyle. It's not like that. I'm after Liz, remember? Mindy and Liz are best friends. Usually, when I see Liz, Mindy is with her. They both work together in this ICU, dumbass."

"Okay, sorry. I guess I'm getting ahead of myself here a little bit. Tell me more."

"Well, I don't know her that well yet, but what I can say is that she is very sweet and shy. I mean, I can tell she is working on her self-confidence and also her physical self."

"Why? Does she look like a troll or something? I thought you said she was cute."

"She is cute. She has a pretty face and beautiful skin. She is just a little meatier than my taste, if you know what I mean."

"That depends, David. Your opinion of a little overweight and mine are drastically different. You like your women tall and tits out to here." He motions to his imaginary large breasts. "I happen to enjoy women with a little curve and a little something to grab onto."

"Well, Kyle, she's got that. She really is adorable, just needs a little firming up, in my opinion. Bro, she is a fantastic nurse and has wonderful qualities. She's the kind of woman you bring home to meet the parents. She's that kind of woman, you know? If I was into that type, I would have grabbed her up by now."

"At least I know she has your approval. Maybe I should try and grab that up. What are my chances?"

"Kyle, I'm not even going to answer that. Let's worry about getting you physically better and getting you out of here. I don't want you getting all worked up about a girl you can't even see."

"Thanks for the low blow, man, just the dose of reality I needed. I appreciate that."

"I'm sorry, little brother. I didn't mean to sound so insensitive. You know what I meant. Let's have the priority be you, and not some girl. Not yet anyway, Kyle. I'm so sorry."

"Yeah, yeah, we're good. Now get the hell out so I can work with physical therapy. I'll catch you later. Go find Mom and Dad and bother them for a while."

"You got it. Work some sexual tension off and I'll see you in a while."

"Let the torture begin. The sooner I heal up, the sooner I can get out of here."

Laughing, I head for the dreaded cafeteria for hospital food once again.

Chapter 17

Icheck on Kyle, and he is already out of bed and sitting in the recliner. Physical therapy spent a lot of time working with him and gaining his trust. It's a little more challenging to assist a patient that can't see. There has to be mutual trust between the patient and therapist for it to work successfully.

Kyle looks amazing sitting out of bed. He looks taller, now that he's vertical. His arms are casually resting at his side, with his legs elevated. He has on shorts and a regular T-shirt. I stop at the entryway to his room and stare at the perfection sitting in the chair. He is napping, and probably unaware of my presence. Of course, I take full advantage of the opportunity to gawk at God's beautiful creation.

I notice his chiseled cheeks, which need a shave in a big way, and his Adam's apple. It's a sign of masculinity I can't ignore. I look at his abdomen, remembering the six-pack hiding underneath his shirt. Hot momma hello, it was beautiful. Then I wander my vision way down to the skin I can see.

I see his thighs. Strong and muscular, like a soccer player. Then I see them. Those beautiful knees at the end of those sculpted thighs. They are bony and defined. I've got this thing for kneecaps. I know it's weird and I can't explain it, but a nice pair of toned and defined legs, with great-looking quadriceps and kneecaps, will start my inner heat flowing. I take a deep breath and exhale slowly. I need to calm the fuck down! My inner sexual self is on fire, and I must tame the lioness within. I back out of the room quietly so Kyle doesn't wake up. My God, he's magnificent.

Kyle's call light comes on and I rush in to see if he's okay. He has never put the call light on before, which makes me nervous.

"Hey, Kyle. You okay?"

"Yeah, I was hoping to get back to bed. I'm starting to get a cramp in my leg and I want to lay back for a while and stretch it out."

"Sure thing. Let me get some help and we'll get you back to bed."

"We don't need any help. I can do it with just you and me. I'm pretty strong and if you just guide me, I can do it with my good leg. That's how I got out of bed in the first place."

"Are you sure? I don't want to drop you and hurt something else. If you fall, I don't know if I'm strong enough to hold you up, Kyle."

"Mindy, I promise I won't fall and I've got you."

"God, I hope so, Kyle. Okay, let's give it a try. I'm trusting you."

Kyle uses his upper arm strength to push himself up and out of the recliner. He is balancing on his good foot and holding my arms for more balance. I guide him to pivot so his back is to the mattress.

"Okay, Kyle, the moment of truth. Bend at the waist and sit down. You have got to stick your butt out and slowly sit. I've got you and the mattress is right there. You won't fall."

"If I fall backward into this bed, Mindy, I'm taking you with me."

"Oh, you'd get more than you bargained for with that, Kyle, so be careful."

Kyle flashes a devilish smile that I've never seen before. It makes me smile, too. "Mindy, you really do highlight my day. And I have to tell you, your perfume scent of amber and rose is so alluring. I can always tell when you're in my room. You leave behind this beautiful light aroma. It makes me smile, among other things, so thank you."

"I had no idea my body lotion was that long-lasting. I don't wear perfume because I don't want it offensive to patients, so I use after-shower lotion. I hope it isn't too powerful. I would feel bad if it's overbearing."

"On the contrary, Mindy. It's delicious."

"I'm glad I brighten your day, Kyle. Are you totally exhausted from today? You had a lot of things going on today."

"No, I'm good. Just waiting for the vision gods to shine down upon me and restore my sight."

"One day at a time, Kyle. Oh, by the way. I've been working some serious overtime this last week. I finally have the weekend off, so I'll be back Monday to take care of you."

"What are your plans this weekend? Anything fun and exciting?"

"No, I lead a pretty boring life. I want to sleep in for sure, at least one day. Maybe I'll go for a bike ride or go to the beach. I love seashells, so scouring the beach for the perfect shell is my relaxation time. But I really have no idea, just enjoy some rejuvenation time. You know?"

"Yeah, I do. That's what this trip was supposed to be all about—relax and rejuvenate. And see what happened? Be careful and don't be reckless, Mindy."

"No, not me. I'm not usually reckless. Maybe I'll read a trashy book. That's about as reckless as I get lately." We both laugh and it sounds great to hear him have a moment of being carefree. "I'm done for the day now, so stay out of trouble and I'll see you Monday. Tell your family I said goodbye. Okay?"

"Okay, I will. Have a good weekend."

"You, too, and work those muscles. I want a good report from physical therapy when I get back on Monday."

Kyle gives me a thumbs up as I head out for a much-needed weekend off.

Chapter 18

It's Friday night and nowhere to go, and no one to hang out with. I'm too tired to care, if I really want to be honest. I take the longest hot shower known to man and scrub the hospital grime from my every pore. It feels so good—hot water and clean-smelling soap. I'm thankful for these little things in life.

I curl up on the couch with the television remote and grab my cell phone to call my mom to check-in. It's been a long week and I haven't talked to her all week. The little notification light is blinking. Two missed calls. I scroll through the call log and 'unknown number' displays on the screen. My stomach lurches, but I'm curious. I'm going to get to the bottom of this, and block this number, too. I check my messages and only one voicemail. I press play and hold my breath, waiting to hear a voice I can recognize, but it's a damn telemarketer! I delete it and block that number. That's enough of that!

I call and check on my mom and dad. My mom worries too much about me. The usual: I work too much. I never come over enough. I don't go out enough. Oh, and of course, the big one—why aren't I dating? Once we cover all those topics, its business as usual. I say goodnight as another call beeps in.

"Hello? Hello? Seriously? What do you want?"

"I want you to notice me, Mindy, because I notice you."

Immediately hanging up the call, I jump up making sure to dead bolt the door and lock the windows. I want to call Liz, but I'll be damned if I'm going to ruin another date night for her. With the sharpest kitchen knife at my side, along with my phone, I'm ready and feel like I'm in the middle of a B-rated horror flick.

It's a restless night for me. I don't really sleep much as my apartment is lit up like New York City at Christmas. Maybe I should get a guard dog. Hell, maybe I should get a pistol. Who am I kidding? I don't think

I could shoot someone. Could I? I'm the one who fixes the crazies after someone shoots them, not the one who pulls the trigger. My mind is in overdrive. Maybe a glass or two of my favorite white wine will help.

❧

I wake up early, 6:00 a.m. again. This is getting old. Will I ever sleep in again?

Since the early bird catches the worm, I am starting my Saturday to-do list now. I may as well be productive. I grab my keys and cell phone and head outside for a bike ride. I glance at my car. There is something on the windshield…again! I walk over and find one purple rose and a note attached.

A purple rose just for you.
Do you know what the color purple represents?
Love at first sight and enchantment.
Let's fall in love together.

I grab the flower and note and bring it into my apartment. This is getting to be too much and now I know this creep knows where I live! I need to talk to Liz and David about this. Liz is going to flip out. I'm not going to let this ruin my day off, and I'm not living in fear. I look around and I don't see anything out of the ordinary. I make a mental note as I go through my checklist: phone, keys, and pepper spray. Check. Feeling prepared, I head out for some peaceful morning biking. I'll call Liz when I return and have a clearer head. One of us will need to be rational. It should be me because Liz is going to freak the fuck out.

Chapter 19

David and I spent a great night getting to know each other. He kept his word, and we didn't have sex on the first official date. I have to admit; it is disappointing. We had talked about how attracted we are to each other, but I'm impressed he really showed restraint. Me? Well, not so much.

I shaved and buffed and puffed everywhere to be prepared for anything last night. I will not let that go to waste. I was honest with him, so now it's my turn to entice this man and be prepared to go the distance!

We're going to meet up for breakfast. This way, we can spend a little time together before he heads to the hospital to see Kyle.

Little does David know, I brought breakfast to him with a little treat. A good nurse is always prepared, especially for the unexpected. I knock on David's hotel door and he opens it. He looks scrumptious in jean shorts and a tight-fitted t-shirt. God, those biceps.

"Well, hello handsome. How are you this morning?" I lean in and give him a little peck on the cheek.

"I'd be better if this was the good morning kiss." He pulls me into his chest, pressing my breasts against his hard pecs, and I'm loving it. He devours my mouth and I feel the heat. It explodes within my womanhood and travels to my toes in seconds. My nipples harden, as I'm sure his does, too. I mean, how can he not? I'm plastered to his chest, for God's sake.

"Now that's a greeting," I say as I come up for air. "I brought you breakfast. I know we were going to go out, but I thought you might like some home cooking for a change. I made you warm muffins, and brought some gourmet coffee and fresh fruit salad, with a little whipped cream, of course."

"Did you now? Whipped cream with breakfast. Now that's ingenious. I'm starved actually. Can we eat now?"

"Sure thing. Grab the basket and let's sit on the floor. I brought this plaid quilt, so let's have a real picnic."

"I love it, thank you."

The muffins were amazing, and now I open the container of fruit and whipped cream. I grab a strawberry and generously dip it in the whipped cream. I attempt to feed it to David, but I accidentally missed his mouth and hit his nose. Oops.

"Well, that's no good, David. You can't go walking around with Cool Whip on your nose all day. Now, can you?"

He doesn't say a word, just smiles and lets me take the lead. I lean in and kiss off the whipped cream. As I lick his nose, he moans that wanting moan of his. It's wonderful. He closes his eyes and I slowly lean in and smother his mouth with mine. We kiss tenderly at first and then animal instincts roar to life. David sits up from leaning on his elbow and pulls off his shirt. My seduction is working perfectly and score one for the ever-prepared nurse!

I grab the entire container of whipped cream and instruct David to lay back down. He obliges and places his hands behind his head as he watches me. I trace the muscles on his chest with a strawberry covered in whipped cream. When I run out of cream, I tell David to open wide and seductively feed him the strawberry. It's a beautiful thing to watch the muscles in his jaws clench as he fights with self-restraint. That little muscle clench turns me on every time.

I trace the curves of his six-pack with my tongue as I lick the whipped cream from its creases. His muscles tighten under my tongue. *Now we're getting somewhere.*

"Liz," he whispers. "I'm on fire here. I'm trying to show some restraint and be a gentleman, but you're killing me. Please be careful. You might push and tease me too far. You know, to the point of no return. I can't guarantee I won't pounce on you in an instant and make you mine."

"Shh, David. Relax and let me take care of you. Remember that's what I do. I've got this, and I'm a big girl. I'm aware of just how on fire you are." I reach down and slowly drag my hand over David's bulging manhood. His jean shorts are full and hard in my palm. Under that zipper is a feast waiting to happen, and I can't wait to indulge.

Straddling David, I purposely position my hips over his zipper, feeling his hardness beneath me. It feels amazing, feeling his heat through his jeans. Jesus, this man really is on fire, literally. Reaching down, I feed him another strawberry, this time following it up with a sensual kiss, tasting the strawberry on his breath. My smiling eyes look into his. "Hmm, delicious."

Slowly kissing his cheek, I work my way to his earlobe. There, I softly nibble and suck as he wiggles and moans beneath me.

With lust-filled eyes, I peer at him. "Not so fast, Mr. Masterson. I'm in charge here. You just relax and enjoy. Now, be still, and let me look at you. I have wanted to see you naked for days. I told you my innermost wish and truths. Now it's time to pay up."

David sits up and pulls at my shirt. Obliging him, I raise my arms, allowing him to pull it over my head. He inhales sharply as he gets the first glimpse of my divine breasts, and my pink lace bra—a push-up, of course. Gotta keep the girls looking perky, and I remind myself to thank the woman at the store who suggested this lace ensemble.

He reaches around to my back to unhook the bra, but I stop him.

"Not so fast, Mr. Masterson. It's my turn."

Reaching for the zipper of his jeans, I ever so slowly pull it down.

"Lizzy, please don't tease me. I'm not in the habit of holding my self-control for too long. I'm warning you, there is a side to me I have trouble controlling. Please be careful."

"David, I have dreamed of having you underneath me every night. Shh, please don't worry about me. I've got this." Pulling off his shorts, a large cock springs free, and I look into David's face and smile. "What, no underwear?"

He smiles and his blue eyes are ice-cold and focused. Focused so intently on me. Reaching for the picnic basket, I grab the awaiting warming body oil.

David hears the opening pop of the lid and grins from ear to ear.

Dribbling the oil over his chest and generously covering my hands in oil, I massage his body from shoulders to that infamous V of his pelvis. David moans in relaxation as his cock pulsates with life. Ecstatic at his reaction, I watch David as I palm his manhood. He hisses in ecstasy as I rub the full length of him, massaging his balls with care. David's hooded eyes give away his pleasure, and I intently smile and stand for a moment.

"Where are you going?"

"Nowhere, Mr. Masterson, just getting more comfortable."

Slowly unhooking my bra, I ease it off each shoulder and drop it to the floor.

David quickly hisses as his dick dances. He softly whispers, "Beautiful, just fucking beautiful. Can I see more?"

Already prepared to give him more, to give him all of me; I just want him to have the slow-motion pain and joy of anticipation. So, I slowly rub my well-oiled hands all over my breasts and abdomen as David's breathing quickens in approval. I reach down and, ever so slowly, shimmy out of my shorts and reveal the prize. Beneath the shorts is a matching pink lace bikini bottom. I glance down at David as my shorts hit the floor and notice he has his dick in hand, stroking it to full length.

"David, do we have a problem here?"

"Oh, hell no, beautiful, no problem. Come here."

"Not just yet, sir. I believe this is still my truth time, remember? I'm not done having you underneath me yet. Sit back and be quiet."

"Yes, ma'am. You're awfully bossy, lady." He admits with a grin.

Straddling him once more, I'm naked except for the lace bikini bottoms. "Remember when I said I would have you underneath me covered in oil?"

"Um hmm."

"Well, I always get my way." I pour a huge handful of oil all over David's chest. Leaning forward, I lay on his chest as our lips meet in a passionate kiss. Tongues find each other and he finds my breasts. He rubs my nipples, which are already rock hard and at attention. Moaning into his mouth with approval, David suddenly sits up with his arms encircling me, his hard cock trying to gain entry into my heat. His hips are slowly grinding as I match his rhythm of the rocking, but don't let him inside. I break the kiss and smile.

"What's the matter?"

"Nothing, but don't get any ideas. I'm still in charge." I quickly shift my hips and stand, pulling off my bikini bottoms as I watch David grin in approval.

"Standing before me is the most beautiful pink nub of womanhood I have ever seen." He reaches for me as he begs, "Come closer, Liz, I need a closer look at your beauty."

Obeying him, I take a step closer and straddle his hips.

David remains sitting up and waiting. He reaches for my ass cheeks and gives me a gentle squeeze. "Oh, so beautiful, Liz. Your ass is perfection and this pussy, well, it's to die for. It's pink, smooth, and naked. Just the way I have dreamed it would be. I like it."

He leans forward and in a split second, he is face-deep in my wetness. I have no time to react. David is losing all control and eating me thoroughly for the second course. His tongue is magic like I've never known it to be this good. It feels divine and I can feel my wetness increasing as he gently sucks on my clit. The steady pressure and rubbing motion of his tongue on my engorged nub sends me into a moaning and panting frenzy. I throw my head back as I lose all control.

"That's it, baby," David encourages. "Enjoy the ride. Let me hear you. Let it out, baby, I want to know how good this fucking feels." I grab his head and get a fistful of hair. I'm holding on tight and rocking back and forth against his tongue while still standing.

"Jesus, I'm gonna come already," I burst out.

"Let it happen, baby, I want to taste you, I want all of you, you are my dessert."

I buck against David one more time and moan in ecstasy as I fall over the edge in the biggest orgasm I have had in a long time. Holding David's head in a death grip, I continue to rub my clit on his tongue harder and for more pressure as I climax again. This time it's longer as I cry his name and tremble from head to toe. David is enjoying every second of witnessing me coming beneath his touch. He is licking and sucking me to perfection, not missing an inch.

"I don't let anything go to waste Lizzy. You ride my mouth until you're done, baby. I want to taste all of you." I have just experienced a complete and utter loss of control, sheer perfection. David moans and laps at my intimate folds as he enjoys every last drop of my hot sweetness.

"Oh, my God, Liz, you taste amazing. Sweet and sexy and I want more."

"And more you shall have, sir. I'm not done with you yet, so now lay back and stay there."

I continue to straddle him as I land on my knees, and notice his rock-hard penis. I mean, how can you miss it? I glance up at him in satisfaction. It's as if he knows my question.

"I know. It's big, but I promise you, it will fit. You will accommodate me. No worries, Liz." He says with that devilish smirk on his face.

"Oh, I'm not worried. I'm just making sure you can handle me."

I lean over and kiss the tip of his cock. David about flies off the floor in need. The audible hiss he makes is confirmation that he desires more, way more.

"Good things come to those who wait, Mr. Masterson, remember?"

"Yea, yea, yea, I remember. I think I have heard that phrase before Lizzy. You're killing me here, baby."

I reach over with my hand and steady his cock. It's in my mouth in an instant. David hisses like a coiled-up cobra ready to strike. He immediately bucks against my mouth and reaches for my hair. With his hands placed strategically on my head, he slowly rocks to the rhythm of my sucking. He is gentle and very much aware of his size. He's focused and self-controlled because he knows if he gets crazy, he will choke the shit out of me with his length. He's being careful and following my lead. I slowly increase my rhythm and watch David as his eyes begin to roll into the back of his head. *Not so fast! I'm not done with you yet.*

I reach over to the pocket on the inside of the picnic basket and pull out a condom. David opens his eyes as he hears the ripping of the foil packet.

"Well, well, well," he says sarcastically. "Aren't you well prepared?"

I give him a serious look and tilt my head. "A real nurse is always prepared for whatever situation might occur, sir." I hold his stare and slowly lick my lips. I reach out and pull his cock to my mouth as I give the tip a quick lick, and a slow hot wet deep suck. I can feel David shudder beneath me. He is watching my every move, perfect, just perfect. With burning desire in my vagina, I roll on the condom with expertise. I glance down as I hear my inner voice cheering.

This, my dear Liz, is a masterpiece. Just the right size, a mouthful made to be remembered. Fuck this man, silly. Take him, all of him, and make this a morning he'll never forget! Hurry, Liz, I need this, too, you know!

I spy the large vein underneath. It's bulging to near explosion, and as an added bonus, he's shaved, smooth, and hairless. Just the way I like it.

I slowly bend over and gently suck on his balls. So soft and tender. They are just hanging there, waiting for their turn to receive some attention. I massage them slowly as I watch his cock bounce in appreciation. *My inner soul is begging for satisfaction.*

I can't take it much more, and I'm sure David is at his limit of restraint. I straddle his waist with my knees on each side of his hips. My throbbing sex hovering directly over his erect cock. I look into those beautiful blue eyes of his and I can't help myself, "Mr. Masterson, may I introduce you to Ms. Bennett. She is on fire, and only you can tame that fire."

"Ms. Bennett, challenge accepted." He says with conviction. I never break eye contact as I slowly slide down his cock. In one slow steady decent, I have completely engulfed him into my awaiting fire. All of his rock-hard erection is deep within me.

"Jesus Liz, you are so tight. I feel every inch of you. You are so fucking wet for me, it's like a river. You have no idea how fucking hot you are, do you Lizzy? I'm going to make you remember this day, Ms. Bennet. All other days and nights will never compare to this moment. You will remember me always."

David's desire was too much to ignore. I began to ride him like my life depends on it. I feel every inch of him inside me, and he rubs me in all the right places. His length hits me on my clit with every push and pull of his cock. It is pure fucking heaven. I lean forward and placed my hands on his chest as I hold his gaze. We pump and groaned in unison, breathing each other in. It is fucking magic. Just as I am about to climax, David grabs me around the waist and flips us over. He is holding himself up by those strong well-defined biceps, looking down at me. I pull myself to him as we kiss, a frantic kiss of need and understanding. I throw my legs around his waist as I begin to feel him slip a little deeper inside me and move faster. He breaks the kiss and his mouth travels downward until he can concentrate on my breasts.

He sucks on one nipple at a time, bringing me to a fiery need, a need I've never had before. I want it harder, harder and faster. I don't want to make love; I want to fuck like mad animals that need each other to survive. To prove to each other that they are meant for one another, and no one else. Hot pounding sex, that's what I want.

"Ms. Bennett, you feel so good. I'm going to ruin you for anyone else, you hear me!" he barks out in between groaning sex breaths.

I look at David and see this strength I haven't witnessed before. He's giving me the orders now, and you know what? I like it. He's a little rougher than before and a lot stronger. There is a change in him, a possessiveness that wasn't there before. It makes me feel empowered and protected, yet claimed and marked. I love this.

"Ms. Bennett, look me in the eyes when I'm fucking you, do you understand me?" he says with cold authority. I do as he orders and the connection is amazing. We stare at each other, and I swear I can see all the way to his soul. A man of many talents, strong and sensitive. A man of mystery, yet a man who knows what he wants. *Jesus, I'm in trouble here. I'm so hooked.*

Our rhythm increases; using the strength in those thighs as we thrust hard into each other. Reaching around and placing my hands on his defined and solid ass, I squeeze his cheeks and pull him into me a little deeper.

David hisses. "That's it, baby. Let me fuck you; fuck you hard and deep. You feel so good, Lizzy. So good and wet. You've got all of me, baby, every fucking inch inside you."

"Yes, I do, and I'm enjoying every hard inch of you. You and that beautiful cock of yours. Now fuck me like you need me to survive, and make me come. I want to hear you, David. I want to hear you loud and clear as I blow your mind."

"Your wish is my command." David increases his depth and quickness of his rhythm. I match him in unison. The thrusting is so strong and feverish that we have worked our way off the quilt and onto the rug, causing a burn on my shoulder blades from the carpet with every pelvic thrust. I ignore the pain, as the pleasure of watching my Greek God come undone right before me is way more exciting.

"Lizzy," he whispers, "are you ready?"

"Bring it, baby! I'm so ready for you." David thrusts a few more times deeper, if that is even possible, as I'm ready to fall over the edge with him. His taught neck muscles, with his head back, he jerks and pulsates inside me. The telltale sign of his undoing. I tighten my grip on his ass for him to dig deeper inside me, as we come in unison. Pure perfection. He rides out the orgasm for my benefit, but no need. I'm already there, one with him.

David slowly lowers himself to me and rolls us over, while he is still inside me, two as one. He lowers his mouth to mine for a tender kiss. He circles my lips with his tongue and gently kisses me.

"My dear Ms. Bennett, I do believe that was the best introduction I have ever had. I look forward to our second meeting." He says with a smirk.

"As do I, Mr. Masterson. I believe breakfast is my new favorite meal."

Chapter 20

I enter Kyle's room, full of excitement. "Hey, Kyle. I have some good news for you. You can officially get out of the ICU and be transferred to the regular orthopedic floor."

"What does that mean?"

"Well, for starters, you are well enough not to need critical care at this point. Your vision issue is stable, although you haven't regained your sight yet. But the only other medical problem you have is your femur, and that has been repaired. So, you just need assistance with physical therapy right now. They have deemed you safe with ambulation, so soon you can get out of the hospital and move on to rehab. Isn't that exciting?"

"Oh, sure Mindy, take me away from everyone I have learned to trust and send me to a floor where I know no one. Where nobody knows anything about me, except I'm some ass who was a fool on a jet ski and is now paying the price. Yeah, sounds like fun times to me."

"Kyle, this is an opportunity to help you learn to become more independent and mobile. You're not leaving this hospital yet, so those doctors you trust are still here to take care of you. In fact, they make rounds on the ortho floor twice a day. Once in the morning and once before dinner. This way, they can check on the mobility progress of their patients. Kyle, we are not throwing you away, if that's what you're thinking."

"Mindy, are we alone here?"

"Yes, we are. Why?"

"Because I want to tell you that I think you are fucking awesome. You just knew exactly how I was feeling, and I didn't even have a chance to tell you. How did you know that was exactly my fear?"

"Kyle, I have been watching you for days. I can see every expression on your face, the slight movement of your eyebrows when you think someone is full of shit, and the clench of your jaw when you are trying to show restraint. I'm an ICU nurse, Kyle. I'm trained in assessment skills, remember?"

"Well, you're amazing at it. You hit the nail on the head. I'm sorry, but I did feel like I was being thrown away."

"Kyle, no! Don't ever think that. I was so excited for you. I just couldn't wait to give you the good news first thing. Trust me, this is a good thing. And you will still be here, so I can come check on you and hang out occasionally if you want."

"That would be awesome. I'm sure I could use a familiar voice. Thank you, Mindy, for everything."

"You are most welcome, Kyle. I do this because I love it. You don't need to thank me. Now, let me get a few other things done and I'll let your parents know your new room number when I get it."

I'm done with my shift so I sneak quietly into Kyle's new room. He's asleep in bed, so peaceful and angelic looking. I sit in the recliner and relax. I think this is the first time I've sat down all day. I don't want to wake him, but I promised him I would stop by at the end of my shift, so here I am. I stare at his face, beautiful as ever, but still in need of a shave. Those dimples are hiding again behind a few days of stubble.

Kyle stirs and stretches as he takes up the length of the bed. I smile.

"Mindy, is that you?"

"Yes, Kyle, I'm here. How did you know? You can't hear a smile."

"What do you mean? What were you smiling about?"

"Oh, never mind. It was nothing. So, I'm waiting. Tell me, how did you know I was here? You were sleeping when I came in."

"I can smell amber and rose, a dead give-away. Nobody wears that but you, so I always know it's you, my favorite nurse."

"Gotcha. I'll remember that for next time. If I want to sneak in, I need to change my body lotion scent."

"Don't you dare! I love that scent. It's sexy and it's a winner. It's soothing to know you're around and very comforting, even though I can't see you."

"Well, thank you. No one has ever told me that before."

"I mean it, Mindy. It's your signature scent. Don't ever change it."

"Okay. I won't, just for you. Hey, a serious question now. Do you trust me?"

"Of course, I do. A hundred percent, why what's up? Because that's a loaded question and now you're making me nervous."

"I want to do something for you, but I need you to trust me. I mean, really trust me. It's a little intimate, but I don't want you to feel uncomfortable."

"Jesus, Mindy, my mind just went to a thousand places with a comment like that. Do I need to think dirty?" He smiles, raising his eyebrows.

"No, Kyle, this is strictly professional, but intimate. I can only do it if you give me your complete trust and follow my instructions."

"Okay, Mind, go for it, but I can't help my mind get out of the gutter. I'll try and be good, but I'm sorry if my little buddy decides to rear its not-so-little head."

"Oh, my God, Kyle! You're making me blush. It's not like that. Stop it." I laugh, as Kyle is laughing and clearly proud of his cleverness.

"I'm going to go get my supplies. I'll be right back."

"I'm not going anywhere, Nancy Nurse. Me and my little buddy will be right here when you get back."

I return to his bedside with supplies in hand. As I set up, I see the inquisitive look on his face, even though he's unaware he is making one.

"Relax, would you? I know what I'm doing. Trust remember?'

"I remember. I'm just second-guessing myself here. That's all."

"You're okay. Just move over to the left side of your bed a little, so I can sit here next to you. I need to be facing you."

"Now you're talking. My mind's visual of this is getting X-rated, Mindy."

"Down, boy! This is strictly legit."

"Damn, I thought maybe me and my not-so-little buddy were going to get lucky and have some fun."

"Kyle, don't call him that. First of all, I've seen you naked many times, remember? I've taken care of you for a while, and little buddy isn't so little now, is he? Second of all, don't give him a name. It's dumb. That is a part of you, not another creature." I scold.

"Mindy, you surprise me. Where is all this coming from? Where is my proper nurse who never says anything unprofessional or off-color?"

"She is off the clock for tonight, and actually, I don't have to behave like that anymore in front of you. You are not my patient anymore, so I'm not your nurse anymore, either. Now I can act like the real Mindy, and just be myself for you, not Nancy Nurse."

"I think I'm going to look forward to this." He grins.

"Now, sit up straight and don't move." I place a towel under his chin in bib fashion. I squirt out the solution and rub it on my hands to warm it up, and rub it on Kyle's face.

"Oh, hell no, I can smell that! That's shaving cream. You are not giving me a shave. No way, no how!"

"Too late, sir. The shaving cream is already all over your cheeks. Just be still. I know what I'm doing."

"Mindy, I do trust you, but this is too much. You could nick me, leave a scar or something. Please?"

"Kyle, listen to me." I lean in closer and whisper slowly in his ear, all breathy, as I say with emphasis, "Trust me, Kyle. If I can take care of your "little buddy" while you were unconscious, and it looks like I did a great job with him, and I don't believe he has suffered in any way, then I think I can take care of your face. Now that you're awake, and you know what I'm doing, it's all about trust. Just breathe, Kyle. I've got you."

Kyle inhales a large breath and exhales in defeat. "Okay, point well made. Go ahead, just be careful."

" I'm always careful Kyle, always."

I sit next to Kyle and the mattress sinks as I get up close and personal. I can feel the heat radiating off his body as I place my hand on his upper cheek to tighten his skin. I make the first pass of the razor. His soft clean skin shines underneath.

"See? No worries."

He smiles and I catch it.

"Hey, I can't shave cheeks in the middle of a smile. Be still, okay?"

"Yes, ma'am."

I let out a small chuckle and continue with revealing the masterpiece hidden below. It's coming to life beneath my very fingers. My Greek god. Damn, I try to keep my composure as I burn this memory into my brain forever, as it may never happen again. I'm almost done when Kyle apologizes.

"Oh, damn, Mindy, I'm so sorry. It does that sometimes and I just can't help it."

"What the hell are you talking about? You haven't moved a muscle; your face is fine."

I double-check his face, thinking I had nicked him somewhere. I see nothing, but hear the whoosh of the sheet as his hands move quickly to cover his crotch. *Oh my God, his "little buddy" has come to life.* I try not to stare, but how can I not look? The pup tent in his sheet gives way to my memory of his beautiful cock, the very one I bathed and held every day while I cared for him. I clear my throat and adjust my position on the mattress and try to hide the fact that my underwear is now soaking wet. I need to remain calm and focused.

I lean in again, on purpose, to tease him a little more, and whisper in his ear again. I want to make sure the warmth from my mouth tickles his ear.

"Kyle, you're a man and this is natural. I told you this was a little intimate. Please don't be worried. I'm good, really."

Before I can sit up, Kyle reaches up and caresses my face. Instantly he sits up and his lips are on mine. It's hot and heavy as I let him take power over my mouth. Parting our lips, our tongues dance. I'm on flaming fire here, the three-alarm kind. He possesses me quicker than I can say "Little buddy," and it feels like heaven. It feels naughty and forbidden, kissing a patient in a hospital room. Who am I kidding? It's erotic as hell, and I love it, but I'm probably going to hell for this. So, sensibility overcomes me, and I slowly pull away. We are both breathless and my heart is pounding. Fuck the tingle in my jingle, the tingle has grown into a full-blown bush fire!

"Shit, Mindy, I'm so sorry. That won't happen again, I promise. I don't know what came over me."

I lean in and give Kyle a tiny peck on the lips.

"It's okay, Kyle. I mean it, really. It was actually spontaneous and nice. This has been the highlight of my day. Please don't worry about it. Now, your face is amazing and back to the way you normally look. How does it feel?"

"It feels smooth and amazing. I don't feel so grubby now. Thanks a million."

"Anything for you, Kyle. I'm off tomorrow, but I have no plans. Do you want me to drop by for a little visit to break up your day?"

"I would love that. Do you think you can bring me the latest copy of the *Sports Player's* magazine?"

His request confuses me. "Um, Kyle, what do you want that for?"

"I thought maybe you could read it to me, you know, while you're here hanging out."

"You got it. I'll drop by in the afternoon. Right now, I need to clean up this shaving mess and head out for the night." I gather my things and clean up my shaving supplies as I admire my handiwork from across the room. Marvelous, just perfect.

"Sounds like a plan, Mindy. Have a good night and be safe."

"You too, and don't give the nurses too much grief. Have a good night and sleep well."

"Oh, I will now! Don't worry about that."

I grin with satisfaction as I watch my masterpiece snuggle under the covers and smile.

Chapter 21

I toss and turn in my bed as I try to relax and concentrate on sleeping. I can't focus on these fucking sheep I'm supposed to be counting because I can't get that amazing kiss from Kyle out of my mind. What the hell is the matter with me? Never fall for a patient, ever. And rule number two, do no harm! It's a conflict of interest, and don't play in dangerous waters. But he's not my patient anymore, right? He's just a patient in a bed and I'm just spending some time with a friend and his family. Right? I debate the argument with my conscience for a few more minutes, and decide, fuck it, I'll go with that. I try to rationalize it as best I can until sleep slowly overtakes me. The thought of his warm lips on mine is the last thing I remember.

I wake to a loud bang in the neighborhood and dogs barking. What is going on out there? I get out of bed, walk to the window, and slowly slide the lace-sheer curtains over just enough to peek outside. There is a bonfire in a metal trash can in the parking lot next door. Teenagers gather around as they all hoot and holler in fun. Someone throws a small object into the fire and bang, another explosion. I look around and no one is paying them any attention. It appears to be just a bunch of teenage kids having fun and obviously out too late. Mystery solved.

Just as I turn to go back to bed, I get a glimpse of a person on the other side of the parking lot watching me. What? He surely isn't staring at me, is he? I concentrate and focus. I really look hard. It's not anyone I recognize, but I take mental notes. He's medium-built, with dark hair, and is leaning back on a parked motorcycle. He's relaxed, arms crossed and legs crossed at the ankles. He looks comfortable and like he's just hanging out. He's not participating in the teenage fun, just watching the activities and watching my window. He lights up a cigarette and takes a long drag as I see the red glow from the tip. His actions appear confident and in charge, because no one is bothering him, although that's just an assumption.

I quickly let my curtains close and step back from the window, but not too far back. Curiosity has a hold on me and I still want to watch. The man on the bike seems larger than life and somewhat dangerous. Maybe because he's on a motorcycle, you know, the bad boy type? He takes a final drag off the cigarette, throws it to the ground, and stubs it out with his boot. He looks up at my window one last time, as he throws his leg over the seat and starts the engine. He purposefully revs the engine hard. It's loud and makes a statement. You know, the kind of statement that says, "Get the hell out of my way because I'm a badass and coming through."

As I watch him ride off, I notice he's got a leather vest on with a bottom rocker only. No center patch that would identify which motor cycle club he belonged to. Damn. Now I have no clue as to who this dude rides with. He could be anybody, anybody at all. I make a mental note of it and add it to my "weird events" folder in my brain. Just another random unexplainable event in the life of Mindy Harper, and just another night of interrupted sleep.

Later that day, I head to the hospital for an afternoon visit with Kyle. When I get there, I find him in the hallway struggling with himself and the physical therapist. He's frustrated, I can tell. I watch from a distance, as I don't want to distract him as he's trying to learn to balance walking and blindness. I sneak into his room to wait for his return and settle myself into the recliner. I'm relaxing for a minute when the familiar voices of Mr. and Mrs. Masterson are approaching. I get up to say hello and I'm greeted with a big hug from both of them. What a welcomed surprise.

"What brings you here, Mindy?" asks Parker, Kyle's dad.

"I came to visit Kyle. He asked me to pick up this magazine for him and I thought I might hang out for a while and read it to him. You know, help break up his day a little."

"That's very thoughtful, Mindy. So, how have you been?" he asks.

"I'm well thank you. I'm excited for Kyle. It's a great day when a patient transfers out of the ICU. He's one day closer to going home. Do you think he's excited about that possibility?"

"I'm sure he'll be happy about not being in the hospital, but when he gets discharged, he will be staying with us for a while. We need to make sure he can function independently before he goes back to his house. You know, for safety reasons."

"Oh, I totally get it. I don't have much experience with counseling the blind, so I'm sure all the support he can get will be gratefully appreciated."

Sam, Kyle's mother, gives me an understanding smile and gazes out the window. I feel bad for her. I'm sure her heart breaks for her son. I truly hope his sight one day will return, for both their sakes.

As I watch Sam, Kyle's voice is music to my ears.

"Hello, Mindy. I'm so glad you actually came. This makes my day." He smiles.

"How did you know?"

"Really? I already told you. Just remember, you can never sneak up on me. I have the nose of a bloodhound, and I'll find you. Amber and rose, my new forever favorite."

I look at Sam and start to blush, and Parker notices, too. I wear my feelings on my face and can't hide it. I'm blushing and I've just been caught, yet again, in a big way.

"Kyle, your parents are here, too. We were just talking about your progress. It's wonderful to watch your daily improvements."

"Thanks, I'm trying hard to strengthen these legs. They have a lot of work ahead of them." He says with confidence.

"They look fine to me." I blurt out without thinking. Then I realize what I had just said and how flirty it sounded. I want to run and hide. *Damn it, Mindy, your filter failed again. You don't always have to say what your dirty little mind is thinking!*

I'm blushing pretty bad and Kyle can sense it and rescues me instantly. "Hey, Mom and Dad, I know you just got here, but do you think you could catch up with David for a while and give me a little time to visit with Mindy? I'm not going anywhere, but Mindy is on a schedule and she's got an appointment later, so when you come back, bring David, too. How does that sound?"

Mr. Masterson stands up. "No problem, son. We have a few errands to run ourselves and then we'll grab David and be back for dinner. We'll bring you a real meal so you won't need to have hospital grub tonight."

"Okay, cool. Thanks, Dad. Catch you in a while."

As Mr. and Mrs. Masterson leave, I look at Kyle and feel a little confused.

"What just happened?"

"Well, Mindy, I told a little white lie. I didn't want to share you with my parents. I wanted some alone time with you. This way I could enjoy some of that spunky non-nursey stuff you do. You know? Let the real Mindy come out."

"So that's what that is called? Thinking quickly on your feet?"

"Yup, I do that pretty well, don't I?"

Kyle and I laugh and I'm starting to feel myself relax. I pull up a chair and scoot next to Kyle, who has made himself comfortable in the recliner, with his legs elevated.

"Gee, Kyle, you have managed to maneuver that pretty well. How does it feel?"

"Um, it's okay. As long as the furniture stays where it is, I can start to get up on my own some. It's weird, but starting to be a little okay, I guess."

"Well, I'll make sure I put my chair back where it came from when I leave. I certainly don't want you to trip. You don't need any more broken bones, that's for sure."

"Always the thoughtful nurse, aren't you?" He flashes that cute flirty smile.

"Hey, I make sure I take care of the ones I care about, that's all."

Kyle reaches for my hand and finds my arm instead. He slowly traces his fingers down my arm.

My blood begins to pump faster at the mere soft touch of his fingers. I say nothing, but the small crisp inhale I try to hide from Kyle is a giveaway to my arousal. A small smile forms on his face. His dimples begin to show and I can tell he's proud of himself.

I watch him closely, never saying a word, just enjoying the gentle touch of his fingers. He traces my arm all the way down to my fingers, giving me goose bumps. We lace our fingers, and he slowly brings my hand to his lips. With the warmth of his lips, he presses a gentle kiss to the back of my hand. He kisses it again as he softly whispers, "I'll never get tired of your scent. It has rescued me more times than I care to tell you. Thank you for coming and spending some of your day off with me."

"Kyle, there is no other place I'd rather be today. Thanks for inviting me."

Kyle slowly releases my hand and rubs his hands through his hair, in an attempt to relax.

Of course, I pick up on the cue. "I found that magazine you wanted. Are you ready to hear the latest in sports news?"

"Sure, give me the scoop."

I read Kyle the entire magazine, and he's delirious with excitement now that he has all the latest sports gossip.

"I don't know how you enjoy all this athletic crap. You can get just as much info from the evening news in half the time. Besides, it's so boring."

"I enjoy it. It's an escape for me. And what, pray tell, do you read to escape?" he asks, all snarky.

"As a matter of fact, I read good romance and drama books."

"Really? If that isn't wasting time, I don't know what is."

"Listen here, mister, in my line of work, where life and death hinge upon good trauma care, a good smutty romance novel is a great escape."

"Okay, give me an example."

"You mean like what are the books about?"

Kyle nods.

"Well, that's easy. There is always some drama, some hot and heavy sex, especially when the main character can't stand being without his woman. And my favorite part is when he finally gets his woman. And then there is always a good sex scene that follows. You know, like when he backs her up and plasters her to the wall, holds her there with his strength, and devours her from head to toe? Like he can't live another minute without her. Then they live happily ever after, the end."

"My God, Mindy, you're hilarious. That is such a cliché scene. Does it ever really happen in real life? Probably not, it's just fantasy."

"Well, it's my fantasy, and hey, you asked! Now don't make fun of my smut books. I happen to live vicariously through them. Someday, I told you, I will be a sexy bitch and my man will plaster me to the wall and have his way with me! When that day comes, I know I will have achieved the goal of being one sexy goddess! I'm going to be a force to be reckoned with."

Kyle and I laugh at my passionate speech and don't hear his family enter the room.

"What's so funny?" David questions.

"Oh nothing. Mindy was just preaching to me about why her smut books are better than my sporting books. It was hilarious as she was trying to justify it."

"Yeah, yeah, Kyle, some day it will happen. And when it does, I'll let you know, and then you can apologize to me. Okay?"

Kyle gives in, and the conversation slows to a regular pace. I graciously excuse myself and tell Kyle I will stop by tomorrow after my shift, for another check-in visit.

~

I watch the interaction between Mindy and Kyle. I know my brother well enough to know when he is full of shit. So, no time like the present to call him out on it, now that Mindy is gone.

"So, Kyle, what's up with you and Mindy?"

"What do you mean? We're just hanging out. I like her. Now that she's not my nurse, she has loosened up a bit. She's actually funny and makes me feel normal and at ease."

"Kyle, I know that look. The one you don't even know you're making. Be careful, man. She could easily fall for you, and then what? When you get your vision back, you won't like her. She's not your type. You won't see her the same way, bro. Be careful, man."

"So, what is my type actually, David? Is it someone like Patricia? Like she can't hold a candle to Mindy. Please! Patricia is a bitch. I'm rethinking my standards and making myself examine my morals. This whole vision loss thing has given me a new perspective on my life. I'm forever changed by this, bro. I know I'll be better. I look forward to being better."

"Just be careful, Kyle. Mindy is sweet and Liz's best friend. Don't hurt her, man. Keep it friendly. Let's not ruin a good thing. Okay?"

"Warning received, big bro. Thanks for the advice, but I'm not sure how this is going to play out, so I'll be cool."

Chapter 22

I patiently wait for the end of the day so I can visit with Mindy. The doctor has permitted me to have my first shower since this whole nightmare started. It feels so good to be completely clean in all the right places. Sponge baths are okay in a pinch, but nothing beats a hot shower and a good scrubbing and shampoo. I even added a little cologne and now I'm feeling more like my old self. If I could only fucking see!

In an instant my mood changes. She's here. I can sense it!

"Hey there, Kyle. How are you? Wow, you look amazing. What did you do?"

"Well, I just had my first real shower since I've been here, and it felt wonderful. I feel like me again."

"Well, you look rested and great, but you do have some stubble. Care for another shave?"

"I'm not so sure I could handle that right now. Why don't you come over here and tell me about your day?" I pat the bed and have her sit down next to me as we chat nonstop for half an hour. We're like two old ladies who haven't seen each other in years.

"Kyle, I probably need to go soon. You need your rest."

"I know, but this is the most relaxed I have been in a while, and I'm enjoying it."

"You know, Kyle, I'm sure you will be heading to rehab soon to work on your vision deficit. It won't be the same around here without you."

"Mindy, do you know when that will happen? I need to know so I can prepare."

"I have no idea. It probably depends on availability at the rehab center, but I bet it's any day now. Why?"

"Mind, I haven't really prepared this well but I need you to hear me out."

"What's the matter, Kyle? You're being weird all of a sudden."

I reach for Mindy's hands and find them in her lap. Holding her hands, I begin the words I had rehearsed in my head all night. "Mindy, in case I don't get the chance to say goodbye, I need to say a few things here. First of all, you are the most kind and compassionate person I have ever met. You place your needs second to those you love and those you take care of. Your optimism has rescued me from depression several times, and your scent, that amber and rose scent, is maddening! In a good way, of course." I inhale deeply and breathe her in. "I can smell you now, and it's so sweet and warm. It's driving me crazy."

"Kyle—"

"Shh, Mindy, let me finish." Taking her face, and cradling it softly, her head tilts and rests into my warm palms. That slight movement is all the permission I need. I gently trace her bottom lip with my thumb, pulling her face closer to me.

"Mindy, I have wanted to do this again for so long."

I kiss her lips. The heat is immediate, and Mindy welcomes the kiss and it quickly becomes more than a gentle kiss. With passion and need, we lose ourselves in the moment. The tender dance of tongues and the pounding of hearts is more than either of us can bear. I can hear and feel Mindy panting heavily and then pulls away.

"Kyle, what are you doing? I can't do this. I'm your nurse. I'm trying to be good here." she says, exasperated.

"I'm a breaker of rules, Mindy. Don't you know that by now? And besides, you technically aren't my nurse anymore, remember? Or did you forget that?" I don't give her a chance to answer as I continue to enlighten her. "I couldn't let you walk out of this room one more time without tasting you again. Last time was too quick. I wanted this kiss to have meaning. I have dreamed of you every night. You have been the one thing that keeps me sane in this place. You mean so much to me, Mindy, I just had to."

"Kyle, you don't even know me, really, not that much anyway. Kyle, if you could see me, you would change your mind. I'm not your typical bikini-clad beach girl that I'm sure you're used to. I'm heavier than some, and I don't wear bikinis. I work a lot and stay home a lot. I'm a work-in-progress, and I'm not shy to say it."

"Mindy, like I'm not a work-in-progress? Look at me? I've got a lot of work to do."

"Kyle, I am looking at you, and I've been looking at you in all ways possible every day. You are stunning, a beautiful creature who, on a good day, would never look my way. You didn't even notice me at the bar that night."

"What are you talking about?"

"I was with Liz the night she met David and turned down his offer for a drink. I noticed you instantly that night. You were the one I spotted first. You were leaning against the bar with your face in your phone. You didn't look up once from your phone. That's all you did. You missed the whole night, and you missed me sitting there with Liz, watching you and David. So, believe me, Kyle, I look at you. I look at you, and you're beautiful. You can't want me. You don't even know what I look like. I'm just a girl who you envision in your mind. I'm sure the real me would never measure up."

"Mindy, you're wrong. I do see you. I see you through my senses. I see you by listening to your every word, and by the inflection in your voice. I see you by the way you touch me, and by the way you cared for me when I was sick. I see you through my touch. How soft you feel, so warm and inviting. And I see you by the way you smell. That amazing scent I will forever have in my memory for you, always. Jesus, Mindy, I can't physically see you, but trust me, I see you in my darkness in every way possible! And I want all of you so bad it hurts. I want to be away from here, just you and me. I want to show you how bad I want you, Mindy."

"Kyle, I would jump you right now if I could. You are so sweet and caring. You are sexy as hell, like the hottest man I have ever seen, kind of hot. But Kyle, I have morals. I was your nurse who became your friend. I nurtured and comforted you when you needed it. I'm so proud of your progress and excited about your prognosis. One day you will look back on this, and remember me fondly as the nurse who cared so much for her patient that she let him go. I can't believe I'm saying this, but in real life, you would never give me the time of day. So please don't worry about it now. Just be focused on your recovery and taking care of you. The best gift to give a nurse is just getting better."

"Mindy, I get it. But I'm not giving up. I'm not that kind of guy. You'll see."

Mindy sits next to me, leaning on the mattress. I pull on her arms to bring her closer to me, but she loses her balance and lands face-first into my lap. I lean down and reach for her face, raising it to mine. Her lips are close to mine; I can smell her sweet breath. I claim her; I need her to know how I truly feel. My lips are hot and wet, and my tongue is roaming, seeking an entrance. Mindy immediately succumbs to the passion she was so intent on hiding. She opens her mouth to receive my tongue and the firestorm ignites.

A knock on the door startles Mindy.

"Hello, housekeeping! I'd like to make my final rounds for tonight."

I'm smiling a wicked grin as I can imagine Mindy's blushing face.

"Sure, come in." Mindy says clearing her throat and probably happy the housekeeper interrupted, saving her. "Kyle, I really need to go. I had a lovely visit, and I'll see you tomorrow."

"I'll be here, Mindy. Have a safe night and be careful."

"Always."

Chapter 23

Walking down the hall to Kyle's room, I'm on a mission. I want to say hello and make sure he doesn't feel weird about last night, and see how the rest of his night went after I left. Entering his room, there is a woman in his bed. What? Who the hell is this? I look around the room and realize it's another patient. Kyle is gone.

Masked in confusion, my heart sinks to my feet. Where is he? Did something bad happen to him? How come nobody told me? Where is everybody?

Leaving his room, I round the corner to the nurse's station and run into Doctor Benjamin. He looks up at me. "Are you ready for patient care rounds, Mindy?"

"I am, but I have a question first. Where is Kyle Masterson?"

"He was transferred to rehab last night. They had a last-minute opening, so I discharged him." Doctor Benjamin answers flatly and with no emotion.

"What? Why would you do that?"

"Mindy, you know just as well as me that Kyle is getting better and needs the benefit of rehab. He needs the expertise of rehab so he can learn to adjust to his new lifestyle."

I stare at Doctor Benjamin, speechless.

"Mindy, I know he was a special patient to you, but seriously, he needed to be transferred. You know that, just look at this objectively. We have many more critical patients to take care of today. Now, let's get to patient rounds, shall we?"

Damn it! I know he's right, but I didn't even get to say goodbye. I would have liked to have seen his parents one more time, and David, too. Oh no! I wonder if Liz knows Kyle is gone? That means that David is gone, too. Shit! How is Liz going to handle this? She is falling for the guy, and now he is ripped away from her. Just fucking figures!

Now I'm in a cranky mood—pissed, depressed, and slightly broken-hearted. I mean, I know Kyle couldn't see me, but I did feel a little something. Maybe a little connection, just a little flirting. I guess it really doesn't matter. He's gone now and he'll move on, too. He has so much to deal with now in his life, I'll be a distant memory. I have to accept the fact that life goes on, and we just move on to caring for the next trauma patient.

I see Liz after rounds and tell her about Kyle. "Liz, Doctor Benjamin transferred Kyle. He went to rehab somewhere last night. Can you believe it? The Greek gods are gone!"

"Mindy, I got you, girl. A sister never leaves another sister hanging. I just found out an hour ago from David and got the 411."

"Why didn't you tell me, Liz? I was worried and I feel sick over it."

"Geez, Mindy, he has really gotten under your skin, hasn't he?"

"I guess it's just because we had a few good conversations and he is really a nice guy. I feel bad for him and I was hoping his eyesight would have improved before he left the hospital. I would have felt so much better if I knew he could see again."

"David said Kyle is in Summer City at a rehab facility, especially for the blind. There, he will learn how to navigate life before he is released home. You know his leg is fixed, so it's really about his vision now. Mindy, I know where he is, and he's only an hour away. I'm sure we can go visit one day."

"You mean you'll be visiting David." I chuckle.

"Girl, you got that damn straight. I need to tell you about my weekend later. It was amazing. I unleashed my inner slut."

"What? You unleashed the I-like-it-all-hot-and-sexy, I-like-it-hard-and-fast-come-get-me- Liz?"

"I sure did. I unleashed her power with some extra baby oil added in."

"Ooh, girl, I need the details later. I'll be on edge waiting for the scoop. Way to keep a girl hanging." I smile and walk away. At least one of us is getting it. All I'm getting is let down, and the crap scared out of me on a weekly basis.

I manage to squeeze in a few minutes for lunch between trauma admissions. My best friend has fully updated me on her sexual activities and her delicious Greek god. Apparently, he lived up to his name. My mind races with visions of Kyle. If I only had that kind of confidence, and Kyle could see, then I would have my way with him, too, but wishful dreaming.

I still need to tell Liz about my purple rose caper, but not now. She is too excited about David, and lunch is just about over. I'll grab her tonight after work for the update.

I'm making my patient care rounds after lunch when I'm paged to the nurse's station. "Hey, Mindy, you have a phone call."

"Thanks, Peg, I'll grab it over here," I yell back. "Hello, this is Mindy. May I help you?"

"I hope you can. I have one question for you."

"Okay, how can I help you?"

"You can tell me why you never talk to me when I call you?"

"What? Who is this? Tell me who you are? What do you want?" I yell back at the phone. I yell so loud that now I have the attention of all the staff sitting at the nurse's station. They are all watching me as I pale and shake frantically. "Who the hell is this? Leave me alone and go bother someone else, you psycho!"

I hang up just in time for Doctor Cooper to catch me as my knees buckle.

"Mindy, what the hell? Are you okay?"

"Yeah, I'm fine. I'm sorry, Dan, I didn't mean for you to have to grab me, but thanks."

"Hey, no problem. Can I get you some water or something?"

"That would be great, and can you call Liz for me? I need to talk to her."

Liz comes flying around the corner a few minutes later. "What the hell, Mindy? What is going on? Dan told me you just about passed out at the nurse's station, and you were yelling into the phone?"

"Liz, we need to talk. Let's grab our break and get a cup of coffee. I could use it."

We head to the cafeteria and I sit with Liz and spill my guts. I tell her about all the anonymous phone calls I've been getting. I told her how I thought they were just kids crank-calling me. I told her about the note and the purple rose. She about flipped her shit when she found out about that one.

"Why didn't you call me right away? You shouldn't have been alone for that."

"I'm glad I didn't call. I would have interrupted that amazing session of body oil sex. Hell no, sex with a Greek god trumps a 911 call, most definitely!" We both laugh and I feel better now that someone else knows all the crazy shit that's been happening to me.

"I think we should tell David. You know he's a detective. This isn't his jurisdiction, but he may know people we can talk to and give us pointers."

I shake my head and try to enjoy my last few sips before we need to go back to trauma drama central. "You know, Liz, there is no pattern to it. At least not one I can tell. It's so random, and I never know when shit is going to happen."

"Mindy, in your free time tonight, why don't you write down the dates, times, and days of the week these things are happening? Maybe together we can find a pattern after all. How about we grab takeout tonight and head to your place? I'll help you with it, and then we can call David. He'll be able to give us a Kyle update, too."

"Sounds like a plan to me. Thanks Liz, you're the best."

Chapter 24

Liz and I are sorting through the dates of all the events. We can't seem to find a correlation. It's all so weird, and nothing overlaps. We call David and fill him in on the newest events. He doesn't seem to have any ideas for leads either. Although two questions keep replaying in my mind: "When did you first start having these crank calls?" and "When did you first start having that uneasy 'gut' feeling you've been talking about?"

I think back to every incident that made me feel uneasy. There is always a good explanation that seems true and plausible. *So why is my gut still in turmoil?* I ask myself. David asks me again. This time he wants to personally hear the answers instead of my writing it all down.

David begins the questioning as if I'm a client. "Mindy, recently you have been having some episodes of 'woman's intuition,' you might say. A time when you may have felt uneasy. According to Liz, this hasn't happened to you in a long while, but when it does, your gut is never wrong. Tell me when you first experienced this."

Liz and I think about it because she knows me better than anybody else, sometimes better than myself. "I'm not sure. I guess when my first crank call happened. It started before Kyle was admitted to the hospital. The phone rang and there was no one there. It made the hairs on the back of my neck stand up, but I blew it off to probably just kids crank calling."

"Wait a minute, Mindy. What did you just say?" Liz asks.

"Which part? The phone call or the part about the hairs standing up on my neck, that uneasy feeling?"

"That's the part! Mindy, you said that to me at work one day, and I remember thinking, hmm, that's weird. Mindy doesn't usually say that unless she's shaken up. So, I filed the thought away, until now."

David listens intently as Liz and I try to work out the details.

"The only time you felt weird was when that biker dude patient wanted to hug you, remember?"

"Yes, I remember, but he shook my hand and was polite as can be. He even sent me flowers to thank me for taking good care of him."

"How did that make you feel, Mindy?" David asks.

"What do you mean? Like weird or something?"

"No, I mean, did you have that 'gut' feeling again? When you got the flowers?"

"No, once I read the card, it was all good. Just a real nice thank you. He was very thoughtful."

"Too thoughtful? Mindy? Do you think the gift was over the top? What I mean is, too much gift for the job that was done? So to speak."

"I don't think so. It was only a bouquet of flowers, David."

"What kind of flowers, Mindy?"

"A dozen yellow long-stemmed roses. Why?"

"Just checking. Yellow roses symbolize friendship, remembrance, and sometimes affection, I think. I was just thinking maybe he wanted to make a statement with the roses."

"Well, if that's the case, David, friendship would be appropriate, don't you think? I'm glad they weren't red ones then.

"Hey, David, I just had another thought. The only other time a face-to-face encounter gave me the heebie-jeebies was when the delivery guy acted like he didn't want to leave. He delivered the flowers to me at work and wouldn't leave until I personally signed for them. Then I caught him staring at me."

"Well, Mindy, you're beautiful to look at. I can't blame him for that."

"Thanks for the compliment, David, but what I meant was, he kept looking back at me. He was watching me the whole way back to the elevator. He kept looking over his shoulder and stopping. He even waved a few times and actually waited for me to wave back. He finally got on the elevator and left, but it seemed like it took a while. It was so weird."

"Okay, so write that down as an experience and we'll have to keep that in mind. Unfortunately, Mindy, there is nothing the police can do yet. No crime has been committed, and you're safe. He's just annoying the crap out of you at this point, so just keep a file of all the events. Okay?"

"I will, David, thanks. I appreciate any insight you can give me along the way. While I have you on the phone, can I have a Kyle update? How is he? I never got to say goodbye, and I felt so bad about that."

"He's doing good. He really wanted to talk to you before he left, too, but it all happened so quickly. He's trying to adjust in rehab and get his strength back in his right leg. He doesn't have pain anymore in the leg, so that helps with physical therapy. He is definitely working hard at getting back in shape and strengthening that leg."

"What about his eyesight, David? Has there been any improvement yet?" I ask with hope in my heart.

"Not yet. He thinks he can see different shades of black now, but it's still black, nonetheless."

"Please give him my best and let him know I was asking about him, okay?"

"Will do, Mind. If we're done, can I have a moment to talk to Liz?"

"Sure, and thanks again." I hand the phone to Liz and her smile is a mile wide. I see a twinkle in her eyes now that wasn't there before. I hope this thing with David continues to be a good thing for her.

Liz finishes her call with David and I can see the happiness on her face.

"How did it go, Liz? All good?"

"Yeah, he wants us to come up for dinner one afternoon before they head back home. David says Kyle is getting around better now and all he needs is an arm to guide him. You know, to be his eyes for him. He said Kyle's ambulation has improved, and he doesn't need crutches or a cane now, just an extra arm for direction. Isn't that wonderful?"

"That's great, Liz, I just wish he could see."

"Me, too, Mind. All hope is not lost, you know. There is still time."

"We'll see, Liz. I hope so every day. So, when do they want us to come up for a visit?"

"David said Kyle should be discharged in about two weeks if he continues to progress this well. He is going to keep me posted on the date, but tentatively plan on two Saturdays from now."

"Okay, I'll put it in my book. Thanks."

Chapter 25

Liz and I arrive at Summer City Rehab Center right on time. David and Kyle are sitting on a bench under a huge live oak tree waiting for us. As we park the car, David escorts Kyle in our direction. He looks amazing. He's still beautiful and is definitely rockin' the masculine fitness body look. It takes my breath away. I inhale deeply and Liz smiles as she hears my reaction.

"They're both beautiful, aren't they?"

"Without a doubt, Liz, without a doubt."

David helps Kyle lean on the car trunk for support. He leaves him there for a minute while he approaches Liz and plants a beautiful, sensual kiss on her lips. I'm embarrassed for watching, but I couldn't help it. I'm envious and feel the tingle in my jingle roar to life. It's been a long time for me... way too long. God, help me.

I walk over to Kyle. "Hey, Kyle, it's Mindy. You look amazing, and you're walking so great, I don't think I would have known you had a leg injury if I wasn't there to see it myself."

"Thanks. Hey, Mindy, can you come closer?" I do as he asks and take a few steps.

"What's the matter, Kyle? You okay?"

"I am actually." He opens his arms. "Can I have a hug hello, please? I have missed you and I didn't even get to say goodbye, so now I want to say hello."

I walk into his arms and give him a big squeeze. "It's so good to see you," I whisper. "I've missed you, too."

He hugs me tighter and whispers in my ear, "Mmm, the smell of you. You wore it, amber and rose. I dream of this scent every night."

"What did you just say, Kyle?" My quick question makes him realize the information he is revealing. He is blushing and appears a little embarrassed.

"Um, nothing. Just that I remember this as the fragrance you always wore, that's all. It always smelled so nice."

"Thank you." I internally smile because I heard every word he said. *He dreams of me every night. Yes!*

I take Kyle's arm and guide him back to the bench under the live oak tree. There, we hang out, chat, and catch up while David and Liz reacquaint their lips. I tell Kyle about work and he listens to every word.

"I was so pissed when I got to work and you were gone. I had no idea your transfer was happening so quickly. I even had a discussion with Doctor Benjamin about it, but it was too late. You were already gone. I didn't even get to say goodbye. I was so upset."

"I wasn't happy either, Mind. I wanted so badly to talk to you, but I didn't have your number or any way of communicating with you. I asked my nurse that day for your number but she wouldn't give it to me, but I still tried."

"At least I know you tried, Kyle. That means a lot to me. Thank you."

"There were a lot of things I wanted to say to you before I left, but now they seem so awkward."

"Kyle, when the time is right, you can tell me anything you want. There is no judgment here. And I'm an open book. Anything you want to know, just ask. Okay?"

"There is one immediate thing I need to ask you before I forget. May I have your phone number, please?"

"I would love to have your number also, but I guess I don't understand. How will you call me? David told me you don't have your vision back?"

"No, I don't, but I do have voice to text, and voice-activated calling. So, once I make the call, I can still hold my phone and talk."

"Oh my, God, Kyle, I would love that."

"Good, now that we have that out of the way, would you like to take a walk with me? I hear this place is beautiful and I would love to get some fresh air."

"Sure, you tell me what to do, and we'll go."

"Okay, just guide me like an usher at a wedding, and we can take a nice easy stroll and catch up." Kyle extends his arm, and I oblige.

We are casually strolling around the beautiful grounds when Kyle asks, "So describe the setting to me, would you?"

"You mean where we are now? Sure, it really is so pretty, Kyle. We are on the sidewalk, walking toward the pond. In the center of the pond is a beautiful fountain. It looks like a petunia pointed to the sky, and its gently spraying water from the center. There are benches all around the perimeter, for relaxing and watching the swans. Oh yeah, there are a few swans in the water, too. I think I count four. They are so majestic and graceful, just beautiful. There is a flower garden at the other end of the pond, with benches there, too. And right now, we are standing under a live oak tree. Just imagine a huge live oak tree with tons of Spanish moss just draped from every branch. It's hanging down like a gentle lace shawl covering every branch. It reminds me of a competition between the branches, to see which branch has the longest moss. It's just beautiful. Just inhale. You can smell the beauty, and listen to nature. It's quite amazing actually, refreshing and relaxing."

"Mindy, you're amazing. I can picture it so perfectly. Are we really under this tree now?"

"Yes, sir, smack dab in the middle."

"Is there anyone else around? I mean, anyone that's going to be walking by us, that we would be in their way?"

"No, just a couple sitting on the far side of the pond, relaxing on a bench. Why?"

Kyle gently turns and faces me. He runs his hand up my arm and finds my neck. His strong hand circles the back of my neck and gently pulls it to him. With one gentle movement, he places his left hand on my cheek. His touch is so soft and delicate, yet with subtle hesitation, as if he is unsure of himself. He lightly pulls my face to his. It's as if he can see me. He knows instinctively what to do and where to find my face. His lips gently touch mine. Instantly, the heat travels throughout me. My nipples harden, my vagina twitches in excitement, and my knees weaken with hot desire. I pull away first.

"Kyle, what are you doing?"

"Oh, Mindy," he looks slightly nervous, "I have wanted to do that since I first heard your voice over at the car. You have been on my mind every day and I've missed our visits. You have been the light in my darkness, Mindy."

"Kyle, please don't take this the wrong way, because I'm not trying to be rude or insensitive, but you can't even see me. How could you have feelings for me if you don't even know what I look like? I'm a ghost with a voice to you."

"Oh, Mindy, you are so much more than that. You have been so many wonderful things to me. Many more things than most people are on a regular day. You have been my caregiver, my advocate, my protector, my friend, and my guardian angel. And, Mindy, just so you know, *I do* see you. I listen to your every word. I see you through your voice, your actions, and your tone. When you are happy, sad, pissed off, and even distracted, I can tell by just listening to you. So, in essence, I do see you. I know you are strong, sensitive, caring, witty, professional, and so loving. I hear you talk and sometimes it just melts my heart."

"Kyle, that is the nicest thing anyone has ever said to me, and so sweet. Thank you, but—"

"No 'buts,' just be here with me now, and enjoy the day. Okay? Just go with it and enjoy."

Kyle leans in and kisses me. A deeper kiss, and one that warms me to the bone, and I instinctively wrap my arms around his neck and allow him to deepen the kiss. Feeling safe and sexual, I lose myself in the moment, and in the deep, passionate kiss that is giving me goose bumps and setting my womanhood on fire. A kiss I will remember for all time, a kiss that will top the charts as my best romantic kiss ever. My favorite kiss, under my favorite tree, with my favorite person. That, my dear, is a kiss made to perfection, which no one can compare.

We break the kiss when laughter approaches and, a deep voice, a man of strength, clears his throat, loudly. Shit, it's David.

"Um, hello you guys. What's up?" he asks.

"Mindy was just describing the grounds to me in detail. She painted me a great picture, unlike you. You just told me 'It looks nice here.' You never said there was a pond and swans and stuff."

David looks at me, and I'm trying to hide my reddened face.

"I guess I didn't. It's a guy thing, you know? I guess because it looks a little too romantic and shit for me when you're here with your brother and not a chick."

"Well, you're here with a chick now, so be gone." Kyle laughs. "Go for a walk and pick us up in an hour, and then we'll go eat. Does that sound like a plan?"

"Works for me." David takes Liz's hand in his and they stroll off toward the flower garden.

"Mindy, I'm sorry if I embarrassed you. I selfishly wanted just a piece of you, a small piece to remember you by. In case I never see again, I wanted to always have this. This vision in my mind of you and me, under a live oak tree, kissing like we were the last two people on Earth."

"Kyle, please don't apologize. I'm thrilled to be here and believe me, you've got me. You've got me all day to make whatever memories you want to make. I'm here. I told you once I am an open book, remember? If you want to know or do something, just ask. If it's in my power, I'll try to make it happen."

"Okay, Mind, I got it. Right now, I want you right here again. Please?"

Kyle points to his lips. He wants me to kiss him again? Wish granted. I slowly lean in and Kyle moans as warmth touches both our lips. Our kiss is slow and electric as it deepens and Kyle caresses the back of my head, his fingers entwined in my wavy hair. He moans louder and whispers, "My God, Mind, you're perfect. You taste amazing, and smell divine. I could kiss you all day. Hell, maybe I will."

I giggle as I take hold of Kyle's hand. "Come on, I'll show you around. We can't stay kissing under the oak tree forever. People will talk."

"Let them talk. It's not every day a Greek god gets to fall for his nurse."

I stop us in our tracks. "What did you just say?"

"You heard me. This Greek god is proud to be kissing his amazing nurse. I hear she's the cutest nurse there is around these parts."

"Okay, first of all, mister," I say with authority, pointing my finger at his face as if he can see it. "Someday I'm not going to be called cute, because I hate that damn word! Someday I'm going to be referred to as a hot, sexy bitch. Second of all, umm Greek god? Really? You're awfully full of yourself, aren't you?"

"Excuse me, Ms. Harper, I have it on good authority that I am known as the Greek god. You know, the man with all the beautiful parts, especially this amazing abdomen." He rubs his perfectly toned six-pack. "And then there is this area," as he is showing me with his hands, "that leads down to that perfect V you love so much." He grins.

"*Oh. My. God.* Kyle, how do you even know this?" I am in supreme embarrassment.

"Well, Nurse Harper, you really should be more careful when you are speaking in front of patients. Especially when you think they may be sedated or under the influence of medications. You see, I was more awake several times when you thought I was heavily sedated. I could hear you at times, and boy, the conversations I heard you and Liz have. They were eye-opening, so to speak. Excuse the pun." He laughs.

"Mr. Masterson, would you care to enlighten me, please? I may need to defend myself here," I say with a guilt-ridden tone.

"Absolutely not. Let's just say I'm glad my physical appearance pleases you so much. I was wondering, do you have that tingle in your jingle yet?" His grin is a mile long.

Holy shit! I'm in trouble and so busted! What else did he hear? He probably told David everything, and now he knows all about Liz and David. Jesus, I have a big mouth. I need to warn her. She's gonna kill me.

"Shit, Kyle, I'm not answering on the grounds it may incriminate me. I plead the fifth."

Kyle laughs so hard, that he actually belly laughs, but I'm horrified. He gains his composure. "Mind that was a perfect comeback. You know I'm a lawyer, right? You got me. Touché."

I reach for Kyle's hand and we lace our fingers. It feels so natural to be holding hands as we walk. We continue our walk with light and easy conversation. I describe what I see in detail, and Kyle absorbs it like a sponge. He asks questions and pictures the scenery in his mind. I hope someday he can see for real because what a celebration that would be.

"So, you said you're a lawyer? I don't think I ever knew that. I was so busy worrying about your vision, I didn't ask you what you did for work."

"You mean what I used to do for work? I don't think I can be a blind lawyer. Maybe a blind advisor, but not a lawyer." He pauses in our conversation as that realization hits him. He stops walking for a minute and hangs his head down, as if to gain his composure. He clears his throat and I give him a moment to pull it together. "I'm a defense attorney. I have a lot of clients, but there is one high-profile organization that keeps me busy most of the time. I worked hard at assisting them to reorganize their company, so to speak."

"What does that mean?"

"Well, their reputation was not the greatest. You know, stereotypical opinions and shit like that. They needed to change their image and become the company they truly are. The stigma would eventually fade away if their company stayed true and portrayed themselves as an organization that does the right thing morally. You know?"

"So, did it work?"

Kyle takes a long deep breath "Well, it's a work in progress. But I will say this: that organization has a good heart. They do great things for the community and other organizations. Hopefully one day, everyone will be aware of that fact, too. Until then, they will need to keep working on it. Come on, enough shop talk. Let's go get dinner. I'm starving."

We meet up with Liz and David and head over to dinner. The Market Place, as it is known in town, is a waterfront area lined with beautiful boutiques, restaurants, and local gift shops. It's quaint and trendy and a fun place to hang out for the evening.

We are going to be having dinner at The Dockside Restaurant. It's a comfortable venue directly on the water at the docks. You can monitor the waterway and watch the boats come and go into the harbor nearby. I love it, but I'm a sucker for anything that has to do with water and the ocean.

As we are walking through the market, we are window shopping and something pink and shiny catches my eye. I stop to look through the window at a new trendy jewelry boutique. I tell the gang, "I'm going to run into this store for a minute. Can you wait for me?"

Kyle is the first one to answer. "I'll wait as long as it takes."

I look up at Liz and she winks and waves me along.

Unfortunately for me, I have champagne taste and a dollar store budget, but I enter and roam over to the display case, anyway. Under the jeweler's lights, the bracelet sparkles like a million tiny stars. I sigh. How pretty.

Kyle wanders in the store with Liz in tow, wondering what has caught my attention. I explain that I spotted this cute pink and gold bracelet and was thinking I might try it on.

Kyle smiles. "Go ahead, I can wait. It's not like I can go anywhere without you." He laughs. "I am your prisoner, drag me around at your will."

I walk up to the case and peer in to view the elegant bracelet. I don't look at the price tag, which is my first mistake. My second mistake was when I ask to see the bracelet and try it on. It fits like a glove, which pulls at my heartstrings even more. It's beautiful and light as a feather. How damn cute. I take it off and look at the price: $450. Well out of my price range. I thank the salesman and hand him back the bracelet. I back up from the jewelry counter and I sigh.

"What's wrong? You sound so disappointed."

"I am. I should have known better. Kyle, I can't afford that beauty on a nurse's budget right now, so I gave it back. It's stunning, but I could do smarter things with my money right now." It takes all the restraint I have to say no thank you to the salesman, but such is life. I have to think of the goal I have to achieve. New body, new wardrobe.

Kyle and I continue to walk down the sidewalk to the restaurant. We're getting closer to the restaurant when Kyle realizes where we are. "We're near the ocean, aren't we?"

"How did you know? We're at a dock and not the beach. You can't even hear it."

"No, but I can smell the saltwater. And I can feel it on my face. It's wonderful. Stop for a minute, please?"

"What's the matter?"

"Nothing, just stop and listen to your surroundings and feel it on your body. Go ahead, stop and feel your senses. Come on, close your eyes and just breathe and feel."

"How did you know my eyes were open?"

"Because I can feel it. It's amazing to me, but since I can't see, it's like my other senses are heightened and aware. I told you, Mind, I can always see you."

"Stop blushing, Mindy. I didn't mean it like that. Now I'm embarrassed. But it is true," he says all sexy as my insides melt. "Seriously though, Mind, close your eyes and breathe. Listen to your surroundings, and imagine in your mind what you would see if you really couldn't see."

I do as he asks. I take a deep breath and try to relax. But how can I when Mr. Gorgeous is standing next to me, all hot looking and smelling fine? His hand slides down my arm from where he was holding me for support and gently takes my hand. He wraps his long slender fingers around mine and lightly squeezes. I think I just peed myself with excitement. *Okay, Mindy, calm down! Relax already and do as he says!*

As I exhale, Kyle says, "Now clear your mind and listen to what you hear and visualize only what you hear, not what you can't see."

Seriously? Because I can visualize a naked, toned Greek god in front of me, that's what I'm seeing! Shit, I'm sucking at this visualization attempt. I need to get my head out of the gutter and really try here.

"Okay, Kyle, I hear water lapping at the dock wall, seagulls in the background, flying around the boat, and a foghorn in the distance."

"Exactly. Except I can see a beautiful orange and pink sunset in the distance with two people in love, enjoying dinner, at a secluded table, sipping champagne."

"Wow, all that from a deep breath of salt air?"

"Yup. What can I say? I may have a crazy stressful job, but parts of me are romantic at heart, while some parts of me are bad to the bone. You never know what you're gonna get."

"Hmm, good to know. That leaves a lot of room for interpretation"

"Yes, it does, my dear, yes it does."

Kyle and I had a wonderful dinner at the Dockside Pier Restaurant. We feasted on fried buffalo shrimp, the best chicken Cesar salad I've ever had, and enjoyed a few cold beers. It was casual and friendly and relaxed. He's really a funny guy and occasionally shy, too. Who would have thought that a man with a body made for hours of hot sex, *I can only imagine*, would be shy and sensitive, yet strong in his beliefs? Oh, and physically strong, too. I can't forget about those well-defined muscles, Holy Mother of God. That six-pack to die for, or to run my fingers over, or to lay on top of, or better yet, to straddle! God, I've got to get my head out of the gutter and back on track.

I'm pulled back to reality when Liz and David are laughing, and Kyle asks, "Are we about ready to head to the car?"

"Whenever everyone is ready, I'm ready," I say.

We all get up and I help usher Kyle back to the car. Before I can open the door for him, he grabs my waist and pulls me in tight.

"Mindy, thank you for spending this evening with me. I'm sure it's not the most romantic time you have ever had, but I hope it was fun and memorable. It definitely was for me, so thank you."

"Kyle, I have had the best time, and yes, it has been a memorable night. I always enjoy hanging out with you. It's the highlight of my day when I get to see you. Thank you for inviting me."

As I blush, Kyle leans in for another tender kiss. His hand is tenderly behind my neck as he kisses my accepting mouth. A gasp and slight moan of approval escape my lips, a confirmation of the spark between us that I'm confident he feels, too.

Chapter 26

It's my day off and I've been looking forward to this all week. It's awesome having a day off in the middle of the week while the rest of the world is working. My to-do list is enormous, but I am more productive the longer the list. Isn't that crazy? But it's a fact, the less items on my list, the slower I am and the less I do. I procrastinate. Go figure.

I jump on my bike for my morning ride and enjoy the peace and quiet. It's my private time and time to plan and examine my life. Thoughts of Kyle enter my mind. I'm happy for him that he is weathering his storm so well and being positive in his recovery, but my heart feels sad for him.... *such a young virile man, successful and in the prime of his life, now blind.* He has to relearn so many things, things I take for granted every day. Like, where is your food on your plate, although he mastered that pretty well the other night at dinner with some help. He can't drive, and he can't join me on a bike ride. He will be missing so much of life. How does he stay so positive? I guess that's part of who he is and his personality. A Mr. "always looking at the cup half full" kind of guy.

I think back to our dinner the other night. God he's so strikingly handsome. That wavy dark hair, those piercing blue eyes, and that chiseled face with the dimples when he smiles. What I wouldn't give to suck on that face again! Jesus, it's incredible. Oh, and those biceps that were peeking out from under the sleeves of his t shirt…holy hell, it brought on the tingle! I close my eyes and sigh just as a loud horn blows behind me.

Shit! I'm startled and lose control of my bike. I fumble with the handle bars to steady myself but no luck. I find myself run off the road into a sand dune. *Nice job, Mindy, way to get distracted and almost end up a trauma patient yourself!* A car almost hit me, and over a day dream. I lose all control over a man that can't even see me, what the hell is my problem?

I stand up and brush myself off. I have sand in places a woman shouldn't have sand. As I dance the jig and try and get sand out of my underwear, I'm reminded of my carelessness as I sit on the bike seat and feel the crunch. Oh man, a sandy who ha is not a great feeling. *Let's rub the cheeks raw girls, and not in a fun way either!* I guess that's what I get for daydreaming and not paying proper attention.

My bike ride is cut short as my thighs can't take the sand exfoliation any longer. I head for home and a shower, so much for a relaxing ride. It's my own fault, but at least I'm safe and not one of my own patients. How would I have explained that one to my coworkers? *Staff nurse has sexual fantasy while riding bike into a sand dune?* I think not!

I've gotten my chore list completed and it's only 4:00 p.m. I've got free time to spare. I think of the extra shift I've worked, rather the shift that Liz guilted me into, and I plan for the use of the money. You know what, I've decided I deserve a little reward. Yes! I'm going to be a little impulsive. That's right, I'm doing it. I jump in my car and drive to that sweet little gift shop near The Dockside restaurant. I'm going to go buy that pink bracelet, the one I saw when I was out to dinner with Kyle. With renewed determination, I walk into the shop ready to spend my hard-earned money. I walk straight to the glass showcase and peer into the case. I inhale quickly as I notice it's gone!! *Oh no, that was mine! Where is it?* Just as I start to internally panic, the salesman approaches.

"May I help you, young lady?"

"Yes please. I was in here on Saturday and there was a beautiful pink and gold bracelet right in that spot. Do you still have it by chance?" I ask.

"I do remember you from Saturday. You were looking at it so lovingly. That was a one-of-a-kind custom bracelet made by a local vendor. I'm sorry but it was sold later that same evening. I could give you the name of the vendor who made it if you like? I have his card, and maybe you'll find it on his website."

Saddened, I say, "Oh no, that's Ok. I probably shouldn't spend the money anyway. I'd like to think that this is a sign I should save the cash."

"I understand that," he says, "but if there is anything else I can show you, please don't hesitate to ask."

"Thank you, sir, I think I'm good. Have a nice evening." As I walk away to my car, I think, *well that's a bummer. Some lucky girl is now wearing my bracelet.*

Driving home feeling defeated and my mood deflated, I make a quick right turn into Dairy Queen. Ice cream always fixes the blues. A peanut butter cup blizzard with extra peanut butter sauce makes me happy. I'll just ride my bike twice as far tomorrow. Working off the ice cream will be a bitch, but at the moment I don't care. It's all about the ice cream and being in a happy place. It's worth it, but tomorrow I know I won't think so.

I snuggle up on the oversized couch with the remote. This is the first time in two weeks I can actually kick my feet up and relax. Binge TV here I come. Now to decide what is binge worthy? A Fifty Shades of Grey movie marathon? Outlander? Or a Vampire flick? I'm not sure. I do know I'm a sucker for a main character who will be strong and fight all forces to defend and protect his woman. He must be the alpha male. But throw in some good take charge sex scenes along with some tenderness and romance, and oh lord, you'd have me on my knees in no time flat! I decide that A Fifty Shades of Grey movie marathon it is. Like I haven't seen this movie a hundred times already, but I'm a sucker for a happy ending.

I awake startled to my cell phone ringing. What? It's 1 a.m. Nobody calls me at that hour unless it's an emergency or someone is dying. My hand is shaking as I reach and fumble for the phone. With my stomach in a knot, I grab the phone and peer at the screen. 'Unknown' shines on the caller id. Do I answer it? I'm a little freaked out, but what if it's a hospital to tell me that one of my family members is in trouble? What if someone has had a bad accident? These thoughts quickly run through my mind, especially when I have firsthand experience as the trauma nurse who has had to make such calls. I can't get that thought out of my mind so I answer the phone.

"Hello? Hello? Are you there?" Nothing. More silence. That's weird. "I know someone is there, I hear you breathing." Still silence. They hang up…damn crank callers!

Sleep evades me now and I'm wide awake. My mind wanders once again to Kyle. I wonder how rehab is going? I wonder if his walking has improved? Is he using a walking stick, will he decide to get a guide dog?

So many unanswered questions I would love to ask him. I close my eyes and I can smell his cologne, that clean crisp manly smell that reminds me of the cool air in the morning at the ocean. So, so, good. I wonder what it would be like to wake up to that smell next to me in the morning? To run my fingers over that well defined chest down to that infamous V? To feel the soft hair that trails from his navel down to his manhood? Jesus, I'm a mess. I jump out of bed and head to the kitchen for a glass of cold water. My mind is in sexual overdrive. No more Christian Grey for me before bedtime I decide, that's for sure.

I have forgotten to get the mail two days in a row at the mailbox, so I head out to grab it. I've been working so late that I just seem to come home, shower, eat, and sleep. Just to get up and do it all again tomorrow. I open my mail slot to see and it overstuffed with mail. Ugh, probably just bills and crap advertisements. That's about all I get lately. I throw the mail on the counter and notice a small padded mailer envelope slip out from under the People magazine. What's this and who is it from? No return address, but it's definitely addressed to me.

I rip open the envelope and a neatly wrapped box falls out. The paper is silver swirl flowers and there is a pink bow attached. The wrapping is exquisite and definitely professionally done. A small card reads:

**For you, Mindy,
because you deserve beautiful things.**

What? Oh my God, a gift from Kyle. How did he know? He was with me, but how did he know the exact bracelet I tried on? The man is a genius. He pulled off such a surprise, and a spectacular one at that! He's secretive and a gentleman. I'm sure he had help. I'm in such shock and surprise that I decide I've got to call Liz. She must know something about this, I'm sure of it.

With renewed excitement and anticipation, I place the bracelet on my wrist. It still fits like a glove and sparkles beautifully. My heart is warm with anticipation of thanking Kyle. My first call is to Liz. "Hey, girl, what are you doing?"

"Not much, I just got home like you. What's up? We've been together all day, aren't you tired of talking to me already?"

"No, I'm not tired of you. But something happened and I'm so excited, I wanted you to be my first phone call."

"What's going on Mindy? Your voice is an octave higher than normal, and you're speaking so fast, slow down."

"You're never going to guess what I got in the mail today? I'm so excited I can't stand it." I scream.

"Porn!" Liz says.

"Seriously? Liz, I can't believe your mind just jumped right into the gutter first thing. NO! not porn."

"Well, that's a shame." she says as I giggle.

"Remember that pink bracelet I told you about, the one I saw when we were all out to dinner with Kyle and David? The one too expensive for me? Well, I got a package in the mail today. You'll never guess what was inside?" I never give Liz time to answer as I speed along in my story. "Yes ma'am, Ding! Ding! Ding! You guessed it! The pink bracelet. It just showed up in my mailbox! Can you believe it?"

"SHUT THE FRONT DOOR!" she yells.

"Nope! I'm not kidding. It's here, on my wrist as we speak. All pink and sparkly and shit. It's beautiful Liz."

"Mind, I'm assuming it's from Kyle, right?"

"It has to be. He was with me when I eyeballed it before dinner that night. He is so thoughtful. He must have gone back with David to get it after we left him for the evening. What do you think this means Liz? You think he's into me more than a nurse/patient relationship?"

"I don't know Mind, but a gift like that definitely sends a statement. What the statement is actually saying, you'll need to ask him for that interpretation."

"I thought maybe you had something to do with this?"

"Nope, I swear Mind, it's a surprise to me too. You know you have to wear it to work tomorrow to show me, right?"

"I will, but not for long. I don't want to crud it up at work or lose it in a glove while I'm doing who knows what to God knows who."

"Right?" she says. "Well, bring the box and the card so I get the full effect, okay?"

"Okay I will, I'll see you in the morning. Night."

I scroll through my phone and call Kyle to thank him properly. It rings and goes to voicemail.

"You have reached the voicemail of Kyle Masterson; you know what to do after the beep. "Hey, Kyle, this is Mindy. I just wanted to say thank you for the thoughtful gift. I hope you are doing well. Please call me back when you get a chance so I can thank you properly. Thanks."

Liz sees the bracelet on my wrist at work and freaks the fuck out. "Holy crap Mind, that thing is beautiful. The pink gems are stunning and the gold accents really make it perfect. It really is a beauty. You are one lucky dog."

"Thanks Liz. I'm just so touched that he thought of me and wanted this for me. It really is special and means a lot."

"Have you heard from him yet?" Liz asks.

"No, I left a message last night on his phone. I really didn't want to leave a message, but I realized my mail had been sitting in the mailbox for a few days and I didn't want to seem ungrateful. What if he was waiting for a callback? Who knows how long it was sitting in my mailbox? What if he thinks I'm an ungrateful bitch because I didn't call him sooner?"

"Oh my God, Mindy, stop it. You're getting freaked out for no reason. Relax, and when you talk to him, tell him what happened. He knows you work long hours for God's sake, he's been there with you while you do it. Remember?"

"I know you're right. See? It's good to have an objective friend you can bounce things off of daily. Thanks, Liz, you always manage to put a sensible spin on things."

"Your welcome girl, now get back to work."

"Yeah, yeah, yeah." I smile and walk away.

The day passes quickly and when I get a chance to go to lunch, I check my phone. No calls, no texts, no voicemails. That's a bummer. Kyle must be super busy because he would have called by now. My shift ends and I check my phone again. Radio silence. Nada, nothing! No word from the

Greek God. This sets my thoughts wandering. Liz sees my face and she can read me like a book.

"What's up, chickie? I know that look and whatever you're thinking, stop it."

"Not much, I just find it weird that Kyle never returned my call. I mean, we don't talk that often, but when we miss a call, he is usually good about returning my calls sooner rather than later. It's just strange, that's all."

"Mindy, I guess I never thought about this before, but how does he call you back on his cell phone? He can't see to text or dial a phone? "

"Ha, good question. David set him up with a new phone. It's a special phone with voice activated calling. When his phone starts to ring, the voice alerts him to who is calling or reads out loud an incoming text. Kyle can also activate it with his voice and just tell it to 'call Mindy' and it will automatically dial my phone number and then he just uses his cell phone like normal. It is super cool and very efficient."

"That's so amazing. Kyle can stay connected to everyone that way."

"Hey, by the way, what's up with you and David anyway? You haven't mentioned him lately. Is he still as buff and beautiful as I remember?" I ask

"Um, that's an understatement sister! That man's kiss curls my toes. How do you say it, Mind? 'He puts the tingle in my jingle?'"

We both bust out laughing and I have tears coming out of my eyes. Liz even snorted and made me laugh so hard I almost peed my scrubs! I even managed to lose all my mascara. Everyone needs a good laugh now and then, especially in my job. It's very therapeutic and cathartic to laugh. Thank goodness for a few rare moments of silliness.

My cell phone rings and I jump. I quickly look up at Liz. "Ooh, is it Kyle?" She asks.

"No, unknown number" I reply. "This happened to me the other night at 1 am too. I forgot to tell you about that because I just blew it off as random."

"Well answer it. Maybe it's Kyle from a different number."

"Hello?" silence on the other end. "Hello? Is anyone there?" Still nothing. "Hello?" and I wait again. "Ok, three strikes and you're out." *Click,* as I hang up. "See Liz, it's nobody. Probably some random kids crank calling. Like we did as kids, only this time it's not 1 a.m."

Liz gives me that look, you know the one. That look when you know your friend isn't buying the shit you're selling. She knows this is bothering me, even though I'm trying to play it off.

"It's fine Liz, really."

"Did you add these events to your weird events list, Mindy?"

"Yes, I did. Don't worry. I still have nothing!" I try and change the subject by asking her about the almighty David. "So, what are you and David doing this weekend? Any hot and heavy plans? You know I live vicariously through you right?"

Liz smirks and her cheeks begin to flush. "Well, right now we are still in the "getting to know you" phase. You know, getting to know your chest, getting to know your lips, and getting to know how much noise you make during hot sex phase."

"That's one hell of a getting to know you weekend Liz. Say no more, enjoy and give me details next week. I want full-on uncensored details girl. And do me a favor, please tell Kyle I said hello and that I was checking in on him. I still haven't heard from him and I'm a little worried."

"You mean he hasn't called you back yet?" Liz asks.

"Nope, it really is weird. I'm not a freak out kind of girl, but that's not like him. Just check on him for me, okay? Like a friend check in, got it?"

"You got it sister." We hug goodnight and smile and wave as we each drive away. Another successful day at work. My patients got better and one patient actually was transferred out of the TICU. That right there is a win in my book. I drive home feeling accomplished and satisfied with today's work. It's been a good day.

Chapter 27

Another uneventful weekend is planned for me. What shall I do? Decisions, decisions. I grab the newspaper and notice an advertisement for the local craft fair. It's today at the site of the old mall. "Vendors galore, and local artisans with unique gifts." Hmm, I'm a sucker for a craft fair. Besides, Christmas is coming in a few months. Maybe I can find some unique gifts. Decision made.

Stress free and happy, I head to the craft fair. I'm mixing with the locals and enjoying the sites. It feels like I've walked ten miles, as this place is huge and I don't want to miss any isles of crafts. The perfect gift may be around the next corner, and how would I know if I skipped an isle? I wander the endless decorated rows, full from sampling all the dips and baked treats available. What a selection. I've bought a few ornaments and a cream cheese pumpkin roll, my favorite. A few small purchases later and I head for my car.

I stop dead in my tracks as I see a tall, muscular man leaning on my car, his arms folded across his chest and his legs crossed at the ankles. He's wearing a biker vest. This looks familiar, only now it's daylight.

Do I approach him, do I run, or do I call the cops? I look around and there are people everywhere. If I get in trouble and need help, surely someone will rescue me, right? I have faith in mankind, so I approach my car. I stand far enough away from it, so this tough-looking biker dude can't snatch me up in one move. I leave several feet between us in case I need to run. So much for my attitude on having faith in mankind, but he really does look scary.

"Can I help you?" I'm purposely looking around at my environment. Everyone is going about their normal craft fair duties. Nothing seems out of place. I eye this man up and down. It's oddly strange that he's a biker dude with no tattoos. His hair is neat, and his face clean-shaven, except for the goatee. He's tanned and muscular. Boy, is he muscular, and a pair of expensive aviator sunglasses complete the package.

"Are you Mindy Harper?"

My brain kicks into overdrive. *Think, Mindy, think. Don't answer that.* My inner sensible voice says, "Who wants to know?"

"It's my duty to present this letter to Mindy Harper, and only Mindy Harper," he states with no emotion.

"And then what?" I ask Mr. Biker Guy.

"And then I leave, ma'am."

Did he just call me ma'am? Who is this guy? A scary biker guy with manners? What the hell is going on here?

"Okay, I'll tell you, but then you're really leaving?"

"Yes, ma'am. I don't lie." He says, sounding all offended.

"I'm sorry, you just look a little intimidating, you know?"

"Yes, ma'am, I get that a lot." He smiles.

"Yes, I'm Mindy Harper."

"Here you go, ma'am. Consider it hand-delivered." He hands me a large manila envelope.

He returns to his bike and starts the engine. Wow, I feel the vibration of that powerful machine down to my bones. I must admit; it feels a little exciting. A little bad to the bone kind of feeling. Hmm, a biker with manners. How fun! I let my mind wander for a minute. *Focus, Mindy!*

I get in my car, start the engine, lock all the doors, and stare at the large unmarked envelope. Not even my name or anything on it. Just blank. What the hell? I open the envelope and pull out the contents. Several eight-by-ten photos fall into my lap. I pick them up and stare. There before me, in living color, is a picture of Kyle and Patricia. Patricia is wrapped so tightly around Kyle you couldn't get a piece of paper between them. They're kissing, more like examining each other's tonsils.

I glance at the other pictures. Why? I don't know, because I already feel nauseous. There he is, my sculpted man of perfection, walking arm in arm with *her*! They're at the beach, which is my happy place, but not today. And then there they are! The ultimate heart-wrenching killer pictures of all time. My Greek god, buried full length into her! Their naked bodies photographed in many positions. You name it and he fucked it. He knows what he's doing, I'll give him that. And he certainly doesn't look like he's having any vision problems either, the bastard.

I throw the pictures back in the envelope and I think I'm going to throw up. My Kyle, who said all the right things, all the time. My Kyle, who made me feel so special and important. Who made me believe his every word is already fucking someone else? Wow! That didn't take long. So much for his ability to "see me!" I think in pure white-hot anger. Yeah, all he saw was a gullible fool. Someone willing to listen to his shit. And the more I listened, the deeper it got. God, I'm so dumb. Here I was thinking maybe, just maybe, I was deserving of someone as beautiful and thoughtful as him. That I finally had my chance to be the envy of every hot girl around, because he would be mine. That I would be enough for him. That I would be the one he called his hot sexy woman. Here's proof, I'll always and forever be the cute, kind, and special nurse.

Chapter 28

I head back to work feeling like shit. It's Monday morning and I have a long week ahead of me. I've signed up for overtime, just so I won't be home, pining over a man I never really had in the first place. All I really had was a dream. A dream that maybe someday he would see, and really see me. See me for the person I truly am and see me for my inner beauty. Fuck! I hate Mondays.

"Hey, sister!" Liz yells down the hall.

Crap! She found me. I'm dreading hearing about her perfect weekend with Mr. Wonderful, her perfect sex, her perfect orgasm, and her perfect happiness. I know that's not fair because I truly am happy for her, but I'm just not in the mood today.

"Hey, Liz, what's up?" I try to sound normal.

"Mindy! What the heck? You look like crap!"

"Thanks, Liz. How was your weekend?" I try to look interested, but what I really want to do is go home and cry myself to sleep and pretend the last two months never happened.

"I had a great weekend, Mind. I'll tell you all about it later, okay? You sure you're okay? I sense you're off, and I want to be here for you."

"Yeah, I'm good. I just don't want to talk about it right now, okay? I've got to get back to work. I'll catch you later."

As I walk down the hallway, I see the flower delivery man approach the nurse's station.

"De-de-delivery for-for Ms. Mindy Har-Har-Harper, please."

I walk up to the nurse's desk and look the delivery man straight in the face. "Can I help you?"

"De-de-delivery for yo-you, if you…you are Mindy?"

"Yes, I'm Mindy. Thank you."

"You're wel-wel-come."

As he walks back to the elevator, he stops, turns, and watches my every move. I catch a glance of his eyes and something is off. He is staring at me, watching me as if taking mental notes. He squints, smiles, and waves at me, but it's not a nice, friendly smile. There is evil there, I can sense it and it's creepy.

"Hey. Liz, you know what? I think that's the same delivery man that was here last time. Remember when I got the flowers from that biker, the yellow roses? That was the same guy."

"How do you know, Mindy? We see so many people, I can never keep track."

"Liz, I'm not so good with names, but I usually don't forget a face, and he stutters. So did the last guy. Remember, he kept watching me and waving? He gave me the creeps back then, too. Made my neck hairs stand up, like today. I'm telling you, Liz, something's not right."

"Mind, you need to add this to your list of weird events that David is asking you to keep. Make sure you say the flower delivery man. Is there anything else you noticed about him?"

"Yeah, I think he must smoke. He smells like cigarettes."

"Okay, random fact, but lots of people smoke, so add it to the list."

"Oh, I will, don't worry Liz. Detective Mindy is on the case!"

"Well, don't keep me in suspense much longer, Mindy, read the card already. You're killing me. Let's see who they're from."

I reach for the card as my hands shake and I break out in a cold sweat. I read the card aloud to Liz.

Memories of you,
My Amber and Rose.
Missing You.
Love, Kyle.

"Aww, Mind, that's so sweet. Don't you just love them? Long-stemmed red roses; they're so romantic, and they smell wonderful." I lean over with my eyes closed and take a big inhale of their aroma.

"No thanks. If you like them so much, Liz, you keep them." I walk away with a lump in my throat the size of a baseball. Liz looks up from admiring the bouquet and stands there in complete confusion. *What the hell just happened?*

After work, Liz catches up to me as I open my car door. "Hey, wait up a minute, would you?" Liz yells.

I sigh and wait for Liz.

"What's going on with you? You've been a bear all day. Do we need to have a sit-down?"

"As a matter of fact, Liz, I would love a sit-down. Wanna come over for wine and cheese and crackers?"

"I'm one hundred percent in. I'll follow you home."

As I drive to home, I notice a motorcycle one car back. It's loud and big, with an even bigger driver. He's burly, full of tattoos, and has a beard. Stereotypical biker dude. I watch cautiously as I drive, and he seems to be following my every turn. Is it just my imagination? I make a mental note of the description of the bike and its driver. When I get home, I will log this as yet another crazy, Mindy is losing her mind, episode.

Liz is curled up on my couch with a glass of wine, feeling concerned about me. I know she is worried. I can feel it. I shower and change into lounge pants before I get comfortable with a big glass of wine. I sit down next to my bestie and take a big swig of wine before I begin.

"Okay, Mind, spill it. What the hell is going on, and why are you so distant and miserable? What happened while I was away this weekend?"

I pick up the manila envelope and throws it on Liz's lap. "This is what happened while you were away, Liz. Look at that shit. Really look at it."

Liz takes the envelope and unfastens the metal clasp. She reaches in and pulls out the pictures. Of course, the first picture on top is the one of Kyle and Patricia, having oral sex.

"*Shut the front door!*" she screams. "No way! There has to be some mistake."

"Liz, seriously, there's no mistaking that dick. I've seen it enough times to know, and that's the bitch I had escorted from his hospital room, remember? These pictures are recent Liz! Look at him."

"Mindy, you don't know that. They have a history. These are probably old photos."

"Look at the scar on Kyle's face, the eyebrow mark. That's from his accident, Liz!" I cry, even though I told myself I wouldn't. Damn him! "I'm such a fool. Why did I let him get under my skin? What was I thinking? I'll never measure up to be good enough for him. Maybe it's a good thing this happened now before he got his sight back. Reality check now rather than later. I guess I should be thanking her, actually." Liz leans over and hugs me as tears that I can't stop run down my face.

"I'm done, Liz. I'm so done. I'm taking care of me from now on and everybody else can just suck it! I'm so exhausted trying to please everyone. It's all about me now. Fuck him." Liz holds me tight as I cry it all out of my system and try and find my new inner strength.

Chapter 29

When I get home, I immediately call David.

"Hey, babe, how are you this evening?" he asks, all lovey-dovey and sweet.

"I'm fine but I have to ask you a question, David, and I want the honest truth, or so help me God!"

"Liz, you're freaking me out here. What's wrong? You know I always tell the truth, especially to you. What's got you so upset?"

"Did Kyle sleep with Patricia since he has been out of the hospital and in rehab?" There is a hesitation and a moment of silence before David answers. My stomach knots up and I know I have my answer long before David admits it. "David?" Now I'm pissed off and my tone lets him know it.

"Yes."

"Jesus Christ, David! What was he thinking?"

"He wasn't thinking, that's the problem, Liz."

"Or he was just thinking with his dick, David, that's all!"

"Actually, honey, no, he really wasn't thinking."

"What's that supposed to mean? I've seen the pictures, and he looks like he knew exactly what he was thinking. His body definitely knew what it was doing, that's for sure! Pictures don't lie."

"What? Waite a minute, what pictures? How did you even know to ask me about Kyle and Patricia, anyway?"

"I just told you I saw the pictures."

"*What* damn pictures?"

"The ones Mindy received on Saturday, those pictures! And let me tell you something, mister, those pictures broke her heart!"

"Liz, I swear to you, I didn't know any such pictures existed. I'm sure Kyle knows nothing about them, either. Who gave them to Mindy? Where did they come from?"

"I don't know. Mindy told me the story. I think it was some biker dude. He showed up and dropped off an envelope to her. She didn't know who he was."

"Kyle will be blazing mad when he hears about this. He cares for Mindy so much. He will never forgive himself for being so careless. We knew Patricia was evil, but this act takes the cake. Let me do some research and see what she's up to, and I'll talk to Kyle. Liz, honey, I'm so sorry."

"Not as sorry as I am. And David, when the time is right and you have all the information, you need to be the one to tell Mindy. She will digest the facts coming from you better."

"You take care of Mindy and I'll be in touch soon, sweetheart. I need to do some disaster control and find out what the hell that wench is up to."

"Will do. Talk to you later. Night." I hang up and close my eyes as I am all too familiar with the pain and hurt Mindy is feeling.

I march into Kyle's room on a mission. I'm going to get to the bottom of this if it kills me. "Hey, bro, we need to talk."

"Sure. What's up?"

"We have a problem and it's a big one. Apparently, someone took pictures of your little drug-induced soiree with Patricia. And then they sent Mindy copies of the pictures. They were very explicit and raw and she saw all of them."

"David, *no!* This will crush her. She will think the worst and think we are back together!"

"Exactly! Kyle, she knows that you two have a history. She knows a woman like that will stop at nothing to get her man back, and those pictures just proved the point. It put the nail in your coffin, so to speak."

"What the hell are we going to do? Mindy will be crushed and so pissed off. That wicked woman will never leave me alone and now she has evidence!"

"Well, we have to be smart and keep our cards close to our chest, so to speak. Your blood test after you woke up was positive for Rohypnol or roofies as known on the street. It proves you were drugged and put into a compromising position. We have the documentation to prove that fact, so that's a plus. If we need to use that info, we will at a later date."

"As for Mindy, bro, you're in a bind, man. The only advice I can give is just be honest with her. Maybe you'll have a shot. I just don't know. She's angry and hurt. You've got your work cut out for yourself, that's for sure. I know Liz is with her now, you know, giving girlfriend support."

"*Fuck!* She is the sweetest woman I have ever met. The last thing I want to do is cause her pain. How can I make it up to her? I can't even look into her eyes and explain myself. How can she believe me when she can't even trust me? She can't look into my eyes and see I'm telling the truth. It's a no-win situation, man. I'm screwed."

"I'm going to call her and see if she'll talk to me. I have to do something."

"If there is anything you need, let me know, Kyle. You got this and good luck."

∽

After David leaves, I pull my phone out of my shorts pocket, feeling for the raised dial button and speak into the phone. "Call Mindy." I put the phone up to my ear. My heart is pounding, drumming through my ears loud and fast in frantic anticipation, but my mood deflates when the call goes to voice mail. "Hey, it's Mindy. Please leave me a message at the beep."

"Hey, Mind, it's me, Kyle. I so badly need to talk to you. Please call me back, please."

Chapter 30

My phone vibrates in my scrub pants pocket, signaling an incoming call. I peek at my phone and *The Greek God* lights up the screen. My insides shake in anger as I immediately dump the call into voice mail. If he thinks I'm going to call him back after the wonderful fan mail I've received, he's got another thing coming!

My inner conscience is yelling at me. *That's it, be pissed off and unavailable. This is a good game to play! Why not face the truth and just have it out? Get it off your chest and move on! Stop whining and be strong!*

The voice in my head is arguing with my heart, and I can't tune it out. I'm miserable. I'm not sure how to handle this, so I'll ignore the call. Maybe then it will go away.

My phone rings again and this time I don't recognize the number. I step into the break room and answer the call. "Hello? This is Mindy. May I help you?"

"Mindy, honey, you're in danger. Please heed this warning. I can't tell you who I am. I need to be anonymous. I don't want to start a turf war, but please be careful. I've been trying to keep you safe, but I fear for you. Someone is watching you. I don't know who yet, so be careful."

"Who is this?"

"Think, Mindy. If you need me, just call me. I'll be there. Be safe." The line goes dead as nausea rises from my stomach.

Who the hell was that and what did he mean, I'm in danger? I'm being followed? I knew it. My gut is never wrong. Fuck.

Who is this man and how did he get my number? The man on the phone was direct and to the point. His voice was deep and crisp and he didn't leave me any time to ask questions. It was as though he was in a hurry to get off the phone. What do I do now? My nightmare is now a reality. I'm being followed by a dangerous person and could be in danger at any moment.

I panic and call David. He's the only cop I know, and maybe he can help, even if it's from a distance.

"Hey, David, it's Mindy. I need to talk to you for a minute."

"Gosh, Mindy, I'm so glad you called. I'm so sorry about those fucking pictures. Kyle has been going mad over this big mess. Do you want to talk to him?"

"No, definitely not! Now, please, stop talking and listen to me! Concentrate, David, this is important. I only have a few minutes."

"Okay, now you're freaking me out. What's going on, Mindy?"

"I'm at work and something has happened to freak me out. You're the only detective I know, so that's why I called you. Otherwise, I wouldn't have bothered."

"Okay already, you've got my attention. Get to it. What's got you all worked up?"

I tell him about the phone call and what the unknown caller advised. "David? Are you there? Say something."

"I'm trying to wrap my head around why such an innocent woman would be in trouble. Mindy, I mean this in the most respectful way, but I've got nothing so far. When you get home, get your list out and call me. Let's do some work and see if we can find some similarities. In the meantime, don't go anywhere alone and have hospital police escort you to your car. Keep Liz in the loop, too. She should be with you. I'll pack up Kyle and we'll come down tonight to help out."

"No! I don't need any help from Kyle. He's done enough. Just stay home and I'll call you later. Thanks for the offer, though."

I hang up and try to finish my day without losing my mind. I have scrutinized every visitor and encounter I've had today and saw nothing odd. My head is pounding, and I am emotionally and physically exhausted. A hot shower and a big momma glass of wine are in order.

Liz and I pull out the weird events list and look at it again…we've got nothing. As Liz heavily sighs, my phone rings and David's number pops up on the screen. Liz answers it first so she can have a quick minute with her man, while I sit there and listen to all the cutesy talk. *Ugh! Sickening sweetness and happiness…save me now!*

"Okay, are you two lovebirds quite done?" I ask with pure attitude. "I'm freaking out here and you're playing kissy-kissy on the phone."

"I'm sorry, Mind, let's get to it." David begins by questioning me about every event I encountered. "Mindy, did you ever see any similarities between the events? You know, same car, same stationery, same penmanship? Anything that would link the stalker to multiple visits?"

"No, every time it was someone different. Do you think all these visits are tied together?"

"I have no idea, but it's worth a try to find a common thread."

"David, all the encounters were so random, but when the biker called me by my full name, it kind of freaked me out. How did he know my name? And another thing, whoever sent those pictures knew exactly where I was. I mean, I didn't even decide to go to the damn craft fair until that morning when I read the paper. And I went by myself. I didn't even tell anybody I was going. It was completely spontaneous."

"Mindy, it's safe to assume that you were already being watched. Someone was watching you that morning before you decided to go. How else would they know to find you there? Someone knows where you live and is watching your every move. Please be careful, Mind. Eyes open and at attention every minute."

"Jesus, David, I'm so freaked out. I'm starting to not want to leave my own house anymore."

"We have enough coincidences to alert the local police. I have a good friend on the force in your town. I'll put in a call and let's see what he says, okay?"

"Thank you. Any advice and help would be appreciated."

"Hey, Mindy!" Liz interrupts. "I just thought of something. Didn't you say the hospital flower delivery man had brought you flowers once before?" she asks, all excited.

"What do you mean, Liz?" David asks.

"Liz, you're right. I forgot about that."

"Give me all the details while I take some notes." David says.

"Well, I didn't think much of it at first, but the guy gave me the creeps from the first minute I saw him. He always stared at me and kept turning around to wave at me when he was leaving. He purposefully waited on me to notice him and wave back before he left. He had creepy eyes that looked me up and down, and not in a good way. And, oh, I almost forgot. He stuttered. He tried not to, but I could tell it bothered him that he couldn't hide it. It was like he was ashamed."

"Okay, Mind, good girl. I think I'll start there. Do you remember the name of the flower shop?"

I get up and look for the card that came with the bouquet as David continues.

"I'll contact the business and find out who was working that day. Let's find out who this guy is and what his deal is. It's the first common thread we've found. I'll get on it and give you an update as soon as I can. Until then, Mindy, stay put, okay?"

"I will. I have a few extra personal days available to me, so I guess I'll be using one of those days tomorrow. Good luck and thanks again, David, for helping a girl out."

"No worries. Now be smart and try to rest. I'll call you as soon as I have something. Talk to you later. Night, ladies."

Chapter 31

The night drags on and Liz and I can't sleep. I tossed and turned. My mind never rested. Liz finds me in the kitchen, staring out the window at 2:30 a.m. I am not moving, just in a trance, concentrating, almost catatonic.

"What's the matter, Mind? Can't sleep? Me either. My mind won't shut down long enough to entertain the idea of sleep."

I continue to stare, motionless. Liz touches my arm and I jump back a mile. Liz scares the shit out of me.

"I'm sorry, Mind. I was just talking to you and you didn't even hear a word I said, did you? Are you okay? And what are you doing?"

"I'm trying to be incognito while I watch that biker across the street."

"What biker? I don't even see anyone out there."

"Right there, Liz! Look…right between those two SUVs. He is squeezed between them on purpose. This way, no one can see him. He's leaning on the bike, just waiting. Constantly looking up at my window all night."

"Oh, my God, Mind, is that why you are sitting here in the dark?"

"Yup. I don't want him to know I can see him. I've been watching, hoping maybe I'll be able to see something to identify him if I concentrate."

"How did you even see him in the first place? He's dressed in black, for God's sake."

"I was up wandering around because my mind can't put the pieces together. Then I walked by the window and saw the red glare of his cigarette. He was inhaling and the burn of the cigarette caught my eye. Otherwise, I would have never seen him. Now I can't get my eyes off him."

"Hey, I have an idea. Can your phone take telephoto pictures?"

"I'm sure it does. Why?"

"Where is it? I'm going into your bedroom and get a little closer and take his picture. We'll have it for safekeeping to give to David."

"Oh, see why two heads are better than one? Maybe we'll actually get some needed information."

Just as Liz is about to snap a picture, the biker's engine roars to life. As he begins to leave, Liz points the phone in his direction and continues to take picture after picture, just on the chance she might catch something we can use to identify this man.

Liz and I are reviewing the pictures together when we realize all the pictures are in the shadows and we really can't see shit.

I exhale in defeat. "Well, so much for that idea. It was worth a try. Thanks for the effort, girlfriend."

Liz continues to scroll through the pictures, scrutinizing every single one. "Hey, Mind, look at this. I might have something here."

We both look at the last picture. Liz snapped it as the biker was leaving and rounding the corner. The streetlight above shone on his bike to catch an image. There was just enough light to see the side of his face and his leather vest.

"Score!" Liz screams in excitement.

I grab the phone from Liz and stare at the picture. It looks like the man has a beard, of course. I touch the screen and blow up the picture. I increase the zoom and can see the side of the man's face. There is definitely a beard and a visible image of a tattoo—a lightning bolt down his cheek. That's unique and something you don't see every day.

"Liz, I can see part of his patch, too. He was turning just as you snapped this picture. Can you make out that design on his back patch?"

"It looks like a dark color, maybe black and green with gold colors? It looks like a skinny arm reaching or pushing into the air. I have no idea. It's so hard to see it."

I blink to clear my vision as I study this picture in an attempt to focus my eyes. It's blown-up to the max on my phone. Now the whole picture is blurry, but I can concentrate on the patch. "Liz, this isn't an arm. I think it's a snake."

"Seriously, Mindy, let me see." She grabs the phone from my hand. "Oh, my God, I think you're right."

"It's a snake. Finally, a solid lead. What motorcycle clubs are around here with that kind of patch, Liz?"

"I have no idea. Do I look like a biker chick to you? I never pay attention to that kind of stuff."

It's morning and we're exhausted. Neither of us slept a wink as we mulled over the details of the weird events list again and the new information we discovered. It's only 7:00 a.m., but we can't wait any longer to call David and give him the news of our latest discovery.

I dial David's number, and he answers on the second ring.

"Hey, Mind how are you? Did you get any rest last night?"

"Nope, we didn't, but I have some news." I tell him about the bike that was camped out in my apartment complex parking lot and the pictures Liz took.

David sounds optimistic and requests I forward all the pictures to him. There are people in his IT department who can enhance the photos for clarity.

"Mindy, at least it's a lead. It could be random, but it's another positive. Good work, girls." David sounds encouraged, and that helps my nerves, for now.

Chapter 32

As Mom escorts me into David's office, he's on the phone deep in conversation.

"Bro? Are you talking to Mindy? Let me talk to her. David, man, let me talk to her. I need to update her on my progress. She'll be so happy. Bro, cut me some slack here, please?"

I can sense his hesitancy, but he places the phone in my outreached hand.

"Hello Mind. How are you?" Silence.

"Mindy, Mindy, please talk to me. I'm begging you, please talk to me!" Silence.

"Mind, please."

"Kyle, I really don't have anything to say to you, nor do I want to hear an explanation. A picture can tell a thousand words, Kyle. And I don't need an interpretation of you fucking Patricia. It's pretty clear, no room for interpretation is needed. Please, Kyle, leave me alone. My heart can't take it. Good luck to you and tell David I'll touch base with him later."

David takes the phone from me. The look of loss and defeat is plastered on my face.

"Kyle, man, give her time. She'll come around when she hears the truth. Give her time and let us get this stalking case wrapped up."

"What the fuck are you talking about? What fucking stalking case! Is she in danger for Chrissake? You'd better tell me everything, and I mean everything, starting now."

"Kyle, let me explain. Have a seat and just listen. I'll tell you everything and maybe you can give me some advice and a lawyer's perspective. Okay?"

I reach for the arm of the sofa and sit down as I try to calm my nerves.

I hear my mom speaks up, as I forgot she was in the room. "Excuse me boys," she blurts out in that tone. "but if Mindy is in trouble, you both need to do something. She's like family. If it wasn't for her, I'm sure Kyle wouldn't be in this good of shape. She is the best thing that has happened to you boys in a while. If she needs help, you boys make sure she gets it. I'm sure, with your police and lawyer backgrounds, you have all the resources you need to help her in whatever situation is going on. Make sure you guys do right by her. I mean it."

"Mom," David says, "We're already on it. Please don't worry. Kyle cares about her, and that's a good enough reason for me to help her. And she also happens to be the best friend of the woman I'm in love with, so that helps."

"Holy shit, bro, you're in love with Liz?

"Yeah, she's amazing. I haven't said anything yet because there is so much going on, but one day I will. I'm waiting for the perfect opportunity."

"Good for you, man. I'm so happy for you."

"Well, I'll leave you two to it," Mom says, excusing herself, leaving us in private. Once we are alone, David starts the story from the beginning. He fills me in on all the details of Mindy's 'weird events list.' Shocked and mad as hell I didn't know about Mindy's issue sooner, I'm feeling helpless but determined to assist David any way I possibly can.

Chapter 33

Sitting with Mindy, having coffee, she tries to relax for a minute, as she stares into space, but she can't fool me. I've known her way too long. This whole mess has gotten under her skin. I can't say that I blame her. If it were me, I'd be a nervous wreck, too.

Without warning, she bolts upright and firmly announces, "I need to make a phone call. Excuse me, Liz, but I need a little privacy for a minute, okay? I'll be right back and then I'll fill you in."

I raise my eyebrows and stare at her. She went from catatonia to a high-speed marathon in two seconds, racing to her room. Considering her state of mind, I wasn't leaving her alone. So, I follow her to her room and stand in the doorway, watching her search through her purse.

She pulls out her wallet, opens it, and pulls out a business card. "Whew, I thought I had lost this," she mumbles.

She turns the card over and then pulls out her cell phone and makes a call.

"Umm, hello, Mr. Turner? This is Mindy Harper. I was your nurse at Memorial Hospital. You said to call you if I needed anything or needed you. I think I need you. Please call me back at 555-276-6699."

When she ends the call, she looks up to see me in the doorway.

"You know, great minds think alike. I was thinking the same thing. Damn, girl, you really did it. You called him."

"Yes, I did, Liz. He was very thankful when he left the hospital and he did say to call him if I needed anything. So, who better to help me with biker issues than another biker? And now that I think about it, I'm betting he was the one who called me and warned me. The voice on the phone said, 'Think, Mindy.' I'm guessing he wanted me to figure it out without his help. This way he wouldn't be implicated if anything biker related went down. Liz, I know I'm right. I can feel it. My gut is right."

"Well, let's hope so, Mindy, otherwise you've just given a biker a lot of room for interpretation."

"I know, but it'll be okay. I'm going to grab a quick shower and be right back. I need to feel awake and alive instead of worried and exhausted. Catch you in a few." She walks past me and down the hall to the bathroom.

As she closes the bathroom door, I move into the kitchen and pour myself another cup of coffee. I go into the living room and peer out the window. There, across the parking lot, is another biker. I'll be damned. Here's proof in daylight that she's being watched. I reach for my phone and snap a picture of the biker. This man is not afraid to be caught and wants to be seen. He looks right at me and waves as I snap the picture. *What the hell? This dude wants to be caught. Who in their right mind stalks a woman and then waves at the camera? Oh, my God!* My internal warning alarm goes off and I run down the hall to the bathroom.

I bust into the bathroom and the door crashes against the wall. Mindy jumps a mile and yells, "What the hell, Liz? You just scared the shit out of me!"

"Mindy, I know who the stalker is!"

"What? How do you know that?" She turns off the shower. I hand her a towel. She dries her face and I shove my cell phone in her face.

"Look at this, Mind. I took this picture one minute ago! He was sitting outside your apartment building, looking right at me. He even waved at me! Ring any bells?"

Mindy grabs the phone and stares at the picture. "Holy hell in a handbasket! Liz, this is the flower delivery guy! What the fuck is he doing outside my apartment?"

"Good question, Mind. And you know what? He saw me and waved at me. It's obvious he wants to be seen."

"There is something really wrong with him. I can sense it, Liz. I sensed it at the hospital both times he was there. I freakin' knew it. Now, what does he want with me? That's the question."

I call David and give him the latest update as Mindy gets dressed. When her phone rings, I hurry to her bedroom. "Who is it?"

She looks at me and shrugs.

"Put it on speaker," I whisper.

She does and answers, with fear plastered on her face. "Hello?"

"May I speak with Mindy, please?"

"This is Mindy."

"Mindy, this is T. I'm returning your call. I was surprised to hear from you. Did you receive the flowers?"

Mindy relaxes her shoulders and silently exhales.

"Yes, I did, and they were beautiful. They were the biggest roses I have ever seen. Thank you so much, but that was not necessary."

"Mindy, I told you. I'm thankful to you and if you needed anything, I'm here for you."

"Actually. Mr. Turner, that's why I called you. I have an issue I would like to discuss with you in private. Can you meet me and my friend, Liz, for a cup of coffee?"

"I would like that very much, Mindy. Tell me when and where and I'll be there."

"How about one hour at the Eggs Benedict Grill?"

"Okay, sounds like a plan. I'll see you then."

Mindy looks up at me.

"We're going to meet him in an hour. So go get ready, girl. We need to find out what I'm up against. Hopefully, he can shed some light on the subject."

Before we head out, Mindy takes one last-minute look around outside. "Nothing. No motorcycles, no funny-looking unmarked cars, no storage vans. I feel safe enough to head out to go meet T."

Chapter 34

We get to the Eggs Benedict Grill and T. has already staked his claim on the best table in the restaurant. A nice table in the back corner, next to a window, where he can see all the comings and goings of all who enter.

As we approach the table, he suddenly stares out the window. I follow his line of sight to see a motorcycle parked across the street. When the rider gets off the bike, I notice the rider's vest patch, a snake. T. reaches for his phone and sends a quick text, and then quickly sets his cell phone on the table. "Good morning, ladies. You both look lovely this morning."

"Good morning, Mr. Turner. Thank you for meeting us on such short notice."

"It's my pleasure, Mindy. I took the pleasure of ordering gourmet cappuccinos for you both. I hope you don't mind. Please, sit and be comfortable. Now, please tell me what I can do for you?"

"Well, when you left the hospital, you said to call you if I needed your help. I'm hoping you can help me. I'm being followed almost all the time. I'm receiving unknown phone calls and notes in the mail. Initially, I had no idea who was doing this to me, but this morning something has come to light and I may have a lead. I was hoping maybe you might be able to help me."

"Mindy, I'm so glad you called me. I did receive some intel that you were a person of interest, but I'm not sure what that means for you. Do you know why you are being followed?"

"Mr. Turner, I have no idea and it scares me. There is no one that I know who does any shady business deals. I mean, I'm a medical professional. I went to college and I work. That's it. I'm an only child. My parents are now retired. I lead a boring life. I really don't have a clue."

"So, Mindy, how can I help you?"

"Well, Mr. Turner, we both, Liz and I, have been monitoring the parking lot at the apartment complex where I live and there has been an increase in the number of bikers who have been showing up. None of them looked familiar until this morning."

"Really?" His right eyebrow raises. "How so?"

"Well, we took a few pictures and wanted to show you. Can you look at these and see if you know any of these gentlemen?" I pull out my phone and show T. the shot of the man with the lightning bolt tattoo. He says nothing, but his raised eyebrows give me hope.

"Hmm," he says. "Interesting."

"And there is one more," Liz interjects. "Look at this one. This man was there this morning, and he is the one we both recognize. He actually waved at us, like he was saying, 'Hello,' and wanted to be caught. We have a few good pictures of him."

T. looks at the snapshot, rubs his chin, and then looks up at me. "So, how do you know this man?"

"Mr. Turner—"

"Listen, Mindy, we're no longer in the hospital. I consider you a friend and have a lot of respect for you. Please call me T."

I glance at Liz, who nods in agreement. "Okay, umm, T. This picture, we both recognized this man. He was the flower delivery man that brought me flowers to work. One time he delivered the flowers from you, and a second time from another patient a few weeks later. Both times, he stared at me and wouldn't leave the unit until I waved at him. Oh, and he stutters. He tried to hide it but was unsuccessful. He had regular clothes on while he worked, but this morning, we got a picture of his leather vest. Check out the patch." I point to the picture on my phone. "It's a snake, I think. Do you know this patch?"

"Mindy. Liz. First, let me educate you on the lingo of the biker world. A vest is called 'a cut' and is never misused. It is respected and to be worn with pride. It is earned and not given. Different motorcycle clubs have different standards one must meet before they are awarded a cut. The patch on the back is earned over time and applied to the cut when one has earned the right to be considered a full patch holder or brother. With that being said, this picture of the biker with his cut on shows us he is a member of the Vipers MC. He is known as John-John. His name is John, but they call him John-John."

"So, this John-John is a full patch and a member of the Vipers MC. What does that have to do with me?" I ask as if T. has all the answers.

"I don't know, honey, but I'm going to help you find out. I also know the biker with the lightning bolt tattoo. He is called Levin. His real name is Scott Levinthal, but Levin for short. He was struck by lightning when he was a kid, and survived, hence the tattoo. But I don't know the connection to you. Let me do some research and get back to you."

"Thank you, T. I have a detective friend working on trying to find some background information on the flower delivery guy, too. At least we have a name now."

"Mindy, be careful. My MC Club is working hard to continue our reputation as a community supporter and nonviolent club. It's not easy to maintain that image when you're a biker. It's a slow process and there is a stereotype about being a biker. Be careful. Bikers don't usually work with the police and if the Vipers find out, it could be a huge problem. Tell your cop friend to be careful."

"Thanks for the advice, T. I will pass it on and I appreciate any help you may have."

T. stands to leave and places his hand on my shoulder. "Listen, Mindy, keep me posted and if you need extra surveillance or protection, please let me know. I'll be in touch. Have a good day, ladies."

As we watch T. walk out of the restaurant, I feel a little safer knowing he is in my corner. The biker across the street monitoring our movements had already left. Finally, we were alone.

Liz and I head for home after picking up the newest trash tabloid to read and a few comfort food groceries.

When we arrive home, I call David to give him the latest information provided by T. Once on the phone, David asks to put us on speakerphone, so he can take notes, think, and scribble all at the same time. He says scribbling and doodling help him focus his mind.

"Mindy, are you sure you don't mind?"

"No, it's fine. Liz is here, too, so I'll put my phone on speaker, too."

"Hi, baby," she yells into the phone.

"Hey, Lizzy. Let's chat in private after this call, okay?"

"Sounds wonderful. Now, I'll let Mindy give you the update."

I tell David about our meeting with T. I can hear him frantically taking notes, shuffling paper as he writes. There is a pause in the conversation that I'm acutely aware of, so I pause in my telling of my story.

"David, everything all right?"

"Um, yes, Mindy. Please continue. I'm listening."

I finish my discussion with David and I'm ready to hand the phone to Liz, when David says, "Hey, Mind. I'm not trying to pry, but you should really talk to Kyle for a minute. He has made great improvements and would love to speak to you."

"David, I understand your concern, but I can't. You, of all people, know how trust is a big issue and so important. I don't have any faith or trust in Kyle right now. I'm sorry. I can't."

"Mindy, he has made such huge progress. Are you sure you don't want to talk to him about it?"

"David, it breaks my heart, but no, I don't want to talk to him about it. I can't right now. Maybe once all this crazy stalking crap is over. We'll see, okay? That's the best I can do for now."

"Fair enough, Mindy. At least it's not a flat no."

"I'll be in touch, David, and thanks again."

"Hey, Mindy, can I talk to Lizzy now? I really need to connect with her. We haven't been able to see each other in a while and I'm going through withdrawal."

"Sure thing, David, hold on a minute."

Chapter 35

"Hey, girl. It's for you. It's your Greek god," Mindy says, teasing me. Smiling, I take the phone.
"I'll give you two some privacy,"

"Hey, baby," I say with excitement. "How are you? I've missed you."

"Lizzy, I've missed you, too. So much is going on. I don't know where to begin. But I need to talk with you in private. Are you somewhere Mindy won't hear you?"

"Yeah, I'm in the bedroom now, with the door closed. What's up?"

"Lizzy, honey, you have to keep this is a secret. Mindy doesn't want to talk to Kyle yet, and he wants to tell her himself. So, swear to me you won't say a word."

"Okay, I swear, but you're freaking me out. What the hell is going on? Is Patricia pregnant? Is that what this is all about?"

"Thank God no! That would be horrible for Kyle. No, Lizzy, Kyle is starting to get a little bit of his vision back. He can see shadows so far. Isn't that wonderful?"

"Holy crap, David. That's huge. How is he coping? Is he excited? Why won't he tell Mindy? David, we need to tell Mindy."

"Slow down, Lizzy. This is Kyle's secret to tell. He is doing better, walking around better, but still frustrated. He wants to be able to tell Mindy himself. But right now, she doesn't want to talk to him, so mum's the word. Got it?"

"Holy crap, David. I promise, but this sucks! She needs to know, but I promise. David, tell me about Kyle. How did all this happen?"

"Well, he noticed that he started to see different shades of black. He thought he was just imagining things, then last week he started to see outlines of bigger objects. One day, Mom walked into the kitchen. He was sitting at the table having his breakfast. When he heard someone approaching, he glanced up. Because it's a built-in response, right? And

163

when he did, he got a vision or outline, you might say, of our mom. He looked in her direction and said, 'Hey, Mom. What's happening?' Needless to say, she freaked out. She had no idea that he could tell it was her just by her outline. Since then, it has slowly started to improve. He can't really see yet, but at least it's something."

"David, it's a freaking miracle. That's so wonderful. I'm so happy for him. You know, Mindy really is a wonderful woman. I hope someday he realizes that. Thanks again for helping her."

"Lizzy, I'd do anything for you ladies. Now let me get back to work and I'll see you soon. Okay?"

"Okay, honey. I'll chat with you later."

"Until later, bye, baby."

I'm so excited about Kyle, but I promised not to say anything, so I gather myself before I go find Mindy. She's in the kitchen.

"Hey, girl."

"Liz, I feel so lost, wandering around the house, not knowing what to do. I am reliving T.'s conversation in my head and I come up with nothing. I'm going stir crazy and I need to get out. I need my happy place, my place where sand and water unite." She sighs and drops her hands at her sides. "Liz, I need a break. Let's go get some food and bust out of here for a while?"

We decide to go rogue and head out for some fresh air. The parking lot is clear of bikers and mischievous looking individuals, so we head out. We decide we are in need of some good burgers and fries and head to Burgers and Buns on the beach. It's a great little place on the boardwalk with lots of activity. A place where people are always around and happy.

As we watch the bodies on the beach, Mindy lets out a large sigh. "Liz, I love the beach. This is my happy place." She looks around and then closes her eyes. "That's such a beautiful sound."

"What is?"

"The rush of the waves. It just soothes me and my inner soul. Normally, I can feel the stress leaving my neck and shoulders when I'm here. But today, it's not working for me. I feel a knot in my stomach that won't go away. I'm waiting for the other shoe to drop."

"Mindy, I know you well enough to know when you are suffering. I see it now and I don't know what I can do to help you. It hurts my soul to see you so sad and worried. What can I do for you?"

"Liz, just being here with me is a huge help. Thank you for hanging out with me. I'm so appreciative and thankful for you."

"What's going on inside that head of yours? I can tell you're thinking too much."

"Aw, Liz, you know me so well. I don't know. I just feel like I'm missing something. I've got that gut feeling. Something is not adding up, and it's driving me crazy." She looks away at the surf and takes in a long, cleansing breath. "Let's just go eat a big burger and forget about this for a while."

"I'm up for whatever you want to do, Mind. You name it, I'm your gal."

She leans in and gives me a bug hug as we head off to burger perfection.

Chapter 36

My brain is exhausted. Liz and I are watching a chick flick and finally relaxing a little. I settle into my favorite place on the couch, put my head on the pillow, and drift off to sleep.

"Stop!" I yell. "Stop touching me."

John-John, the flower delivery man, has me cornered at the hospital. He drags me by the arm and shoves me into the family bathroom, and locks the door.

"What do you want with me? Why am I here? Don't touch me!" I yell as he closes in the distance between the two of us.

John-John holds his palm over my mouth. *"Not a word or I'll kill you. You got it?"* I remain calm until I can flee. I will play into John-John's feelings and won't fight him. At least not yet.

John-John moves closer and gets up in my ear and whispers, "Oh, my dear, I've watched you for so long. Now it's my turn to have my revenge. What shall I do first, cut you or fuck you? Hmm, decisions, decisions. I'll think I'll cut you first. I'll cut off all this beautiful hair."

He grabs my ponytail and wraps it around his hand, pulling it tight, and yanking my head back. With precision, he shaves and cuts it off with his large switchblade, right at the other side of my hair tie. I try not to cry as I remind myself to stay calm, even though I am super pissed.

"Aww, see this cute Mindy. She's fading away. Just like my life," he says with anger. He tosses my ponytail on the floor and kicks it into the corner.

"Second, I'll cut off these clothes." He reaches for my scrub top and slices it easily from the bottom to the top. He gives it a good yank open to reveal my bra and shoulders. "Now for this bra. Jesus, Mindy, your tits are to die for. This lace bra is killing me. Let's get rid of it, shall we? Let's let these beautiful breasts free."

He slices the straps and pulls the bra off in one quick motion. My breasts bounce freely. John-John stands back and gazes at the gloriousness before him. "Goddamn, Mindy, your breasts are perfect. Soft melons, just ripe for the picking. I'm getting hard just looking at them. Just fucking perfect." He whispers as he reaches up to touch my breasts.

I slap away his hand seconds before he gets a handful. "Don't fucking touch me! You can look all you want, but don't touch! I mean it, John."

John-John looks up in amazement. "Well, aren't you feisty? Don't worry, sweet Mindy. I'll touch you if I want, and I'll earn it, too, and you'll love it. You'll love every fucking minute of it. You'll be yelling my name and asking for more by the time I'm done with you."

John-John grabs the waistband of my scrubs and pulls me into him, pressing my naked breasts against his chest as his hand is holding the tie of my scrub bottoms. "Mindy, don't move." He slices the waistband and the scrubs fall to the floor. Pink bikini underwear reveals my round ass cheeks and full thighs. "Holy mother of God. If you aren't the most beautiful fucking thing I have ever seen. I'm going to enjoy every inch of you, that's for sure."

I try to think and remain calm. *Think, Mindy,* I tell myself. "John-John," I say in a sweet tone. "If you want to see all of me, then why are we here, in the hospital bathroom? Wouldn't you rather be in a place of comfort? Let's go back to my place where there is a bed at least."

John-John looks at me in bewilderment. "You would go out with me?"

"Sure, if you ask nicely. I just need to change my clothes and put on something a little sexier for you, that's all. Hospital scrubs are so unattractive. Don't you think? Let me borrow your shirt to cover myself up and we can leave together. Okay?"

John-John falls for the bait and puts his switchblade down on the bathroom sink. He reaches around his neck to grab the cuff of his shirt, to pull it off when he suddenly hits the floor. I give him the old kick-in the-groin shot and frantically reach for the switchblade when he grabs my ankle and pulls it out from under me. I tumble to the floor and roll to escape.

When I get over the shock of hitting the floor, I come up swinging with the switchblade in my hand. John-John grabs me again and I ferociously swing out. This time I connect the switchblade to his flesh.

John-John lets out a big yelp as blood runs down his arm. "You bitch! I'll get you for that."

I have just enough time to scream bloody murder for help as John-John tries to get his bearings. He is so busy tending to his bleeding arm; he doesn't see me coming at him again in full self-defense mode. I stomp on his foot with my nursing clogs and kick him in the shin with everything I have, inflicting enough pain to take him by surprise and push him off balance. He stumbles and hits his head on the sink as he falls to the floor. He is conscious but visibly stunned. I manage to unlock the door, just as a huge weight plow through the door. It's Mack, the security guard.

"What is going on in here?" Mack yells. "Mindy, honey, are you all right?" He takes one look at me and this gentle giant is on the offensive. His choice of language rings in my ears as he reaches down and grabs John-John by the collar. "Wake up, you scumbag! You are under arrest." He spins John-John around easily and handcuffs him until local police can take him away. He takes one look at my nakedness and does what any gentleman would do. He takes off his shirt and wraps it around me, sheltering me from intrusive eyes. I cling to Big Mack for dear life as I shake like a leaf.

"Mindy, honey, come on. Let's get you out of here."

As we walk out of the bathroom, I look up, and in front of me is an all-too-familiar silhouette. "Kyle, it's me, Mindy. Please turn around. Kyle, look at me." The man turns around and so does his companion.

"I'm sorry," he says. "Do I know you?"

"What? Do you know me? Yes, you know me, it's me. Mindy Harper. I was your nurse. Kyle?"

Kyle looks at her with a blank stare. "Honey," he says to the other woman, "do you know this woman?"

I look at the woman and recognize her instantly. It's Patricia. A very pregnant Patricia.

"No, darling. I've never seen this woman before in my life."

Kyle looks at me with a blank expression. "I'm sorry. You must have me mistaken for someone else. Excuse us, we have an appointment," he says as they walk off.

"Kyle, come back!"

Liz is shaking me awake. I bolt upright and a fog encases my brain. I fight to focus as Liz calls my name. I look at her and I'm sweating and short of breath.

"Mindy, honey, wake up. You were dreaming. Are you okay?"

"Yeah, I'm okay. That dream seemed so real. I could have sworn I was really living it. The events were crystal clear and familiar." Jesus, I'm a mess. I look down and I still have my lounge clothes on, and I'm safe at home on the couch.

"Well, what the hell was it all about, Mind? Because you woke screaming for Kyle. You're in a cold sweat, shaking, and looking horrified."

I look at Liz and focus and tell her about the dream. Liz listens and hangs on to every word.

"Jesus, Mindy, I'm glad I was here. What do you think the nightmare was trying to tell you?"

"That someone is after me and I have lost Kyle. I guess I care for him more than I want to admit. What am I going to do, Liz? How can I spend time with Kyle when there is a potential psycho on the loose? I certainly don't want to endanger him or anyone in his family. My problems are not his problems. He has enough happening in his own life right now. He certainly doesn't need to worry about me."

"I've been meaning to ask you. Have you spoken to your parents about any of this yet?"

"Oh, God, no. My parents would freak the fuck out. Are you kidding me? First of all, I'm being followed, and second, I've enlisted the help of a biker! Jesus, let's give my mother a heart attack, why don't we? I guess someday I will tell her, maybe when it's over and done with, but not yet. She really doesn't even know about Kyle."

"What? Why not?"

"Don't get me wrong, Liz. I love my mother, but she can be a pain in the ass. You know she asks me fifty questions about my social life now. Can you imagine if there was a man in my life to talk about? I'd never get any rest. She would want every detail, in living color."

Liz laughs as she knows it's true.

"But I love my mom and I'm so appreciative of her. But when I have something to tell, I'll fill her in on the Kyle saga."

"It's a deal, Mind. By the way, while we are talking so openly and honestly, I have another question for you."

"Go ahead, ask away. You know I'm an open book, and you're my best friend. I don't keep secrets from you. What's on your mind?"

"Well, I don't know how to ask this, so I'm just going to say it, and I want you to know I'm asking out of love."

"Liz, just ask already, geez."

"Okay, Mind. I'm really worried about you. I've been watching you for a few weeks now. How much weight have you lost? I get the impression you're not eating much."

"Funny you should ask that, Liz. I didn't even realize I wasn't eating much until I put on these shorts today. They used to be a little tight around the middle, and today I had to wear a belt. I actually got on the scale, and I was down twenty-one pounds. I didn't even know it, because you know how I hate that fucking thing and avoid the scale at all costs."

"I mean, Mindy, that's awesome, but I'm still worried about you. It's the way you lost the weight. I don't think you're eating enough because of all this stress, and you have been riding your bike like a mad woman. I think you only eat when I'm around."

"You're probably right. We do seem to go out a lot and eat. I guess in hindsight, that's a good thing. And I ride when I can to clear my mind. I'll try to be more careful about eating properly."

"Mind, I love you, girl, but I'll be watching you. I know you want to trim up, but starving is not the way to do it. Promise me you'll be more careful and aware."

"I promise, Liz. I mean it."

Liz leans over and gives me a much-needed hug.

Just then, my cell phone rings. I grab it off the coffee table and glare at the screen. Unknown Caller. "Fucking hell, here we go again. Do I answer it?" Before Liz can answer, I announce, "I might as well get it over with."

"Hello?"

"May I speak with Mindy, please?"

"This is Mindy. Who's this?"

"My identity is of no concern to you. I'm calling regarding one of my brothers. He's in turmoil and it's all your fault. You need to fix this.

He's angry, and it's because of your family that he's an orphan," he yells into the phone.

"My family? What does my family have to do with anything? We're a quiet, normal, mind-our-own-business type of family."

"My brother is an emotional mess. He's fucked up and coming for you. You need to fix this!"

"How do I fix something I know nothing about?"

"Oh, you know, I'm sure of it. Big Joe knows everything. Fix this, Mindy, or else!"

I look up at Liz and the phone goes dead. "Liz, what the hell was that? Did you hear all that? I don't know anybody named Big Joe. Another missing piece to a puzzle I can't solve. Now what the fuck do I do?" I start crying.

"Mindy, breathe, girl. Take a deep breath and calm down. Let's think for a minute. Do you know anybody at all named Joe?"

"Nope, I have no clue. But you know what? The man said 'my brother' and he used the nickname 'Big Joe.' Do you think those could be biker references? Bikers often call their fellow club members brothers." Before Liz can answer, I say, "I'm calling T. He'll know what that means and how I should proceed from here. And Liz, while I call T., can you call David with this latest information? I would really appreciate it."

"Anything for you, love. I'll call from the bedroom, so you don't get distracted while you're out here on the phone with T."

"Sounds good. Thanks, Lizzy."

Liz looks up at me with a smirk and I can't help but smile and wink back.

Chapter 37

"Hey, T., this is Mindy Harper. How are you today?"

"I'm fine, honey. What's going on? Something must have happened for you to call me. Are you alright?"

"Well, I had an interesting phone call a few minutes ago and it kind of shook me up. I thought if I told you about it, you may be able to shed some light on the conversation."

"Sure, Mindy. I'll be glad to help you in any way I can. Give me the scoop. What's going on?"

"I received a phone call from an unidentified man. He told me that his brother was coming for me and that his brother was in turmoil and a mess. Then he told me I needed to fix it, and Big Joe would know everything. T., I don't know much about the biker world, but I thought those terms "brother" and "Big Joe" may be some words for a biker code? I thought I had heard bikers use the term "brother" before, so the first person I thought of was you."

"Mindy, the term "brother" is used as a sign of respect and acceptance. It's a respectful salutation to someone inducted into that particular motorcycle club. Each club is unique and like a family. So, when someone earns their patch, they are often referred to as a brother. "The Big Joe part I'm not so sure about. It could be the name of a former club member or a member who is still active. I certainly don't know every biker's name in town, but I'll do some checking and see what I can come up with, okay?"

"That would be great, T. I really don't know what I did to put this man in turmoil, but the sooner we find him, the better I'll feel. Thanks a million, T."

"You got it. Oh, and by the way, based on our conversation the other day, I decided you needed some extra security. And now I'm sure of it. I don't like the tone of the phone call you just received so I'm going to have two of my men tailing you for the next few days to keep you safe. Each man will be unidentified in the biker world. No cut to wear and no biker identifying marks. This way, they won't stand out as a person of interest. Both bikers ride a Harley, and one bike is white, and the other one is red with lots of chrome. Just in case you see these men, they are with me to keep you safe. Got it?"

"So, I should just go about my normal business?"

"Yes, Mindy, business as usual, honey. I've got you, okay?"

"Thanks for letting me know, T. I look forward to your call with hopefully some more information. Good night, T."

"Night, Ms. Harper."

Chapter 38

I hang up the phone and rake my hands through my hair. "Shit! This is going to start a fucking war, I just know it," I say to Hammer, my vice president.

"What's going on, T?" I explain the story.

Hammer's only response is, "Jesus Christ, if we get involved with the Vipers, we're screwed. Maybe we need to run this by the advisory council?"

"Hmm, good idea, Ham. I think I'll give him a call. But first, I want to do a little research on this Big Joe reference. I know I have heard this name before, but I need more details. Especially if I'm going to ask for a sit down with the Vipers."

I know I have heard that name before, Big Joe, Big Joe…

I'm not sure if Big Joe is one of the brothers from many years ago or a Viper. There is only one way to find out. I need to go to the safe deposit box and review the old Motorcycle Club records. There is a master list of all its members who were ever inducted into The Creeks Motorcycle Club. It's kept under strict lock and key for obvious reasons, and only MC presidents know of its hiding place.

I grab my keys and look at Hammer. "I gotta make a run. I'll be back later. Hold the fort, and keep surveillance going on Mindy. Okay? She's in more danger now than she was before. I'll be back."

"You got it, T. Be careful, brother." We hug and I head for my bike.

The thunderous rumble of the engine brings all eyes to me. I step on the gas, hit the throttle, and spin out of the parking lot, sending pebbles and sand flying.

I arrive at the bank with a few minutes to spare before closing time. The teller escorts me into the safe deposit room. I unlock the box and quickly thumb through the pages of the membership book when a newspaper clipping falls out of the book. I pick it up and read the headline:

Biker Kills Biker During Shootout

Short on time, I replace the safe deposit box in its slot and take the book with me, I quickly mount my bike and head back to The Creeks Clubhouse where I can concentrate in my office, undisturbed.

I roll up to the clubhouse, say my greetings, and head for my office. But first, I grab a beer and leave strict instructions not to bother me until I am ready to emerge. Hammer looks at a few other guys and nods. I'm sure they think shit must be going down because I only close my door when shit is getting serious.

I look at older pages of membership information and see nothing that jogs my memory. Thoroughly examining the last decade of members, I'm finding nothing. *I know, I know that name. Why do I know that name? How do I know that name? Where have I heard it before?*

I throw the empty beer can across the room and it hits the door. "Damn it!" Rubbing my eyes, they are tired and feel gritty from reading over this book for the last two hours. I get up to get myself another beer and accidentally knock the book and some papers onto the floor. As I grab the stack of newspaper clippings off the floor, that same clipping from before had fallen to the top of the pile. I grab the papers in anger and throw them on his desk, and walk out of the room.

"T., how are you getting along in there? Do you need anything?" Hammer asks.

"Yeah, I would love a big, fat cheeseburger and fries. Do you want to take a run to Burger and Buns on the Beach and grab me some takeout? I think I'm going to be busy in there for a while."

"Sure thing. I'm on it. I think I'll get myself some, too. Thanks for the suggestion. Be back soon."

Hammer is out the door faster than you can say cheeseburger, and I am back at my desk. As I sit down with a new ice-cold beer, I pick up the stack of newspapers I threw on my desk. I glance down and read the headline again:

Biker Kills Biker During Shootout

The date of the article is July 22, 1988, well before I ever became a member of The Creeks. The article described a turf war between The Creeks MC and The Vipers MC.

Apparently, The Vipers gained unlawful entry to a storage facility The Creeks owned. One night, there was a break-in at the storage unit. The Vipers broke in and were unaware that there were Creek members inside. The Creek members were hanging out playing a little betting poker and having a little game night.

When The Creeks heard the commotion, they got up and explored the building. They heard voices and found men in the front office space of the building. The Creeks yelled and started chasing the Viper members. The Viper members scattered, all but one. John Marxx confronted Creek member Joe Harper, President of The Creeks. A heated discussion ensued, and John attacked Joe first. He cut up Joe's face pretty badly and broke his arm. Joe fought back and got in a few punches that caused John to stumble. John came back with a vengeance and pointed a .38-caliber pistol in Joe's face. There was a struggle, and a shot rang out. "Man down," the paper said. John Marxx died instantly. There were witnesses and it was ruled self-defense. No arrest was made, and no time served was ever logged for Joe Harper.

"Holy mother of God! She's a fucking legacy. A legacy! What the hell do we do now? I'll tell you what we do. We protect her with our lives. That's what we do! Fuck me! I've got to call the advisor!"

I barrel through the doorway out into the open clubhouse. Four members are hanging out, relaxing, and drinking beer, and Hammer walks through the door, carrying a bagful of burgers.

"Hammer! Call all the brothers. I don't care what they are doing. They need to report to this clubhouse within sixty minutes. It's a 911 emergency, got it?"

"I'm on it, T. Care to enlighten me?"

"No time, just trust me. I'll update everyone in sixty. I gotta go make a call to the advisor!" I slam my office door and reach for my phone. "Holy shit!" I drink my beer in two gulps and run my fingers through my hair. "This is going to get real in a big way."

Hanging out on the couch, listening to the sports channel on the TV, in an attempt to catch up on what I've been missing, the phone rings. I lean over to answer it.

"Hello?

"Kyle? Kyle Masterson?"

"Yes, this is he. How may I help you?"

"Mr. Masterson, this is Todd Turner, President of The Creeks Motor Cycle Club."

"Yes, sir, I know who you are. What can I do for you?"

"I have a situation and I need your counsel. I know we haven't met in person, but you and your firm have been representing us for many years."

"This is true, Mr. Turner. Your motorcycle club has done wonders in turning your reputation around. You haven't needed our services for a while now."

"I know that, sir, but you are still on retainer, are you not?"

"Yes, we are. Therefore, I am legally your counsel. I'm not sure I can help you, though. I may need to refer you to one of my associates. You see, I'm recovering from an accident and not actively working at this time. But I can listen to your issue now, and refer you to the appropriate associate, if that's okay with you?"

"That would be wonderful, because I'm at a loss, really."

"Well, Mr. Turner, it's always good to start at the beginning."

"Okay, right. So, there is this woman—"

Kyle interrupts. "There always is," he says, snarky.

"No, Mr. Masterson, it's not like that. She is an acquaintance of mine. Someone I respect and care for very much. She is being harassed, followed, and receiving anonymous phone calls. Now she is being threatened, and seriously threatened. She has no idea who is torturing her, so she came to me with some intel and to ask for advice."

"Why didn't she go to the police if she had important intel?"

"Mr. Masterson, you know bikers don't involve the police. We try to handle things amongst ourselves…legally, of course."

"Of course, Mr. Turner. Please proceed."

"Well, this friend of mine has received a present in the mail from this stalker—flowers—and he was staking out her apartment complex. She managed to get a picture of the man, and he even waved at her, like he wanted to be caught on film. He wants to be known. The thing is, she had no idea who he was, but she knew he was a biker. So, she came to me for advice."

"And what did you tell her?"

"Well, I met with her and her friend. They showed me the picture of this man and he happened to be wearing his biker cut, so I got a good picture of him. His name is John-John, and he's special. You know what I mean?"

"Special, like you're in love with him special?"

"Oh, hell no! I mean, special like small-minded, you know, not well educated, has difficulty in society, etc."

"And how would you know that, Mr. Turner?"

"Everyone knows that. That's why his road name is John-John. He's always stuttering. He tries to hide it, but when he can't, he gets all frustrated and shit."

My stomach lurches and the hairs on my arms stand at attention, as I get the worst case of goosebumps I have ever had. Mr. Turner is describing the life of *my* nurse, and I don't like it. *What the fuck is going on?* Now I'm putting the pieces together and it is freaking me out, as Mr. Turner reveals the whole damn story.

"So how is this John-John person a threat to your friend? If he's so special, is he even capable of being a threat?"

"Mr. Masterson, this is why I called you. I just found out that my friend's father was involved in killing John-John's father accidentally years ago, and now John-John knows who she is. He is out for revenge, and Mindy is in danger. And to make matters more complicated, she is a goddamn legacy! The Creeks are going to protect her, and if we need to fight off The Vipers to do it, we will. I wanted you to know the reason why we are defending her. This way, if we get in deep, you'll be there."

"Oh, I'll fucking be there, don't you worry." My blood pressure is rising. "Mr. Turner, you said Mindy? Right?"

"Oh, did I? I didn't mean to."

"I need you to tell me the names of the people you are protecting, and why?"

"Well, Mindy's father was our president at the time of the shooting that killed John-John's father. He is actually the one that killed John Sr. She is a child of a president. That makes her a legacy. Someone we protect and respect for life."

"Mr. Turner, I'm getting a very uneasy feeling about this case and I'm never wrong. I think there may be a conflict of interest here, but I can still help you. Mr. Turner, let me be very, very clear. Listen to me, I might have some insider information on this case. And if I do, that means I am emotionally involved in this case. I promise you I will go balls to wall for you, if you and your friend need me. Do you understand me?"

"Yes, sir, I do, and thank you."

"Now, Mr. Turner. What is the name of your friend you are trying to protect?"

"Her name is Mindy. Mindy Harper."

I inhale sharply and hiss as I am just about to pass out. "Mr. Turner, do you mean Nurse Mindy Harper?"

"Yes, how did you know?"

"Holy fuck, Mr. Turner. I am deeply involved in this woman's well-being. I need to help her in any way I can. I know you don't work with the police, but my brother, David, is a detective, and he has been helping Liz Bennett, Mindy's friend. We need to pull our resources together and fix this situation."

"Mr. Masterson, the police issue might be a problem. I'm going to have a hard time selling that to my brothers."

"Well, you're the president. Don't give them a choice. Besides, we live an hour away. Your town is not in David's jurisdiction. He can just use his connections if we need them. Right now, we need to get Mindy safe."

"I agree. I'll work on The Creeks."

"Mr. Turner, does Mindy know the connection between her dad and this Viper Club you mentioned?"

"No, not yet. You were my first phone call. I was going to call her next and have her come to the club and explain it to her."

"*No!* Listen, I need to be there with her, along with her friend, Liz, and my brother, David. Please, wait for us. I will inform my brother, and we will pack a bag and drive down tonight. We can be there within two hours. She will need support, Turner. She's an only child and if she doesn't know about her dad, she's going to freak the fuck out. Please wait for us, for Mindy's sake."

"Okay, we'll wait for you. Go to her place and pick her up, and then you all need to come here, where we can protect you. We have men on her now for protection, but now that I know the connection, I feel like there should be more. If she's here, she'll be protected."

"Turner, text me the address and we'll be there soon. We'll have Mindy in tow, whether she likes it or not."

"See you in two hours. Don't be late."

I hang up the phone. "Fuck me!" I yell, as I panic for Mindy's safety.

Chapter 40

"David!" I yell from the hallway. "David, where the hell are you?"

"I'm right here. Jesus, Kyle, what's all the yelling about?"

"We need to pack a bag and head to Mindy's now! She's in danger and we need to be there for her. She's going to be getting some bad news, and she's going to freak the fuck out. I want to be there for her, and you need to be there for Liz."

"What are you talking about? She was fine yesterday when we talked."

"I have a client, a big client, that I represent. You don't know him and I have never told you because I didn't want a clash of conflict of interest to be in the way of our careers. I mean, shit, you're a detective, for Christ's sake."

"Yeah, and you're a lawyer, Kyle. Big fucking deal. It never got in the way before. So, what's the problem now?"

"Well, hopefully, there won't be a problem, but my firm, and mostly me when appropriate, represents The Creeks Motor Cycle Club."

"You mean *The Creeks*? As in the biker club in Mindy's town?"

"Yes, David, one and the same. The president of that club just called me. Mindy went to him with some questions and a possible new lead. She has been getting threatening phone calls now, too. Anyway, the president of The Creeks has just figured out why Mindy is in danger, and she needs to know. And we need to be there when she finds out. She will be a basket case, David. She is going to need Liz, too."

"Kyle, I'm all for going, but she doesn't want to see you, remember? How will you explain that?"

"Bro, I'm going to be honest and tell the truth. I know she thinks she doesn't want to see me, but I'll be there just in case. It's okay. I'm going for her, not me. And, as counsel for The Creeks, I should be there for them, too. Hopefully, she will come around and realize she needs me, just as much as I need her."

"You mean just as much as you want her? Isn't that what you really mean?"

"Well, yes, there is that factor, too, David. But remember, I don't want her to know of my vision progress yet. It's still not good, just better. I still struggle and still can't see colors yet. Promise me, you will keep that a secret still. I want her to be herself around me. She needs to trust me, and one day I want to surprise her."

"I'll keep it a secret, but you know how she feels about the truth. She's just as passionate about it as I am, I'm afraid."

"This little truth just needs to sit on the back burner for a while, that's all. This is about Mindy, not me and my small progress, got it?"

"Loud and clear, little bro. Now, let's go get ready and I'll fill you in on the rest of the details in the car. We need to be at The Creeks Clubhouse in less than two hours with Mindy."

"How are we going to do that? Kidnap the poor girl?"

"If we have to, yes. It's for her safety."

The one-hour drive is agonizing. My mind is reeling with new information, and I have so many questions. Like, how does Mindy know T. in the first place? Why does she have his phone number? Why did Mindy's father kill John-John's father? And so many more questions, and I have to admit, I'm feeling a little envious of Mindy's relationship with T. She went to him for help. This sits a little uneasy with me right now, but I'm trying not to feel like a jealous teenager.

My thoughts are with the girls, but I am trying to piece it all together, but I am still missing many of the details.

"You know, we'll be able to figure all this out when we're all together in the same room. Each of us has different bits of factual information that Mindy needs to put the whole story together. There are still pieces missing, Kyle. Stop trying to do the puzzle in your head when you don't have all the pieces."

"I know. You know me so well. I'm trying to rest until we get there, but I have a feeling it's going to be an uncomfortable night for everyone."

"I heard that."

I settle in for a long emotional night. Being the thorough detective he is, David informs me he put into motion measures to ensure Mindy's safety. Plans that even I'm not aware of, or T., for that matter. This is going to be a long night.

David calls Liz from the car and puts her on speaker. I hear the concern in the tone of his voice as he speaks to her.

"Hi, baby. How are you?" She sounds all smitten and shit.

"Hey, Lizzy. Listen, I'm calling on official business, okay? I don't have much time, so just trust me, and listen. Okay?"

"David, you're scaring me. Are you okay?"

"Yes, baby, I'm fine, but Mindy is not. So, listen to me closely. I want you both to pack a bag, enough clothes for a few days, and whatever you ladies might need. Put on comfortable clothes and be ready to leave in forty-five minutes. We are on our way to pick you both up, and should be there soon."

"David, what the hell is going on?"

"Lizzy, we will explain everything when we pick you girls up. Now get ready and get Mindy ready. She's not going to want to leave, but she doesn't have a choice, Liz. Do what you need to do and convince her, or I will. This is no joke. Her life was threatened and we're coming to get you both. Trust me when I say this is serious, and we'll be there soon. Now move it, okay?"

"Okay, but you know I'm going to have a hard time convincing her, but I'll do it. Please be careful. See you soon."

Chapter 41

I hang up. My pulse is rapid, and now I'm perspiring. *Be calm, Liz, it's just like at work. Handle the emergency first, then collapse later when the emergency is all finished.* Instincts kick in and I'm now on a mission. I walk into Mindy's bedroom to find her looking through a trash tabloid, trying to lose herself in the "problems" of the over-privileged.

"Hey, Liz, what's up? You have that oh-shit look we give each other at work when we know things are bad."

"Mindy, don't give me shit. Just do what I say, no questions. Okay?"

"What the hell, Liz? You're all pale and shit."

"Listen, David just called me and said you are in real danger. We need to pack a bag with a few days' worth of clothes and any other items we may need. He said they will be here to pick us up within the hour. Mindy, he said this was no joke and not to fight him on this. He said this is serious and for us to get a move on and get ready."

"Come on, Liz, how much danger could I really be in?"

"Mindy, I'll drag you out to his car if I have to. David said they would fill us in when they get here. He sounded extremely official and serious, and was definitely not joking around. Now move it, girl, let's go!"

"Hold up a minute. 'They?' Who the fuck are we talking about here, Liz? Who are 'they?'" There is a definite hesitation in the response. "Liz, answer me!"

"Umm, I didn't ask, actually, if you want the truth, but I'm assuming he meant Kyle, too."

"Fuck, I don't want to see him. Nor do I want him involved in my shit drama. That man has enough of his own crap going on without me getting in the middle of it."

"Mindy, we can't worry about that now. Just pack your damn bag and throw me some extra clothes of yours that I can borrow. I have no idea where we are going, so I'll grab the toiletries. Move it, sister!"

"Jesus, my heart is pounding, Liz. I haven't seen Kyle in a long while. I look like crap, and I'm certainly not in a cutesy nurse mood."

"Mind, please. It's nighttime. Who cares what we look like? And it's not like he can see you yet, anyway, so relax."

"Oh, thanks for the reminder that the man I care about is blind, Liz."

"Shit, I didn't mean it to come out sounding like that. I'm not trying to be insensitive, honey. It just popped out of my mouth. I'm sorry. But I did hear you admit you care about him, right?"

"Of course, I care about him. He's amazing, caring, and gorgeous, too. What's not to like about him? I really got to know him for him. I could see him for who he really is, not just the physically beautiful attributes he so amazingly possesses."

"I'm sure he can say the same about you. He got to know the real Mindy, not just the nurse who took care of him."

"Maybe so, but at least I could see him."

"Yes, but I'm sure he can see you, too, just in his own way. Didn't he tell you that?"

"He did, but I'm having a hard time believing him, you know? He's just so hard core handsome. I'm afraid when he does get his sight back, I'll be such a disappointment for him."

"Aha! That's the real problem right there, Mindy. You don't believe you're worthy of his love. Right?"

"I guess so, Liz. I mean, look at him. He's absolutely stunning. And I'm just me, cute little me. No one like him wants an average girl like me. For a blind man, I'm a gem, the whole package, etc. For a seeing man, I'm just an average cute girl, nothing special. That's why I hate that fucking word, cute! Cute is for puppies, not women."

"Mindy, you are so much more than cute. Please don't sell yourself short. You are perfect in every way. Never doubt that you are someone's everything! And never doubt Kyle. If he says he sees you, then believe him. A person can see in many ways, Mind. It doesn't always have to be with their eyes. These men believe in trust and honesty, just like us. Kyle wouldn't lie to you. I feel that in my bones. Please, just listen to him, okay?"

"I'll try, Liz, but I'm scared. All I can do is say I'll try."

"That's a start, Mind. Now get packing and move your ass."

The doorbell rings just about an hour later. As Mindy heads for the door, I yell, "I got it. You finish up." I look through the peephole to see my Greek god waiting patiently. I pull the door open and pull my man to my awaiting lips.

"Mmm, you taste divine."

"Um, excuse me, do you not see me here?" Kyle asks.

"Actually, I didn't. I was so happy to see your brother. My mind was elsewhere."

"I got that impression. Now, can you put your mind back on this moment?"

"Please, come in. Mindy is just about done. We need like five more minutes."

As the Greek god brothers enter Mindy's apartment, she comes barreling around the corner with her bag swinging on her shoulder. She stops short at the sight of Kyle, and her bag tumbles to the floor from the quick stop. She inhales sharply at the sight of him. "Kyle, you came."

"Of course, I did. If you're in danger, I want to be here for you, Mind. I'm always here for you. I hope you know that."

"Thank you. You both didn't need to come, but I'm really glad you're here. Now, what the hell is going on?"

"Mindy, I received a phone call from an extremely reputable client, looking for some legal advice. It was determined that you are a common link between my client's problem, a biker club, and me."

"I'm so confused, Kyle. How are you involved with a biker club?"

"Well, one of my firm's biggest clients happens to be The Creeks Motorcycle Club, and this just so happens to be my account."

"What?" David and Mindy say in unison.

"Why didn't you tell me this earlier, bro? You knew I was working on this case from a legal perspective. It would have helped."

"Bro, I never want my job and your job to come between us, or have a conflict of interest. So, I don't talk about my job at home, hardly ever. Until now. We all need to sit down and discuss some new information that has come to light. Mindy, T. called me earlier. We shared some intel, and now we all need to go to his clubhouse for a formal sit down. This is serious shit, Mindy, and we need to all share our information."

Mindy looks between Kyle, David, and me, and the tears just start flowing.

"Oh, Mindy, honey, don't cry," I say. "It will be okay. You have so many people on your side. Look, you have a lawyer, a detective, and a biker all on your side. I'd say you're well protected and loved. Wouldn't you say?"

"And a kick-ass nurse, too, Liz, let's not forget that." She tries to laugh a little.

"Do you have everything?" David asks.

"I think so."

"Let's go then." David grabs Mindy's bag and they head for the door. Kyle stands there waiting for direction. Mindy steps over and reaches for Kyle's hand to guide him to the door.

"Wait. Can I have five minutes with Mindy while you both wait for us outside?"

"Sure, bro, but make it fast. We have a schedule. I wouldn't want to piss off the bikers."

"Gotcha. Thanks."

Leaving the apartment, David closes the door behind us. He pulls me into a close, warm hug and we wait quietly for Mindy and Kyle.

Chapter 42

"Mind, I've played this moment over a million times in my head, and now that you're here, right in front of me, I'm weak in the knees and sweating."

"Just say what you want to say, Kyle. Just get it over with," I say with sheer coolness.

"Mind, I never, in a million years, want to hurt you. Please know that Patricia means nothing to me. Those pictures you saw mean nothing."

"They didn't look like nothing to me, Kyle. You looked all too happy, enjoying every minute and every position imaginable."

"Mind, I don't even remember that night. Somehow, Patricia drugged me and had someone take those pictures. It was a setup, Mind, I swear."

"That's the oldest story in the books, Masterson. You expect me to really believe that?"

"Yes, I do. When David figured it out, he demanded I get drug tested. He was adamant about it, just in case we needed the information for future proof. Proof in case Patricia tries anything in the future. You know, like blackmail, etc. And you know what, Mind? The fucking test was positive. It showed benzos and Rohypnol in my system. She fucking roofied me! Please know, I hate her with a passion. I would never have spent a night with her, ever, especially like that. I would never do that to you."

"Kyle, we better go. Liz and David are waiting." I reach for the door as Kyle reaches for my hand. He gently entwines his fingers with mine and I lead him out the door. *Hmm. That was so natural, like he could physically see me. Like he knew exactly where to find my hand. How did he do that?* I immediately dismiss the idea once I get a look at Liz, who is watching our every move, scrutinizing everything.

What? I mouthed to her.

Liz looks at Kyle and just shrugs as we head for the car.

We arrive at The Creeks Clubhouse right on time, not one minute to spare. Two burly men, tattooed and friendly, welcome us to their "home."

As we enter, this biker hangout isn't at all what I expected. It's a neat and orderly space, with couches, tables, a pool table, and a functioning bar. It's organized, and the décor is classic artwork fitting for a motorcycle enthusiast.

T. emerges from his office. He prances in, like the well-deserved title he has earned as president, and comes right over to me. "Mindy, honey. Thanks for coming. And who do we have here with you?"

"T. you already know my friend, Liz. This is Mr. David Masterson and his brother Kyle."

"Ah, the lawyer. We have met via telephone. Nice to meet you in person, Kyle." T. extends his hand and Kyle shakes it with confidence. *What the hell was that?* I think, watching Kyle's every move. He shook his hand so easily. It is as if he could see it. Can he see? Just as quickly as the thought pops into my mind, I dismiss it.

"Please, everyone, have a seat. Make yourselves comfortable. Billy Boy here will bring you all drinks. What will it be?" Kyle reaches for the edge of the furniture so he can find his way to sit down. There is no mistaking that.

"I'll have water," I say, and Liz, David, and Kyle echoed.

"Mindy, I know you're scared, but let me assure you, this is the safest place for you right now. We have men positioned in various places designed to keep you safe and to monitor the whereabouts of some of the Vipers. We've got you covered. Try to relax and let's go over all the facts together, shall we?"

"T. you don't even really know me, and you have taken so much effort to protect me. I thank you, but I really don't understand why. Why Me?"

"I told you that day in the hospital, Mindy. You earned my respect and took care of me as if I was your own flesh and blood. That, my dear, was all I needed. I knew there was a passion in you to always do the right thing and stand up for your patients. That is a quality that only one in a million possess, my dear. I never go back on my word, and when I left the ICU, I told you that if you ever needed me, to just call. So, here I am, and all my brothers, too. Now, since that first call, Mindy, we have learned so much more, and that is why we are all here. Those of us who care for you, and want to protect you."

"I'm humbled by the dedication of your men, and I'm so thankful to you all. How do I fit into this whole mess?"

"So, you called me about a threatening phone call you received?"

"Yes. The man said I was the cause of a "member's undoing." That he needed help, and it was my responsibility to fix it. Then, the name Big Joe came up, but I don't know anyone named Big Joe."

Kyle, David, and Liz listen intently as T. and I hash out the details. It isn't long before Kyle and David have more to share.

"So, the name Big Joe kept bothering me. I knew I had heard that name before, but I just couldn't place my finger on it, so I did some Creek investigating. I pulled old records and couldn't find anything at first. Then I discovered this old newspaper article. Mindy, do you know anyone named John Marxx?"

"No, I don't think I have ever heard that name before. Why?"

"Holy shit," Kyle says. "Um, excuse me T., but can I interrupt here for a minute?"

"Sure, Kyle, what's the matter? You're as pale as a ghost. You okay, man?"

"I'm not sure. You said John Marxx. Is this John Marxx, married to Suzette Marxx, mother of John Marxx, Jr.?"

"Yes, why Kyle?"

"I think I'm going to be sick." Kyle stands as David reaches for a napkin to hold up to Kyle's mouth.

"Bro, what the hell? You okay?"

"No, I'm not okay. I have more information to tell, and I'm just starting to put it all together. This is a big fucking mess. T., I think I know these people, but please continue and I'll interject when appropriate, if you don't mind."

T. nods. "John Marxx, Sr., was a Viper gang member. The Vipers were a troublesome gang and caused town chaos and turf fights between themselves and The Creeks. The newspaper article talks about a break-in at a Creek-owned storage facility. Now, The Creeks were there, minding their own business, playing poker, when a confrontation occurred. There was a fight, and a gun was pulled on a Creek Member. The Viper drew first blood, but in self-defense, the Creek member fought back and shot and killed the Viper. That Viper was John Marxx, Sr."

"That's horrible, T. I'm so sorry for their loss, but I still don't see the connection to me?"

"Mindy, there's more. Listen to me, honey. I found the Viper member who was following you and stalking you, at least most of the time. That picture you showed me of the Viper waving at you, the one who looks like he wanted to be caught?"

"Yes, I remember why?"

"Actually, Mind, you have met him several times. Remember I told you they call him John-John. I didn't tell you why he was given that name. He is called John-John because he stutters."

"*Oh, my God!*" I look at Liz and total fear washes across our faces.

"The flower delivery man!" Liz yells.

"T. This man was at my work. He was the guy who brought me the flowers you sent me, and then he showed up again when Kyle sent me flowers. He saw me leave work, knows my car, knows where I live, and he has my phone number! How did all that happen? Work never gives out phone numbers."

"He got your name from the delivery order," David interjects. "T., when you went to the flower shop to order the flowers, you needed Mindy's last name. How did you find out her entire name?"

"That was easy. She had to sign all my paperwork at the hospital. Her name is on my records as the ICU nurse."

"Son of a bitch," Kyle mumbles.

"It's okay, Kyle, it is standard procedure. There is nothing wrong with that. What does bother me is how easily John-John figured out the rest of my personal information."

David shook his head and shrugged. "It's too easy nowadays to use social media and reverse lookup online to find out information on people. Mindy, you were just a victim of the times. It can happen to any of us."

"Okay, so why is John-John after me? I'm still not understanding that piece of the puzzle."

T. looks at Kyle and David, and nods. "Mindy, you've never heard the term Big Joe before? I really need you to think, honey."

"No, I told you. Not that I can recall."

"In the article that I found, the shooter of John Marxx, Sr. was a Creek member called Big Joe. That was his given road name by The Creeks, but his legal name," T. pauses and looks up at the Masterson brothers, "was Robert Joseph Harper."

I gasp in disbelief, and Kyle is at attention. "What the fuck are you talking about, T.? That's my father's name. He has never been in a biker club in his life. He doesn't even know how to ride a motorcycle. You have got to be mistaken. Robert and Joseph are such common names. T., there is no way in hell my dad was involved in killing someone! No way. I don't believe it."

"Mindy, let me fill in some more of the blanks for you, honey. Robert Joseph Harper was president of The Creeks from 1985 until this unfortunate event on July 22, 1988. He graciously retired from The Creeks Motorcycle Club because of this unfortunate event, and coincidentally, because his wife was pregnant. His daughter was born on September 28, 1988. Mindy, isn't that your birthday?"

"Yes," I whisper, still in denial. I can't believe any of this.

"Mindy, honey, you are what we call a legacy. In our club, a legacy is a child born to a president of The Creeks. Legacies are cherished and well taken care of by Creek members. They are protected and forever welcomed here. That is another reason why we have given you extra surveillance."

"And because I ordered it, too," David pipes up.

"What is that supposed to mean?" T. asks.

"Well, on a different note, I have known for some time that the Vipers have been attempting to blackmail The Creeks for situations that were beyond their control. Specifically, from events in years past, and the current members are paying the price. The Creeks Motorcycle Club's reputation and members are on the 'up and up,' and I'm going to prove it. This club's social acceptance and reputation has greatly improved over the years, and I'm sure your current members had something to do with it. Mr. Turner, meet special agent, Timothy "Boots" Dixon. The member who has always been in your corner."

Boots waves from the seat at the bar, and T. looks at David. "No shit.

Boots, you're a cop?"

"Yes, sir, and a damn good one, T. I am also a faithful member of this club and proud of it. I want you to know I'm loyal and dedicated. I've got you and my brothers, T., no worries.

"That's another conversation we'll have later, but please just know you're doing good here. Keep up the good work. Now we need to get Mindy squared away."

"Mindy, your dad was a revered president who never did anything wrong. He happened to be in the wrong place and defended himself. Any normal human would have done the same thing. It was one hundred percent self-defense, and no charges were ever filed. I think your dad suffered the most. He felt horrible about the loss of the Viper. He couldn't forgive himself, so he resigned from the club."

"I still can't believe he was a member of a motorcycle club."

"Mindy, the article states your dad was badly injured in the face and suffered a broken arm. Does any of this make sense to you?" T. asks.

"Well, it didn't until you just said that. My dad has a large scar above his right eyebrow that he said he got as a kid. He told me he got a fishing hook stuck in his eyebrow, and they had to cut it out. Jesus, he was lying to me this whole time."

"Now we know why John-John said you would know what happened. Big Joe is a reference to your dad. At the time, your dad was a member. There was already a member named Robert, so your dad used his middle name. And when he became president, the members added the 'Big' in front of it, because he was the big man, you know, the president. It was a term of endearment, so to speak, that just stuck."

"So how do I fix John-John's problem? He wants me to pay for the death of his dad? That makes no sense. I wasn't even born yet! How the fuck am I going to do that? I'm not even sure what he wants yet."

"He wants you, Mindy," Kyle says with confidence.

"Why would you say that?"

"Because, think about it, Mind. He can't have his father, so he'll make your father pay, in some way. What better revenge for him than to hurt the ones you love?"

"I still don't understand. Why now? I mean, I'm thirty-three years old. Why didn't he figure this out sooner? What made him decide to do it now?"

"My love for you, that's what made him decide to do it now."

Liz gasps.

"Kyle, what the fuck are you talking about?"

"He knows I love you, and seized a perfect opportunity to torture me, and your father, at the same time. He thinks he could kill two birds with one stone."

"He doesn't even know you. How would he have known we even knew each other?"

"Actually, Mindy, he knows of me. He doesn't know me personally. I just put this whole nightmare together while I've been sitting here listening to all the pieces. You see, John Marxx Sr., had a son, John Marxx, Jr. We just established that, but what you all don't know is that he also has a daughter, a fraternal twin to John Jr., and her name is Patricia Marxx. The one and only. You guessed it, my ex-girlfriend, who just can't seem to go away."

The color drains from my face, as I remember those pictures of her and Kyle having sex. The visions creep into my memory. I sit there emotionless, staring at Kyle as I try to listen and focus.

"Shut the fucking front door!" Liz yells. "That bitch is his sister? Now, this is making some sense."

"Let me put some light on their relationship, if I may," Kyle requests.

"Please do, by all means," T. replies.

"I have never met John Jr., but I knew he existed. Patricia mentioned him occasionally as an estranged brother. Apparently, he never really matured as quickly as Patricia did, and school was always difficult. He was constantly being made fun of because of his speech impediment. He also had a severe learning disability. Because they were being raised by a single working mom, she never paid much attention to John Jr. and his special needs. He became more withdrawn, so momma gave her daughter all the attention."

I smirk. "Well, that explains her high and mighty, I'm better than you, attitude."

"I'm willing to bet Patricia put John-John up to this to help get back at me. She is sadistic enough to know she can hurt two people in the process. She can hurt Mindy's dad, for killing their father, and Mindy will be the casualty. She also knows if Mindy gets hurt in some way or leaves me, then I will also be directly hurt. I don't think Patricia has it in her to physically hurt someone, so she enlisted her brother. But she also knows how to effectively hurt a woman without being physical. So, how would you hurt Mindy without physically hurting her?"

"You send her pictures of you and Patricia together in compromising poses," Liz answers.

"Exactly. Proving the point. It drives Mindy away. Hoping to leave me vulnerable so Patricia could get closer to me, or so she thought. All it did was drive Mindy away from me and solidify my hatred for her. I'm so sorry, Mind. If I could take it back, I would."

I look at Liz, and then at Kyle. Tears well in my eyes. I can't help it. Without a word, T. reaches over and hands me a tissue.

I clear my throat, so it doesn't sound like I've been crying. "I thought Patricia was estranged from her brother? How did she enlist his help? And what does that mean for me? I'm still getting threatening phone calls. Isn't that why I'm here, too?"

"That is one piece of the puzzle we have yet to answer. Yes, that is why you are here, and now we know why you are in danger. Now we just need to have a plan to fix it," T. says.

"I don't really remember Patricia mentioning her brother much. Just sometimes she would make these comments like 'He will do whatever I want to keep me happy,' and 'Because I'm the only one who pays him attention and loves him,' Kyle remembers.

"So, she basically is using him. She probably doesn't even love him. How typical," Liz blurts out.

"T., I need a minute. Is there somewhere I can be alone for a few minutes to digest all this? It's a little bit overwhelming."

"Sure, honey. Here, use my office. There is a nice chair and couch in there. Take as much time as you need. We will all be right here when you come out."

"Thank you, I appreciate it." I get up to walk toward T.'s office. I stop mid-stride and turn around. "Um, excuse me, Kyle. May I have a word, please?"

"Oh, ah, sure. Someone point me in the right direction."

"Here, take my hand." I place my hand in his and escort Kyle into the office. "Here, sit down."

"I'd rather stand. It's been a long day and I'll just lean right here against the edge of the desk if that's okay."

"Okay, suit yourself. First of all, I've heard a lot of information tonight, some of it confusing as hell. My dad's story breaks my heart, but I will handle that with my parents. There is one issue that needs clarification, and maybe you can shed some light on the matter."

"I'll try my best, Mind."

"I think I recall hearing you say you loved me. Am I correct about that?"

"Ms. Harper, you are one hundred percent correct about that, ma'am."

"Really? How come you have never shared that information before, Mr. Masterson?"

"Well, there was this trust issue, you see, and people need to earn trust back in order to make a relationship work. I was just waiting for the correct moment, Ms. Harper."

I stealthily make my way in front of Kyle.

"I don't care how quiet you think you are being; I know you're right in front of me. I can smell you. My amber and rose angel. My God, I have missed your scent and your company."

I position myself between his open legs and reach for his hands, placing them on my hips. I can hear Kyle slowly control his exhale. My insides are beginning to simmer and the warmth I am feeling is traveling down to my pelvis. Dear Lord, I have missed him.

I place my arms on Kyle's shoulders and pull him closer to me, placing my well-moistened lips against his. Kyle's grip on my hips instantly tightens, and he pulls me to him. He reaches up and finds my face. My tender kiss has turned into a deep, passionate kiss of want and need. Hearts are pounding and breathing is heavy as our bodies are entwined. I can feel his cock as it hardens under the zipper of his jeans.

I press against him, my waist perfectly aligned with his, and I can feel the growing hardness beneath. Kyle moves his hands with precision to my back, and in one quick movement of his hands, he unclasped my bra. He embraces my back and gently pulls my chest to his. I can feel his heart pounding as he gently rubs up and down my back. His tongue, warm and tender, is exploring every inch of my mouth.

My tongue dances around his as he slowly reaches underneath my shirt and caresses my firm, pointed nipples. They are as straight as a pin and rock hard. He circles his thumb around the base of a nipple, causing me to moan. He breaks the kiss and his mouth finds my full breasts. His tongue is hot and wet. He squeezes gently and kneads my breast as I tilt my head back, giving full access to my bare chest. Kyle grabs the other breast, and in unison kneads them well. He pulls my nipples gently, applying enough pressure to make them harder between his fingers.

He kisses my neck and sucks on my earlobe. I turn my head and gain entry into his mouth. It is my turn to take control, and he allows me. I am a savage to his mouth, tasting every corner possible. I pull his shirt out of his pants when he firmly grips my wrist.

"Don't."

His words stop me cold. "What? Did I do something wrong?"

"No, Mind, on the contrary. My God, you did everything right. Honey, if you touch me there, it's all over. That's the point of no return. I have dreamed of you so often. I'm afraid if you go there, I'll never be able to contain myself with you. I will have you on this desk in a fucking hot second. But you know what? I want to do it right. I want it to be special for us both, and not in a biker club. God, I want you now, can't you tell? I can't believe I'm the one saying slow down when all I've wanted for months was to have you. But not now, especially with my brother ten feet away. Mind, come here. I see you. I see all of you, and I miss you. You are magic and mine. Don't you ever forget that. Now, we better put you back together before people get the wrong idea about what goes on behind closed doors."

"Oh, I'm already thinking the cat is out of the bag on that one."

"Girl, please put these gems away before I suck the nipples right off them. They are fucking perfect, Mind. You are fucking perfect. How I've missed you, you have no idea." He wraps his hands around my cheeks and pulls me in close for another kiss. "Jesus, I can't wait to feel my way around your body. You're amazing."

"I better stop now, or pretty soon this whole club will know what I'm doing to you behind these closed doors."

"Kyle, stop it. You're making me blush. Good things come to those who wait."

"I think I might have heard that phrase before, Mind."

"I bet you have, Mr. Masterson."

"Before we head out, I just have one final question for you, Kyle. So, let me ask you again. Did I really hear you say you loved me? I just want to be sure my hearing is correct."

"Miss Harper, I am definitely in love with you. You are mine, woman, and I am yours. I promise."

Chapter 43

"T., I need to go see my parents. I need to talk to my dad and figure out the truth. Maybe he can help me figure out what John-John is after, or how to stop him. I need to know about this side of my dad. It's killing me to think my parents may have kept this from me all these years."

"I understand, Mindy, but it's late now, and your parents are probably asleep. Nothing will change the facts. Why don't we all get some sleep, and in the morning, we will ride with you to your parents' house, all of us. This way, they will get all the information presented to them."

"Okay." I casually look around. I don't see any bedrooms in sight. "So, umm, where do you want us to hang out, T.?"

"Follow me. We have two rooms and a full bath upstairs. You are more than welcome to hang out and rest your souls here. We'll catch up in the morning. Now, there will be members here all night, so don't worry about safety. Just try to rest. How about I'll see you at 0800? We'll grab food and head over to your parents' house after?"

"Sounds good. Thanks."

"No worries, you're family. Clean towels are in that cabinet on the wall. Sleep well."

I look at Liz and she's holding David's hand with intent in her eyes. Jesus, she's being a little obvious, giving me the evil eye. I know what that means, so I just announce the plan and save her the effort.

"Liz, why don't you and David take that room and we'll take this room?" *Like I don't already know her answer.*

"Sounds like a great idea, Mind. See you guys in the morning." She winks at me appearing all too anxious to continue this night behind closed doors.

Kyle holds my hand, and says in a soft caring voice, "I guess that means I'm staying with you. Are you okay with that? I can stay downstairs and hang out on the couch. It's not a problem, Mind, really. I don't want to make you feel uncomfortable."

"Kyle, I would never be able to sleep knowing you were downstairs on a couch when you could be here with me. Please, come with me."

"How can I turn down such a sweet offer? I'll follow you anywhere, Mind."

"Will you follow me to the shower, because all this talk of revenge has made me feel dirty? I would love a hot shower."

"You do realize you're killing me here, right? I will try to be good. I'll wash your back, I'll wash your hair, etc. I'll try to show restraint, but I make no other promises. I mean, I am a man with needs, you know."

"The only need you will have tonight, Mr. Masterson, is the need to keep your hands to yourself." I giggle.

"We'll see, Ms. Harper. Don't even challenge me, because I love a good challenge."

Adjusting the temperature of the water, we agree that a little hot is better than a little cool. The water is perfect, and the room is toasty warm. Steam fills the air and fogs the mirror as Kyle reaches for his shirt. "Here, let me help you." I pull the t-shirt up and over his head. He stills with the touch of my hands on his shoulders. His shoulders are firm and muscular. I freeze as I get a good look at his naked chest. It is smooth, sleek, and hair free. I look down and notice his six-pack and slowly glide my hands over his firm chest. His pecs are rock solid, and I see his nipples harden to a small point as I continue to touch him. I shyly look up and see Kyle has clenched his jaw and I watch as the muscles in his cheeks twitch as I roam his chest. A small smile forms on my lips. With renewed confidence and empowerment, I am pleased with myself. No stopping now. He's alone with me and I have his full attention.

I stroke over his abs, feeling the ripple in every muscle of his wondrous six-pack. The ridges separating each section are firm and smooth. As he slowly inhales, I can tell he is restraining himself, as I slide my hands up his stomach. I massage his shoulders and can feel the tension underneath. I give a gentle squeeze as I rub and massage down his muscular forearms.

They are strong and defined, with a few lovely veins thrown in. A nurse's dream. Pure heaven.

"You know, by the time we get in the shower, there will be no hot water left at this rate," Kyle interrupts.

"I know. I just want to look at you from another angle."

"What does that mean?"

"Well before, I was your nurse and had to be all professional. I bathed you several times and saw all of you naked numerous times. I could admire your beautiful body, but only in a medical professional kind of way. But now, it's different. Now I can touch you the way I have always wanted to touch you, in a seductive way. I want to look at you in a non-nurse kind of way, you know, in a hot sexual Greek god kind of way. The way I only imagined in my dreams. Because, quite frankly, Mr. Masterson, you make me feel hot in the most erotic way."

"Mindy, you make me feel hot and carnal every minute. Just look at what you're doing to me." He points to his pants and the big bulge at the zipper.

"I see you have a problem here, Mr. Masterson. Please let me help you with that. You see, I happen to be very knowledgeable in the area of caring for the human body. I feel this problem needs some serious attention. I'm afraid you are suffocating your anatomy. You see, things of this nature need to breathe and be free."

Kyle doesn't say a word as it appears he's trying to maintain some self-control.

I gently pull-down Kyle's zipper and his jeans down around his ankles. He steps out of them while holding my shoulders for support. He remains still as I pull them off and throw them to the side as his belt buckle loudly crashed to the floor. I swear they probably heard the noise downstairs, but I don't care.

"So, Mr. Masterson. I notice you prefer the commando approach. You are to be commended for your choice. It's not every day I get to appreciate a creature so beautiful as yourself. This," as I reach for his hard cock, "is a work of beauty. It needs to breathe and be appreciated and worshipped. I'm so glad I have the chance to release it, for I was in fear of its suffocation behind the wall of those jeans. Although, Mr. Masterson, you should know, just like any ICU nurse, I am certified in mouth-to-mouth resuscitation. Should there be a real medical emergency, I am willing and able to bring him back to life."

"Ms. Harper. Just a quick reminder, as I have warned you before. Tread lightly, as I am barely hanging on here. You have made me feel human and very sexual since the first day I could hear you. I knew then you were something priceless and special. Now that I have you, one day I will make you mine in every way. But for now, I need you naked and in that shower."

I take a step back and look at Kyle in all his glory. He is one fine, beautifully sculpted man. From head to toe, amazing perfection, and I'm the one who gets to soap him up. *Holy hell, this is going to be fun. Make it memorable*, my inner voice yells. *You've got this woman!*

"Yes, sir, follow me and I will guide you."

I enter the shower first and guide Kyle as he steps into the shower. It's large enough for both of us, how convenient. I grab the shampoo and tell Kyle to turn around. I pour a moderate amount of shampoo into my anxiously awaiting hands. I create a good lather and begin to run my fingers through his dark, wavy hair. As I work the shampoo into his scalp, I purposely rub and massage his scalp. I watch his shoulder drop in relaxation and his head falls forward on my shoulder. His muscles loosen under my fingertips. "You are so beautiful, Kyle. Never in a million years did I imagine you would really be here with me. You're fucking perfect."

"As are you, Ms. Harper. Now, let me wash your hair."

He massages the shampoo in my hair like a skilled cosmetologist, moving down to my shoulders, melting away the stress. His fingers work magic below my skin in every way. I tilt my head back and let the water rinse my hair. As bubbles flow over my breasts, Kyle moves in closer. Turning my back to him, I rest my head on his shoulder as he cups my breasts. He moans and groans in my ear as his arousal pushes at my buttocks. There is no mistaking—this is a needy, virile man.

Kyle lathers my breasts and massages my nipples, twisting the soft nubs between his fingertips. They respond instantly and harden under his touch. He remains gentle as his hands trail down my sides. I relax into him with my head back against his chest. He takes this opportunity to extend his arm and reach around to find the junction of my thighs. That wonderous area where woman take extra care of themselves. That forbidden V of pure heaven, where a man can get lost in eternal bliss. I feel his hand as it slides over my shaved nakedness and he hisses in approval. His touch made me jump and bring fire to my core. I'm wanting more, much more.

"I'm sorry. I didn't mean to scare you."

"You didn't scare me. I just wasn't expecting that kind of response from you, that's all."

"What do you mean, my response to you? You mean my hiss of excitement? Mindy, I'm a man who is extremely turned on by your sensualness and sex appeal. You feel wondrous under my fingers. I love touching you. And when I reached my favorite spot, I was not expecting you to be shaved. I happen to love soft and smooth lady parts. Your softness and warmth have sparked a fire in me that will not be easily extinguished. You feel so soft and erotic. I feel like I could come any minute if I'm not careful."

"Maybe I don't want to extinguish your fire. Did you ever think of that?"

"Be careful what you wish for, woman. I am a man in need, after all. A man who is so in love with you, and this wonderful body of yours. You feel so good under my hands. I just want to get you under my tongue. I want to taste every inch of you, from your luscious lips to those amazing breasts, to this amazing hot spot I feel getting wetter by the minute."

Kyle rubs my hardening bud as he whispers to me. "My God, your response to me is overwhelming. Let yourself go, relax, and become one with me. Let your body do what it was made for. Let me feel you, all of you, and let me touch everything. I want to know every inch of you and make my very own road map to your heat."

Kyle continues his rhythmic thumb dance over my nub, rubbing and applying gentle pressure as my inhibitions drain away with the water in the shower. I close my eyes and lose myself in this wonderful moment.

"That's it, love, relax into me and just feel. Feel me touching you and just enjoy it. Enjoy the moment and let me have this pleasure of knowing I can make you come undone."

Kyle continues to work my clit to perfection as he slips his middle finger into my awaiting wetness. The feeling sets me ablaze as I gasp and twitch beneath his touch. "Jesus, you are so fucking wet for me. I'm going to taste you all night."

One finger leads to two, and I'm in heaven. The firmness of his fingers provides a gentle stretch and pressure that I have been missing for a long time. I flex my hips and ride his fingers in a slow rhythm as I clench around him. "Good God almighty woman, you will have me on my knees any minute if you keep that up."

"I can't help myself; you found the spot. It's all your fault. God, you make me feel alive."

Kyle's fingers dive deeper into my wetness. My legs are weakening, as though I may fall. I grab the front of his thighs in need. I can hear Kyle moan as his fingers dance within me.

"That's it!" he declares as he pulls his fingers from me and spins me around to face him. "I warned you, sweetheart. Now it's my turn to have my way with you. Lean up against the wall for support."

"I thought you were already having your way with me?"

"Hardly! That was me being a tease and warming you up. Just wait, Mind, and trust. You do trust me, don't you?"

"How can I not? You have had to trust me for months. I think I can trust you, especially tonight."

Kyle sighs as he strokes my arms and down to my breasts. He bends over and sucks on my nipple, softly at first, and then teases me with a little bite. *Hmm, such a beautiful sound you make when aroused.* He straightens up and grabs my head to pull it close to him. Lips meet lips in a slow-burn kiss that makes my toes curl. *Where did he learn to kiss like that? Never mind, I don't really want to know. I'm just thankful, oh so thankful.* The heat between my legs is incredible. It's becoming a storm I may not be able to control. My knees start to buckle and Kyle reaches for me to hold me up before I end up on the shower floor. "Oh no baby, you're not done yet, and neither am I. I'm going to taste you, and I mean really taste you."

I grab the front of his muscular shoulders in support, and Kyle pulls me in closer. His hardened cock pushes against my abdomen as my hips take on a mind of their own. My hips start to grind and push against his enormous, hardened cock. I cup his manhood. *Holy mother of God, this man is more than I ever expected. He certainly didn't look like this lying in his hospital bed, that's for damn sure! I'd swear his cock has grown at least two inches in the last five minutes.* Kyle inhales sharply at the touch of my hand. I caress his cock from base to tip. I gently twist my palm around its girth as I pump him up to the tip. His smooth tip is wet with the sweetness of pre-cum and hot. I watch Kyle shudder as I slowly rub my thumb over its head, stimulating him more.

"I've dreamed of touching you like this since the first day I saw you leaning against that bar. I remember it like it was yesterday. Now I'm going to make my fantasy come true." I bend over to take him in my mouth when Kyle interrupts.

"Not so fast, woman. I'm having my way with you first. I was always taught, ladies first."

"Who am I to argue with etiquette? By all means, sir, please proceed." I giggle.

Kyle holds my arms for support and kneels in the shower. He begins by roaming my abdomen, to my hips, and then my thighs. He slowly traces up my inner thighs as he finds my sweet spot. I swear he can sense it. He instantly found the split in my lower lips. The place I dreamed of him being since I first saw him.

Kyle inhales slowly. "I have wanted to be in this spot since the day you shaved me. Every night I dreamed of you and your scent. Now here I am, and I want all of you, Mind. This will forever more be mine, and only mine."

He places his fingers on each side of my swollen lips and gently spreads me open. I instinctively place my hands in Kyle's hair and hold his head in place. I hear Kyle inhale as he whispers, "Mmm, fucking perfect. The most beautiful scent I have ever needed and wanted." He leans forward and finds my magic spot. The clit. That nub of pleasure that has been known to drive a woman mad with need.

Kyle opens his mouth, and with a little gentle pressure, his tongue works magic. I writhe to the momentum Kyle has set. He sucks gently and a gentle bite sends me into a fit of moaning and grinding. I tighten my hold on Kyle's hair and push his head harder against my throbbing vagina. Kyle obliges and inserts two fingers into my depths. I'm soaked in sexual pleasure and so damn tight. It's been a while for me, I'm sure he can tell.

"Lord, have mercy, woman. You are tight and just right for the picking. I want to be inside you so fucking bad. I'm going to come right now just listening to you moan."

"Kyle, my heart is racing. You're killing me. I want you inside of me, too. You have no idea."

"Yeah, I do. But not here. Not yet. Just let go and enjoy baby. I want you to relax and enjoy the feeling. I want to taste you, remember? Let me have this. Come for me. I want to taste all of you."

Kyle's instructions hit a nerve in me, and I realize just how much he wants me. With confidence and anticipation, I enjoy myself more and let go. I let go of the stress, the insecurities, and the depression. I focus on just feeling. Just feeling the heat of this amazing man kneeling in front of me. I'm on fire like never before, and he is the reason.

Kyle returns to playing with my clit and pumping my vagina. He withdraws his fingers and licks them clean. "Mmm, your delicious, baby. I'm going to make you come like you've never come before." He continues with his feast as my thrusting tempo increases with need. I can feel myself getting closer to the edge, but I just can't relax enough to climax. I know Kyle can sense it. Unspoken words. Kyle reaches around and places his finger at the entrance to my ass. *What the hell?*

"Kyle?"

"Shh, baby. Let loose and enjoy. I've got you. Just experience the feeling. Let your inhibitions fall away and trust. Trust me to save you, and trust me to help you feel amazing."

""I'm not sure about this. I've never…"

"Mindy, relax and feel. I promise I will not hurt you. Close your eyes and feel."

Trust? Okay, I take a leap of faith and take a slow, cleansing breath. I can feel my muscles relax enough for Kyle to make his move. He massages my ass cheeks as he works his way closer to my tightened anal entrance. His tongue is working miracles on my clit and I am reaching for his head. I entwine my fingers in his hair as I grip his head in place, thrusting against his oral assault.

He reaches my anal entrance and applies even more pressure. *Whoa! What the hell was that shockwave?* A new thread of pleasure is building within me. In perfect tempo, he sucks on me firmly with just the right amount of pressure as he slowly inserts one finger into my anal canal. I grab his head and press it tighter to me, riding his face to the perfect tempo.

"Fuck, baby…come for me. Show me how good I can I make you feel. I want to taste all of you. Come to me." Hearing those words pushes me closer to the edge. Kyles presses slightly deeper into my backside as I lose all control.

"Oh, my, God, Kyle. Please…"

He smiles into my pink folds.

"I'm coming, baby, all for you." My climax is like lightning to my system, exploding inside me like a runaway train that will never stop. The strength of this orgasm is something I have never experienced before. The heat traveled up from my toes and ignited a fire deep within my core. A fire that caused such an erotic explosion, my whole-body trembles. I'm in shock at what my body is capable of, and I'm amazed at what I've been missing. Completely sated and relaxed, I grab the bars in the shower to steady myself as I wait for the tremors in my legs to slow down. Kyle is still kneeling on the floor, enjoying the fruit I so generously offered.

"Baby, you taste so good, so sweet and creamy. I could stay between your legs all day." Kyle reaches for the bars as he stands up and steadies himself. "I need you so badly, but I refuse to take you here."

I lean in and plant a tender kiss on his lips as he grabs himself. He strokes himself to facilitate his release. I pull away from his lips as I watch the show and moan in my pleasure. His stroking becomes more frantic at warp speed. I know he must be getting close.

"Don't you dare, Mr. Masterson. That's mine and I'm going to have it. It's my turn to get what I've been waiting so long to have. I've been imagining this day, and now it's here. I want to feast upon you."

I drop to my knees in front of him and take in the view. His dick is rock hard and standing at attention, pointing directly at me. *Holy hell, I can hang a flag on this thing.*

I gently grab the monster cock at its base. Its head is smooth and round, and the vein on the underside is full and engorged. I lick my lips in anticipation. *Oh, this is going to be so much fun.*

With my hand on his well-developed thigh for support, I stick my tongue out and trace the length of his vein from the root to the head, moaning in pleasure all the way. I watch Kyle's expression and I'm quite pleased with myself. The Greek god has a weakness. He likes his cock sucked. Well, I aim to please.

He is nearing climax when I say to him, "Let me taste you, Kyle. It's only fair. You had me, now I want you." I stretch my neck to take all of him. It was a slow struggle, but I managed the task without gagging. I continue sucking, but it's time to turn up the heat. I reach for his balls and give them a slow massage, and its game over.

"Christ, Mindy, I'm coming for you, baby. You have all of me, now and forever." Kyle pumps a little harder and faster as he jerks in my mouth. The dead giveaway he's reaching his max, he is coming with pure strength. He thrusts deeper once more; the jerking of his manhood spurts the warmth of his seed down my throat. I give his balls some extra massaging and suck him more to ensure I have drained him properly.

Kyle reaches down to my face and whispers, "Come here, baby. I want this to be shared in every way." He pulls me to my feet and finds my awaiting hot mouth. He kisses me deeply and inserts his tongue, exploring my entire mouth. "Hmm, Mindy, we are delicious together. Let's do this again sometime, shall we?"

"Mr. Masterson, I believe spontaneity is the key. You never know when I might drop to my knees for you. You should always be prepared."

"I'll remember that, Ms. Harper. But as a lawyer, you should know, I'm always prepared." I lean in and hug Kyle as he kisses me tenderly. There we stay, entwined, enjoying each other's bodies until the hot water runs out and there is a knock on the door.

"You going to stay in there all night, Masterson?"

I reach for the water nozzle and turn off the water. "Shit, we're busted. I'm so embarrassed."

"I'm not. I've just had the best shower of my life. I'm feeling fucking fantastic." Kyle whispers in my ear. "Yeah, be right out!" he yells back.

I open the door and Liz and David are staring us in the face. Liz glances at me with that look and raises one eyebrow.

"Did you all have a good time?" she asks sarcastically.

I give no response and blush. I look at David and he's all smiles but doesn't say a word. I'm guilty as crap and they know it. I take Kyle's hand to guide him to our room.

On our way down the hall, Kyle yells over his shoulder, "Hey, David, you both have a good night and sleep well. I know I will. Oh, and by the way, we're out of hot water."

Chapter 44

We, including T., arrive at my parents' house at 10:00 a.m. sharp. T. drives up on his loud-as-hell motorcycle, and proudly parks it directly in front of their house. There is no mistaking which house this biker is visiting.

I didn't warn my parents we were coming, so this is a total surprise to them. We enter through the garage and find my parents relaxing on the back patio with coffee and the morning paper.

"Hey, Mom and Dad. What's up?" I ask, trying to be all casual.

Dad puts down his paper and looks up at the group of visitors following me through the yard. He gets up and hugs me tightly. "So, what brings you and your bright smile out here today? This is unexpected, and I'm so happy to see you."

"Hi, Dad. Hi, Mom." Mom gets up and hugs me, too. "I'm kind of here on official business. These are my friends. You already know Liz."

Liz gives them a polite wave from across the patio.

"This is Mr. Kyle Masterson. He's um," I pause, as I'm not sure what to call him.

"I'm Kyle, Mindy's boyfriend. It's nice to meet you."

I reach for his hand and lace my fingers with his. "And this is Kyle's brother, David Masterson."

"Nice to meet you, sir."

"And Dad, this is Mr. Todd Turner, President of The Creeks Motorcycle Club."

T. extends his hand.

Dad accepts with a firm grip. "Nice to meet you, Mr. Turner."

"Please call me T., everyone does."

Dad and Mom exchange glances and looks of concern but say nothing.

"What's going on Mind? I get the distinct feeling something bad has happened. Are you okay? Are you in trouble, honey?"

"Mom, Dad, it's a long story and I'll fill in the details as best I can, but all these people are here today to help me. David is a detective, Kyle is a lawyer, and T., well, he's a hell of a nice guy and my protection."

"Wait, what? Protection from what? What the hell is going on, Mindy? Why do you need protecting?"

"Dad, recently I have been getting weird phone calls, notes in the mail and on my car, and even gifts in the mail. I've been noticing people watching me and staking out my apartment."

"And you didn't go to the police with this craziness, Mindy? What were you thinking?"

"Well, Dad, David is the police, so to speak, remember? So, I spoke with him first. Then Liz got a good picture of two of the guys that were staking out my apartment. One of the men had a Viper's Motorcycle Club's cut on. I recognized one of the men, so I called T. for his input."

"With all due respect, T., but Mindy, how the fuck do you know and have the phone number of a biker?"

Mom is now out of her seat and standing next to her husband, with her hands on his shoulders, attempting to calm him and bring down his anger a notch or two.

I look at T., and he is aware of the permission I am seeking. T. gives the nod of approval and I continue. "Dad, T. was one of my patients once. He was critically wounded, and I took care of him in the ICU. When he left the ICU, as a gesture of thanks, he gave me his business card and said if I ever needed anything, I could always call him. So, when I discovered the man following me was a biker, I called him. I needed his advice, Dad. I had no idea what to do. And as it turns out, he discovered a lot of information. He can explain why we think I'm being stalked. That's why we're all here. This involves all of us, Dad."

Mom looks pale and visibly shaken. "Mom, are you alright? You don't look so good. Here, come sit down."

"I'm fine, honey. I just need a minute to breathe and get my bearings. Please continue, and please, will all of you sit down? I'm sorry we didn't offer you seats when you first got here, but please, sit. This is going to be hard on all of us, I can tell."

T. inhales deeply and begins. "Mr. and Mrs. Harper, first, let me tell you that you have a wonderful daughter. She is an amazing nurse and personifies the words caring, empathy, and professionalism. If it wasn't for her, I'm sure my stay in the hospital would not have gone as smoothly. So, thank you for raising such a wonderful daughter."

Mom smiles. "Thank you, T. We really are so proud of her. It's nice to know others love and value her as much as we do."

"Now, let me start at the beginning. Mindy called me to assist her with identifying a biker. She hoped by showing me a picture of the biker and his patch, I just might be able to identify the man who had been casing her apartment parking lot. As it turns out, I did know the name of the biker, but I had no idea why there would be a connection to Mindy. That is, until she received an anonymous phone call with a tip. The caller said that Mindy knew why his brother was in turmoil, and if she didn't fix the problem, then he was coming after her."

Mom gasps in horror, and a tear streams down her cheek. I scoot over next to Mom and hold her tightly in a hug. "Mom, I'm okay. It will be all right. Just listen to the rest of the information, please."

T. looks up at Mom, and she nods to continue. "The anonymous caller told Mindy that if she didn't know how to fix the problem, then she needed to ask Big Joe because he would know the answer."

With that comment, Mom lets out a huge gasp and looks at Dad. She cries hysterically. "No! No, no, no, this can't be happening. My baby can't be in danger from a psycho that doesn't exist any longer. NO! He's dead. He can't hurt you, Mindy."

"Mom, calm down. Nobody is going to hurt me. It's okay. Please, Mom, what's wrong? We didn't even finish the story yet? Why are you freaking out and who's dead?"

Dad looks at T., and he continues. "I couldn't get that name Big Joe out of my mind. I knew I had heard it before, but I just couldn't make the connection and it was driving me crazy. So, I did some club research and, Mr. Harper, I found evidence that the name Big Joe refers to you. Is that correct?"

I watch Dad so intently, assessing his every move, as I hold my breath and wait for his answer.

"Yes, Mr. Turner, I am Big Joe."

I gasp, covering my mouth. Tears fill my eyes. "Are you fucking serious, Dad? You were in a motorcycle club and never told me? What the hell?"

"Mindy, honey, it was a long time ago, in another lifetime. It was before you were even born. There was no need to ever tell you about it. Some things are better left buried, and my life as a biker was one of those things."

"But, Dad, now that secret is out and here to haunt me. If I had known about it sooner, I might have been able to see it coming, and not be taken by surprise. I could have been prepared. Now I'm clueless, and this guy is tormenting the crap out of me."

T. continues. "Mr. Harper, we suspect the man stalking Mindy is John Marxx Jr."

Mom continues to sob and stares at Dad.

"Do you know of such a person?" T. asks.

"Unfortunately, I do, Mr. Turner. Although I was unaware there was a John Jr. still in the picture. I knew of a daughter once, but I haven't heard anything of a son since the accident."

"Dad. So, the newspaper article was true? You killed a man?"

Mom jumps up and points at me. "Now you just wait one-minute, little girl. This was not your father's fault."

"Mom, calm down. I'm not accusing him. I just want the truth. I'm thirty-three years old and I've never heard this story. Now my life may be in danger because of it. At least give me the whole damn story, please."

Mom looks at me, as I'm now holding onto Kyle's arm for dear life.

"Mindy, honey, I've read that newspaper article one thousand times until I've wanted to vomit. Unfortunately, for once, the paper had its story correct. Mr. Marxx and a few of the other club members attacked a bunch of The Creek members at our storage facility. We were ambushed, and he attacked me first. I tried to just get him off me, but he kept coming at me. Eventually, he connected with my face, as you can see by the scars that were left behind.

"When he pointed that gun at me, all bets were off and I fought him off me like a wild animal. I broke his hand as I twisted the gun back just as he pulled the trigger. He never had a chance. The bullet hit him under the chin and went right up into his brain. It was at just the right angle to cause instant death. It was a total self-defense accident.

"The Creeks never carried guns, so the only form of self-defense we had was our own strength. He almost overpowered me, but I thought of you, who wasn't even born yet, and your mom. Somehow, I got the extra strength I needed to wrestle him off me. It was just enough to weaken him so I could point the gun away from me. I had no idea he was pulling the trigger at the same time."

"Oh, my God, Dad. You could have been killed."

"Yes, I could have. But instead, another man died. Another man, who was already a father and a husband. Mindy, that accident changed me. It changed me forever. As much as I loved being a Creek brother, back then, their reputation was not as good as it is today. Let's just say we were a rowdy bunch back then. It was more important to me to be alive and be a good dad and husband than it was to be a Creek member. So, I resigned from my position in the club and left. I've never looked back."

Mom looks up at T. "I'm sorry that you and your brothers must experience this drama again. Robert tried hard to distance himself from the club as much as possible. It breaks my heart to know this nightmare has surfaced again."

"Mrs. Harper, I'm just happy to help. When I found out the truth about who Big Joe really is, I knew we needed to protect Mindy. She is, after all, a legacy."

Mr. Harper looks at T. in astonishment. "I forgot about the Legacy Tradition. I'm thankful she has you and the brothers to help look after her. Although, I'm sorry I have put you all in this position once again."

"Mr. Harper, John Jr. has been making threats to Mindy, and we need to come up with a plan to catch this guy. The brothers and I are willing to assist in any way possible, but it's going to be tricky. He hasn't done anything illegal yet. He's just been annoying to Mindy." David states.

Dad looks at David. "With all due respect, Mr. Masterson, how do you fit into this mess? Last I knew, motorcycle clubs didn't really do business with cops."

"Mr. Harper, I'm sort of here by default, and because I have resources available to me, that may help. I'm Liz's boyfriend and that's how I initially got involved. I have a few cop friends on the local force that are doing a little OT for me. They are adding extra surveillance to Mindy for her safety. They are plainclothes cops, always keeping Mindy in their sights. So far, there has been no attempt on her life. We want to keep it that way, but something has got to give, and soon. I propose we put a plan in place. Something to entice John Jr. and see what happens. We need to know what he is up to so we can nail him when he least expects it."

I pipe up and add my two cents to the conversation. "Like a plan to make me the bait? I can do that if I know for sure you are all watching me, and I have nothing to fear. I can do it."

"Absolutely no fucking way!" Kyle spouts off. "I finally have you. I'm not going to risk you for some nut job with an axe to grind."

"Excuse me," Dad interrupts, "but I think I need to be involved here. I agree with Kyle. I don't want Mindy involved. I mean, if it wasn't for me, we would never have to be here. Let me be involved. Please, let me help. Maybe I should be the one to confront this John Jr. person."

"In due time, Mr. Harper, but we really need all the facts before we decide on anything," David reminds him.

The gang and I talk about the events that had occurred up to this point. All the phone calls, anonymous notes, and biker visits to my apartment's parking lot.

Mom and Dad are now up to speed on all the details, and they are not happy I have kept all this a secret from them.

As we sit and discuss our options, my cell phone rings. I look up at T., petrified, and see all eyes on me. I grab the phone and close my eyes with anxiety.

"It says unknown," but I answer it. "Hello, this is Mindy." Silence. "Hello?" Again, silence. "What!" I yell into the phone. "What do you want from me?" Still, no response. "I can hear you breathing, you asshole. I know you're there!"

"I'm here, listening to you and getting all hot and hard for you, Mindy. I can see you, and you look more beautiful than yesterday. Your hair is soft and wavy, and your ass looks delicious in those jeans. I can't wait to put my fingers in all that hair as I pull your head back and fuck you so hard. Mmm…the thought of that ass, naked before me, makes me want to come any second. I want you so fucking bad. And that pink tight t-shirt, it shows off your perky tits to perfection."

I look down at my chest. I pale instantly as I realize I'm wearing my favorite pink T-shirt.

Standing up, I look around, seeing nothing in my parents' backyard or the neighbor's. As I struggle to see over the line of hedges my father has so meticulously manicured over the years, Kyle says, "What the fuck is going on, Mindy? What the hell is it?"

"He can see me! He knows what I'm wearing, Kyle. He can fucking see me right this minute."

T. and the men jump up with concern in their eyes. Instantly they case the property and all around the neighborhood.

T. hears that all-too-familiar rumble and runs to the front yard, and we all follow him. We see the bike in the distance as it jets out of sight.

"Son of a bitch, it's a Viper!" T. takes a large breath and exhales heavily. "And so, it begins."

Kyle finds me, reaches for my hand, and I enclose my arms around his waist. "Okay, I wasn't scared before, but now I'm freaking out, Kyle. He got this close to me, with my family and protection right here. What if he can get all the way to me? What if he does get me and we're not prepared? Then what? You didn't hear all the sexual things he said he wants to do to me. He's creepy as hell, and he's not going to stop unless we stop him first.

"Kyle, I want to make a plan. I don't want to be caught off guard. I can't live my life in fear every day. What if we make him think he is getting what he wants? What if we make me more available to him?"

"Mindy, I don't know if that's a good idea. I'm not too keen on putting my girl at any more risk, any more than you already are. I'm positive that using you as bait is not a good idea."

"Oh, hell no!" Dad barks from across the yard. "I heard that, and I'm not going to let that happen. Are you out of your freaking mind, Mindy? You're not going to offer yourself up so easily. That's a bad idea. This is not television. It never really works like that in real life. Hell, no!"

"Have you got a better idea, Dad? You're the biker, let's figure this out. T.? I need some help and input here. I thought you were on my side?"

"I am, Mindy, but I don't know about this self-sacrifice idea. There are so many variables that could make a plan go south, and fast. I'm not sure we have the manpower to pull off a plan like that. We would need a lot of help and a solid plan."

"Consider it done, T.," David interjects. "Don't forget, we've had a man on the inside for a while now, and he's just itching to get involved and get this done. We've been watching the Vipers for a long time. If we need manpower, we've got it."

T.'s eyes light up. "Hey, Mindy, how do feel about biker women?"

"Excuse me? I don't have a problem with any biker person, male or female. Why?"

"Well, I have an idea, but you would need to come out of your girlie "goodie-goodie" shell. Can you do that?"

"You mean like play a part? I can do it. What do you have in mind?"

"Well, next week is the big bike rally, and several of the area clubs will all be out and about on Saturday for the rally. There will be bikers galore in town, and activities to raise money for the non-profit. The main event is the concert and swimsuit competition at The Biker Burn Out Bar."

"No way, T. I'm not entering the swimsuit competition. No way in hell."

"Mindy, although that's a great idea, that's not what I had in mind. I was thinking more along the lines of you being a hot biker chick hostess."

"And what would I have to do?"

"Well, you would have to dress like a biker bitch. You know, tight pants that hug that ass, and lots of cleavage hanging out everywhere. Then you can walk around selling tickets for the 50/50 raffle drawing. The more tits and cleavage you show, the more tickets you sell. You will be seen for sure, and we will be watching you like a hawk. Do you think you can dress a little slutty and be super flirty for the night? You will need to stand out. Catch my drift? We'll watch John-John and wait for him to make his move."

"T., this would really be stepping out of my comfort zone for sure, but maybe with a little help, I can do it. I need Liz to accompany me on this endeavor. You know, two sluts are always better than one."

David just about chokes on his coffee, but Liz is grinning from ear to ear.

"Count me in," she says with a wicked, eager grin.

Chapter 45

Kyle and I return to my apartment with Liz and David. T. escorts us home and does some quick surveillance of the area. He catches nothing out of the ordinary, nor does he see any bikers hanging around.

"Hey, Mindy, remember, I've got some guys watching you and your place. If you need me, just call and I'll have them at your door in five seconds flat."

"You got it, T. Thanks for everything, really."

"Well, don't thank me until it's over. You know, the big fat lady needs to sing first."

"I got it. I've got you on speed dial, T. Thanks and be careful driving home."

"Always." He fires up his bike and rides away.

"I don't know about you guys, but I'm exhausted. This has been one heck of a day. I'm still in disbelief about my dad. How crazy is that? All those years and I never knew."

"I think your dad misses it, Mindy," David says.

"Misses what?"

"Riding motorcycles, belonging to a group where you have so much in common. You know, the male bonding and camaraderie. He didn't come right out and say it, but I can tell he misses riding. It's ingrained in his bones, like nursing is in yours. I can sense it."

"Yeah. I get that. Maybe I'll have to chat with him about it when this is over. I would love a ride on a bike. If he started riding again, he could take me. That would be so cool. Maybe I would turn into a biker bitch after all?"

"Mind, would you mind if David and I head out for a while? Maybe go back to my place and grab a nap or something?"

"Sure. The 'or something' should be fun. See you all later."

"How about you guys meet us later for dinner?" David asks.

"Sounds like a plan. Call us with the details," Kyle answers.

As Liz and David leave, I dead bolt the door and make sure the lock is set tight. It clicks tight under my fingers and I lean back against the door and just breathe. Inhaling deeply to get rid of some of today's stress. I'm watching Kyle, and his movements are slow and precise. He's not fumbling around as much as usual, but still needs guidance. *Hmm, that's unusual.* I know my assessment skills are as sharp as a tack. I'm on to him. Something about his movements is off. He's improved, and he hasn't said anything to me about it. Is his vision improving? *Hmm, let's play.*

I watch Kyle as he is casually sitting on the couch. He's got one ankle propped up over his knee and one arm draped over the back of the couch. He looks fucking delicious. *Let's begin playtime with a devious little plan.*

"Hey, Kyle, I'll be right back. Are you good there for a minute?"

"Yeah, baby, I'm just chillin'. I'll be here when you get back."

On the way to the bathroom, I walk behind the couch on purpose. I have taken off my pink T-shirt and jeans and replaced them with a matching bralette set of black satin. I've freshened up and applied my infamous amber and rose body oil. *Game on!* exclaims my womanhood with excitement.

I walk back into the living room in stealth mode. There I stand and watch the show. My scent finds its way to Kyle. I watch as he deeply inhales and hums to himself. I catch a slight whisper in his voice as he mumbles, "Jesus, she smells divine."

My inner confidence is smiling brightly as I watch his every move. His breathing pace increases slightly and he leans his head back against the couch cushion. His eyes are closed as he continues to just breathe me in. I walk one step closer and I can see over the back of the couch. I glance down and I notice Kyle's manhood.

His cock is hardening right before my eyes. It's a beautiful thing. To watch the man you want so badly, respond to you in this way, and see the evidence that he obviously wants you, too. It's simply magic, and it makes me wetter than a sponge on car wash day! I've never been this excited before.

I remove my bra and toss it on the couch next to him. He casually turns his head toward where my bra landed. He reaches over and casually picks it up and smells it. "Fucking divine," he mumbles. My mind is racing. *What? What is he up to? How did he know the exact location of where my bra landed? Did he see it land? Hmm…think, Mindy. What next?*

I walk into the kitchen braless, tits hanging out everywhere, and watch Kyle. I see nothing unusual; I wonder what he sees, because he's awfully quiet.

"I'm gonna grab some iced tea. Do you want some, babe?"

I continue my research and watch for any clues.

"Sure, I'd love a glass, thanks."

I pour his glass first and sit the glass down on the coffee table and purposely don't tell him where I put it. I continue to watch. Nothing happens. Plan B is now in effect.

"I forgot my phone in the bathroom. I'll be right back." As I walk to the bathroom, I watch him as I close the door.

Kyle sits right up and takes the glass of tea to his lips and drinks. He replaces the glass perfectly in the same spot.

Son of a bitch! He's so busted. I can't believe it. He can see. Well, I'm going to give him a show, and if they want me to be a biker chick, I might as well start practicing now.

I yell from the hallway, "Hey, do you want some music?"

"Sure."

I grab my phone and select the soft ballads channel from my Pandora account. I begin to walk into the living room and my favorite song begins. Take My Breath Away by Berlin. *Oh Mr. Masterson, game on! You have no idea what you're in for. Sit back and enjoy the ride, because I know I'm going to.*

I start dancing, seductively swaying my hips to the music in the kitchen as I pour myself another glass of iced tea. I'm exaggerating my hips and rolling my stomach like a belly dancer on purpose. If he can see me, how long will he have restraint?

I continue with my enticing dance, boosting my self-confidence, as I also need to practice my part as an uninhibited biker chick.

Kyle doesn't make a move except to tap his foot and occasionally sing a bar or two. He's acting like normal Kyle, with subtle movements until I bend over and remove my silk underwear. I gently roll it into a ball and throw it in the direction of Kyle's lap. He catches it in mid-air before it lands on his hardened cock.

"Kyle! You are so busted!" I walk over to Kyle, in all my naked glory, and straddle his lap, one knee on each side of those gloriously toned thighs. I look Kyle in the eyes as I rub my breasts and then pull my hair up into a ponytail.

His manhood increases in hardness through his pants. I slowly place my hands on each of his cheeks and bring Kyle's lips to mine for a soft, loving kiss. Just enough of a kiss to make him want more.

I pull away and look deeply into those crystal blue eyes of his and begin his torture.

"Why, Kyle Masterson, you can see me," I say, soft and whispery. "I think I may have to punish you for that. And by the way, just how long have you been able to see?"

Kyle tries to look down, but I lift his chin.

"Kyle, please answer me."

"It was supposed to be a surprise. I can't see you fully yet. What I can see are shadows, some occasional outlines, and shades of darkness and contrast. I can see your silhouette and your outline. Your body is screaming, *come fuck me now*. I did all I could do to be still while you were doing your little dance. You're killing me here."

"Oh, Mr. Masterson, just wait. I'm not done with you yet." I kiss him fully on the lips. I unbutton his shirt and he happily obliges by sitting up and letting me push his shirt off his shoulders. He quickly pulls out each arm, never breaking the contact between their lips.

I lean back and take in the view as I run my hands over his solid pecs. The smooth warmth of my hands on his chest makes his dick twitch with excitement under his zipper.

"Mmm, someone's feeling happy. I believe somebody wants to come out and play. But first, Mr. Masterson, you do know, it's not nice to keep secrets, especially from your girlfriend, right? Didn't your mom ever tell you that?"

"She may have mentioned something like that once." He smiles as he's reaching to touch my breasts. "But it wasn't a secret, it was a surprise. Two totally different things, Miss Harper."

"Mr. Masterson, I do believe you're trying to coerce me into agreeing with you. You may not touch me, not yet. I'm in charge here. This is my house, and I'm the one completely naked. That means this is my show. You just sit here and enjoy the activities. I'll let you know when I'm ready for you to participate."

"Mindy, I feel like I've waited a lifetime for you, and now you won't let me touch you? Seriously? I'm dying here." He pleads.

"Good things come to those who wait, Kyle."

"Jesus, whoever said that I'm going to hunt them down and shoot them. I'm aching for you, woman."

"As I am for you, see, feel this." I take Kyle's hand and guide it to the opening of my thighs. The heat is tremendous. He slips a finger inside with complete accuracy.

"Fuck, Mindy, you're soaking wet. You're so ready for me. Please let me inside."

"Not yet, dear Kyle. Let me play. It's my turn. Here, stand up for a minute." I help Kyle off the couch to a standing position. I immediately grab his belt and undo the buckle with ease. With a small tug, his pants fall around his ankles. "Mmm, perfection." I look dreamily at his engorged manhood. It is standing straight out and pointing up to his abdomen. "This is the biggest, most beautiful piece of art I have ever seen, and it's all mine."

Kyle twitches with anticipation and his cock dances to my words. I help him step out of his pants and then order him to sit back down. As he sits down, his cock rocks in rhythm with his pelvis and gives a little come here wave.

"Now, Kyle, you are to sit back, relax, and don't touch until I say so. Got it?"

"I'm not sure I can do that, Mind, but I will try. You see, my cock has a mind of his own, and when he really wants someone, he has a difficult time listening to reason. He wants to be invited inside; you see. He will stop at nothing, and he will be very creative until he gets that invitation. He always gets what he wants Mindy. I can tell you right now with complete certainty, he wants all of you. He's going to be on his best behavior, but I can't guarantee for how much longer. He can kind of be impatient."

"Mr. Masterson, it's time for you to surrender. You've made a good argument on his behalf. Now I know why you're a lawyer, but give it up.

I'm in control." I straddle him once more and hold his face as I look into his eyes again. "And Mr. Masterson, I'm the one on top. This is my favorite place, at the top, so I can watch your undoing. I will have you, believe me. I've waited my whole life to feel this amazing. I'm so happy it's with you."

I lean over and take his mouth to mine. I kiss him with the need of a woman who hasn't fucked for years. I devour him, every inch of that lovely mouth I have claimed for my own. Kyle's excitement grows against my crotch. His need is evident as I gyrate on his manhood. Back and forth, slowly, with just the right amount of pressure as I share my wetness. He rocks his hips in unison with mine, together as one. Mmm, so nice.

"Mindy, honey, he's begging for an invitation. Please let him in."

"No, dear Kyle. He is not allowed in. I will decide his fate. You must keep him in line. He cannot break free."

I lean over and kiss Kyle's neck and suck on it gently. I want to mark him, but below the collar line, where no one will see it but me. As I suck, the pressure of my pelvis on his lap grows stronger. Kyle grabs my waist and holds on as if he is going to flip us over.

"Don't you dare, Mr. Masterson. I will not be on my back for you today. I'm in charge, remember?"

"Ms. Harper, I told you he was creative in his ways. He's trying desperately for an invitation."

"I see, Mr. Masterson. I'm not sure he is ready for such a big responsibility. There have only been a select few that have ever been invited to that kind of party. You see, it's quite an event, and something not taken lightly. The invitation comes with huge responsibilities, and I'm not sure he is up to the task."

"Oh, my dear Mindy. I believe he has waited a long time for you and your invitation. You see, he really has a special talent, one that you won't want to miss. He, like you, rarely accepts invitations. It must be a very special invite indeed. I do believe he is ready, willing, and able to accept all responsibilities you may require."

I can tell Kyle is enjoying this game. He has a huge smirk on his face and is awaiting my reply. He is so witty and clever, but he has met his match.

I can't bring myself to ignore it any longer. I can feel my desire and need for him escalating. It's running through my tight nipples, down my abdomen, and straight to my pulsating vagina. The tingle in my jingle is about to bust! I'm flaming hot, wet, and full of need. I want all of him and bad.

"I can feel your heat and wetness on my cock. You're dripping for me. It's the hottest fucking thing I have ever felt. Please, let me feel you all around me. Let me feel deep inside you."

I move my hips back and forth, working my clit on his hardened cock, teasing him.

Kyle whispers, "Fuck it, Mindy, I'll play along. But I need to touch you."

My pelvic rhythm continues, torturing us both, but that's the idea. Kyle wraps his arms around my back and pulls me in for contact. We are chest to chest and kissing passionately and deeply. I have never felt this emotionally close to a lover before, I'm feeling safe and wanted.

With renewed confidence and power, I break the kiss. Kyle is breathing heavily and reaching for my hardened nipples. He finds them and lightly rolls them between his thumb and fingers, setting off a firestorm in me as I yell out in pleasure. I have reached my maximum level of restraint and now I want all of him.

Kneeling, I reach around to find Kyle's hardened dick. I grab it with perfect execution and center it perfectly below my craving entrance.

"Mindy? Mind, please. I want you to be sure. Don't do this if you're not ready."

"Why, Mr. Masterson, I am so ready. I'm ready for all of you. Consider this your personal invitation." Kyle smiles, with a faint blush on his cheeks, as I lower onto his shaft. He hisses in approval as I slowly slide down to his base with conviction.

I moan as his fullness touches me in places I never knew existed.

"My God, Kyle, I'm so full. You feel so amazing."

"Mindy, you're amazing. You're so damn tight, it's like no one has ever been here before. Remember, you're all mine, every inch of you is mine, and you have all of me, in every way."

I move my hips and feel Kyle growing harder as he slips in a little deeper. "Jesus, you are all the way in. There is no more room, Kyle. I'm so full, I love this feeling. Pump for me."

Kyle is all too willing to thrust in rhythm with me as I ride his cock. I grip his shoulders as he sits back and enjoys the ride. I'm in charge and riding him like the stallion in heat he is. Our breathing quickens together as Kyle grabs my hips for added leverage. He is pulling me down harder with every thrust. We match each other's rhythm in perfect unison, two becoming one.

Our breathing has become quick and deep as we both moan in pleasure. Kyle quickly sits upright and encircles my back and pulls me in closer to his chest. Chest to chest, we touch, rock, thrust, and pant together.

Sweat forms on our skin. The sounds of hot, wet lovemaking fill the room. Skin on skin and the slapping of thighs against thighs brings me close to the edge.

"Mindy, honey, I'm getting close."

"Me, too. You feel so good. I'm going to explode all over you."

Kyle pushes harder and finds a part of me that has been untouched until now. I cry out in pleasure as Kyle pumps me hard. He jerks his pelvis deep within my folds, dropping his hot seed safely within. I hold on tight as I ride out the best orgasm I have ever had.

"Don't move, Mind. I want you to sit here on top of me for a minute. I want to hold you. I feel complete with you like this. Let's just have this minute. I adore you and want to feel you wrapped around me in every way."

I lean into Kyle and lightly brush his lips as he holds me in a tender embrace. "This is what dreams are made of," I whisper to him.

Kyle chuckles and hugs me tight as he whispers, "Can we grab a quick shower before we have to meet the other love birds?"

"Sure, because you know they are doing the same thing. Nothing like a good piece of ass in the afternoon, I always say. Although, morning sex is the best. That's my favorite. Start the day off right."

"I'm liking the way you think, Ms. Harper."

"Yeah, well, I like the way you feel inside me, Mr. Masterson. How's that?"

"Just fine with me, Ms. Harper. I'll fill you up anytime you want." We laugh as we head to the shower.

Chapter 46

Everyone is at Mindy's apartment for the drive to the Bike Rally. Her parents are present, along with Kyle and David. I arrive earlier and I'm helping Mindy with her biker outfit and the overall look of a 'biker bitch.' T. and his men are scattered around, some in her neighborhood and some of them are already at the Biker Burn-Out Bar.

I get dressed first and I'm sporting short shorts and a black leather lace-up corset. "Liz, if you bend over too much, your ass cheeks will fall out of your shorts, for God's sake."

"I know, Mindy, but I need to look the part, remember? The more skin you show, the bigger the tips and the more raffle tickets we sell. It's a cool game, don't you think?"

"I'm not so sure about that. I know I need to play this part, but how do women have this confidence all the time?"

"I think most of the women don't care. They are rough and tough and they run with bikers. They ooze confidence. But I think for me it would be a lot easier if my man was open to it. You know what I mean? It would be as if David said, 'Yeah, baby, you look fucking hot like that. Let's go show you off.' Then I would probably feel more comfortable with it all the time. Does that make sense?"

"I guess so. I'm just not that comfortable in my own skin to show that much of it off in public."

"It's only a show, Mindy. You have the look; I mean just look at you? You're fucking gorgeous in this outfit. Now you just need to have the attitude to pull it off tonight. So, think like a hot sex machine, and put sweet Mindy away for the night. Bring out confident, slutty, hot as fuck Mindy, instead."

"I'll see what I can do. I mean, I have to, in order for this to work, right?"

"Are you ready to go show off the final look? Let's see what the guys say."

"Oh dear God, my parents are out there Liz. How am I going to do this with them around?"

"There's going to be so many people around, you won't even notice them once you get there. We have a job to do, that's all."

We walk out of her bedroom and into the living room.

"Holy fucking hell," says T. "You guys look amazing. You will both fit in perfectly. Man, Liz, you nailed it. Those clothes are spot on. You both will blend in perfectly. Nice job."

Kyle tilts his head, probably trying to get a silhouette of Mindy in her outfit.

She walks over to him and reaches for his hands. "Kyle, feel this. This is a red leather lace-up corset. It's really pushing up my boobs, that's for sure. I've got more cleavage than Liz."

"I'm not buying that one. I don't think anyone has more cleavage than Liz," David says, all proud as he winks at me.

"Gee, Mindy, you feel amazing, and yes, lots of cleavage."

"Um, excuse me. Mindy's father is in the house and I'm standing right here. I saw that, mister, that little extra squeeze you gave her. Watch where you put your paws, Masterson," Mr. Harper barks.

"Yes, sir. Just trying to participate. My apologies."

Everyone in the living room laughs as Kyle turns three shades of red.

Mindy is wearing short black boy shorts and the red corset. Her hair is in a high ponytail with a bright red bow at the top. Her makeup is glamorous but not cheap. She looks sexy, and the red bow and corset make her easy to see and follow.

Because so many people wear black, T. recommended that she wear something that would be noticeable in a crowd, so I dressed her in red. Red is sexy, and Mindy is on fire tonight. *If only Kyle could see her.*

Mindy's phone rings and everyone freezes. She grabs it off the table and looks at the screen. "Time to play my part," she says as everyone stays silent and waits. "Hello?"

"Hello, Mindy. We haven't spoken in a while. I thought I would call and see if you were coming to the Rally tonight?"

"As a matter of fact, I am. Will you be there?"

"I will be waiting for you. I want to take you away and make you mine. I need to settle the score and taking you away from Big Joe forever should do the trick."

"And if I don't want to go?"

"Honey, you don't have a choice. You see, me and Big Joe have an issue. You will be collateral damage."

"Why not just call Big Joe and settle this like two grown men? Why involve me? I'm a nobody."

"Oh, honey, you are everything to Big Joe. The best revenge is having something of his taken away. And I will take you in every way possible. Tell me, are you shaved? I love a naked pussy."

I watch as Mindy's face pales and she immediately hangs up and throws the phone on the table. She is shaking and hyperventilating. I know the signs and I need to stop her from spiraling out of control. I reach for her hands and hold them tight. I talk her down from her anxiety and help her focus. "Breathe, Mindy. Look at me, we've got you. Just breathe."

"I don't know if I can do this. He says revenge and taking something away from Big Joe is the best way to settle the score. I'm just collateral damage. He said he wanted me in every way possible. You can figure out the rest."

"Mindy, you don't have to do this," Kyle admits. "No one will be angry if you decide to forget it. It's scary being the center of a dangerous plan."

"David, how many men will be there to help me? I need to know how I will be protected."

"Mindy, there are six undercover police and civilians looking like bikers with their eyes on you. Plus, all the guys T. has there. And don't forget all of us."

"Are your men armed?" she asks with a shaky voice.

"The undercover men are armed and will be carrying their pistols. T.'s men are not."

"Okay, let's do this. I have pepper spray and my cell phone in my pocket, nothing else."

"Liz, do you have that red lipstick I can borrow? This should add the final finishing touch."

"You look amazing, Mind. I'm your partner in crime, so let's go get this fucker."

"Hey, guys, there is one more thing I noticed tonight. I almost forgot to tell you. And come to think of it, now in hindsight, it's kind of weird," Mindy states.

"What's that?" David asks.

"The man who has been calling me, he's not stuttering on the phone. John-John always stuttered in person. But on the phone, he never stutters. Why is that? It's weird."

"Hmm, that's interesting. Thanks for the info," David says.

As we all walk out to the cars to leave, T. grabs David's arm. "Hey. Can I have a minute?"

"What's up, T.?"

"Are you thinking what I'm thinking?"

"Yup. There may be more than one person looking to grab Mindy. Please be careful."

"I'll notify my men. All eyes on the girl with the red bow."

Chapter 47

The Biker Burnout Bar is jammin'. There are bikers and people everywhere. It's a great turnout and Mindy and I are selling tickets like hotcakes. Men are loving big tits and this red corset. It was a great idea.

We have been at the rally now for two hours and nothing unusual has happened. It's getting dark and the swimsuit competition is beginning. The stage lights come up and an enormously tall and muscular man walks up on stage.

"Good evening, everyone, and welcome to the Fifth Annual Bike Rally. Tonight's proceeds go to benefit the local Miracle House. A place of rest and recovery for sick children and their families. Donations are always accepted and please don't forget to buy your 50/50 raffle tickets. See the lady in red for your tickets. So far, we have accumulated over one thousand dollars for the raffle, and you only have one hour left. So go see Miss Red Bow, check out her tits, because they are beauties, and grab an arm's length of tickets. It's worth it. So, remember, the lady with the red bow, you can't miss her. Now let's get this competition started."

Liz and I are working a small group of bikers when a swarm of loud men descends on me. "Shit." They encircle me and I lose sight of Liz.

The men crowd around me and are buying up raffle tickets like crazy. Most are pleasant and cooperative, but some get handsy and give my ass a little pat and grab a handful. I ignore it for the sake of selling the tickets and playing my part.

Most of the men buy their tickets and go on about their business, but there is this one man who stands off to the side and just watches. He is patiently waiting for his turn. He is constantly watching me. I can feel the burn from his glare. It's like he can see right through my clothes and it's making me uneasy. My gut is in a knot as my adrenaline rushes. I'm acutely aware of my surroundings, so I continue to play my part to perfection.

"Hey, handsome, how about some raffle tickets? Can I interest you in an arm's length? It's for a good cause," I ask and watch as he puts down his drink and walks over to me, looking at me like I'm the last woman on Earth. He reaches into his pocket for his wallet, or so I thought.

"Hey, beautiful, you look fucking stunning in red. How much are the tickets?"

"Twenty dollars for an arm's length."

"I'll take that arm then," he says.

I stretch out my arm to measure an arm's length and to get ready to pull off the tickets. Just as I look down to rip the tickets from the roll, cold, hard handcuffs snap around my wrist. "What the hell?"

"This is me, darling, finally having my way. I've been watching you all night. Don't struggle or the handcuff will get tighter on its own. Now put your arm casually down and hold my hand. Look normal and walk with me. No funny business."

"So, now that you have me, do I at least get to know your name? I see you have this cool tattoo of a lightning bolt. It must mean something?"

"My name is not important. I finally have you after all these weeks. This is going to be so much fun. Just wait, you'll see."

I walk with him to the back of the picnic area, where there are several outbuildings used for storage. As he reaches to open the door to the largest of buildings, there's a familiar voice.

"Hey, hey, Levin. What-what are you doing-doing there? Isn't that-that the nurse-nurse from the hospital? I know you. Hi, I'm John-John. It's so nice-nice to finally meet-meet you."

"Hello John-John, I'm Mindy. How are you? I thought you looked familiar. You brought me flowers at work one day."

"Yes-yes I did. They were-were the biggest flowers ever. Yellow-yellow roses."

"That's right. You did a great job. Thank you. Can you tell me where am I?"

"Oh, this is the-the medical building. This is where we-we fix-fix up people."

"Well, that's appropriate since I'm a nurse."

"John-John, you can go now. Crazy Harry said it was okay for you to go home now. We are done with the fundraising now, so Mindy is done with work."

"You don't think-think crazy Harry will be mad-mad at me-me if I go-go home now, do you? I'm kind-kind of hot and-and want a bath."

"No, John-John. You're good. Crazy Harry will be okay with you. Go home already."

"Okay, see-see you guys-guys later."

"Oh, and John-John, take this thing and throw it away, would you? It's like a fucking beacon and it's fucking annoying." Levin reaches up and pulls the red bow from my hair.

My heart is racing as I watch him walk away with my red bow. I look at tattoo guy and he is oblivious and not paying John-John any mind. John-John is waving goodbye to me and then points to the big school bell on top of the building and turns away. *Hmm, that's weird.*

Levin yanks me back to reality as he pulls on my wrist and the cuff tightens and pinches my skin. "Hey, go easy, that hurts," I bark out.

"Well, if you didn't chat with that simple-minded jerk so long, I wouldn't have to hurry you along. Now move it." Levin pushes me inside the building and down the hallway to a door on the left. We enter the room and it looks cold and sterile, like a mini operating room.

"What the hell is this, an operating room?"

"If it needs to be, now move."

Levin slides the medicine cabinet over and behind it is an electronic keypad. I watch him as he enters a few numbers and the opposing wall slides open.

"Is this like some secret hideout? I feel like I'm in a movie or something. What are you up to, and where are we going?" I'm trying to stay calm and not freak out. I remember the number combo on the keypad just in case, but we're walking further away from safety.

Think, Mindy, think. Be careful and not stupid. What would David advise you to do?

I observe my surroundings and the direction we are heading. There are no windows, no doors, just a long hallway. At the end of the hallway is another locked door. The keypad code is the same, good for me. Only one number sequence to remember.

I try to remain calm and observant, but my jitters are getting the best of me. I tremble and feel light-headed. *Shit, don't pass out now, then you'll really be at his mercy.*

Levin opens the door and pushes me inside. He shoves me onto the stretcher and yells, "Stay put! You move and I shoot. And don't worry, no one will hear you in here. It's soundproofed for a reason."

I look around and see all sorts of surgical instruments hanging on the walls.

Great, just fucking great. I'm in a fucking horror movie episode, and I'm the dumb chick who ends up sliced to shit. Well fuck that, I want to be the smart chick who gets away at the end. Be smart, Mindy. Play along and do what you need to do to survive.

I look around and notice a desk in the corner of the room with a computer and a landline telephone. There are security monitors on the desk, watching the hallway and the outside perimeter of the Burnout Bar. He's got all the property staked out. He'll know if anyone is ever coming for me. He'll see them first. Shit. *Be calm, and hopefully, T.'s and David's men are in hot pursuit of my ass.*

Chapter 48

Irun up to David, out of breath, and he's on the phone, frantically yelling at T. "What do you mean, you lost her? She was just standing right here!" He points to the ground. "We had twelve sets of eyes on her. How does a woman in red just disappear? Find her damn it! No one is wearing red but her. She's not that hard to spot!"

"David, a group of men surrounded me and Mindy. They were buying up raffle tickets like crazy. I had eyes on her, and then the next minute she was gone! How did I lose her? I was watching the whole time. One of those men must have her, David! We need to find her."

"Liz, I'm on it. She has to be somewhere close. She couldn't have gone far."

"David, what do you mean, you lost her?" Kyle asks. "I heard you on the phone with T. What the hell is going on?"

"Listen, Kyle, I don't know what happened. One minute she was here, the next gone."

"Are you fucking serious right now, David? You promised her and everyone else she would be safe. You promised her parents, for fuck's sake. You mean to tell me all those men don't know where she is?"

Before David can answer, a biker wearing a Viper cut approaches, and David is on hyper-alert. David tells Kyle to chill out and listen and calm the fuck down. He doesn't want to appear out of control in front of any bikers that may have some information.

"Excuse me, sirs, are-are you-you friends of my-my girl Mindy?"

"Your girl? What did you do with Mindy, you piece of shit? Where the fuck is she?" Kyle snaps.

"I'm not-not a piece-piece of shit, sir. I really-really like her, and-and I just want to-to help."

"Are you John-John?" David asks.

"Yes, sir, that's my name. Don't-Don't wear-wear it out."

"Why you stalking piece of shit! I'm going to fucking kill you!" Kyle screams and lunges for the shadow in front of him. Kyle barrels into him, knocking them both over.

They land in a heap and Kyle gets a good punch into John-John's cheek before John-John reaches back and, with one swift punch to Kyle's jaw, knocks him out.

"Fuck!" yells David. "What did you go and do that for? The man can't even see. He's fucking blind and harmless. He never would be able to hurt you."

"Well, I didn't know-know that. He-he was just coming-coming to-to hurt me. I was de-de-defending myself."

"Yes, you were John-John. I'm sorry he hit you. Here, let me help you up." David offers a helping hand and John-John grabs it for support as David pulls him back on his feet.

"I came to-to give-give this to you-you. I was told to get-get rid of it, but its too pretty to throw-throw away." John-John reaches into his pocket and pulls out Mindy's red ribbon bow and gives it to David, just as Mr. and Mrs. Harper walk up to see what all the commotion is about.

David is bending over and checking on Kyle, as he remains knocked out cold. Mrs. Harper bends over and sits down next to him. She props Kyle's head up on her lap and watches him sleep. "I'll protect him from further injury and make sure the poor guy will hear a familiar voice when he comes to," says Mrs. Harper.

T. and a few of his unmarked men walk up and join the conversation. Just as T. opens his mouth to speak to John-John, Mr. Harper beats him to it.

"What are you doing with Mindy's bow?"

"I was-was returning it. I didn't want to-to throw it-it away."

"Oh, my God, you stutter. You're John-John," Mr. Harper realizes.

"Yes, sir, my name is John-John Marxx Jr. Nice to meet you. I just-just needed to give you her-her bow back."

"John-John, where did you find this bow?" Mr. Harper asks.

"It came from-from Mindy's hair. It looked so-so pretty in her hair. But then he-he-he took it-it out."

David's detective instincts are on high alert and don't miss a thing. "Who took it out, John-John?"

"Levin took the bow-bow from pretty Mindy's hair. He-he-he said it was-was a beacon and I-I-I needed to-to get rid of it. But I just-just couldn't throw her pretty bow-bow away, so here I am. Do you-you want-want it?"

Mr. Harper reaches for the bow as tears come to his eyes. "Thank you, John-John. I think we need to talk, John-John. Do you have time to talk to me now?"

"No-No I need-need to go home. Crazy Harry said I can go-go home and take-take a bath. I'll see-see you all later-later."

John-John walks away and Mrs. Harper is crying as she tends to Kyle and looks at Mindy's red bow. "What are we going to do, T.? David? Robert? Anybody?" she yells as she hysterically cries.

I sit down next to her and give her a hug for support. "Mindy is a strong woman. You have never seen her in action like I have. Trust that she is being strong. She will find her way back to us." I look up at David with tear-filled eyes, saying nothing as the message is understood.

David's phone rings and he grabs it on the second ring. "Masterson here. Yeah, I got it, thanks. Keep eyes on that building and find a way in the back. We'll head to the front."

Kyle stirs and awakens. "What the hell just happened to me? Did I hit a wall or something?"

"Actually, bro, it was the fist of John-John. You lunged at him and he punched you and knocked you out. How are you feeling?"

"Like I've been hit by a truck, again. Shit, man. Where is Mindy? Did he say anything that would help us?"

"Yeah, Levin, the lightning bolt tattoo guy has her."

"Well, let's go get her. Where are they?"

"We don't know for sure, but I just got a lead on a storage building at the back of the bar's parking lot. We're heading there now with T.'s men."

"Okay, I'm coming. Hold up." Kyle goes to stand up and loses his balance, and lands back down in the lap of Mrs. Harper.

"Whoa, Kyle. You aren't going anywhere. You need to stay here with me. You can keep me company, because I'm losing my shit, and I'll keep you safe. Just stay down until you recover."

Chapter 49

"I've been waiting a long time for you, Mindy. You see, I have watched you grow up, just waiting for the right time to do my picking. I've wanted you for fucking years, and now I'm going to have you. You are one fine specimen of a woman."

"Well, thank you, Mr. Levin. I appreciate the compliment, but why have you been watching me for so long? I mean, I don't even know you. Why have you been watching me?"

"Well, it's a long story, but you see, Big Joe took something away from me, and now I'm going to take something away from him. Something he loves and cares deeply about. No turning back now."

"Mr. Levin, I would be so much more comfortable if you took this handcuff off my wrist, please. I'm tired of being pinched by it. I'm not going anywhere. You have us locked in here. Wherever here is. I have no idea."

"We are in the escape room of the Vipers Motorcycle Club."

"Ah, somewhere safe where no cops will find you, in case you or your men get into trouble, is that it?"

"Well, something like that. But it's a safe room, too. You can only get in by the keypad code, and only a few of us know the code. There is a special way to call for reinforcements, if needed, but that's a club cherished secret."

"No, no, I get it. It pays to be smart, Mr. Levin. You never know when you might need help down here. Smart thinking. You Viper men are pretty tight, huh?"

"Well, it's a brotherhood, you know. We are all family. Some of us are real family, like genetically related and shit."

"Is that why you guys always call each other 'brother'?"

"Yes, because we mean it. We are all brothers, and we will do whatever it takes to keep our family together."

"Is taking me part of a plan for keeping your family together?"

"No, that's just pure and simple revenge. I have been watching you since you were a baby, and you were so cute back then. Now you are a woman. I fucking need you. I need you to touch me, suck me, and fuck me. And then when I'm done with you, maybe there will be something left of you to bury. I'm not sure yet. It all depends on your behavior."

"Mr. Levin, I can't be all those things to you if I'm in pain hurting. If you really want to enjoy me, then let my arms free so I can feel my way around your muscular body. Really give you a massage and treat you right. You deserve it. It's the least I can do if you have been waiting so long for me."

I watch him as his eyebrow raise in disbelief, but his cock is answering for him. I can see his arousal and his curious look. It's as if his conscious is saying, *Why not? It's not like she can get out and go anywhere.* I monitor Levin as he looks around the room and notices, yes, the door is closed and sealed, with the code safely tucked in his head.

He walks over to me and licks my neck as he lets out a groan. I try not to react in disgust, as this would ruin my plan and make my acting obvious.

"Mindy, you smell amazing. I can't wait to taste all of you."

I instantly feel nauseous and bile fills my throat.

I give myself a pep talk. *Swallow that shit down, Mindy. If there was ever a time to be a psych nurse, it's now. Play along and be cool. Look for an advantage and be smart. Stay cool for God's sake.*

"Um, Mr. Levin, please release the handcuff. I'll be good. You won't be disappointed, sir. You know, I'm a nurse, right? I'm very knowledgeable about relieving pressure points and the male anatomy."

"I'll bet you are, Mindy. Now, there's nowhere for you to go, so if I release this handcuff, you need to obey me and be good."

"Of course, Mr. Levin. I'm at your mercy."

"Yes, yes you are, my dear. Now, let me see you. I want to see what I've been missing all these years." Levin walks over to me and pulls on the red shoelace at the top of my corset. He unlaces the top of the garment and relieves all the pressure that was keeping my breasts lifted and in place. He pulls open the corset and looks at my full breasts.

"Well, hello there. Aren't these just perky and fucking beautiful?" Levin touches my breasts and kneads them like a roll of dough as he moans. I notice his manhood responding and realize if I don't figure something out quickly, he will soon be at the point of no return. There is no way I'm letting this man fuck me!

"Mr. Levin. The handcuffs?" I ask softly, using the best sex voice I can manage under the circumstances.

"Fine, Mindy. I'll do it in a minute. But only because you are the most fucking beautiful thing I have seen and I'm going to enjoy every inch of you."

"Thank you, sir. I appreciate your trust."

"Wow, and you're polite, too. How did I score such a perfect woman?"

"Why am I here? Did I do something wrong, sir?"

"Oh. No, my dear, you are perfect and have done everything right. Me, taking you, is just settling an old score, and now I win."

"Well, since you have won. Can we just relax and enjoy ourselves then? Let's not worry about anyone else." I now have renewed determination.

"I couldn't agree more, my dear. Now, let me see those tits again." He leans over and sucks on my nipple and pulls it hard in his teeth. I refuse to cry out.

"I can't play along with you when I'm still bound. Don't forget about me," I say sweetly.

"I won't forget. You'll have your chance to touch me. I'm on fire for you. You'll touch me when I'm ready. Don't worry."

As Levin works on my other nipple, I look around the room for clues to help me. *I will get out of this room. I just need to assess the situation and pay attention.*

While Levin has his way with my breasts, I notice a desk on the other side of the room. There is a landline telephone and a computer. There is also a row of buttons on the wall, hidden behind a glass case, like a fire alarm. I assume they must be important if they are protected behind glass. *Note to self: find out what the fuck those are.*

Levin comes up for air and slowly takes the corset off me, totally exposing my bare skin from the waist up. He's rubbing my shoulders and feeling his way back down to my breasts. There is a cool chill in the room and my nipples respond. I'm getting the goose bumps, and my nipples are pointing hard and straight. Of course, Levin notices and thinks this is a direct response from his touch. Silly boy.

"I need you completely with me, Mindy. You got that? If I release this handcuff, I want you on my side and consenting to my touch."

"Mr. Levin. There is something exciting about being with a big biker man such as yourself. I'm with you, don't worry." I'm still feeling so sick to my stomach I can't stand it, but I need to play this part. If I need to be a little slutty in the process, then so be it. My life depends on it.

Levin releases my handcuff and I rub my wrist where the red mark is evident. It's swollen and sore, and bruises from the metal are becoming apparent. I try to ignore it as I focus on finding a way to getting the fuck out of this room.

"Mr. Levin, I noticed there is a desk over there. I don't know about you, but one of my all-time favorite fantasies was to be taken by a large man, such as yourself, on a desk. You know, push all the papers on the floor, in the heat of passion, like in the movies, and fuck like animals on top of the desk."

"Holy fuck. You are reading my mind. Come here." He grabs my wrist and I wince, but follow. He turns me around and sits me on the edge of the desk, spreads my legs open, and walks himself into my V. I breathe slowly and deeply and try to calm myself down, as I look around again at the magic buttons on the wall.

Levin moves in for the mouth-to-mouth kiss when I turn away and interrupt. "Mr. Levin. I have another fantasy if you would like to hear it."

"I've got time, baby. You are so fucking hot. I'll be ready when you're done. I've been ready all day just waiting for this moment. What's a few more minutes? Let me hear it."

"I have always wanted to be a secretary, taken by her boss. Can we role play? I'll ask some questions and you can be my boss? You will be more than willing to answer me, because you know I will be giving you myself in the end. What do you say?"

"I say, you are making me so crazy horny, I'll do whatever you want. Now, let's play."

"Okay, here we go. I'll go first." I turn on the dumb blonde charm and play my role to perfection. "Why, Boss Levin, I'm so happy to be here sitting on your desk. This makes me so horny and hot for you."

"Mindy, I'm burning for you, too."

"Well, you are my boss, so I expect a raise when we are done here. I will service you with pride, sir. You have such a lovely office, and such a big desk."

"Honey, that's not the only big thing I have."

My heart is pounding hard and fast, as it's time for drastic measures. If I want to stall for more time, I need to sell it. With as much courage as I can muster, I grab his hard cock and give it a little rubbing and a gentle squeeze. There's an immediate response beneath his blue jeans.

Work it, Mindy.

"Why don't you tell me about all these little toys you have on the wall, sir? I love buttons. They turn me on."

"Seriously, toys turn you on?"

"Oh, yes, sir. There is something about adult toys that gets a girl wet with hunger, you know? I like to break things when I'm in heat. I'm all about breaking things and breaking the rules. That's what makes me so wet."

Levin loses his self-control and plays perfectly with me. He is so hard for me that his cock is controlling his brain, and he forgets I am the "prisoner."

"Miss Mindy, my buttons are special. They will call my men and alert them to danger. I can ask them to come here if I need them."

"So, if I wanted you, and more of your men, to play with me, I could just push the buttons? I might want more cocks to play with, boss. Can I push it if I want?"

"Of course, the more the merrier."

I continue to rub his cock as I purposefully whisper softly. "And since this is your safe room, will this button call for help?" I ask as I point to the red button behind the glass.

Levin quickly pushes me down on my back on the desk and is towering over me. Not a position I want to be in, that's for sure.

"My dear Mindy, that my dear is the school bell. It only sounds when the Club President is in danger. It will bring the house down, so to speak. We never push that button unless we want the whole fucking club here."

"No, sir, I don't want the whole club here. I feel you will be enough for now, sir. I think I only want you." I slowly sit up and reach for Levin.

I pull him in for lip-to-lip contact. He happily obliges and grabs my head with some force, and pulls me closer to him with brute strength. I let him hold me there, encased in his hands. I allow him to feel like he is in control because now I have my plan.

My hands are free to roam his body and keep him occupied. I grab a fistful of Levin's hair. I return the favor and hold his head in place as I return his kisses. Kissing him roughly and deeply, keeping him distracted.

I slowly wiggle my hips to his deep throating, as if I were in hot need. All the while, making it easier to gain access to my back pocket. I slowly loosen my hands on his head as I place my hands on his hips. Levin pulls my waist in tighter to his, bringing us chest to chest. That quick movement gave me all the time I need. I reach into my back pocket and pull out my pepper spray. I can't believe he never checked my pants. He was so interested in my tits and that red corset; he forgot about my ass.

I moan as if I'm on fire for him, all the while looking around and trying to keep him occupied. I moan a little louder this time, just to give me cover as I quickly attempt to get the top off the pepper spray. I pull away to catch my breath and Levin looks at me in excitement.

"Girl, you can kiss. I can't wait to fucking taste you."

My nerves snap and I yell, "I don't think so, asshole!" as I pull the trigger on the pepper spray and aim it right in Levin's face. I push him back off me as I simultaneously kick him in the balls.

He doubles over in pain, grabbing his crotch as he tumbles to the floor, yelling, "You fucking bitch! I will get you. You'll never get out of here! I'll find you; I will have you, and then I will fucking kill you!"

While Levin is rolling around on the floor, screaming in pain and holding himself, I run to the wall and, with the other end of my pepper spray, I break the glass, and push the red button for the school bell. "Fuck this!" I yell as I slam my fist on every button, cutting my hand deep on a piece of glass. Blood drips on the floor as I run past Levin and spray him again for safe measure. I run to the keypad and enter the code number I saw him type in. I stand there, holding my breath and my hand. My hand is still bleeding and oozing blood.

"Come on!" I impatiently wait to see if the code I entered was indeed the correct code. Then I hear the electronic click of the lock. I grab the door and yank it open. I slam the door closed behind me, as I run for my life up the long hallway. I make it back to the makeshift operating room and punch in the code. Droplets of blood line the hallway from my quick escape, giving away my escape route.

The door unlocks, and I have a fleeting sense of relief. At least here I can gather up some supplies for myself, and instruments and tools I can use as weapons.

Just when I think I might have a few moments to regroup my thoughts, the lock on the door clicks. I hide in a panic. *Fuck! He's here for me. Do what you need to do to survive, girl. Take no prisoners and defend yourself!*

Chapter 50

Outside on the grounds of the Burnout Bar, we are frantic, covering ground, trying to find Mindy. We collectively head to the largest storage building on the premises. As we approach, the school bell on top of the building sounds. The bell is loud and old-fashioned, like a school bell from an old one-room schoolhouse.

The gong of the bell is distinctive and can be heard over the entire property. Viper members gather outside, awaiting direction.

"What the hell is going on?" T. asks.

I look at T. and announce, "It's an alarm. It means the Club President is in danger and inside. All Vipers must respond."

"I get that, David, but how the fuck did you know that?"

"We'll talk about that later, T., but for now, we need to find Mindy."

"Hey, David, the Viper president is standing over there under the tree. See all the members swarming around him? He doesn't look in danger to me. If he's here, who the fuck set off the alarm? And where are they?"

I look at T. and then at Mr. Harper. "Mindy!" we all say in unison.

"T., we need to get in that building and now!" Mr. Harper yells.

"I agree, let's go."

"And I'm coming too," Liz yells in grief. "If you all think I'm waiting outside, you can forget it. Mindy needs me! She'll be a wreck and panic-stricken. I'm going!"

"Hold up!" T. shouts. "There is a right way to deal with bikers. There is a code to follow. We just can't bust in there, with all these Viper members present. We need to do this right. Give me a minute and I'm on it."

On his heels, we follow T. as he briskly moves toward the Viper's president. He catches his attention. "Crazy Harry, may I have a word, please?"

Crazy Harry looks T. up and down and looks at his club members gathered all around.

"We have reason to believe that Mindy Harper, our legacy, is in danger and in that building, with one of your brothers. We need access to get in there and find her, with your permission. I want to do the politically right thing here, but respectfully, you need to know we are going in there with or without your permission."

T. stares at Crazy Harry, holding his gaze. He never falters and waits for an answer.

"What's it gonna be, Crazy Harry? I'm asking out of respect for your house and your family. She's our legacy, man. Think long and hard about this before you answer. Now is the time to fix old wounds and do what's right. Harry, we would do this for you in a heartbeat and you know it."

"Permission granted, *but*," he hesitates, "we will accompany you. You are not entering our private building unattended."

"Done! But we need to move now."

T. turns and looks at Liz. "Liz, honey, a biker safe house is no place for a woman. They will not grant you entrance anyway, so do me a favor? Look after Kyle and go with Mrs. Harper to the hospital. Mindy will be more at ease knowing her favorite nurse is looking after her man."

Reluctantly, Liz nods in agreement.

Crazy Harry unlocks the door to the storage building and T., Mr. Harper, me, and several other Viper club members quickly enter.

T. yells for Mindy as Crazy Harry unlocks various doors looking for her. "Mindy! Mindy! Where are you?"

Nothing. There is no sound.

"What the hell? Where is she?" I question. "How big is this place, anyway?"

Crazy Harry pipes up and admits, "These rooms are soundproofed. She will never hear you yelling for her."

"Then we need to check every inch of this place, room by room," Mr. Harper states.

I watch over Crazy Harry's shoulder as he walks over to the monitor controls and pulls up the footage of the hallway. There is no sign of any open doors, but then I catch a glimpse of light as it is turned off in the examination room. "There!" I point. "Someone just turned off a light in that room. And look, there is a trail of blood in the hallway leading to the door! Let's start there."

Crazy Harry leads the way and punches in the code to the examination room door. He opens the door cautiously, and the room is pitch black. There is no sign of anyone, and at a glance, nothing looks disturbed. Crazy Harry slowly takes two steps into the room. There is a loud scream and a weight crashes into me. The momentum startles me and knocks Crazy Harry off balance. Pepper spray is everywhere as we choke and gasp for air. Crazy Harry got the brunt of the pepper spray as he is coughing and then yells, "What the fuck and who the hell was that?"

I get a vague vision of someone running toward the open door, arms lifted to shield their face from the blinding hallway lights. I recognize Mindy as she bolts out the door into the hallway. She doesn't get far when she runs smack dab into a large, solid chest. I watch helplessly as she crashes to the floor, appearing disoriented and gasping for air.

"Mindy! It's me, T. Holy shit, girl, are you all right? Christ, Mindy, you're bleeding and you're half naked."

Mr. Harper and I run up behind T. as we watch him console Mindy. "What the hell is going on?" Mr. Harper asks.

Mindy doesn't answer as she shakes and cries profusely.

"Here, give me your hand. Let me help you up. Come here, honey." T. helps Mindy up off the floor as he pulls off his t-shirt. "Here, put this on. You need to be covered, sweetheart. I don't want anyone gawking at my girl." He pulls a bandana from his pocket and hands it to her. "Wrap this bandana around your hand. It will help stop the bleeding and we will need to have that looked at later."

T. holds her tight. "Let it out, girl, I've got you. It's my turn to take care of you. You're safe, honey."

"I got away, Dad, I just got away." She sobs out as she keeps crying and shaking.

Mr. Harper steps in and hugs his daughter tight as she grabs his shirt. "It's okay honey. You're safe. But you got away from who?"

"Oh, my God, where is David? I need to tell David."

"I'm right here, Mind. I'm with you. We are all with you. You need to tell me what?"

"The man, the man who took me, was Mr. Levin, the lightning bolt tattoo guy. Not John-John. He took me down there to a room. He called it the escape room or safe room, something like that. He said it was a place for the Vipers to go to be safe, where no one would find them. I got away because I played his game and I pepper sprayed him. He's still in there! I left him in there. I kicked him in the balls and pepper sprayed him. He's sick, David, mentally sick. Please, get the cops in there. He handcuffed me and dragged me there. Go get him! Don't let him get away!"

Crazy Harry is listening to her story as he is trying to focus and recover from being pepper sprayed. "T!" he yells. "Get the fuck over here."

"I'm right here. What's up?"

"I can't see great at the moment, but I can hear just fine. I heard what Mindy just said. Do you have men here to help you?"

"Yes, sir, I do."

"Alright then. Tank, you, and Bear accompany T. and his men down to the safe room, and do whatever you need to do to bring out Levin. We need a word with him. And do whatever it takes to keep him attentive and grounded. He will not be a flight risk tonight. Got it?"

"Yes, sir. Understood," Tank and Bear answer in unison. Tank and Bear, the two biggest Viper brothers I have ever seen, wait as me and T. join them.

I can feel Mindy's eyes on my back as we all disappear down the hallway.

Chapter 51

"Come on, Mindy, you don't need to watch this. Let's get you out of here and into the fresh air," Dad says as he guides me outside into the night air.

"Dad, where's Kyle? I need to see him."

"Actually, Mindy, I need to talk to you about that. Your mom is with him, and she took Kyle to the hospital."

"What? Why? What happened? Is he all right? I need to be with him, Dad. Can you take me there now?" I am nearing hysteria.

"Mindy, honey. Calm down. He's fine. He got in a little altercation with John-John, and John-John threw a punch and knocked Kyle out."

"What? Are you serious? Is he okay?"

"He was only knocked out for a few minutes. He knew his name and where he was and all that stuff. Your mom has been with him the whole time, along with Liz. They took him to the hospital just to get checked out. Since he's already had a head injury, Liz thought it was best."

"Damn right it was best. Can you take me there?"

"Of course, honey, let's go."

❧

I arrive at the hospital twenty minutes later and burst through the emergency department's doorway looking for Kyle.

"Mindy? Is that you?" came from behind me.

I turn around and see Doctor Benjamin walking in my direction.

"Yup, it's me. I know I look crazy. It's a long story. Do you happen to know what exam room Kyle Masterson is in?"

Doctor Benjamin goes over to the admission log and checks for me. "Hey, Mind, according to this admission log, he was sent to his room about thirty minutes ago. He is in room 203."

"Thanks, I'll catch you later and update you another time. I know this is nuts and I look crazy, but look the other way, Doc. No questions now, please? I gotta run."

"I'm sure there's a good story here, and I can't wait to hear it. But hey, you need to have that hand looked at! Let me see it really quick. You can't run off just yet. You're bleeding, Mindy."

I unwrap the bandana and look down. Shit. This gash is bigger than I thought. Doctor Benjamin looks up and makes eye contact with me. No words are needed, I know the answer. When you work with someone long enough, you know the plan just by a glance, and I'm reading his mind.

"Stitches." We both say in unison.

Damn.

"Mindy, honey, that needs washing out and stitches before you go anywhere. You'll bleed all over the hospital if I don't get you stitched up first. You know I'm right."

"Fine! Make it quick, okay? I really need to go see Kyle."

Ten stitches and a gauze wrap later, and I'm on my way. Doctor Benjamin shakes his head as he watches me disappear down the hallway to the elevator.

I head for Kyle's room with nerves shot to hell. I'm emotionally exhausted, haven't eaten all day, and now all I can think about is making sure Kyle is okay.

I slowly open the door and enter Kyle's room quietly. I wave to his parents, my mom, and Liz. Mrs. Masterson gets up and gives me a big hug, but we exchange no words. Kyle is sleeping and no one wants to wake him. I sit by his bed as everyone quietly gets up and leaves to give me a moment with him.

Liz and I exchange knowing glances and just watch Kyle breathe. Easy, light breathing. He is resting. I start to relax and start to come down off my adrenaline high. My breathing slows and I can feel my shoulder tension ease up a little. Just as I close my eyes to say a prayer of thanks, I hear him.

"Mindy, honey, you're here. I can smell my favorite nurse. Ode to Mindy with amber and rose mixed in. How are you, baby?" Kyle whispers.

My eyes cloud with tears as I get up and lean over to kiss him on the lips. Kyle reaches up and finds my ponytail. "Mm, there's my nurse. I've missed you," he says tenderly.

"And I've missed you. Are you okay? I heard you got knocked out?"

"I did, babe, but it was my own fault. I heard John-John talking and thought he was your stalker, so I lunged at him. In his defense, he thought I was dangerous, so he threw a punch and caught me in the chin just right. It knocked me out immediately and down I went. Your mom and Liz have been with me ever since."

"How did you even see him to lunge at him?"

"I really didn't see him. Well, not like you're thinking. Only a silhouette, but I knew the direction of his voice, so my instincts kicked in and I went with it. I lunged in the direction of his voice, but I got my ass kicked in the process."

"I'm so sorry, but thank you for defending my honor."

"Always. Anything for you, Mind. Now sit down and tell me all about your night. Are you okay? What happened?"

"Kyle, can I have some time to process it all, please? I really don't want to talk about it yet. I just know David and T. went to go get the guy, and hopefully he is behind bars by now."

"So, John-John wasn't your stalker?"

"I don't know that for sure, but the man who took me tonight was that Viper, Mr. Levin. The guy with the lightning bolt tattoo on his face. I'm sure when David gets here, he will have more information for us. Now, Kyle, how is your head?"

"My head is just fine, honey. It's my vision that is all fucked at the moment," he casually admits.

I instantly look at Liz and our ICU Nurse instincts kick into high gear.

"What exactly does that mean, Kyle? How is your vision different?" Liz asks, because she knows I can't. I can't begin to think something is wrong with him again. What if this has caused more damage? I'm screaming inside, watching Liz do her unofficial assessment of him, and Liz knows it.

"Well, at the moment, it's darkness. Like how I used to see. No variations in shadows or silhouettes. Just blackness. But my senses are keen and I can tell that Liz is looking right at you, Mindy. Don't be worried. It's all good. Just a little hiccup in my recovery plan. Stop worrying, please. Just come here and sit beside me, please? I need to feel you."

I do as he asks and I get up to sit next to him. Kyle scoots over to make room for me as he pats the bed. "Please, Mind, come here beside me and put your feet up. I want to hold you. I want you to rest for a minute. You have been through hell."

I lay on the bed next to Kyle as he wraps his arms around my shoulder and pulls me in close. The warmth of his body warms me to my soul. I take a slow, relaxing breath as I rest my head on his shoulder. Every muscle in me aches, and I need a shower, but I'm not going anywhere until I know Kyle is stable and can be discharged to go home.

Chapter 52

Doctor Benjamin and the team round early in the morning and enter and see me napping in the recliner.

Doctor Benjamin taps me on the shoulder. "Good morning, sunshine."

I startle and focus on the group. "Hello, everyone. I'm sorry, I fell asleep for a minute. How is our patient doing today?" I ask.

"His CT scan was negative, no evidence of a head bleed or any other abnormalities. His neurological exam is back to baseline, post-trauma, from his last admission. I'm just waiting for the final exam by Doctor Keller. Once he signs off, then Kyle can probably be discharged later today."

"Why does Doctor Keller need to see him again?"

"It's just a precautionary measure since his vision has changed. It should be nothing, just a formality, Mindy. We'll keep you posted, okay?"

"Um, okay. Thanks."

"Mindy, don't sound so worried, honey. I'm fine. Let's just wait and see what he says and then let's get out of here, okay? Oh, I almost forgot. David said he has some updates for us. He will be by later to catch us up on the new developments."

Doctor Keller arrives two hours later and reviewed all of Kyle's images and performed a bedside exam on Kyle.

"Kyle, I would like to give you my findings and recommendations in private, if you don't mind. I really feel you need to be the first person to hear my assessments."

"Actually Doc, Mindy here is my better half, and she knows the medical lingo, so if you don't mind, just lay it on the line and tell me."

I make eye contact with Doctor Keller as my eyes fill with tears. He gives a slight nod of his head. Dear Lord, I know what's coming next.

"Okay, Kyle, Mindy, I have examined all the test results. Yes, your CAT scan was negative, but I'm worried about your vision. In my experience, when someone has made progress, and then loses partial or all their progress, the resulting vision loss is usually permanent. Now, there have been rare exceptions, but I don't want you to get your hopes up. Kyle, I'm sorry I have to deliver such a bleak prognosis, but you need to know."

"There are no more medical treatments available to me at this time, Doc? So, you're telling me my vision change is permanent? How can that be? I was starting to get some vision back. I'm not ready for this to be final. I won't accept that, Doc."

"I understand, Kyle, and I'm sorry to have to be the one to deliver this news. I'm never ready to give my final diagnosis to a patient. I just wanted to be honest with you. There are always exceptions, so hopefully one day you will beat the odds. I'll make you a follow-up appointment with me in my office in three months, and we'll see how you are doing then. Hang in there, and we'll see then if things have changed. I'll see you both soon."

Doctor Keller leaves the room and I can see the deflation in Kyle's hopes. He is shattered and worn out. Small tears develop in my eyes as I ache for him. His hopes of recovery are squashed. I'm heartbroken for him and me.

"Kyle, can I get you anything, honey?"

"No, I just want to be alone for a few minutes, Mind. David will be here soon and I want to talk to him. Can you go hang out with Liz for a while? I'll let you know when we're heading home, okay?"

"I'll be in the cafeteria if you need me. Liz and I will grab a coffee." I lean over and kiss Kyle gently on the lips, as I know he is wrestling with his emotions over his new diagnosis.

Chapter 53

I quietly enter the room, carrying a vanilla milkshake for my brother, Kyle.

"Hey, bro, the coffee here sucks, so I thought you might like a milkshake instead. They are actually pretty good."

"Thanks, man, I'm not really hungry, but you know I love ice cream, so give it here. I'll try it."

"How have you been doing? Any news?"

"Yeah, the bottom line is Doctor Keller said this new vision loss is permanent. What the hell am I going to do now? How will I work? How will I live the life I'm used to living? I guess I won't, will I? It's a whole new world for me now. David, how can I give Mindy the life she deserves and the life I want to give her when I'm blind? She deserves so much more. She's going to stay with me out of pity. She's gonna try to fix me. She's a fixer, and there is no fixing me. She can't cure me. Not this time. She will never get over that."

"Kyle, Mindy loves you for the real person that you have shared with her. The true Kyle. The man who loves music, the beach, and respects those people who truly help themselves. You have a good heart, Kyle. You're a lawyer with morals. A lawyer who represents the underdog, because somebody needs to, and you're amazing at it. Your reputation is impeccable and well respected. You will be amazing and do the right thing. You always do."

"Yeah. Doing the right thing is what I'm afraid of. How can I be selfish and keep something that deserves to be showered in love and goodness by someone whole? Not stay in a relationship out of sympathy with someone who is permanently defective. I need to think about this, David. I mean, really think. I need to examine morals and do what is right."

"Kyle, for God's sake, don't do anything stupid that you will regret, man. I see your wheels turning. I know how you think."

"I just need some time. I need to process all this."

"I know this is huge, and you probably have a million emotions going on right now, but take it one step at a time. Now, you need some nutrition. I haven't seen you eat since yesterday. Drink this amazing milkshake before it melts, please? And remember, they are planning on discharging you later this afternoon. I'm sure Liz and Mindy will be here to visit and follow us home. I think they want to help you get settled in at Mom and Dad's."

"Well, that won't be hard. I grew up there. I know my way around pretty good."

Chapter 54

David is driving Kyle home, with me and Liz in hot pursuit. I'm quiet and watchful as my stomach is in a knot, waiting for Kyle to crack. He hasn't said much to me all day and appears withdrawn. I look at Liz in worry, and she knows. Silence understood. I sit there and observe, waiting for the other shoe to drop because my gut knows it will.

I help to escort Kyle inside and to the couch. Fresh flowers fill the room and Kyle's parents are there as a receiving party. Mrs. Masterson is trying not to hover over her youngest son, but the concerned momma is not too far away. She looks up at me and fakes a smile, unspoken words break my heart. She knows.

Mrs. Masterson breaks the ice with the announcement that dinner is ready. She has made bacon cheeseburgers with killer onion rings and French fries. Apparently, a favorite of Kyle's.

Small talk and light conversations keep the time moving as night slowly approaches. I'm anxious and want to get a few private minutes with Kyle, so I offer to walk Kyle up to his old room and help him get ready for bed. He willingly accepts, and hope blooms within my aching heart, although my gut is telling me something different.

"Kyle, baby. Please let me help you get undressed and get ready for bed. This is what I do. Let me help you."

"No, Mind," Kyle says forcefully. "I can do it. That's the point. I don't want you to take care of me. You take care of people all day. I don't want you burdened when you come home and have to take care of me. Mindy, can you please just leave me alone? I need you to go."

"Kyle, please don't push me away. I love you and it doesn't matter to me if you can see or not. You told me once that you could see me, even in the darkest of times, you could still see me. That is enough for me."

"It's not enough for me, Mindy. And it's not fair to you. You deserve so much more. Someone who can give all of himself to you in every way. Someone who can be independent and love you, and take care of you the way you deserve. Not someone who will be dependent on you for the rest of your life. That's not a life partner, that's a burden. I refuse to be a burden to someone as beautiful and independent as you. You deserve more. You deserve the dream, Mindy."

"Kyle, honey, don't—"

"My God, Mindy, I never expected to fall in love with such a wonderful human being like you. You are everything I have ever wanted. You're thoughtful, caring, sweet, and selfless. You give one hundred percent of yourself to your patients and their families. I can't ask you to come home and give more of yourself to me. I won't do it. Even if you want to. I refuse to put you through that. I love you so much, so much that it hurts me to let you stay. I must let you go, sweetheart. You have to go, even if you don't want to. I'm not giving you a choice, Mind. You have to leave and never look back. You must, and save yourself for someone deserving of you. Someone who can be your better half, not your dependent, needy half. Someone who can give you everything. Someone who can actually physically see you. Mindy, this is me telling you to leave. Now! Please!" Kyle points toward the door and whispers, "Please, Mind. Go. Be free. Leave me alone. Goodbye, my love."

"Kyle, honey, I'm not leaving you. I took care of you at your worst when you were my patient. I certainly can take care of you now that you are healed. I can be your support and your rock now."

"That's just it, Mindy. You don't get it. I'm not healed, and I don't want you to take care of me. I want to take care of you, and I can't. So leave. Now!" Kyle raises his voice and begins to shake. "Mindy. Don't make me be ugly. I don't want to be mean. But if that's what it takes to make you leave, then I will."

"Kyle, I know we can work this out. Just let me—"

"*No!*" Kyle yells.

I crumble emotionally as I look up and see David in the doorway. He probably heard Kyle raise his voice and came running to his rescue. David gives a slight nod as he slowly backs out of the room.

"Mindy no! Just go. I don't want your pity or your help. I just want to be alone. I don't want you. This is me setting you free. Don't look back, just back away!"

Chapter 55

I quietly remain in the hallway. I inhale sharply as I hear the distraught tone of Kyle's voice. I know my brother, and I know how much this is killing him. I had an idea Kyle would do this, save Mindy from a lifetime of wondering what could have been. I just didn't realize Kyle would do it this soon. I slowly creep away and sneak back downstairs to Liz.

"Hey, Liz, I need to chat with you for a minute. It's really important."

Liz looks up and excuses herself from the casual conversation she is having with my mom.

"Hey, what's up?"

"Honey, Kyle is going through a lot, and I'm afraid he is taking it all out on Mindy. She is going to need you in a minute. Take her home and be with her. Support her and be there for her. Okay? Take care of her for me and Kyle, please?"

"David, what's going on?"

"I think Kyle is cutting her loose. Setting her free, so to speak. It's going to get ugly before Mindy gives in. I'm afraid Kyle is going to say things that will make her leave. My heart is breaking for them. Please, Liz. I'm so sorry for her. Take care of her for us, please? And I'll call you later to check-in. I have a feeling she'll be down here in a minute. I just wanted to give you a heads-up."

Liz looks at me and tears are forming in her eyes. "I'll try to be tough for Mindy. But David, this sucks and you know it."

"It certainly does, baby. It certainly does. Be careful, and I'll call you later."

As I finish that thought, there is yelling coming from upstairs.

"Mindy, I'm not your next nursing project! You can't fix me! I'm a fucking man. I'm broken forever. I don't want you anymore! How much plainer can I say it? I'm done with you. Take your fixer attitude and leave. Don't look back. I don't need you, so just fucking go!"

Liz looks at me and mumbles, "Holy shit. David, those are the words that will break her forever. Her pride and joy are the love and care she gives to people. He did it, he really did it. He just broke her."

I sigh in agreement as I know the devastation those words just caused.

Chapter 56

I have no words left. How do you argue with a man when they say they don't want you anymore? There is no argument. He has broken me and he knows it. I'm done. I look at my Greek god one last time, never realizing how weak he could be, and run out of the room. I never say goodbye. I just leave and head for the front door. Liz looks up at me as I grab the front door handle. No words needed.

Liz finds me at the car, hunched over, hyperventilating, and crying. She grabs the keys from me and orders me into the passenger side. "You're in no shape to drive today. I've got you. Just relax and let me take care of you for a change."

Hearing those words opens my floodgates. I cry all the way home and half the night. I'm up all night, tossing and turning and pacing as Liz attempts to comfort me. Finally, around 5:00 a.m., I drift off to sleep. My journal is at my side, open on my bed to the last page I was writing.

Today I lost what was the love of my life. Kyle is such a wonderful man. He is warm, considerate, and fucking hot as hell. He loves me! He told me so. Finally, someone who loves me for me, just as I am. I've waited my whole life for him, and now he's gone. He is so selfless that he is depriving himself of happiness to set me free. Now I don't feel free. I feel trapped in a new, loveless, lonely life. I'm so heartbroken. I saw this coming; my gut knew it was going to happen. My damn instincts are never wrong. Shit! This one time I wanted them to be wrong. My heart is just in denial. How will I ever get over My Greek god?

Chapter 57

I send off a text to David. I know it's wicked early, but if he's anything like me, he'll be up. He probably stayed up all night taking care of Kyle.

Good morning. I hope you are doing ok. Not so good on this end. Up all night with Mindy. How's things with you?

Her phone immediately pings back. *Same here. Kyle feels like shit. Didn't want to hurt Mindy. He loves her.*

I know he does. He's setting her free for her own good. Not sure she will ever accept that.

I agree. Want to meet me this afternoon for a break and some us time? I need to see you.

I'm in. Let's see how it goes today. Maybe after lunch? I'll call you.

David sends back a heart emoji and my heart melts. *I'm so lucky.*

Chapter 58

I sleep in until ten and awaken to silence. My life is back to "pre-Kyle status." Boring, quiet, and alone. I grab a shower and get a good look at myself in the mirror. *Jesus, I'm a disaster. My eyes are sore and red and puffy as hell, and my nose looks like Rudolph's. I don't think I have any tears left to cry.*

I walk out to the living room and Liz is waiting for me with a cup of hot coffee. She's the best. She wraps me in a big hug and holds me tight as I exhale loudly and attempt to keep my emotions tucked away. I'm tired of crying and being angry. Just plain old tired.

"Hey, Liz, thanks for staying, honey. I know I haven't been great company, but just knowing you are here helps. I'm sorry I haven't said much."

"No need to explain. I get it. I'm here whenever you need me. Just get it together at your own pace and when you're ready to talk, I'll listen."

"Liz, you know my life will never be the same now, right? I mean, I love him. Our relationship started as being off limits, and then it miraculously had a chance to slowly grow into something more. I never in a million years thought the Greek god would ever be mine. I felt so lucky, and now not so much. Whoever said, 'It's better to have loved and lost than to never have loved at all,' is full of shit. I could strangle that person. They obviously have never lost someone because this sucks. I'll never be the same, Liz. I'm so angry and I'm done."

"Mindy, honey, don't let this ruin you for someone in the future. You never know what the future holds. Please don't be bitter."

"I'm not bitter. I'm sad he tossed me away so quickly. That he didn't want to fight for us. That he gave in to his fears instead of giving us a chance. It could have been great because we were already great. I'll compare everyone to him, always. I'm done searching for men, I'm done looking at men in that way, and I'm done caring about what people think. I'm just done. I'm living for me now. Fuck everybody else."

"Mindy, that's not like you, honey. Just give it time. I promise this will get easier."

"Yes, well, fuck that person who said, 'Time heals all wounds,' too! I'm getting angry at everyone and everything. I think I might take a week off and just go away. Just me, and go hibernate. Learn to work on Mindy, and screw everyone else."

"That sounds great in theory, honey, but I don't know if you have it in your genetic makeup to do that. You're an ICU nurse, for God's sake, a selfless job. You wouldn't be doing that if it wasn't part of who you are."

"Well, I've been thinking about that, too. Maybe it's time for a job change, too. Enough about caring so much for people. I need a break. Maybe I'll become a florist or a dog sitter. A job where things don't talk back. I don't know, Liz. I feel so lost."

"I'm heartbroken for you, Mind. I really am. I know there's nothing I can do to make it better, just know that I love you and I care."

"I know that, and thanks. You really are my best friend. I'm truly sorry I have been such a needy friend this year. This is not like me and it's going to change. Thank you and I love you, girl."

"I love you, too. Would you mind if I took off for a while? I want to go see David for a bit and I'll be back later. Are you okay with that?"

"Absolutely. I could use a little alone time, no offense."

"None taken, my dear. I won't be gone but a few hours. I'll see you in a bit." Liz grabs her keys and heads for the door as she takes one last look at me.

"I'll be fine," I say as I stare into space, just holding my coffee cup. "Go have some fun with David. I'll be okay, I promise. And stop giving me that look."

"What look?"

"The one you give patients' families when their loved one is going to die. That sympathy look. I'm not dying, Liz. Just heartbroken. Big difference."

"I know, Mind, but my heart breaks for you. But you are one of the strongest people I know. Take a deep breath and clear your mind to make a plan. You always do."

"I think you're right. I'm going to make a plan. I'll share it with you when you get back. Go and enjoy your day, please. I'll see you soon."

"Love you, sis," Liz shouts as she closes the door behind her, and I'm alone again.

Chapter 59

I'm sitting on the couch zoning out when my phone rings. It startles me back to reality. "Unknown" shows on the screen and I think I'm going to puke. *Oh, my God, not again. I can't do this again.* I take a deep breath and answer the phone.

"Hello?"

"May I speak with Miss Mindy Harper, please?"

"This is she. How may I help you?"

"This is Private Detective Officer Randi Newman from Beach City police department. I need to inform you that your presence is requested at the police department tomorrow at noon. You will need to give a statement regarding the events that took place on Saturday night. Please bring with you any witnesses or persons that can corroborate your story. I will meet you there at noon sharp. Do you have any questions, Miss Harper?"

"Um, just one. Where is Mr. Levin currently?"

"Ma'am, he is behind bars until his arraignment later this week."

"Thank you, Officer. I'll see you tomorrow." I hang up and relief floods my system. My head feels like it's going to split open, but I can finally breathe. The hold this man has had over me is finally easing up. I need to learn to relax and begin to redefine myself again. But who is Mindy Harper now? I have no clue. It's time to find out.

With renewed determination and a little bit of leftover anger, I decide to continue the crusade to take charge of my life and be selfish for once. I grab my laptop off the coffee table and search for quick getaways. I'm going to take a trip. To really do it. To have a week of selfish Mindy time. No one to take care of, no one to answer to, and go where no one will know Mindy Harper. I can define myself in any way I want. I can become someone else for the week. *I'm doing it!*

I search the web and come across an all-inclusive resort in St. Maarten. Hmm, now that's an idea. Half French and half Dutch. The best of both worlds. I continue my search as more information comes across my screen. Luxury villas with private pools, private chefs, and private charter service to other islands. What better way to escape than to really escape?

I book the villa for Wednesday's arrival, thinking this will give me time to meet with the police on Monday, and pack on Tuesday for departure on Wednesday. Renewed excitement flows through me. *This is going to be awesome!*

Liz returns from her outing with David and I'm relaxed and smiling. "What's going on, Mind? When I left, you looked like death warmed over, and now you look like the real Mindy."

"I did something totally out of character and I'm so excited about it. I'm taking a trip and I leave on Wednesday."

"What? You're kidding, right?"

"Nope, I'm not. I need a break, and I want some alone time. I leave Wednesday for a week. I'm going to St. Maarten and I booked a private villa. Its activities are amazing, Liz. I booked a spa day, a day of sailing with other guests, a snorkel day, and of course, a day of touring and shopping. This is going to be epic."

"You really did it, didn't you? Do you want me to come?"

"Liz, honey, I love you, but I need to do this myself. I need you to cover one of my shifts for me, but I'll be back next week, just in time to work the rest of my schedule. Will you do that for me?"

"You know I will, Mind. I hope this helps you recover from these last several months."

"It's a start. One day at a time, right?"

"That's what they say. Oh hey, David told me you would be getting a call from an officer about an appointment tomorrow."

"Yeah, he called right after you left this morning. I need to meet him with my witnesses at noon tomorrow. Are you coming?"

"Of course, I am. I watched that freak torment the shit out of you. Of course, I'll be there. David has already contacted T. and his men, along with the Vipers' president, Crazy Harry. I think they have their appointments later in the afternoon, though."

"I want to see T. I really need to thank him. He was wonderful and so were his guys."

"David said he's coming at noon during your meeting."

"Good. Although I'm not ready to see Kyle again, Liz. I'm not sure I can handle that. How am I going to get out of that one?"

"Actually, Mind, David already took care of that, too. Remember when Kyle said his firm represented The Creeks?"

"Yes, he told T. that he was on medical leave and one of his associates would be happy to follow up with him."

"Exactly. So, Kyle's medical problem still exists, and he has arranged for one of his partners to be present for The Creeks tomorrow. Kyle will be staying home with his parents while David comes and gives a statement on your behalf."

"Wow. Kyle says he doesn't want me, but he's still taking care of things from the sidelines. If only he had faith in us and himself. It's so sad, a chance for happiness just dismissed so easily. I hope one day he can beat the odds and see again, for his sake."

"Me, too, Mind. But I have to say honestly, I don't think letting you go was an easy decision for him. I think he loves you so much that he had to let you go. I'm not taking sides by any means, Mind, but try to think about what you would do if you were in his position. It's a tough decision, isn't it?"

I look at Liz and I can see her point. She amazes me as the ever-objective sense of reasoning. When my emotions cloud my judgment, she can always help me clear the fog and make a rational decision. Best friend ever.

"Hang in there, honey, and remember, I love you."

"Love you, too, Liz, and thanks for always being honest with me."

"I got you, girl, always."

It's the Monday meeting and everyone is in the waiting room on my behalf. The clerk comes out and calls me, my mom and dad, David, T., and Liz into the conference room.

"Please take a seat and the officer and scribe will be with you all in a moment."

My gut is in a knot and my heart is pounding in my ears.

Liz looks over at me and sees me trying to keep it together. "Mindy, look at me. You got this, girl! It's just a formality. Just close your eyes and breathe."

I do as Liz suggests and exhale slowly as I try and relax until the door to the conference room closes and Liz gasps. My eyes immediately spring open to see John-John walking down the aisle toward me.

"John-John, what the hell are you doing here?" I ask in a fit of nervousness. "Miss Harper, let me introduce myself. I am Detective Officer Randi Newman with Beach City Special Forces."

"What? What are you talking about?" Dad asks.

"I have called you all here to explain what is going on and to answer your questions, and yes, to also definitely take your statements."

"How are you not stuttering? I'm so confused. You are such a different man. You don't even look the same. John-John, what happened?"

"Let me start at the beginning, if I may. Yes, my name is John Marxx Jr. Yes, my father is John Marxx Sr. of the Vipers Motor Cycle Club and yes, your father was in an altercation with my father and was shot. It was definitely not your father's fault, Mindy. That I am one hundred percent sure of."

Detective Newman looks at Mr. Harper and addresses him directly. "Mr. Harper, there is no way that accident was your fault. I have examined the evidence a hundred times, and you were not at fault. Please know that and forgive yourself, because I have. I moved on long ago and losing my dad, in retrospect, made me a better man."

I look up at my dad to see his eyes glazing over with tears. He is struggling to keep it together as my mom holds his hand. He patiently listens.

"After my father's death, I was sent away by my mother to a home for orphaned children. She was embarrassed by me and my speech impediment, so she sent me away so she wouldn't have to listen to me and my imperfection. There, I learned to speak properly with the assistance of a wonderful teacher. But my sister, Patricia, was allowed to stay behind and was raised by my dysfunctional mother.

"After high school, I changed my name to Randi Newman and enrolled in the police academy. I became John-John Marxx again last year in order to do some undercover work. I had to fake my stutter for Patricia and Levin to believe I was back in the picture, and that I truly was John Marxx Jr. You see, Mr. Scott Levinthal, lightning bolt, as you call him, Mindy, is my uncle. His brother was my father. I had learned he was abducting women and torturing them in the escape room. When he found out you were still in town, he made you his next target. Mr. Harper, he wanted revenge, and there was no way I was going to let that happen."

I glance around the room and watch everyone as we all listen in silence. I try to swallow down tears, as I can't believe what I'm hearing.

"So, John-John, I'm sorry, I mean, Detective Newman, all those times you came to the hospital and sent me notes and the bracelet, you weren't the stalker?"

"Actually, Mindy, many of the times you saw me, I was there to ensure your safety. I was watching and following Levin almost constantly. It was easy to do when you're his nephew and in the same biker club.

"There were several times he got mighty close to you, and so "John-John" would step in and throw him off your track. The nights I watched you in your apartment parking lot, that was to keep you safe. I had other Intel that led me to believe he was going to kidnap you, so I set up extra surveillance to protect you.

"The notes and the pink bracelet were truly from Levin. I needed to let some events really play out, otherwise he would have known something was not right. I'm sorry you were frightened by those events, but I had to let you experience real feelings. Otherwise, we would have blown the whole plan.

"When I came back as John-John, I needed to play the part to perfection. So, I joined the Vipers as a legacy and became a member like my uncle and father. It was then that I began to put all the pieces together. I had some help from David, also. Would you like to explain from here, David?"

All eyes switch to David as he clears his throat to begin.

"When Mindy came to me and told me she was being followed, I put in a call to my undercover agent. He had been in town for a while and could see the tension between the Vipers and The Creeks growing.

"The Creeks have made tremendous changes within their club for the better, but the Vipers always seemed to have an axe to grind, putting tension on the two clubs. When my department got wind of a possible human trafficking situation within the two clubs, I activated our special agent and put him in place within The Creeks. He has been there for about a year gathering Intel, observing, and recently, protecting Mindy from a distance. He is the one who noticed Levin as a person of interest and started to monitor his actions.

"We have been able to rescue several women that he has abducted, with Mindy being the last woman he will ever touch."

T. looks at David and says, "You're shitting me, right? We vet all our prospects and none of them came back as cops."

"T., this is what detectives do. You wouldn't find any information on him if you tried. Now that this case is closed and we have our man, the integrity of The Creeks Brotherhood has been safely restored and is intact. T., your organization should be commended on its high standards. It truly is a wonderful brotherhood and I wish you all the best with it."

"You're not going to tell me who it is, are you, David?"

"No T., I'm not. That is something we need to discuss in private at another time. This individual is loving being a part of your organization and is truly a dedicated brother in every sense of the word and is very happy there."

"My statement should keep him behind bars for a long time, right?" I ask David.

"Yes, honey, your statement and testimony, if you decide to testify, will be the proverbial nail in the coffin. We have statements from his other victims, but you have many witnesses to assist in giving an account of the events. That is definitely helpful for a possible conviction. Kyle's law firm will represent The Creeks, and I will assist you in getting proper representation."

"Count me in, David. I'll do whatever I need to do to keep Levin off the streets and from touching another woman."

"Thank you, Mind. Now, we will need to question each of you individually, so relax. This is going to take some time."

I'm trying to wrap my head around all this new information. I need to stretch my lags and get up and walk around for a few minutes when Detective Newman calls to me.

"Mindy, can I have a word in private for a minute, please?"

"Sure, what's up?"

"I just wanted you to know how truly sorry I am for the damn pictures I had to send you of my sister, Patricia, and Kyle Masterson. That was not my intention to hurt you like that. It was a shitty thing she did, and there is no excuse. I was stuck in such a position that I couldn't stop the process and the investigation. I really am so sorry."

"It's okay, Detective. I got over it and Mr. Masterson is no longer my concern, so please don't worry about it. Just nail this Levin dude to the wall and I'll be grateful."

"I'll do my best, Mindy."

I see T. talking to David, so I walk over and thank him personally. I grab his arms and give him a big hug.

"What's that for, Mind?"

"I just wanted to say thank you. I had no idea how much you cared and how you and your men were keeping me safe. I'm so thankful."

"Anytime, my dear. That's what we do for family."

Mr. Harper walks up to T. just as Mindy hugs him.

 T. can read the look in his eyes

"T., my heart is full, knowing my daughter is now safe. I am well aware that it's the actions of these men, and The Creeks, that kept her safe."

T. nods and extends his hand to Big Joe, aka my dad, and shakes his hand firmly. "Don't you think it's time to come back to the brotherhood, Big Joe?"

I snap my head up and look at T. and my dad in amazement. *Did he just invite my dad back to become a member of The Creeks Motor Cycle Club? Did I just hear that right?*

Dad looks astonished. "I'm not sure I'm ready for that just yet, T. I'll need to speak with my family first, but it warms my heart to know I'm still welcome."

"Big Joe, you left The Creeks based on an emergency situation. You're in good standing with the club. Think about it. If you want to come back, I'll present it to the club. It's a no brainer, in my opinion."

I'm exhausted and finally home. My statement took three hours, and I think I must have answered a thousand questions. David was there the whole time as my support. He was wonderful and kept the conversation focused. Having a well-known detective in your corner is always a positive thing.

As the night fades, I crawl into bed, barely able to focus. My thoughts are with Kyle and wondering how his day was today. I can't help myself. I don't want to think of Kyle, but I care too much. It's in my nature. It's in my damn DNA.

I'm packing for my trip and Liz is helping me with my wardrobe selections. "Hey, wear this," she yells out from the closet as she flings a dress at me.

"I'm not so sure about this dress yet, Liz. I mean, look at it. It's off the shoulders and it pushes my tits to high heaven. I'm not sure I want to send that kind of message yet."

"Oh, you mean, *I'm fucking hot and I know it* kind of message, Mind?"

"Yeah, that's the one. I mean, I do love this dress. The white with the red flowers, it's stunning and my favorite, but I'm just not ready."

"Mindy, throw in some red come-fuck-me pumps and you'll get laid for sure. Don't you just want to go crazy and let it all out when you're away?"

"I do, but I'm not going to get laid, Liz. I'm going for me. I need some time to reset myself and plan new goals."

"Who says you can't have a little fun in the process? Jesus, you're not dead. Just broken-hearted. What better way to fix a broken heart than a fling with a hot island man? Just imagine, tanned skin, smelling of coconut oil, wavy blonde hair, and sex on the beach! Oh, girl! I can feel the tingle in my jingle now. It's going to happen!"

"Oh, my God, Liz, you're a mess. I can't wear that dress yet. That dress represents sexual confidence to me, and I'm not going out in that dress yet. But I will wear this bikini. It's high-waisted but definitely shows off my assets. You know what I mean?"

"Mind, okay, it's a deal. I still want you to pack some condoms and get laid any chance you get. Fuck like a rabbit and have fun. Take care of you, be carefree, and for God's sake, enjoy yourself. When you get back, I want exact details of every dick you get."

"Oh my God Liz, I can't take it. You're too much. But I promise you will be the first person I tell if I find and conquer a hot island dick! Actually, I'm thinking hot beach surfer dude." I crack myself up at my admission, but it's true.

We are laughing out loud when Liz busts out in a surfer voice.

"Hey, beautiful. I'm a surfer, baby. Want to see my board? It's long and sleek. All waxed and shined up for a slippery wet trip on the folds of the waves. Why don't you come feel my long board? You know you want to."

Liz can barely stop laughing as I'm doubled over holding my stomach laughing so hard.

"I think I might pee myself, Liz. You're freakin' hysterical. I can't take it."

"Actually, Mindy, you can take it and you *will* take it all, and like it. Remember, when the board is hard, long, and sleek, you *will* accommodate it. You can take it, you always do."

"Oh, my God, stop it, Liz. I can't breathe. You're killing me!"

"Ah, remember me when you reach down and feel his long board. You will smile and think, 'Damn, Liz, this long, hard, sleek board is mighty fine indeed. Thank you for suggesting I feel it and examine it. It is very pleasurable indeed.' And then, Mindy, stop thinking of me and have the best rebound sex you have ever had in your life!"

"Okay, it's a deal, Liz. But you do know that I'm not going there to get laid? I'm going there for self-reflection, rest, and emotional growth."

"So you have said, but who says you can't have a little stress relief in the process?"

"Oh, my God!"

Chapter 60

Iarrive at The Villas in St. Maarten and am immediately more relaxed. The air is crisp and clean and warm. The soft breeze tickles my hair and slowly blows across my face. As I put my hair behind my ears and reach for my carry-on bag, I look up into the eyes of Oh, Hello! I'm Mr. Sex Machine. I immediately get that hot tingle and smile as I try to look away from his beauty.

"Hello."

"Hello, ma'am. Welcome to the Villas. I'm Stefan, and I will accompany you to your room. Please, come this way to check in, and then follow me."

I'll follow you wherever you want to go, mister. You are screaming hot, oily, all-day sex in every way. Lord, help me. Maybe Liz was right? Have as much sex as I can and forget my life. Just live in the moment? Hmm, I really need to think about this. He's divine. My inner sex voice is yelling, *Yes, baby, don't think, just enjoy and let's have lots and lots of raunchy vacation sex. Uninhibited hot, off-the-chain, incredible sex!*

I'm watching Mr. I'm Screaming Sex get all my bags and arguing with myself. The uninhibited Slut Mindy versus Miss Goody Two Shoes Mindy.

Miss Goody Two Shoes: *Mindy! Reel it in, girl. Focus! You've been here all of five seconds and you're already eye fucking the help. Get it together, girl! Now that's the sensible Mindy I know and love.*

Slut Mindy: *Already giving this man the 'I'm easy and hot for you. Come fuck me now,' look.*

I'm in so much trouble. This self-reflection stuff may be harder than I think.

Stefan escorts me to my private Villa and opens the door for me. "Welcome to paradise, Miss Harper. I hope you enjoy your stay with us here at The Villas."

"Thank you, Stefan. I plan to." I reach in my purse and give him a tip. As I put my hand in his with the money, I can't help but look him up and down as I repeat "I plan to" and close the door behind him. I exhale heavily as I reel in my hormones and decide it is time for some sunshine and a trashy novel. I change into my swimsuit and coverup and grab my beach bag. I'm planning to roam the grounds and find a secluded spot where I can read and escape reality.

It doesn't take long before I spot a hammock tied between two palm trees. Just like in the brochure. I grab my towel and line the hammock with it, then apply my sunblock. Just as I nestle into the comfort of swinging carelessly between two trees, Stefan appears out of nowhere.

"Miss Harper, may I interest you in a cocktail?"

Hmm…I would love to see your cocktail, Slut Mindy thinks.

"I would love a Piña Colada and a bottled water, please."

"Coming right up, Miss." He disappears as quickly as he came and I have no idea what direction he even came from.

"Here you go Miss Mindy. A Piña Colada and water. Enjoy."

"Stefan, how did you know where I was?"

"It's my job to know where you are, Miss. I am to be at your service, but hidden. This way, you can enjoy your time on the island."

"And what if I didn't want you hidden?" Slut Mindy asks, all flirty.

"It's my job, ma'am. Although I'm very good at keeping secrets." He flashes a sultry smile.

"I bet you are. I'm sure this is not your first time servicing a guest."

"I guess it depends on your definition of servicing, Miss Harper."

"Hmm, I bet it does." I look him up and down again over my sunglasses and my tingle is in full force and the jingle is on fire today!

"Thanks, Stefan. I'm good for now, and please call me Mindy."

"Yes ma'am. Enjoy, and I'll check on you later."

I read all day and work on my tan. I napped, flipped over a few times, and relaxed as I listened to the music from the pool bar. The sun is warming my inner soul as it seeps down into my bones. The smell of coconut sunblock acts as an aphrodisiac and I'm secretly wishing for a hidden afternoon delight, but I'll never admit that to sensible Mindy, that's for sure.

Time has passed quickly, and its already dinnertime as sunset is fast approaching. I stay on the beach a little longer and watch the beautiful sky colors of pink and orange fade into the night. The twinkle lights on the trees pop on, and it takes my breath away. It's stunning and romantic and there are thousands of them entwined in the palm trees. I look up and begin to cry. If only Kyle were here to see this. *I hope and pray every night he will be able to see one day.*

I head for my villa to take a long bubble bath and call room service. I unlock my hotel room door and enter to find a large bouquet of flowers awaiting my arrival, along with a fresh fruit and cheese platter. I reach for the card and hold my breath, waiting to see the words.

Remember, we love you.
Enjoy yourself and take care of you.
Love Mom and Dad.

Tears leak out of my eyes because I know my parents are worried about me. They were so sweet to send me something so nice and thoughtful. But truth be told, I was hoping for an olive branch from Kyle. Something that would have an apology attached or a shred of hope. Anything that would make me feel like I wasn't discarded so easily. But nothing. Nothing from Kyle. Instead, my loving parents keep me grounded, forever making me feel like I am the most important person in the world. Thank God for them.

Tears of thankfulness turn to tears of realization. It's really over. He meant every painful word he said to me. I ache all over as I head for the tub. A hot bath should help cure that, and who needs room service when there is fruit and cheese?

An hour later, I get out of the tub. I'm wrinkled like a raisin, and my muscles are weak from floating in the Jacuzzi for so long. I feel light and clean and soft as silk. The Villa bath lotions are to die for. I make a mental note to check out the brand so I can buy some online when I get home. Soaking in this scent at home would be a nice treat.

The hotel robe fits like a glove. It's warm and fluffy and soft and makes for a wonderful snuggle robe. Who needs clothes when you have a room all to yourself? You can dress or not dress. There is nobody to please but yourself, so naked under the robe it is.

I grab myself a glass of white wine and walk out onto the patio and lean down on the railing. I'm enjoying the night and watching the twinkling lights down by the beach sparkle under the palm trees. The view, even from my first-floor villa, is stunning. I can hear and smell the ocean. Perfection.

As I'm leaning on my elbows on the railing, I close my eyes and inhale the night. It is soft and warm and with an occasional slow breeze. My nipples harden as the breeze gently blows, and I realize the top of my robe has fallen open. No one can see me, so I continue my slow yoga breathing as I breathe in the night and listen to the music around me.

Suddenly I get the feeling I'm being watched. My neck hair is at attention and my eyes fly open. There he is, stopped on the pathway next to my villa, watching. I recognize him instantly. It's Stefan and he can pretty much see all of me. It's too late to cover myself now, as that would be obvious, so I do nothing and enjoy the moment. I make no effort to hide myself. It's time for confidence building.

"Hey, Stefan. Nice night for a walk."

"Yes, it is, ma'am. You never know what amazing things you might see on a beautiful night walk like this."

"Will I see you tomorrow?"

"That's a definite. Have a nice night." He waves and smiles a devilish grin as I watch him stride back toward the main building of the resort.

I smile as I look down at my open robe. Holy shit, the breeze had pushed the lapels of my robe open even further, and one whole boob was completely visible. Hard nipples and all. Well, that explains the devilish grin. Thank you, Caribbean breeze.

Day two is spa day. I scheduled a full day of pampering, complete with a one-and-a-half-hour hot oil massage, a facial, a mani-pedi appointment, and a seaweed wrap. I'm not so sure if I want the mud bath or spray tanning. The nurse in me can't get past the fact that I might get mud in certain nooks and crannies that are inappropriate, so I'm doing the spray tanning. No sense in getting a sunburn when I can enjoy a spray tan, too. I also book a beauty appointment. It is time for a hair and face makeover. I enlist the expertise of the spa salon to add strawberry blonde highlights to my hair and wax my eyebrows. I'm even getting eyelash extensions.

Tony, the salon expert, hands me a mirror. "My dear, just look at yourself. You are stunning. You were pretty before, but my God. You are a vixen now!"

I look at myself in the mirror and I'm speechless. "I don't even know who this is looking back at me, Tony! You are a magician. How did you do this?"

"My dear, a little highlighting perfection, and just some eyebrow magic. The rest is just your natural beauty. You are stunning, and don't let anyone ever tell you otherwise."

"Thank you, Tony. You have no idea how much I needed this. I am forever grateful."

"It is my pleasure, my dear. We aim to please here at the villas."

I leave Tony with a big hug and a big fat tip to boot. I have some renewed confidence in myself and can't wait to show it off tomorrow.

Day three is another adventure. Sailing day with ten other people aboard the catamaran *Majesty*. Even the name sounds relaxing. I continue with my new sense of self and break out the bikini. I haven't worn a two-piece bathing suit in a million years, but it's time.

Feeling and looking amazing in my new cover-up, I strut to the dock to board the boat. With my head high and perfect posture, I reach for the hand offered to help me safely board the boat. When I look up and say "Thank you," I look into Stefan's eyes.

Surprise and hidden heat make me lose my footing and balance as I attempt to step onto the boat. Stefan grabs me by the waist to steady me and safely guides me off the steps onto the boat deck.

"Stefan, good morning. Thank you for catching me. I almost fell."

"No problem, Mindy. I'm here to assist in any way I can."

"What are you doing here? I thought you worked in The Villas?"

"I do miss. I mean, when I'm not the captain of this catamaran."

"What? You're the captain of this boat?"

"Yes, ma'am. This is my boat and we sail three days a week. The other two days I help out in the lobby of The Villas."

"Oh, so this is really your boat? I'm so surprised."

"Why is that? Were you expecting the Gorton's Fisherman?"

"Something like that, but this is a pleasant surprise. I'm happy to be here."

"I'm happy you're here, too. Now please, watch your footing around here, okay? And have a great time. I want you to enjoy yourself."

"Oh, I will. Don't worry."

I gather my sea legs and walk down to the seats and claim my spot, a few rows in front of the captain's wheel. A perfect spot where Stefan can't help but see me all day. *Perfect!* my slutty inner voice is yelling. *Now slowly take off your cover-up and sensually put on your sunblock. Make sure you flip your hair and really rub the sunscreen all over your chest. Be sure to lower your straps just enough so your cleavage is showing, and rub the girls good. Don't want sunburned tits. Don't be afraid to show more skin, you'll have him steering this boat with a boner all day!*

Be quiet! I yell at myself. *I want to have fun. I'm not here to pick up men, although a little flirting never hurt anyone.*

The sun is full and hot with not a cloud in the sky, as the ocean delivers perfect sailing conditions. I, and a few other guests, spread out on the catamaran's canvas and sunbathe. I'm relaxed and enjoying the rhythmic movement of the boat as I watch Stefan occasionally through my sunglasses. He's tall and tanned, with a toned muscular body. Lethal combinations.

I wonder what he is thinking. He sees so many vacationers every day. I'm sure this is just another workday for him. But for me, it's definitely eye candy.

I am thoroughly enjoying lunch and casual conversation with other passengers. Everyone is so nice and happy. Not a negative thought or conversation all day. How wonderful. I excuse myself as I head for the ladies' room. When I open the door to leave, I look up and physically run into Stefan.

"Oh, hi, Stefan. How's it going?"

"I'm good. Are you having a good time today, I hope?"

"This is amazing. Your boat is beautiful, and this place is so cool. The Caribbean island décor and atmosphere is just perfect. I absolutely love it. It's just like I imagined it would be."

"I'm glad you're having a great day. Be careful on the way back. You look like you're getting a little pink. You may need more sunscreen."

"Thanks for the tip. How long does it take to get back?"

"We'll be at sea another two hours at least. It really depends on the winds."

"Thanks. I'll see you soon." I head back to the table.

The trip home is uneventful. I stretch out on the canvas before Stefan, slowly applying sunscreen in all the right places, and soaking up more sun. I eventually take a nap under the Caribbean sun, but not before staring at Stefan for a while through my sunglasses.

Stefan helped me off the boat as we disembark upon returning to The Villas' dock.

"If you need any aloe lotion put on that sunburn on your back tonight, just call me. I'm at your service," Stefan whispers to me.

"I'll remember that and thank you for a great day."

"It was my pleasure, Miss Harper."

Day four is all about resting and relaxing, with a little shopping thrown in. I can't go home without buying my family and Liz a gift. I wander around town and see the island folk. As I shop my way through town, I come upon a jewelry store. In the window is an emerald and diamond bangle bracelet. I walk in and asked if I can see the bracelet. It's amazingly shiny and beautiful and reminds me of the islands. On my wrist, it fits perfectly and sparkles like the twinkle lights I love so much. I strike up a deal with the salesman and leave with the bracelet safely on my wrist. I'm proud as a peacock and happy with my only purchase for myself. Now I can get rid of that pink bracelet that was gifted to me. It has such bad memories, and I'll replace it with something stunning. Mission accomplished.

I buy linens for my mom and a typical island t-shirt for Liz and my dad. I'm having so much fun just browsing around. I don't realize how far I've walked until I notice a sign that reads: Welcome to the French Quarter. I cross the street and I'm now on the French side of the island. *How cool is this? Maybe I need a tour?*

I grab a car service and ask the man for a tour of the French side of the island.

"What do you want to see? There are mainly resorts and a few nudist beaches. Otherwise, it's all the same."

"Excuse me, did you say nudist beaches?"

"Yes, ma'am. We have clothing-optional beaches on the French side. Even a clothing-optional restaurant."

"Really? Okay, that's where I want to go. I think I want to have an afternoon cocktail and appetizer at that restaurant."

"Yes, ma'am, but be prepared. If you're dressed, you're the minority."

"Thank you, I'll consider myself warned."

The driver drops me off in front of The Full View Bar and Grill. *Seriously? This is gonna be epic!* I walk in and immediately notice everyone who is sitting down and eating is naked. The wait staff is clothed, for health reasons, but not the patrons. I immediately feel overdressed and uncomfortable.

The hostess approaches. "Would you like to eat indoors or out on the patio in the sand?"

"Oh, I'll take outside, please."

The hostess shows me to my table and there is not a dressed person in sight.

The hostess leans over and whispers, "Ma'am, if you would like to change, the restrooms are over there. Please feel free to express yourself and be comfortable."

"Thank you. Is it that obvious that I've never been here before?"

"Yes, ma'am. It's a clothing-optional beach, but as you see, no one is using the option to stay dressed. No one knows you here, so you might as well look like everyone else. If you stay dressed, you'll stand out even more. But it's just an option. Hence, clothing optional."

"Thank you for the advice. I'll think about it."

I sit and try to relax as I look around and watch the beachgoers. They are in total bliss and act like there is nothing wrong with being naked. People are sitting together and playing cards, sunbathing, and swimming, all naked and comfortable.

I've check out the menu, place my order, and then head to the ladies' powder room.

"Well, when in Rome," I tell myself. I strip down and place my clothes in my shopping bag, and head back to my table. I'm butt-naked, feeling weird but strangely free.

I look around to see if anyone is staring at me or checking me out, because that will be a hard stop, and I will dress in an instant. But as I look around, nobody cares and nobody is watching me. Life continues as normal and nobody is paying any attention to the woman sitting at the patio table in the sand, wearing only an emerald and diamond bracelet. Nobody except the man walking out of the water. He is looking straight at me and no one else. I can feel it. He sits on his beach chair, facing the sun, and just watches me. I can feel it, but something in me is intrigued by this man, but not afraid.

He's tanned, muscular, and blonde. He's the epitome of a cross between a surfer dude and a lifeguard. Basically, a gift from the heavens. He sits back and reclines in his chair and places his straw hat over his face. Just enough to hide his face from onlookers, but enough to see out. He looks like someone who fell asleep, but he's mysterious and still watching.

I'm drinking my cocktail and waiting for my food when I look around and people watch, seeing all shapes and sizes, men, and women alike. I try not to stare, but how can I not when everyone has their "everythings" hanging out for the world to see? It's a good thing I still have my sunglasses on, otherwise, people would yell at me for staring.

And then I realize the way men have to put on sunblock! It's crazy. Who would have thought they need to sunblock their junk? I have never seen anyone do that. It's the craziest thing I've ever seen. *There is something definitely wrong with pulling it that far out, and then rubbing it all the way up and down with SPF 70! This is not normal, but I guess it's better than a sunburned dick. That would be horrible.*

I smile to myself as a thought crosses my mind. *Explain sunburned penises to Liz. Oh, my God.*

I take another sip of my drink as I catch a view of the straw hat man. Whoa! My vision halts and I watch. He's beautiful and tanned everywhere. I mean everywhere. He has no tan lines, just a six-pack line on that amazing flat stomach of his. That abdomen is priceless and holy hell. There is no sunburn on that masterpiece hanging between his legs either. The size is generous, and it's a work of art. Perfect in every way.

Between my legs is suddenly on fire, and my pulse quickens. *Jesus, Mindy, calm down, girl! You're naked, for fuck's sake. Don't you dare! Save it for the bedroom. Now shut that shit down, slut sister!*

I adjust my position in my seat in an attempt to become more comfortable. The man in the straw hat watches and waits. He sees me staring at him. He takes out the sunblock and reapplies it all over, all the while never cracking a smile. I try to look away, but I can't. I'm so fascinated by all this naked freedom. I need to watch as much of it as I can without being too obvious.

I watch as the straw hat man sits back and relaxes, never deviating from looking straight ahead. I'm starting to relax in my new nakedness and I'm enjoying my meal. I'm enjoying my second cocktail when I see him make his move. The straw hat man gets up and approaches my table. Just as he gets in front of me, he takes off his hat and politely asks me, while I'm drinking my cocktail, "May I join you, please?"

I look up at the beach beauty and choke on my Piña Colada. I cough and spit my drink across the table. I'm mortified to see that the gorgeous man standing beautifully in front of me, in all his glorious nakedness, is Stefan.

"Um, I'm so sorry," Stefan says. "That's not the answer I was looking for. Are you okay, Mindy? I didn't mean to startle you and make you choke. I'm so sorry."

"You didn't startle me. I'm just so embarrassed. I've never done this before and I was staring at you forever. You must think I am a stalker. I would have never stared so long and been rude if I knew it was you. I just thought you were some random naked beach guy that I could just enjoy watching while I did something new and crazy. This whole experience is fascinating to me."

"So, you enjoyed watching me, did you?"

"How could I not? Look at you. You're beautiful."

"Mindy, you are just as beautiful. Stunning actually."

"Well, thank you, and yes, please sit down. Your junk is eye level and in my face. I can't keep eye contact with that distraction calling out to me, '*Look at me, look at me, here I am for your enjoyment and distraction!*'" I throw my arms in the air like I'm waving at someone.

Stefan lets out a belly laugh and pulls up a chair. "That was the best answer I have ever heard, Miss Harper."

"I'm figuring honesty is the policy here, since there is nothing to hide behind. No clothes to protect me, and no villa to go run to in embarrassment. I'm letting it all hang out, so to speak, literally, so I might as well really let it all out and own it."

"Miss Harper, you're hysterical. I find you so refreshing. Please let me buy you another drink, since you just lost the last one all over the table. It's the least I can do."

"Thank you, Stefan. That would be lovely. Tell me, what brings you here to naked city?"

"It's my only day off this week, and I wanted to do something free spirited and go where no one would find me. That is, until you showed up."

"I'm sorry to bother you on your day off. I was just out shopping and wanted to do something different. My cab driver suggested this place. This trip for me is all about self-examination and doing things boring old Mindy wouldn't do. I thought I could add this to my list of wild and crazy moments."

"I think you definitely should add it. Finish your drink and I'll help you add something else to your list." Stefan smiles.

"I'm not sure I like the sound of that. It sounds a little devious, if you ask me."

"You wanted wild and crazy. This isn't crazy at all, just free styling and relaxing. Come on, trust me. We're not going to be doing anything illegal."

"Okay, I'll go. Let me go change and we'll be on our way."

"Oh, no, Mindy. Where we are going, no clothes required. Come on." Stefan tells the waiter to put my bill on his tab as he grabs my hand. "Come with me, over here."

I follow Stefan to a wall of small lockers.

"Here, put your stuff in here with mine and let's go."

I place my bag on top of his and stare at him. A million questions come to mind.

"What's the matter, Mindy?"

"I don't know. If I really think about this, it's crazy. I'm following around a naked stranger in a foreign country, and I'm supposed to trust you? And I'm still naked! This is nuts. You can see everything!" I wave my hands in front of me.

"Yes, I can, and you're exquisitely beautiful. Every inch of your nakedness is spectacular. But Mindy, you can see me, too. Every inch of me."

"Oh yes, I can. And boy, is it glorious." I look down and take in the sight of his hardware. "I can't believe I just said that. I'm so embarrassed. I'm so sorry. That was so shallow of me."

"I'm glad you did. It's normal, Mindy. Relax. Come on. You've got to see this." Stefan reaches for my hand and holds it tight. He places my hand over his chest. "Feel that? My heart hasn't beaten that fast in a long time and it's all because of you. Now follow me." He walks me down the beach, hand in hand, to a small rock wall that leads out into the surf.

He continues to hold my hand as he leads me into the ocean. The water is warm and inviting and the clearest crystal blue I have ever seen. I can see all the way to the bottom. It's spectacular. We walk out until we can't touch the bottom anymore.

"Aren't you afraid of the fish?"

"Why would I be afraid of fish?"

"Well, you know, they might think your penis is a worm and bite it. Aren't you nervous about that? It's the epitome of the words: live bait."

"Mindy! Seriously?" We are crazy silly and laughing so hard that he loses his breath. "My dear, Mindy. I have grown up in these waters. Never, ever, have I heard of a man losing his rod to a nibbling fish. You are priceless, my dear. I will remember you always for that assumption. Now come on. Stop worrying and just enjoy yourself and let the stress float away.

"Now, see that small sandbar out there with the palm trees on it? That's where we're going. It's not that far away, so just relax, and swim over here with me and hold my hand and just float. The current does most of the work and we will be there in a few minutes."

I hold Stefan's hand tight as I let him lead the way. We are floating in the ocean and getting closer to the sandbar. I feel light as a feather and Stefan is right. The current did most of the work and we arrive in no time.

Stefan continues to hold my hand as he draws me up on the beach. We rest under a palm tree, laying in the sand, facing each other. I'm quiet as I just relax and breathe, taking in the sights.

"You know we will have sand in places that are unmentionable, right?" I say to the wandering eyes of Stefan.

"I suppose we will. But that's what couples' showers are for. Did you not see them back in the locker room?"

"No, I didn't. But that's interesting. Hmm, I'll have to remember that when we get back."

"Tell me, Miss Harper, if I ask you a personal question, will you answer it truthfully for me?"

"I guess I need to. Like I said before, nothing to hide now. What do you want to know?"

"What did the man in your life do to you to make you want to come here alone? I'm assuming you're tending to a broken heart?"

"Very perceptive of you, Stefan. He broke my heart. It's a long story, but the down and dirty version is that he has a medical condition and he thought I would be better off without him. He said he didn't want me coming home from work, after taking care of patients all day, and then take care of him, too. He said I deserved someone whole and not broken."

"I'm presuming you're a nurse, then?"

"Yes, a trauma ICU nurse."

"I see."

"What does that mean?"

"Nothing. I'm not trying to make you angry, Mindy. It's just that I can understand where he is coming from, that's all."

"How so? Can you please explain it to me, because I just don't get it?"

"Is he a strong man with strong beliefs and virtues?"

"God, yes. He is physically strong and in shape, and he is career strong. He is a lawyer. Not just any lawyer, a lawyer for the common man.

For people like us who need fair representation but can't afford the big expensive firm to represent them. He is a strong believer in doing the right thing, always telling the truth, and community service. More people should be like him, I suppose."

"Mindy, listen to yourself. He did the right thing, at least as he saw it. Listen to me for a minute. If his beliefs are that strong, he would want to take care of you every minute. He would want to be your breadwinner, and the one you collapse on every night when you've had a bad day. It would not be enough for him to watch you take care of him, even if you wanted to. His beliefs are that the man should provide and take care of his mate. How can he do that if he is feeling less than a man? How can he do that if you are always taking care of him? He can't. His selfless heart let you go. To be free and find a new path."

"Are you a therapist or something? I was so heartbroken, and then mad, I couldn't understand his reasoning. I thought he just gave up on us and threw me away."

"I'm sure he never wanted to do that. I'm sure this was the hardest decision of his life. You need to think about that and maybe one day you will be able to forgive him and move on."

"I hope so, because if there are more men like you around, I don't want to miss out much longer." I giggle.

"I'm the one and only Stefan, but feel free to work out any frustrations on me. I can be your rebound man."

"Ha, that's funny you should say that. My best friend back home told me to go on vacation and get some good island rebound sex. You dirty dogs all think alike."

"Well, we're halfway there. We're already naked. You could just come over here and jump on. I'm sure my body will respond most appropriately." His smile sports the most amazing white teeth and dimple.

"Stefan, you're killing me here. I wish I could just come over there and fuck you silly, because holy hell, you're beautiful, but it's just not in my nature. I'm not a one-night stand kind of girl. But neither is all this openness, quite frankly. But here I am, in all my nakedness, just hanging out on a beach with another naked stranger, talking about sex. What the hell am I doing?"

"You're healing, Mindy. The best way you know how, one day at a time, and one hour at a time if you have to. Just enjoy the day here with me, and each and every day moving forward will get a little easier. I promise."

The rest of the afternoon was relaxed and comfortable. We spent a few hours under the palm tree in easy conversation. We talked about our careers, our families, and our aspirations. It was non-threatening and just good company.

The incoming tide helped push us back to shore and onto the beach. It was a short walk back to the lockers, and our clothes.

"You know what, Stefan? After a while, I forgot I was naked and just relaxed while I was with you."

"I'm glad you feel that comfortable now. I would say your trip to the clothing optional beach was a success. But truth be told, I never forgot you were naked. Your every curve and softness is burned into my memory. You're amazing, and my offer still stands, if you change your mind."

"Aw thanks, Stefan, you really have helped me in so many ways. I had the best day today. Thank you."

"Why don't you go get dressed and I'll give you a lift back to The Villa? I need to go that direction, anyway."

"You got it. I'll be right back."

Later that night, I really review and think about what Stefan had said to me. I never really thought about what Kyle must be feeling deep down. And he certainly never really voiced those worries. He just kept pushing me away and saying he wanted me to have someone whole and not defective. I think I'm beginning to understand him and maybe I can slowly start to forgive him. I have a new respect for Kyle's words and some understanding, but I'm still hurting. Maybe now I can start healing.

Day five is relaxing by the pool with yet another trashy book, Piña Coladas, and an occasional swim in the ocean. I'm really trying to work on the tan today. My bikini is tight in all the right places and I can feel my confidence showing.

Just as I turn over onto my belly, I spot Stefan. He is coming back from an afternoon sailing trip with his guests. He looks tanned and his hair is perfectly windblown. And those aviator sunglasses just add the right amount of mysterious sex appeal to his personality.

I can tell Stefan is watching me through his sunglasses as he pretends to be busy at work. A guest suddenly distracts him, so I use this opportunity to sneak down to the dock. I watch him as he is tying up the last life jacket and sighs in relief. He spins around to exit the catamaran, but sees me at his dock entrance.

"Permission to come aboard, Captain?"

"Permission granted, Miss Harper. What is with this personal visit, ma'am?"

"Are you free tonight?"

"As a matter of fact, I am. What were you thinking?"

"Well, I leave tomorrow and I would like to go out tonight. Do you dance?"

"I happen to be a very good dancer, ma'am. Would you like to go to the hottest club on the island?"

"Yes, sir. Would you take me there?"

"I would love to. How about I pick you up in the lobby at 8:00 p.m.?"

"It's a date. Thank you, sir."

I walk away, working it and strutting my stuff, as I can only imagine Stefan's manhood yelling from under his zipper, *Let me out, I'm aching down here!*

It's 8:00 p.m., and I look and feel like a new woman. My hair is wavy, and my makeup is chic sexy. I have just the right amount of red lipstick to look sexy, but not slutty. I have on my favorite little black dress that shows off my round ass and nice tits but hides the thighs I'm always so self-conscious about. And to finish the outfit, black pumps with rhinestone accents, and my emerald bracelet. I feel fucking fantastic.

Stefan pulls up right on time and gets out and opens the door for me. His car of choice is a vintage red mustang convertible. My favorite car and color. *Oh, boy,* my inner voice yells. *Are we feeling a little over confident tonight? I mean, look at this man. He has on white pants, a pink shirt, and smells divine. It's as if he got into your head and knew every little detail that makes you a horny bitch on the prowl. Be careful, girl. This could get too hot any minute. Are you ready for a close encounter of the big dick kind? If not, you better back down now, woman!*

I smile as I put my inner voice to bed and just enjoy the scenery. The night is beautiful and warm. The lights are amazing, and the overall tone of the club is electric. The music is pumping and people are beginning to filter in. The electricity of the night is just beginning and I can't wait to experience it.

Stefan goes to the bar and grabs us some drinks-fruity drinks with an umbrella, of course.

"What's this one?" I ask.

"Sex on the beach."

"Of course, it is."

"Try it, you'll like it." Stefan winks at me.

I sip my drink and find it refreshing, cool yet smooth. I follow Stefan as we head for a quiet table in the back, as if there is such a thing at a club. The conversation remains easy and playful.

"I'm sad you are leaving tomorrow. I was really hoping to win you over, and make you want to stay here forever and be my naked beach partner."

"Stefan, I bet you say that to all the women you chase while they are here on vacation. I'm surely not the first girl you have tried to capture with your amazingly sexy ways."

"Actually, Mindy, you are. I know that is hard to believe, but in my job, people come and go so quickly, I never really pay attention to them for more than a minute. But you, you are different. Something about you grabbed at me and won't let go."

"It was the fish that grabbed your dick as we were swimming," I reply with a huge smile. A smile that crackles heat between us, yet understanding that tonight is all about letting loose and just having fun.

"Come on, let's dance." Stefan grabs my hands and pulls me out onto the dance floor.

The music is pumping and has an awesome beat. Stefan can really dance and now I have the best dance partner ever. He enjoys all the same songs as me. It's a perfect match.

We dance for several hours, and time seems to stand still. We dance as if we are made for each other, couples in perfect unison. The music finally slows, and we decide to take a break and walk off the floor to rehydrate.

Watching couples slow dance pulls at my heartstrings just a little. Stefan notices the change in my smile and offers a walk outside on the patio.

"Let's go get some fresh air, Mindy. Grab your drink and follow me."

The walk outside is amazing. There is a lighted path down to the beach and twinkle lights line the underside of the patio umbrellas. It's romantic and beautiful. We walk out to the end of the pathway and sit on a bench.

"You doing okay? I saw you zone out when the music changed and thought you could use a distraction."

"You are so perceptive, Stefan. Thank you for sharing my last night here with me. You have helped me in so many ways, and you're a sweet man. Thank you, really."

"It has been my pleasure, Mindy, honestly. I've learned a lot from you, too. I'd say we both needed each other, and I'm glad we found each other."

"Me, too. Now that I'm sitting down for a while, I can really tell how tired I am. Can you take me home now?"

"I'd be happy to escort you home, ma'am."

Stefan walks me to my villa door without the prying eyes of staff watching. "Mindy, do you realize it's 1:00 a.m. already? We were dancing for hours, and it didn't even feel like it."

"No, it didn't. I had the best time. Thank you so much." I look into Stefan's eyes and caress his cheeks. I pull him in for a tender kiss. His lips are soft and warm and inviting. His tongue slowly traces the outline of my top lip and I melt. The fire deep down between my legs is blazing and I'm wet.

Stefan pushes his abdomen into me. His hardness twitches against my waist. His mouth dances with mine and his tongue finally gains entrance. A slow moan escapes me as my tongue willingly explores his. I gently lace my fingers into his wavy locks. I hold strong as the quickness of Stefan's breathing increases.

We melt into each other perfectly as Stefan slides his hands under my dress. He finds my underwear and slides it to one side, and I let him, wanting more. He kisses me deeply as he eases a finger into my wetness. He is quite experienced, I can tell. His actions are flawless and without hesitation. This man knows his way around a woman's body.

"My God, Mindy. You are ravishing. Your response to me is maddening and I know you want me as much as I want you. Just feel me, feel how bloody hard I am for you. And you, you are so wet for me. Do you know how much that turns a man on? Knowing his woman responds to him in that way? It's just fucking beautiful. You, are just fucking beautiful."

"Stefan, stop for a minute. Please."

"What's the matter, love?"

"Stefan, I'm so attracted to you it scares me, but I'm not the type of woman who bed hops around. I'm leaving tomorrow morning and I just can't have a one-night stand. As much as I want you, it's not in my nature. I just can't do it. Please understand."

"Oh, Mindy, I do. You are emotionally not ready, and I get that. But can I tell you something? Don't you ever doubt yourself again. I'm here to tell you that you are beautiful, inside, and out. You are one exquisite woman, and stunningly beautiful. You are so unaware of your sex appeal that it just makes you even more seductive. Please allow yourself time to heal and grieve for the love you have lost, and then get back out there. Because you will make some man extremely happy one day. I know it. I wish it was me, but I know you need to return to your life and your reality. I truly hope I have helped you see the beauty in yourself and that you are worthy of a wonderful love."

"Stefan, you have been amazing. I hope you know I truly enjoyed your company and being with you. You have helped me in so many ways, you'll never know. I will be forever grateful. I can credit you with my new fondness for nude beaches now, too. And Stefan, if I wasn't so broken right now, I would stay here with you. Know that my feelings toward you are mutual, so thank you."

Stefan leans in and gives me a tender kiss on the lips that sends the heat down to my toes. "Be well, Mindy. You're extremely attractive and amazing. Don't you forget that, and if you change your mind, you know where to find me. Travel safe, my nude woman."

Stefan leans over and places a tender kiss on my forehead and then turns to walk away.

"Hey, Stefan?"

"Yeah?" He turns around.

"Thank you and remember, protect your worm from the fish. You never know when a big one might get hungry. I'd hate to see you lose that work of art to a damn fish."

Stefan laughs out loud, heading to his car. I stand motionless, as the engine of the mustang fade in the distance.

This has been an amazing week. I'm so happy I did this for myself.

My flight home was quiet and uneventful. The time on the plane was a gift. Time to process my life and confirm my desires and make a plan. I've decided a new job is in order. As much as I love the ICU, I think I'm ready for a break. The operating room has always been in the background, calling to me. Maybe I should really check it out. I think once I get back to work, I will check out the career board and see what new options are available.

My renewed strength and convictions are a direct result of the conversations Stefan and I shared. Understanding a different man's point of view was very helpful. Forgiving Kyle and accepting his decision to break up is getting a little easier every day. I have finally realized that this is not about me. It's not about being thrown away or that I was unworthy. It's the opposite. Kyle's words make so much more sense now.

I'm at peace with my independence and will embrace this time for growing and exploring new career opportunities. I exhale slowly as I rest my head back on the headrest and close my eyes, at peace with my new life decisions.

Liz pulls up to the arrivals gate at the airport and jumps out of her car when she sees me. She takes one look at me and is grinning from ear to ear with a huge ass smile on her face. "Holy shit, Mindy! You look fabulous! What exactly went on down there on the islands? Is this the look of terrific vacation sex?"

"Gosh, Liz, you should be a man. I swear that's all you ever talk about. Cool your jets, sister. I did not have sex, but man oh man, I wanted to.

This girl was feeling the fire and if I could have done it without feeling like a slut, I would have. But no, single goodie-two-shoes Mindy played the morals card."

"I thought I told you to have fun and go have a lot of good rebound sex. What happened?"

"Oh, lots of stuff. I had a wonderful time. I'll fill you in on all the details at dinner. You're going to have dinner with me tonight, right?"

"Yes, girl, definitely! I can't wait to hear about your adventures. Give me at least a little detail of something to hold on to until we get to Burgers and Buns. Then you can spill it."

Liz helps me put my luggage in the trunk and smiles a devious grin.

"Here's a little ditty for you." I sarcastically drop, "I went to a nudist beach and had a wonderful time."

"Shut the front door! You did not!" Liz screams. "I don't believe it. Seriously?"

"Serious like a heart attack! It was the best day ever!"

"I'm sure it was. Who needs to fuck like a bunny when you've got the whole litter right in front of you at your disposal? You could pick and choose which hottie you wanted based on the size of their junk. I'll take that one, and that one, and oh yes, that one for dessert for sure! I'd be slutting it up all day, Mind! How fun would that be? I'm getting hot just thinking about it."

"Oh, my God, Liz, you're hysterical. Sitting there looking at everyone naked was so fascinating to me. I couldn't help but people watch and make up stories in my head about them. These naked people were carefree and just going about their normal day. They were letting it all hang out and unphased by their nudity. It was their normal. It was so crazy to me that I just had to try it and experience their wardrobe freedom.

So, I excused myself and went to the ladies' room and stripped down to nothing. When I emerged, I held my head high and went about my day. I had the best time and I have a whole new respect for nudity. I rather enjoy being in the buff!" I giggle as I watch Liz's mouth hanging wide open.

"You know what else, Liz? I spent the day with another naked beach enthusiast. We swam and talked all day while I tried not to stare at his amazing body. He was a masterpiece of perfection. Do you want to guess who it was?"

"I can't even begin to guess, Mindy. Just tell me. I'm dying over here."

"It was, Stefan. My villa waiter and the catamaran captain. He was chillin' on the beach on his day off and he spotted me. I saw him, too, from afar, but I had no idea it was him at first. We spent the day together and had a wonderful time, and I learned a lot about myself and men in general. We talked about Kyle some and he has an interesting perspective on how men think. It was very productive. I wish I was a little more carefree because when the day was over, I would have invited him back to my room in a hot minute. Lord, I wanted to, but I used all my restraint and was a good girl."

"I'm proud of you, Mindy, because if it was me, I would have jumped on that ride the minute it was available."

"God, Liz, you kill me. I wish I had half your fearless attitude sometimes." We chat and belly laugh as I share my stories of the week. Just when I think my naked beach story wins the prize for the week's most exciting story, Liz tops me and blows me out of the water.

"Mindy, honey. I have something serious I need to talk to you about. I've been waiting for the right moment. Now that I know what happened to you during your week, I need to share something important about my week."

"Oh, Liz. I'm so sorry. I was being selfish, and all I did was talk about me. Please, tell me about your week."

"Well, Mindy. I have just one question. Will you be my maid of honor?" Liz holds up her left hand and is sporting a beautiful three-stone stunning engagement ring.

I scream in excitement as I jump up from the dinner table and run over to hug my best friend. "How did you keep this a secret all day? I want all the details, Missy. Every last one!" I screech.

We laugh and carry on for three more hours and just about close the restaurant. We shared every detail of every day of the week we were apart. Liz even has a newfound respect for the island man named Stefan.

Chapter 61

"Hey, Liz, are you coming with me to the courthouse? You better move your ass or we're gonna be late!" I yell up the stairs to Liz's bedroom.

"I'm coming, girl. Hold your damn ass!"

"Do you think Levin will be in the courtroom?"

"David said he will be there with his lawyer. But don't worry, Mindy. You have all of us there to support you. David has all the pieces in place and Levin will most likely get the maximum sentence. Don't forget, Mind, there are three other women that have been saved from his capture. He's not getting out of jail anytime soon."

"I hope not. I really want to put this nightmare to bed. My parents are going to meet me there, too. Hopefully, this will give my dad closure. I'm sure Randi Newman will be there. He will want to see justice served, too."

"Mindy, you know Kyle would be there if he could. He has an emergent appointment he can't miss. He said to tell you to be strong and deep breathe, that it will all work out."

"I know. Please be sure to thank him for me. I appreciate the sentiment. Now, can we go, please?"

We arrive at the courthouse and it's flooded with photographers and reporters galore. I keep my head down as I make a beeline for the front door of the courthouse. Just before I reach the top step, the loud rumble of motorcycles is coming up the street. It's loud and thunderous. Not just one motorcycle, but a large parade of bikes. The noise is deafening and an attention getter. Leading the formation is T. Behind him is the rest of his club in executive order. They all pull up and park right in front of the courthouse building and dismount their bikes in perfect unison. I watch as I see his familiar face, and turn to run down the stairs into the arms of my rescuer, T. This is where I feel safe.

"You came? I'm so happy you're here. I was petrified to go in there without you. Now I feel safe and protected. Thank you so much for coming." Tears roll down my cheeks.

"Mindy, honey, I'm always here for you. We all are. All you have to do is call me. I'll be there every time, no questions asked." T. pushes my hair behind my ear and wipes a tear from my face with the soft padding of his thumb. "You just go in there with your head held high and be the confident beauty you already are. This will all be over shortly. And remember, honey, I've got you. We've all got you. Just breathe."

The judge begins and addresses the court and the defendant. The trial was over last week and he was found guilty of four counts of kidnapping and one count of stalking.

"In the matter of the State versus Mr. Scott Levinthal, the jury has found him guilty on all counts. The maximum sentence one can occur on each count is twenty years, and a maximum sentence of ten years for stalking shall also be incurred. Therefore, Mr. Levinthal, your maximum sentence will consist of ninety years consecutively served. There will be a chance of parole after fifty years consecutively served, providing good behavior is well documented. Bailiff, remove the prisoner and prepare him for departure to Canyon Park Incarceration Facility." The judge banged the gavel on the wooden platform, and I jump. I have just witnessed justice being served and I'm finally feeling free.

I look over at David as he leans down and gives me a warm embrace. "Mindy, you're shaking like a leaf. It's over, honey. He will never hurt you or another woman again. Just breathe, come on. Close your eyes, and breathe. I know you know how."

I lean into David, giving him a warm hug, and finally feeling some stress subsiding. I watch as my parents are shaking hands with T. and David. "Thank you both so much for what you have done for our daughter. You both have gone above and beyond to keep us all updated and safe. We truly appreciate you all."

T. looks at Dad and extends a welcoming handshake. "It's what we do, brother, you remember. We hope to see you around soon." He winks at my mother.

Out of the corner of my eye, I see Officer Randi Newman approach my dad. "Sir, may I have a word with you and your wife, please?"

"Officer Newman, anytime. I think it's me that needs a word with you. I'm so sorry, son. I'm sorry I had an altercation with your father and he lost his life. That accident left you a partial orphan, and that moment has haunted me for thirty-three years." Tears fill my dad's eyes as he looks at Randi.

"Mr. Harper, that's why I wanted to talk to you and your wife. Please know that I have never blamed you for my father's death. Not once. I truly believe things happen for a reason. Now, at the time, I had no idea how I could become a better person. Being sent away gave me the love and support I needed to become a better man than my father. I am proud of the man I am today. My father was a piece of shit hoodlum. He was not a loving father, ever. So please, heal your wounds and move on, because I have and I'm better because of it."

My dad leans in and gives a big bear hug to Randi as he finally cries tears of healing. I'm watching this story unfold with T. by my side. "Maybe now my dad can heal. He has been given permission to move on."

"I hope so, Mindy. Maybe he'll revisit the notion of coming back to The Creeks Motorcycle Club."

"Seriously? He can do that?"

"Yup. Work on him, Mindy. His reputation was flawless. We could use a good man like him back in our brotherhood."

"I'll see what I can do. Thanks, T."

My mom acknowledges the group of bikers and friends that have gathered around me. "Thank you all for the love and support you have given Mindy. None of this would have been possible if it weren't for each and every one of you. Thank you all so much from one extremely grateful mom." My mom gives T. a huge hug as a tear escape down her cheek.

"Okay, enough with the crying," my dad announces. "Come on, lunch and drinks are on me. Let's hit Burgers and Buns on the Beach and get some damn drinks!"

"Then we're all in," says T. "We never pass up an opportunity to hang with a brother for free grub and booze!"

Chapter 62

"How do you like your new job, Mind?" Liz asks.

"It's really cool, but a lot to learn. You know I love the operating room. I love watching people get put back together. It's amazing what a skilled surgeon can do with a scalpel. I freakin' love it."

"I'm so happy for you, Mind. I know this has been a year of big changes and growth for you. I just want you to know how proud of you I am. You have shined in the face of danger and heartache. You're one strong chick and I love you!"

"Thanks, Liz. I love you, too. Now stop it or I'm going to cry. I don't want to ruin my makeup or have Rudolph's nose. You know I can't hide it when I cry. Now, I have waited a long time to wear this dress. Does it look okay?"

"Mindy, that is a killer dress on you. The big red rose pattern on this dress is just stunning. And those red shoes, oh girl, you look amazing."

"Thanks. I'm trying not to freak out here. I know Kyle will be there, and I haven't heard his voice in six months. I'm getting nauseated just thinking about it. I hope at least to see him and get a chance to check in on him. I'd like to hear how he's doing from the horse's mouth; you know?"

"I understand. Don't worry, he'll be there. He's not going to miss his only brother's engagement party."

"I know. I can't believe you and David are engaged. Who would have thought you would be marrying one of the Greek gods? It's insane when you think about it."

Liz and I ride together to the engagement party. We are planning on meeting David and Kyle at 4:00 p.m. sharp. I'm excited and very nervous about seeing Kyle. I need to tell him I understand his reasoning behind our break up, and it's okay. I get it. I also really want an update on his medical progress. It will take some getting used to, but I'm dedicated to becoming a good friend to Kyle. After all, we are going to be in each other's company a lot, considering my best friend will soon be his sister-in-law.

Before I get out of the car, I give myself one final check in the rearview mirror.

"Stop fidgeting! You look freaking amazing. I'm so glad you saved that dress for this occasion. It's my favorite, and it shows off your figure perfectly. Your hair is wavy and flows so tenderly. You look relaxed and on fire. Please, Mind, just enjoy the day. I think you will be pleasantly surprised."

"That's my goal, Liz. Come on, let's do this." I hold my head high as I grab Liz's arm and we escort each other to the garden patio.

The patio is decorated with white linens with red accents. Poppies and white roses are worked into the centerpieces and twinkle lights are wrapped around all the railings and lampposts to complete the decor. From across the patio, I see the Masterson brothers standing side by side. They are sporting dark blue dress pants with white collared shirts and their dark sunglasses complete the Hollywood model look.

"Liz, if you had told me two years ago when we first saw these beauties that they would be ours one day, I would have told you that you were full of shit. But look, here they are in all their Greek god hotness, looking hotter and better than ever. Lord have mercy! You're actually marrying one of them! How perfectly things work out. Remember how the first night you blew off David when he asked you for a drink? And now look at you both. So smitten with each other, it's romantically sickening, but I'm so happy for you both. And I love you, Liz!"

"And I love you, Mind, and I'm happy for you, too."

We walk up to David. He instantly removes his sunglasses and gives Liz a huge hug and a passionate kiss on the lips.

"Hello, my darling. You look marvelous."

"Thank you, honey. I'm feeling so lucky today." Liz moves over in front of Kyle and leans in to hug him. "You both look amazing."

"Well, thanks, Liz. David dressed us. He said he wanted something timeless and sexy as hell."

"Well, I'd say he achieved the look. You both look so handsome. Good job, David."

"Why thank you, Mindy. I'm glad you approve."

I watch Kyle closely as he inhales deeply and takes one step forward toward me and stops. He's just standing there, motionless, and breathing deeply.

"Kyle, are you okay? Do you need to sit down?" I ask.

"No, thank you. I'm fine. I can smell your perfume, my favorite. I'm just taking it all in, Mindy. I'm a very lucky man and that scent is a big reminder of just how important people are in life."

"I'm sorry, Kyle. I didn't even think when I put it on today. It's just a habit to wear it every day. I didn't even think that it may upset you."

"Oh, Mindy, it doesn't upset me at all. On the contrary. It totally accents the whole package. Your scent is amazing, but that dress is a fucking killer! You look so beautiful and elegant, but those red come-fuck-me pumps really do the trick. You're screaming hot, beautiful sex appeal in every way."

Liz is standing off to the side, arm in arm with David as they watch the show unfold before them. She grabs David's hand and squeezes tight as they watch us interact for the first time in months.

"Excuse me? Wait a minute. Did you just say my dress is killer?"

"Actually, I said it was a fucking killer!"

"Kyle, don't play with me. What does my dress look like? Describe it to me," I demand, shaking.

"Your dress is amazing. The white fabric compliments your tan, and the red rose pattern is beautiful. The off-the-shoulder neckline brings a new meaning to beautiful shoulders and your perky beautiful breasts. And those red come-fuck-me pumps, they scream, come take me home now, because I need you and can't stand to be another minute without you."

I'm frozen in silence, but find the energy to take a few steps closer to Kyle and approach him. Kyle stands still, frozen, and doesn't move. His breathing is fast and erratic. I remove his sunglasses and instantly see those amazing ocean-blue eyes. *God, how I have missed them.*

I place his glasses on the table and touch his cheeks. He immediately relaxes into my palms and just breathes with his eyes closed.

"Kyle. Kyle, open your eyes. Can you see me?"

Kyle opens his eyes, and immediately they are coming into focus on me. Gasping, I inhale quickly as I tremble. I'm staring directly into the bluest eyes I have ever seen. "My God, Mindy. I have always seen you, but now, when I see you, I'm breathless. You are stunning. There aren't enough adjectives to describe how I feel when I see you."

"You can see me!" I cry out. "Oh, my God, Liz, he can see me!"

"I know, honey. Surprise! A lot has happened over the last few months."

"Oh, my God, Kyle. This is amazing. I prayed for you to be able to see. I'm so happy for you." I stand there just looking at Kyle's blue eyes and feel myself cry. "I can't believe it. You can see, but how?" I wipe the tears of joy off my face.

"Listen, Mind, I'll tell you everything, but a little later. Right now, I just want to kiss you if that's all right?"

I'm in such shock I can't even answer. I stand there frozen, blown away. A slight nod is all Kyle needs to move closer to me. He caresses my cheeks and leans in for a soft, passionate kiss on my lips. I melt with his touch and instinctively put my arms around his neck.

Loud cheering and clapping resounded over the soft drum of the music and it brought me back down out of the clouds. I pull away and slowly focus on Kyle.

"You can really see me. This is like the real first time you can actually see me."

"Mindy, I always saw you, even in my darkness. Now, I can see you in my light."

Kyle looks up at David and Liz. "I know this is your party, but do you mind if I steal Mindy away for a little bit? We have some catching up to do, if you both don't mind?"

I look at Liz and David in amazement. I'm speechless and smiling from ear to ear. Liz leans over and hugs me as she whispers in my ear, "I told you to relax and enjoy the day. Now you know why. Go, spend some time with Kyle."

"Are you sure? This is supposed to be your day."

"Believe me, we are one thousand percent sure. Please go be with Kyle, David says as Liz nods in approval.

I look at Kyle and a small tear escapes my eye. Kyle instinctively brushes it away with the softness of his thumb.

"Don't cry, my dear. Please, come walk with me." Kyle has his arm outstretched as he is asking for my hand.

I reach for his hand and our fingers lace together perfectly. The warmth from his hand sends shockwaves to my heart. *Play it cool, Mindy.*

"What are you so smiley about, Mr. Masterson?"

"Why, Miss Harper, it's a beautiful day and I am walking around these amazing grounds with a beautiful woman holding my hand. How could I not be smiling?"

"Kyle, what happened? What are you doing?"

"Mindy, I never stopped being interested in you or your life. I have been watching you from a distance. Liz and David give me updates, but only when I ask. They were very good at keeping things a secret until I was ready. I want you to know that I really wanted to be there, that day in court, for the sentencing of Mr. Levinthal, but that was the day I went for my surgery."

"What surgery? Are you okay?"

"Yes, I'm perfectly fine. That was the day I went for laser eye surgery. My parents took me while David was with you in court. During a follow-up appointment, Doctor Keller noticed that there was a lot of scar tissue on my optic nerve, possibly contributing to my blindness. I agreed to laser eye surgery in the hopes of possibly restoring my vision. The results were amazing. I was seeing fifty percent better by the second day after surgery and every day since it has gotten better. My sight is ninety-five percent restored. I'm so grateful, Mindy. I have a new outlook on the miracles of medicine. I truly am thankful and humbled."

"I wondered why you weren't there. I just assumed you didn't want to be there with me."

"Never, Mindy. I have always wanted to be with you. Please don't think I discarded you. I was only trying to set you free. Let me tell you my story first, and then I'll answer any question you want, okay?"

"Okay, I guess that's fair. But I bet I'll have many."

Kyle walks us over to the park bench below the Live Oak tree covered with twinkle lights. "Here, please sit down for me."

"Sure, I love this spot. I could spend forever on this bench."

"Mindy, please let me start by saying I am so sorry to have hurt you. I never, ever wanted to do that to you. It broke your heart, and it broke mine to set you free. I pushed you away because I felt you deserved so much more than I could give you. Mind, I'm a strong man. I want to take care of my woman and provide for her. I want to be the breadwinner and the caretaker. I wanted to give you everything. I didn't want to worry about you having to give me everything. I felt less than a man and so dependent on people. I couldn't stand it. I thought the most selfless thing I could do was let you go. To give you a chance at finding someone who could give you the dream."

"What dream, Kyle?"

"You know, the dream of being treated like a queen. Of having a man worship you and give you everything, to fight for you, defend and protect you, and have the happily ever after ending."

"Kyle, you sound like a little girl who is looking for her prince."

"Mindy, I'm a romantic at heart and I know my philosophy is old school, but I grew up watching my parents be in love. I know this is so corny for a man to say, but I want the kind of relationship my parents have. I want to give my woman everything and be her everything. Is that too much to ask?"

"No, Kyle, it's not. It's just not common for a man to express his feelings that way. I understand your feelings. I just wish you had explained them to me earlier. It might have saved us so many months of heartache."

"I'm not saying you're wrong, Mindy. It took me a while to get over the anger. I just couldn't accept the final diagnosis Doctor Keller was giving me. I'm so sorry I was an asshole to you. I knew you would stay and take care of me because that's the kind of person you are. I knew if I said things that would hurt the most, then you would have no choice but to leave. So, I attacked the one thing you are most proud of, your career and your ability to be an amazing nurse. You see, Mindy, I wanted more for you. I wanted you to have a chance at the dream and fairytale. I couldn't think of any other way."

"Kyle, you know I'm a firm believer in the old saying that things happen for a reason, right? I have grown so much since then. That breakup, as heartbreaking as it was, forced me to reexamine my life and aspirations. I took some time for myself and just went away. I learned a lot about myself, my life, and men. It was very cathartic, and I began to heal and understand your reasoning and forgave you."

"You went away? By yourself? That's huge, Mindy. I'm proud of you and surprised."

"It surprised me, too. I did it out of anger at first, but then I started to get excited about the possibility of self-reflection and growth. It was a great experience. That trip forced me to make new decisions. I came home with renewed energy and worked on myself. I changed jobs and got in shape. I feel better, happier, and healthier. I'm okay, Kyle. You don't need to worry about me. I'm okay, really."

"I know you are, Mind. I've been keeping tabs on you. Please don't think I pushed you away and then forgot about you. I never did that. You were in my thoughts every day. I wanted you to live your life, but secretly I wanted to get better and come back to you. I just prayed that when I could come back to you, you would have me."

"What exactly are you saying, Kyle?"

"Mind, I'm saying that I never gave up on us. I never quit. I just wanted you to have a complete man, or in my mind, what I thought should be a complete man. I want you, Mindy. I've always wanted you. I would like another chance to prove to you that I see you. I have always seen you, Mindy. And now, I can really show you how I see you. If you'll let me have a second chance. Do you think you can do that?"

"Kyle, I have always wanted us to be together. But if we do this, you need to understand something about me. I will understand your feelings better when you communicate with me. And you need to cut me some slack when I want to take care of you. There are times when you need to just give in and let me do it. I take great pride in being a nurse. It's in my DNA. Think of it this way, Kyle. When you take care of me, it gives you great satisfaction, right? Well, I'm the same way. So just enjoy and know that I do it out of love and just go with it. Do you think you can you do that?"

"So, you love me?"

"Is that the only thing you heard me say out of that whole speech?"

"No, I heard every wonderful word. It's just the one I want to hear the most. Yes, I can do that. And Mindy, for the record, I love you. I have never stopped loving you for one second."

Kyle stands up and pulls me to my feet as he wraps his arms around my waist. We still fit perfectly together and the heat is instant. Kyle looks down into my eyes and I can feel his sincerity. "My God, you are amazing and just as beautiful as I imagined. I really want to kiss you right now and ravage every inch of you. May I kiss you? Please?"

"Yes, please. Please kiss—"

Before I can get the rest of my sentence out, he is on my lips. His lips are warm and tender to the touch. He holds my head gently in his hands and pulls me slowly closer to him. His heat radiates to my heart instantly, along with other places, as my knees buckle. I place my arms around his neck and pull him in closer as he holds me tight, safe, and secure in his arms.

For the first time in many months, I'm feeling relaxed, whole, sexy, and confident. I am content in the arms of the man I have craved from the first moment I saw him. That deliciously looking Greek god, who is now finally mine to explore in every way.

Epilogue

Chapter 1

One week after my big surprise to Mindy, we go on our first official date.

"Mindy, I want to take you to The Dockside Pier Restaurant. I have wonderful memories of that place. Are you okay with us going there for our first post-blindness date?"

"Kyle, any date with you will be wonderful. You can take me to the park bench and I won't care. As long as I'm with you, I'll be happy."

"Then the Dockside it is. Come on."

I grab Mindy's hand and we lock our fingers. Something so comfortable and casual that sends waves of warmth through me, and right to my manhood. I smile as I look at Mindy, soft and warm, and aroused. Her snug-fitting top is giving away all her secrets. I feel proud and wanted as I wink at her in approval.

"You can't hide from me, Ms. Harper. I see everything now. Every little detail of you is engraved in my soul. For example, that beautiful summer knit top is showing off your curves, even those wonderfully hard nubs on your breasts. My, my, Ms. Harper, I believe you may have caught a chill."

"Mr. Masterson, please don't think you are winning back all your good graces so easily. You will need to work for it, and prove you are worthy of my invitation. Remember, dear sir, only those of the highest standards receive an invitation. The last gentleman who was invited, broke my heart. You will have to outwit and outsmart him to receive another invitation." she proclaims with a devious grin.

"Ms. Harper, I am up to the challenge. I'm sure you will not be disappointed."

"That's a lot of confidence, coming from a man who is on an official first date, don't you think?"

"I'm very comfortable with myself and my current situation, Ms. Harper. I know I can win you over. I think you will be pleasantly surprised."

"Let the challenge begin, Mr. Masterson. I enjoy some friendly competition."

We share a wonderful and comfortable dinner. Our conversation is playful and flirty, but I have a few questions I need to ask her. I certainly don't want to spoil the mood, but I need to clear the air.

"Mindy, can I ask you a question? It's really none of my business. You can choose not to answer and I will not be offended, but something is bothering me. I kept up with your life when you were away from me by asking Liz and David for updates. I know it was wrong of me to ask them, but I couldn't help it. They never really said much in detail, but enough for me to know that you were doing okay.

"I know when I pushed you away, you were not doing well. I'm so sorry, Mind. How did you get over me? What did you do? I asked Liz for info and she would never answer me. Did I push you into the arms of another?"

I fire off these questions in record time, not giving her a chance to answer before I ask the next question. I'm afraid if I don't ask them all out at once, I'll never have the nerve to ask them again. Mindy looks at me and her face falls. My pulse is pounding and I'm regretting bringing up this subject. I may have just ruined the moment and this date.

"Mindy, I know when we were apart; that was your personal time, but I feel so guilty about pushing you away. I just need to know. If you're willing to talk about it."

"Kyle, I'm willing to talk about it, but not all of it. Can you respect and accept that? Because if you can't, then we will just skip over the question."

I swallow the large lump in my throat as I prepare for the worst. I asked, now I'll get the answer, ready or not. "I can accept that. I'm the one who pushed you away and broke up with you. That's a guilt I need to live with, not you."

"Well, first, I didn't ever get over you. I just came to an understanding of how you felt when you sent me away. You see, for so long, I felt like something was wrong with me and you were just discarding us without ever trying. I felt like you never really gave us a chance. You didn't even let us try to be a couple before you dismissed the very idea of us."

"Oh, Mind, I didn't discard us. I told you that, honey. I assure you; it wasn't you. I couldn't live with myself." Mindy reaches across the table, taking my hands into the warmth of hers.

"Listen to me, Kyle. I understand you now, but let me say this before I lose my thought."

I nod and let Mindy continue.

"I was heartbroken at first, and then I became angry, for many reasons. So, I decided it was time to take care of myself. I booked a trip to St. Maarten and went away for six days by myself.

"I examined my life, decided what I wanted to change, and then made plans to do so. I decided to look for a new job when I got home. I also decided to dedicate time every day to my own health, both physical and emotional. I needed time for me to do the things I love every day. And you know what Kyle, the biggest thing I learned was how men like you, successful and driven men, think. That was really helpful and the biggest a-ha moment for me. I began to understand your thinking and why you broke up with me. I began to forgive you, but I didn't forget the pain. I started to heal, but slowly."

As she explains her journey, her pain is evident in her eyes. She is revealing her innermost feelings to me and I so respect that. My heart aches for the pain she endured as I cradle her hands as she continues.

"Kyle, please know I forgave you months ago. I have no ill feelings for you. Things happen for a reason. I truly believe that. I didn't understand it at the time, but now I get it, and I'm thankful. Those days that followed our break up made me a better person for myself. I probably wouldn't have taken the chances I did if I didn't learn to make changes and grow."

"You amaze me, Mindy. You truly are one of a kind. You find the silver lining in things, don't you?"

"No, but I try. Working in the Trauma ICU has taught me that life is too short. You never know if today will be your last day. So, I'm choosing to live each day to the fullest, and learn and move forward every day."

"Mind, I want to move forward with you, if you'll let me?"

"What did you have in mind, Mr. Masterson?"

"First of all, this has been wonderful, but let's get out of here and grab dessert to go. I would love to take you back to my place and show you around if you're up for it."

"Oh, Mr. Masterson. A true nurse is up for anything. We are prepared like girl scouts."

"Then let's go see if you can pitch a tent, Ms. Harper."

Mindy chuckles as she deviously smiles and whispers in my ear, "I believe the real question, Mr. Masterson is, can you pitch a tent? And how big of a tent would it be?"

Chapter 2

We arrive at my apartment building, hand in hand. The building is a refurbished old brick apartment building built in the 1800s. There is a front stoop with five large steps and black wrought-iron hand railings. The craftsmanship of the ironwork inside the railings is amazing. The scrolls are beautiful and create an intricate geometric design.

As Mindy walks into the lobby of the building, she looks up at the crystal chandelier hanging directly overhead. It's huge and sparkles like twinkle lights.

The bellman nods and smiles at Mindy as she enters the elevator. "Goodnight, Mr. Masterson."

"Goodnight, Sam."

"You know your bellman's name?"

"Sure. He has worked here for me for the last ten years. I hired him when I bought the building."

"You own this building, too?"

"The city was going to tear it down and put up some sort of store, but I found out about it and bought the building instead. I have always loved this area and didn't want to see it overdeveloped and become a shopper's paradise. I wanted to preserve the old-time nostalgia of the neighborhood. So, I bought it and remodeled it into several apartments, with mine being the top floor and the roof. I own other buildings in the area, too. I want to try to maintain the charm and refurbish this area. The old-school charm is trending now and a popular sought-after look. I'm proud of the improvements this area has undergone."

"Well, I absolutely love it, Kyle. It's stunning."

"Thanks, now come on in and welcome to my place. We are on the tenth floor and overlooking the marina. Follow me. I want to show you something." There is a hidden stairwell behind the kitchen door. I hold her hand as I guide her as she climbs the stairs. "Watch your step. It's a little dark up here."

Mindy hits the top landing and takes the last step. "Oh, I can smell the fresh air and ocean. It's wonderful."

"Well, close your eyes, and don't open them until I tell you."

Mindy squeezes her eyelids shut as I flip the wall switch on the rooftop. The magic happens and the strands above her head light up. Hundreds of twinkle lights glow into the night and set the mood. A round table is in the center of the roof, set with crystal, china, and an ice bucket of champagne standing next to the table. A dozen red roses in a crystal vase anchor the white linen-covered table.

"Okay, Mind, open your eyes."

She opens her eyes and looks around in wonder. She inhales sharply as she looks around at the setting. "Wow, this is beautiful, Kyle. I feel like a princess. When did you ever have time to do this? It's amazing. I love it, thank you."

"Please, sit down, Mind. This is our moment. This moment I want us to remember as our first date. The date we deserved months ago. The date I don't ever want to forget."

I lean in and kiss Mindy on the lips. The heat and passion are instant. Entwined in each other's arms, we kiss like it's our last moment on Earth. I'm sure she can feel my arousal as I pull her closer to me. Her soft moan sets me on fire, and before I lose all self-control, I slowly pull away from her.

"Before you lose all respect for me, woman, I need us to slow down a minute. I have had this planned for weeks. Let me show you. God, Mindy, you are stunning. I love you so much."

"I love you, too, Kyle. Let me show you how much." Mindy leans closer and drags her hand over my hard manhood.

"Woman, don't test me. I'm already weak. I've longed for you for months. It won't take much to push me over the edge and take you now."

"I'm not afraid of you, Mr. Masterson. Remember, I told you that you need to win me over. I'd say you are off to a good start."

"Please, come sit with me. May I pour you a glass of champagne?"

"Yes please, I would love some." Mindy accepts the filled glass I hand her and a soft smile touches her face.

"What?"

"I'm just thanking God for you. I wanted you from the first moment I saw you. I thought you were larger than life and unattainable. Yet here you are, and I can reach out and touch you. You're my wish answered, right here before my very eyes, and I'm so thankful."

"As am I, sweetheart. A toast to us. To the woman I love, from my nurse to the most important woman I love. May we always have nights like these."

We clink our glasses and never break eye contact as we gaze at each other and sip our drinks. Such joy and contentment.

"Kyle, can anyone see us up here? We are facing the marina, and we're so high. Is this the highest building in the neighborhood?"

"Um, there are other buildings behind us that are apartments. I guess if someone really wanted to see us, they could. Why?"

"I just had an idea. That's all."

"Oh really? Do you care to enlighten me?"

"Actually, Mr. Masterson. If you are up to it, I'd like to show you."

"Mindy, honey. I'm always up to it. What did you have in mind?"

Mindy gulped down the rest of her champagne and smiles a devilish grin. She unhooks her bra through her shirt. I lose my breath as she pulls off her bra and throws it in my direction. I catch it midair and smile as I bring the bra to my nose and close my eyes as I breathe her in. I moan in appreciation as I unbutton the cuffs of my dress shirt and roll up the sleeves.

"Please, Ms. Harper, feel free to continue. No need to stop there. Or would you rather continue this inside?"

"Actually, Mr. Masterson, I believe a tour of the inside of your house is in order, don't you?"

"I'll grab the champagne and glasses, my dear. You grab your flowers and please follow me."

"Why certainly, sir. You are such a gentleman. How could I refuse?"

"My dear Ms. Harper, refusal is not an option. Only enticing actions will be entertained this evening."

"Let the games begin, Mr. Masterson. I'm up to the task." Mindy snickers as she follows me back down the stairs and into the kitchen. She gently places the beautiful flowers on the counter and grabs one long stem red rose and pulls it out of the bouquet. She leans forward, closes her eyes, and inhales deeply. The rose is so fragrant, and its petals are as soft as silk. She runs the rose down her cheek and her neck as she enjoys the soft sweetness of the rose. What Mindy doesn't realize is that I'm watching her every move. My jaw muscles clench as I struggle to control my urge to strip her naked on the spot.

"Follow me, my dear." I show her around my apartment, from the large plush living room to my study/office and the guest room. "The master bedroom is my sanctuary. This room was designed for restful sleep and relaxation, with pure luxury in mind. What do you think?"

Mindy stands in the center of my bedroom suite, staring in awe. She is slowly turning in circles as she examines every corner of detail. In the center of the main wall, there is a large king-sized four-poster bed covered in a plush comforter. The bed is filled with amazing pillows and a soft throw blanket is angled and draped at the foot of the bed. On the wall opposite the bed is a fireplace with a large screen television above it, complete with Dolby surround sound. The woodwork on the furniture and headboard is a deep cherry and the carvings on the headboard are elegant. The tray ceiling, with its small twinkle lights encased within its perimeter, adds an extra touch of elegance to the room.

"It's amazing, Kyle, and so beautiful. And this walk-in closet is huge. It's almost as big as my bedroom in my apartment. It really is beautiful. You did a great job decorating this place. I can see why this is your sanctuary. You could get completely lost in here and never want to come back to reality. Especially with this amazing bathroom. And this Jacuzzi tub is monstrous, just elegantly perfect."

Mindy looks up to find me watching her, concentrating on her every move. She smiles at me as she walks over, holding my gaze with every step.

"Do you know what is really amazing about this whole place, Kyle?"

"Well, I think what is amazing is that you are really here with me, alone, in my place. I see you, Ms. Harper."

"And I see you, Mr. Masterson. Although, it has been a long time since I have had the opportunity to see all of you, if you know what I mean." She winks at me.

"That is a problem easily remedied." I unbutton my shirt and throw it on the bedside chair nearby.

Mindy inhales as she stares at my bare chest. She looks up and my eyes focused on her. I say nothing; I do nothing, and I move nothing as I wait for her next move.

I'm frozen in place as Mindy slow-walks over and stops right in front of me. She looks down at my chest and caresses it. The contact makes me jump and form goosebumps as I inhale sharply. I remain still, allowing Mindy complete control. Mindy looks up to find my eyes frozen on her. She doesn't break eye contact as she feels for my belt buckle, undoes my belt, and proficiently pulls it from my pants.

"Ms. Harper, please be aware there is a fire inside of me waiting for you. Should you tease me more, there is no telling what I might do with you."

"I see. Thank you for the warning. Well, let's be patient, shall we?" She giggles and bats her eyes at me. Mindy feels for the zipper of my dress pants. She purposely, and painfully slowly, I might add, unzips my pants so I can hear every click of the zipper as it slides down. My pants fall and hit the floor as she reaches for my hips and pulls them in closer to her. My hard cock is now free from its enclosure and is long and erect, pointing straight at her like a flagpole.

"I see some things haven't changed, Mr. Masterson. You still enjoy going commando?"

"I do, Ms. Harper. It's nice to feel light and free. You should try it sometime."

"How do you know I haven't? Maybe I'm commando right now? After all, I'm already braless."

"Yes, yes you are, and it's a wonderful sight. Your hardened nipples have been tantalizing me all night. I must say they are so perky and beautiful poking out of that soft knit sweater. You wear them so well."

"Why thank you, Mr. Masterson. May I entice you to get one free feel? I will give you an opportunity to cop a feel. You decide where you would like to feel. Up high, where you know there is no bra, or down low, where you might find me commando, too. It's up to you. You have a fifty-fifty chance, sir."

"My dear Mindy, I shall choose down low, always. For that is your sweet spot and where I can tell if I have successfully put the tingle back in your jingle!"

Mindy pushes on my shoulders, pushing me back a few inches. "What did you just say? Oh, my God, how do you even know about that?"

I laugh out loud as I look at Mindy's blushing face. "I may not have been asleep as much as you thought I was, my dear. You should really watch how you talk about your muscular and sexy patients, especially to other coworkers. I heard lots of things you said about me. Like how you love my dimples, my six-pack, my Adam's apple, my bony knees, and muscular legs. Do I need to continue?" I grin from ear to ear.

"God, no! I've heard enough. I get the idea. I'm so embarrassed."

"Now, please come here and let me touch you the way I have been aching to touch you for months."

Mindy's breathing quickens as my hands get closer to her womanhood.

"Mindy, sweetheart, it's my turn to touch you. Baby, I have wanted to feel you forever. I have missed you." I slide my hand down under the waistband of her skirt and follow her warmth. I find her center and gladly rest my hand upon the V of her pelvis and feel a wondrous surprise.

"My God, woman! You don't have on any underwear either! You're very risky my dear, but I like this daring side of you." I kiss her earlobe and work my way down to her neck as I reach the junction of her thighs and she moans softly. She is waxed and naked, soft and smooth to the touch. I palm the folds of her velvety entrance. I don't ask permission as I insert my middle finger into her pool of wetness. Her heat is like fire as I hiss with controlled desire. *She is ripe and oh so ready for the taking.*

Mindy pushes her pelvis against my hand with encouragement and permission. She palms my erection. "Two can play at this game," she announces as she strokes me firmly from base to tip. I lean into Mindy and bend my face to take her lips gently. The heated passion is sending us into a dizzy frenzy. Her walls contract around my finger. It's too much to bear, as she slowly approaches climax. I'm aware of her body's response and pull back to look at my beauty.

"Oh no, my dear. It's not time for that yet. We will come together. We have both waited too long for each other not to enjoy it together."

"Why, Mr. Masterson, whatever are you talking about?"

"It seems to me that we are severely lopsided here, Ms. Harper. I'm naked and you are not. I need to rectify this situation. Lift your arms, please."

I watch her every move as my beauty giggles at my soft, caressing touch. I lift her sweater over her head and study the beautiful sight before me. I suckle her right breast and gently tease it. Mindy grinds into me, feeling my cock against her pelvis, wanting entry. I pull her skirt down in one quick yank. Mindy is naked before me, standing only in her stilettos, gazing into my eyes.

I look into Mindy's eyes and I'm aching to have her. She's studying my eyes as I admit my desire for her, and only her.

"My God, Mind, you are so fucking sexy I can't stand it. I'm going to make you mine and ruin you for any other man. You shall be mine and mine alone, Ms. Harper." I work my way to her ears, and then down to her neck, where I tease her. I find her nipples a delight as I suckle and bite tenderly on each one. Mindy's knees weaken. I'm there to catch her. "I've got you, baby. I'll never let you fall."

I grab Mindy around her thighs and lift her as she wraps her legs around my waist and locks in place. Her hands are around my neck, firmly in place. We kiss with heat, passion, and intimacy that I have never felt before.

I walk her back against the wall as I devour my love. Mindy's eyes pop open.

"What's the matter, baby? Are you okay?"

"Nothing, nothing at all. You have made all my dreams come true and you don't even know it. I'm so happy."

"Ms. Harper, I believe you have made my dreams come true. I have you in a precarious position. I believe there is no escaping now. You're mine, in every way. My angel, you're fucking amazing and sexy as hell. You are my captive and I'm coming to get you." As my hips grind against her heated wetness, I lean in, heated skin to skin, and devour her. I pull her arms up over her head and hold her hands against the wall, taking charge and playing by my rules. I will have this woman today and forever. I will make her mine. I will mark her for life.

I carry Mindy to my bedroom and lay her on my king-sized bed. She gently sinks into the plush comforter as I crawl up between her legs like a lion after a steak. My eyes aren't losing contact with hers as I grab her ankles and spread her wide open.

"Ah, what a work of art you are, Ms. Harper. I'm so in love with all of you, but I can't wait any longer. I must have you. I must taste you."

"Please don't wait any longer, Kyle. I've been wanting you since the first night I saw you. You may have all of me. Take me now, please."

"All in due time, my dear. I believe the phrase is good things come to those who wait. Isn't that your favorite line?"

"Actually, it's, put the tingle in my jingle, if you want to know the truth. Now, Mr. Masterson, consider yourself invited. You have officially received your invitation, so stop wasting time. Please show me."

"Show you what?"

"Just how much you have missed me."

I make love to her for hours, devouring every inch of her, until we are both sated and exhausted. Mindy is wrapped safely in my arms when I notice a few tears roll down her cheeks. She tries to hide it, but I catch her motion as she tries to wipe away the tears.

"Oh no, I've hurt you, haven't I? I'm so sorry, my love."

"No, you didn't hurt me at all. Just the opposite, actually. That was the hottest, most romantic sex I think I have ever had. You said and did all the right things, Kyle. These are tears of happiness. You have made me feel so special and loved. You really did always see me, didn't you?"

"Yes, Mindy, I did. And I have loved you for a long time. Now we can both believe that good things really do come to those who wait. And Mindy, you will never have to wait any longer, I promise." I place a tender kiss on Mindy's lips and reach for the soft red rose she left on the edge of the bed.

I stroke the rose petals across Mindy's chest and her nipples as she sighs.

"That feels so good. They are so soft and sensual."

"Just like you, Mind. Close your eyes and relax and let me play."

Mindy is almost asleep when a loud crash comes from the kitchen. The sound of shattered glass is loud and clear as we both hear footsteps running through the house. The front door slams shut as I jump out of bed and grab my pistol from the nightstand drawer. I place my finger to my lips to motion her to be quiet and look at Mindy. I motion with my fingers—thumb to ear, pinky to mouth—and throw my cell phone on the bed while I slowly walk down the hall, pointing my pistol in front of me, ready.

I case the place and find no one. The front door is closed, but the vase of roses crashed through the living room sliding door and landed on the balcony. I lock the front door again and walk back to Mindy. I find her wrapped in my robe, huddled in the closet corner.

"Mindy, honey, come here. No one is here. I checked. We're okay. Look at me, it's okay."

"It's not okay, Kyle. Someone was here. In your house, while we were here, having sex! They could have killed us. Who would do that? The only person I know is Levin, and he's in jail. What now, Kyle?" She is visibly shaken and tears are rolling down her cheeks. I pull her up off the floor and hug her desperately. It kills me to know that she's scared.

"Did you call 911?" I ask.

"Yes, then I called David, but I got his voice mail so I left a message."

Just then, there is a loud pounding at my front door. Mindy jumps at the noise and I grab a pair of lounge pants to put on and a t-shirt as I head for the door. I look through the peephole to see the police and Randi Newman standing at my door.

"Detective Newman, what are you doing here?"

"Kyle, I was in the office when I heard the 911 call come through, so I jumped in the car with Officer Sayers, and here I am. When I heard it was Mindy Harper calling in the break-in, I got concerned. Are you all right?"

"Yeah, we are. Mindy is shaken up, but okay."

"Can we talk to you both and find out what happened?"

"Sure, I'll go get her. Please, have a seat. I'll be right back."

I disappear to go tell Mindy and I notice Randi and Officer Sayers looking around. They see the vase and the flowers, and the broken window. They both make notes.

Chapter 3

"Hello, Detective. Please don't take this the wrong way, but I thought I was done with the police for a while. The events of last summer were enough for me."

"Oh, Mindy, no offense taken, honey. I just came to make sure you were all right. I heard the call come in and didn't want just anybody coming over to your place. Can you tell me what happened?"

Mindy looks at me for approval as I nod. "We were in the bedroom and all of a sudden, we heard a loud crash of glass and then there were footsteps running and the front door slammed closed. Kyle came downstairs to check things out, and that's when I called 911."

"Was anything taken?"

I shook my head. "No, but other pictures I had on the coffee table, along with a stack of magazines, were all thrown around the room. Nothing appears missing. I opened the door to see if I could see the person, but they were already long gone."

"Well, there appears to be no forced entry. Does anyone else have a key to your place, Kyle?"

"Just my brother and Mrs. Smith, the housekeeper. But I have known her for ten years. She would never do this."

"Mindy, do you have a key?" Randi asks.

"Um, no. This is my first time at his place."

"Okay, I will need to question your brother and Mrs. Smith, of course. But for now, you two be careful. We have taken pictures and dusted for prints already. Does this building have security cameras?"

"Yes, they do. Mr. Garrett from Beach Security is my contact person. I'll text you both his number and Mrs. Smith's number."

I send him the contact information as I see Mindy trying to keep it together. She reaches for the kitchen counter to steady herself.

"Mindy, I've got you. Are you all right?" I lower her into the kitchen chair.

"I'm fine. I just had a little flashback to when Levin kidnapped me, and I freaked out a little. I'm okay, really." Mindy looks up at Detective Newman. "You're sure he's still in jail, right? He didn't escape or get let out, did he?"

"I'm sure, Mindy. I was just on the phone with the correctional facility yesterday. He's safely behind bars. We'll figure out who did this, I promise. Take a deep breath and be safe. Here is my card and my personal cell number is on the back. Call me anytime. I mean it, seriously."

"Thank you, Detective."

Randi nods as he heads for the door. "Keep her close to you until we figure this out, Mr. Masterson."

"I will, Detective, no question about that. Thanks for coming." I escort them to the door while I see Mindy get up and look at her flowers strewn over the outside patio. "What a mess," I hear her mumble.

"Mindy, honey, don't worry. We'll figure this out. Why don't we go back to your place? I'm sure you will feel safer there."

"I would love that. I know it's only our first official date, but considering our history, would you like to spend the night at my place with me?"

"Mindy, I was hoping you would ask. That's a definite yes. Come upstairs with me and help me pack a bag. I can work from home anytime, so if you need me, I'm here."

"I would like that. I'll race you!" she yells as she takes off in a sprint for the bedroom.

Chapter 4

We arrive safely back at her apartment, and all is as it should be. I receive the grand tour and I'm getting comfortable on the couch when my cell phone rings. Mindy looks up at me and the color drains from her face.

"It's David, honey. Relax. Give me a minute to update him, and then we can return to our night."

"Okay, and have him update Liz. I'm sure they are together. She should know what's going on, too."

I give her the thumbs up as she pours us both a glass of wine. I watch her as I talk to David. She glances over at her mail. She rifles through several envelopes and a magazine. But then she stops, analyzing this one envelope. Her hands are shaking and she's not looking well. The color has drained from her face. Still on the phone with David, I get up and move toward her. Standing behind her, I look over her shoulder as I'm seeing what she's seeing. It looks like an invitation. It's unaddressed, just mixed in with her regular mail. She stares at it and begins to shake. I wrap my arm around her waist as she slowly opens it. I watch my love pale instantly. It's a note written in red calligraphy ink. The penmanship is beautiful, but the words shake her to her core.

You may have him now
But I will have him forever.
His child is my child, a bond never broken.
So run away, bitch. Run now, or die!

Mindy drops the note on the counter as I quickly hang up with my brother. She spins around and glances up to see me watching her. "I knew you were too good to be true. Everything I've ever wanted my whole life has been such a struggle. Why should you be any different? I knew it. I wanted to believe you were mine. I really did. But you were just on loan.

Just a dream I have had, but not one I'm going to be able to keep." Mindy cries through tears.

"Here!" she yells as she plasters the note right in front of my face. "You tell me who this is from! I'm thinking Patricia! Tell me I'm wrong!"

The moment I saw it, I knew it has classic Patricia written all over it. She is a professional calligrapher as a hobby and her favorite color is red. Damn it! I say nothing and look up at Mindy.

"Go ahead, deny it! Tell me this is not from your lover!"

"Ex-lover Mindy. That was ages ago, for God's sake. You know how much I despise that bitch. This is just another one of her tricks to win me back."

"Well, according to her, she'll have you for life. It seems to me she's pregnant. Look at the words, Kyle. Interpret them! You'll be tied to her for life!"

"Mindy, honey, there is no way she is pregnant. I haven't been with her in fucking forever."

"Well, not since I received those pretty pictures of the two of you. It's possible."

"Not probable, honey. If you want the honest truth, I never came inside her. I used a condom."

"And how would you know that? You said you were drugged, that you didn't even remember the incident!"

"I don't remember. I just know that I found the condom wrapper in my pocket of my pants the next morning. I always use condoms. There is no way I had sex with her without one, even drugged."

"You had sex with me without one. You could be wrong!" Mindy yells at me.

"Mind, I had sex with you without one because I love you, honey. I have for months. Even back then, I knew I loved you. I would have never done that to you. Of that, I'm positive."

"Kyle, let me ask you something. Does Patricia have a key to your place?"

My gut lurches, and nausea ensues. Holy fuck! I look up at Mindy and no words need to be spoken. She watches me and she knows. Her gut is *never* wrong.

"Kyle, please go home. I need you to leave me alone. I can't do this. I won't be someone's second choice. I won't ever do that again. Please get your bag and leave. Now!"

"Mindy, honey, this is just a big misunderstanding. Please, trust me. Please. I'm your forever, and you know that. I would never hurt you."

"Tell that to Patricia. I'm not in the mood to die, so I guess she wins. Have a nice life, Mr. Masterson. Now get your shit and go home." Mindy points to the door.

"Mindy, I'll straighten this out and I'll be back for you, I promise. I never go back on my word. Especially not to someone I love. I'm not going to lose you again, I swear."

"Whatever." She closes the door behind me. I hear her sobs through the door and I'm broken. My Mindy…devastated again, at the hands of another woman. I need to fix this, and now!

Chapter 5

After washing my face and brushing my teeth, I retreat to my bedroom and snuggle up under the covers, fully clothed, as I have another crying session. Just as I finally drift off to sleep, I hear Liz's voice.

"Mindy? Mindy, honey, where are you?"

Silence. I don't answer as I try to dry my face with the pillowcase. My pillow is soaked and my eyes are bloodshot.

Liz opens the door to my room. "Oh, Mindy honey. I'm here." She sits on the edge of the bed, facing me. "Do you want to talk about it?"

"What's there to say? Go read the note. It's self-explanatory. Fucking Patricia is pregnant and Kyle is the father. I leave or I die. Seems pretty black and white to me. I've been someone's second choice far too many times, Liz. I'm not doing it again, ever!"

"Mind, Kyle is a mess, too, honey. He is so pissed at Patricia and heartbroken. He is going to fix this, you'll see. I know in my heart he loves you, and so does David. They will get to the bottom of it, I'm sure."

"Liz, if she's pregnant, then game over and you know it. She will be tied to him for life, making my life miserable. She's a wench and we'll never get along, not with her high and mighty attitude. You know I have no patience for that."

"No, you don't, but you do have patience for Kyle, and isn't he all that matters?"

"He is unless he has a kid. His child will be his number one priority, as it should be, Liz. I'm not afraid of that, but Patricia will always find a way to make me number two, and never let me forget it. She will use the child to her advantage and always make Kyle choose sides. It will be impossible for Kyle and it will always be in her favor. I'm not sure I'm up for that kind of fight. I don't know if I have the energy to fight her like that for the rest of my life. It's such an unfair advantage."

"Mindy, then don't fight her. That is Kyle's job. You be the stronger woman and rise above her. Always be the untouchable one. Be the woman Kyle chose to be with, not the woman he is obligated to have a relationship with. Be the woman who is proper, respected, and perfect for Kyle. The one who got her man and made him the happiest he has ever been. Make her see what she has been missing. Make her be the envious one, the one who knows she let him get away and there is no chance in hell of ever getting him back. Child or no child, you won Mindy, and all you did was be yourself. You won the fucking biggest prize of your life, The Greek god of all things. The perfect man for you in all areas, and all you did was to be your charming, adorable self. Don't let some insecure hoity-toity bitch take that away from you, ever!"

"How am I going to do this, Liz? I pushed him away and I don't know if I have the strength to stand up to her."

"You did it once. You can do it again. Remember in the hospital how you kicked her out of Kyle's room? You did that for his protection because it was your job as a patient advocate and his nurse. Well, now you're personally involved with him and it's still in your nature to take care of him and protect him whenever you can. So, take this job of being his girlfriend just as seriously. Stand up with him, a united front, and protect each other. It's easier than you think."

"Liz, I feel like shit. I really didn't give him a good chance to explain, or for us to figure this out together. I just felt so betrayed. I wanted him gone. He knows about my last relationship and the issues I had. I just couldn't believe he would do that to me, knowing my past."

"Mindy, he didn't, really. I have some other news you might want to hear, if you're up for it?"

"Sure, my night is crap anyway. You may as well update me on your happy life. I would love to hear about you and perfect David."

"Actually, it's about you, smartass." Liz sticks out her tongue at me, causing me to laugh, just a little.

"David did some research with Detective Newman a while ago and they found security footage of Kyle's building. They pulled the video from Kyle's hallway and you can clearly see who entered his apartment."

I sit up and hold my breath as I wait for Liz to finish the story. I'm white-knuckled as I hold my comforter to my chin. "Go on, tell me! You're killing me, Liz."

"It was Patricia. She tried to get in using her key, but when it wouldn't work, she took out a small packet of tools and picked the lock. She went into his apartment illegally, Mindy."

"So? What does that mean, Liz?"

"It means she can be arrested for breaking and entering, destruction of property, and now with an added death threat. Save that card, Mindy. It's evidence she threatened you."

"I have it. I threw it on the table when I was yelling at Kyle. I think it's still there."

"Good. Let's get it to David in the morning. He is seeking a warrant for her arrest and is on his way there, as we speak, to arrest her. Hopefully, she will be at home and we can all rest easier tonight with another one of life's sad lessons behind bars, even if it's for only one night. It will be satisfying to know she slept in jail. Don't you think?"

"It would make me happier," I say with a little evil twinkle in my eye.

Liz hugs me as I feel my muscles relax underneath her hug. The comfort of a friend is a welcomed relief.

"Mind, you need to lay back and rest. I'll stay the night and we'll face this together in the morning. Deal?"

"Deal. Thank you, Liz. You always manage to show up when I need you the most. I love you, girl."

"Love you, too. Now close your eyes and sleep. I'll see you in the morning." I reluctantly do as I'm told. Liz hangs out in the living room waiting for a call from David as I snuggle into my comforter and finally drift off to sleep.

Chapter 6

"Hi, honey. How are things going?" I ask David when he calls.

"All is well. This was a lot easier than I expected. We picked up Patricia at her place. She was packing a bag to get out of the country for a month-long woman's retreat in Cabo when we intercepted her. She is now in county lockup and Kyle is on board with pressing charges. He is all in. He wants to do whatever it takes to get this woman off his ass as quickly as possible."

"How is Kyle doing? I'm worried about him, and Mindy is a hot mess over this event."

"He's angry as hell that she got into his apartment and created this mess. If it wasn't for her, Mindy and he would be together right now, and Mindy wouldn't be heartbroken. It makes him sick to know that she doesn't trust him."

"David, did Patricia admit to anything? I mean, she was caught, so did she confess?"

"Liz, this is in the strictest confidence and top secret. You have to keep this under your hat. Can you do that?"

"Haven't I kept many secrets already?"

"Yes, you have, and hopefully, this will be the last. I did something kind of evil, but I couldn't stand what this wench has done to my brother, so I put my meanest, biggest, and most intimidating officer on her to question her."

"You did what? Oh, David, that's brilliant. How did that go over?"

"Let's just say it didn't take long before she cracked and crumbled like a squished potato chip. I was watching from behind the two-way mirror and it was awesome to see. She is not so high and mighty when authority reigns down upon her. She admitted to everything and faking a false pregnancy, too."

"What? That's awesome. Mindy will be so relieved."

"Liz, you can't tell her. Kyle will be there to clean up this mess and explain it all to her first thing in the morning. Keep her home and calm, Liz. He will be there at 0800."

"I will, David. This is awesome. You know I hate to see my friend in pain. She will have her man back in no time. I'm so happy."

"Liz, let's hope she'll take him back. He needs to clean up this Patricia mess once and for all, and it may take a few trips to court to do it. You don't know if Mindy will be up for that. She's already been to court once. You don't know how she'll react."

"Oh, David, have some faith in me. I had a little conversation with her tonight. I think she is seeing the light. I know she will rise to the occasion and be the unattainable partner of Mr. Masterson. Patricia never had a chance once I got done talking with Mindy."

"Well, that's a relief. I'll let Kyle know."

"*No! Don't you dare!* Mindy needs to see him work for their relationship and he needs that, too. They both need to see how strong they can be when they need each other. Let Kyle work to win her back. It's good for him."

"Okay, point taken. I love you, Liz Bennett."

"I love you, too, David Masterson. Now go to bed and I'll see you in the morning. I'll see you at 0800 and you can buy me breakfast. How does that sound?"

"Sounds like a date to me. See you then, my love," David whispers as he hangs up the phone.

"Night sweetheart," I whisper back.

Chapter 7

It's 0800 sharp and I knock loudly on Mindy's front door. I hear heavy footsteps quickly coming toward the door. The door opens with a whoosh as I lay eyes on Liz, of course.

"Morning, Kyle, come on in." She opens the door wider for me to enter. In my hand is a huge bouquet of roses. Every color of every rose possible. They are all fragrant and beautiful with tons of baby's breath woven between all the buds.

"Wow. These are amazing, Kyle. They smell so good. Mindy will love them."

"Well, I hope she'll love me more, and let me explain. I'm not leaving here until we make up and get back together."

"Kyle, we had a good talk. I hope you get what you're after. Now go get your girl! I'm heading out to meet David for breakfast. Will you just let Mindy know, so she doesn't worry?"

"Sure will. Does she know that I was coming over this morning?"

"No. I never told her. I let her sleep in and now she's in the shower. Fight for your woman, Kyle." Liz winks and closes the front door.

I take a deep breath and head down the hall to Mindy's bedroom, flowers in tow. I can hear the shower water running. Decisions, decisions. *Do I walk into the bathroom with the flowers in front of me, or sit on her bed and wait for her?* My inner voice is conflicted. Of course, I want to see her naked, but she was so hurt and angry last night. She may get more pissed if I scare the shit out of her in her own bathroom. *Maybe it's better to wait here, on her bed for her?* The sensible side of me plays it safe and stay put. *Let her enjoy her shower, worry free, and then go for the relationship rescue once she comes into her room to get dressed. But that's so boring, but safe is best, for now.*

I hear the shower water shut off and hear Mindy singing her favorite song, something about taking her breath away. I smile to myself as I picture my love dancing nude in the bathroom. I inhale quickly as I look up and see Mindy, stopped dead in her tracks in her doorway.

"Kyle, you're here."

"I am. I was hoping we could talk."

"Please, talk away. I just need to get dressed first. Do you mind waiting in the living room for me?"

"Not at all. I'll be waiting for you. Take your time." I gaze upon her only in a towel.

I walk to the kitchen and place the flowers on the kitchen table. The big picture window in the kitchen has a beautiful view, so I head in that direction to lean on the window and look out. The courtyard below is buzzing with morning activity as the world comes to life.

Mindy walks into the kitchen and bends over and picks up the bouquet. "They smell amazing, Kyle, and they are so huge and beautiful. Thank you."

"Anything for you."

"Can I make you a cup of coffee? I'm going to have one, so it's no trouble."

"Sure. I would like that." I move closer to the kitchen counter and take a seat on the bar stool and watch Mindy at work. "You are lovely, you know that?"

"Thank you, you're not so bad yourself, Mr. Masterson."

"Mindy, can I start by saying how sorry I am that Patricia has interfered with our lives yet again? I have taken measures to ensure that will never happen again. I hope you will let me explain."

"Kyle, I had a great talk with Liz, and she pointed out some important facts I needed to consider if we're going to make a go of this. I'm sorry I reacted so quickly. I was hurt and felt betrayed again. I didn't know what to do, so I sent the person causing me pain away. I'm so sorry."

"Mindy, I love you desperately. Please know I did not cheat on you and Patricia is not pregnant. She admitted she lied to trap me and get rid of you. She was arrested last night on multiple charges. She was packing to leave the country when police caught up with her. She finally admitted everything and is currently behind bars. I plan to press charges and ensure she will not interfere with us anymore."

"Maybe being arrested is enough humiliation to keep her away from us? Maybe you really don't need to press charges?"

"We'll see. But I'm prepared to go the distance if I need to. That is, as long as you'll be there right by my side?"

"I will be. As long as you'll have me?"

"Ms. Harper, I would love to have you. I would love to have you right here on the couch, right here on the kitchen counter, and have you in my bed."

"Mr. Masterson, that's not exactly what I meant. But I have to say, the counter idea is a very hot idea."

"Why, Ms. Harper, I believe you have too many clothes on for a Sunday morning. You need to be free and comfortable. It is, after all, a day of rest and relaxation."

Mindy giggles as I pull her sweatshirt off and throw it to the floor. She is braless underneath and her nipples are hard in anticipation. "My God, woman. You get sexier every time I see you."

"As do you, Mr. Masterson. As do you."

Chapter 8

It's the three-year anniversary of when we met. That infamous day in the Trauma ICU when all I can remember is hearing the voice of an unknown angel softly speaking to me. I close my eyes and remember the faint smell of her perfume of warm amber and rose. Hmm, it was so soft and amazing. That was the one comfort I clung to every day before I could see. The comfort of knowing she was near, just by her soft scent. *God, I love this woman! How did I get so damn lucky?*

"Come on, lady. Bust a move or we're going to be late!"

"I'm coming, Mr. Masterson, hold your horses! Are David and Liz meeting us there?"

"Yes, they're on their way. This fundraiser should be an exciting event. The Rehab Facility hired a deejay, has a silent auction, and has catering by the best restaurant in town. It's going to be fun."

Mindy walks around the corner in her black strapless cocktail dress. Her hair is down and pulled over to one side, and is flowing gently around her shoulders, held in place by a rhinestone hairpin. Her scent is amber and rose, of course, and her black rhinestone stilettos complete the package. A dash of red lipstick never hurt anybody, and Mindy uses it to her advantage.

"My God, you take my breath away every time I see you. You get more beautiful every day."

"Why thank you, Mr. Masterson. You're one fine-looking specimen yourself. Those abs and what's below them are to die for. I mean, what woman wouldn't want to touch you, especially here?" She gives my growing package a gentle rubbing caress and a light squeeze.

"Um, Ms. Harper, you better stop it or we'll never make it to the fundraiser. I have been known to avoid these types of events. I could easily blow it off and not show up, and just carry your ass right up those stairs to that king-size bed instead."

"No, no, Mr. Masterson. You are the keynote speaker. You must show up. Now come on and put your lovely hard-on away. There's no time for that now." She says over her shoulder as she heads to the car, laughing.

∾

We've made our rounds welcoming everyone to The Summer City Rehab Facility and I've given my speech to the crowd. The crowd is welcoming and receptive to every detail of my rehab experience. There is profound thankfulness from me and my family. So much so that my family has made a generous donation on my behalf to the center. That announcement brought applause and cheering from the staff. The center can now make some needed updates and improvements to its facility.

Now that the formalities are over, it's some alone time with my woman.

"Mindy, walk with me?"

Mindy gently takes my hand as we stroll by the pond and fountain in the garden.

"These grounds really are beautiful, just as you once described them to me. I can remember your description and this totally matches what I saw in my mind. It's amazing, and these twinkle lights are perfect. They certainly set the tone for romance, that's for sure."

"It really is a beautiful place. People get married here and often take pictures here. The director said couples often use this as the backdrop for their portraits."

"I can see why. This old live oak tree with the moss hanging down is so romantic, don't you think?"

"You know it's my favorite, Kyle. You know I'm a sap for a good southern live oak tree."

Mindy looks away and points to the fountain in the middle of the lake. A pair of white swans are gracefully floating, never leaving each other's side. "Kyle, look at how pretty that is."

I don't answer. Silence.

Mindy turns around in the silence to find me on bended knee, right below the branches of the live oak tree, holding a ring box. She gasps as I reach for her hand and I begin my description of our beautiful journey.

"Miss Harper, I am a man who has been wishing for a woman like you for many years. It was an accident that brought us together, which I realize wasn't an accident at all. I believe a higher power knew we needed each other. I have seen you in my mind, clear as a bell. And I see you now, before me. When I see you, I see a strong, vivacious, nurturing, beautiful woman. The woman I have always seen. And when I see you, my body and soul are content. You relax me and you are my perfect fit. Will you do me the honor of marrying me and becoming my wife? I want to see you, because I have always seen you, forever."

Mindy looks at me with tear-filled eyes as she glances up and sees Liz and David watching from the patio. Liz has her hand over her mouth, crying as David is all smiles.

Mindy looks back at me. "Yes, Kyle. I will. I will marry you. I want to be your forever, too."

I stand up and grab Mindy by the waist and spin her around as she plants a big kiss on my lips. I pull away and slide a one-carat solitaire ring with a ruby and diamond jacket on her finger. It fits like a glove and sparkles like crazy. Cheers and clapping echo throughout the garden, as the guests watch from the patio terrace.

"I can't believe this, Kyle. Never in a million dreams did I think you would be mine forever. I think back to that day at the restaurant, and I lose my breath. You were bigger than life and untouchable. Just a dream and a wish I thought would never come true, but here you are."

"Here I am, Mindy. Seeing you. Seeing every little detail about you that makes me feel alive and complete. When I see you, I breathe. I breathe because of you. I love you madly, Mindy, and I can't wait for you to become Mrs. Masterson."

"And I will forever be thankful for you, Mr. Masterson. My Greek god and Prince Charming all wrapped up in one. You're here in the flesh. God, how I love you."

"Not as much as I love you." I tenderly kiss her. "Mind, I just have one more question."

"Sure, what is it, Ky?"

"Do I still put the tingle in your jingle?"

"Always, Mr. Masterson. Always."

The End.

About the Author

C.L. Haynes is a full time critical care nurse, clinical instructor for aspiring nursing students, wife and mother. She resides on the coast of South Carolina where she can often be found reading or shelling on the beach. The beach soothes the soul and restores harmony.

Visit C.L. Haynes online:
www.clhaynes.com

C.L. Haynes on Social Media:
Twitter: @clhaynes3
Instagram: @c.l.haynes

Contact C.L. Haynes:
email: clhyanes@clhaynes.com

www.ingramcontent.com/pod-product-compliance
Lightning Source LLC
Chambersburg PA
CBHW020920110726
47900CB00001B/223